MIDNIGHT ANGEL

Slowly Luke stood up and came to her. His eyes were filled with seduction, his smile an invitation to wickedness. "Miss Billings . . . I beg you not to leave. There's a place I'd like to take you to. A cottage hidden deep in the woods. We could stay there, just the two of us, and shut out the rest of the world for as long as you want . . . a day, a month . . . forever."

"And what would we do there, just the two of us?"

"Sleep by day, and wake when the stars came out. Drink wine . . . share secrets . . . dance in the moonlight . . ."

"With no music?"

He bent to her ear with a confidential whisper. "There's music in the forest. But most people never hear it. They don't know how to listen."

"Are you offering to teach me?"

"Actually, I was hoping you would teach me."

Avon Books by
Lisa Kleypas

LISA KLEYPAS

Midnight Angel

AVON BOOKS
An Imprint of HarperCollinsPublishers

This is a work of fiction. Names, characters, places, and incidents are products of the author's imagination or are used fictitiously and are not to be construed as real. Any resemblance to actual events, locales, organizations, or persons, living or dead, is entirely coincidental.

AVON BOOKS
An Imprint of HarperCollins*Publishers*
10 East 53rd Street
New York, New York 10022-5299

Copyright © 1995 by Lisa Kleypas
Front cover art by Fredericka Ribes
Inside front cover art by Max Ginsburg
Back cover author photo by Larry Sengbush
Library of Congress Catalog Card Number: 94-94469
ISBN: 0-380-77353-8
www.avonromance.com

First Avon Books printing: January 1995

Avon Trademark Reg. U.S. Pat. Off. and in Other Countries, Marca Registrada, Hecho en U.S.A.
HarperCollins® is a trademark of HarperCollins Publishers Inc.

Printed in the U.S.A.

20 19 18

To Jennifer Gold,
a wonderful friend!
Thanks for the visit to Russia.

Prologue

❧ ❧

St. Petersburg, Russia
1870

"They say you're a witch." The guard entered the shadowed cell and closed the door. "They say you can read minds." A coarse laugh erupted from his throat. "What am I thinking now? Can you tell me?"

Tasia kept her head down, while her muscles went rigid. It was the worst part of her confinement, having to endure the frequent encounters with Rostya Bludov. He was a disgusting lout, swaggering around the prison as if the guard's uniform buttoned over his fat girth could fool anyone into thinking he was someone of consequence. He hadn't dared to touch her—yet—but every day his insolence grew worse.

She felt him staring at her as she sat curled in a straw-stuffed pallet in the corner. She knew the past three months of imprisonment had taken their toll on her. Always naturally slender, she was now painfully thin. Her ivory skin had faded to a stark white that contrasted sharply with her heavy sable hair.

The guard's footsteps came closer. "We'll be alone tonight," he muttered. "Look at me. See what you've got coming. I'll make your last night something to remember."

Slowly she turned her head and gazed at him without expression.

There was a grin on Bludov's pitted face. He was fondling the crotch of his ill-made trousers, arousing himself as he stared at her.

Tasia focused on his face. Her unblinking eyes were deep-set and slanted at the corners, the legacy of a Tartar ancestor. They were the cold, pale shade between gray and blue, like the water of the Neva in winter. Some people feared she could steal their souls with her gaze. Russians were superstitious. Everyone from the lowest peasant to the tsar himself treated anything that was out of the ordinary with deep unease.

The guard was no different from the rest of them. His smile died away, and his erection collapsed abruptly. Tasia stared at him until a clammy sweat broke out on his face. Stepping back, Bludov looked at her in horror and crossed himself. "Witch! What they say is true. They should burn you instead of hanging, burn you to ashes."

"Get out," she said in a low voice.

Just as he moved to comply, a knock came on the cell door. Tasia heard the voice of her old nursemaid, Varka, asking to be let inside. Tasia's composure nearly cracked. Varka had aged visibly during the ordeal of the past months, and Tasia found it difficult to look into her grief-stricken face without crying.

Pulling his lips back in a sneer, Bludov admitted the servant and left. "Filthy, black-souled witch," he muttered, closing the door behind him.

Varka's bulky form was swathed in gray, and

her head was covered with a cross-patterned scarf that would ward away evil spirits. Crossing the threshold of the dank cell, Varka rushed forward.

"Oh, my Tasia," the old woman said brokenly, staring at the girl's shackled legs. "To see you like this—"

"I'm all right," Tasia murmured, reaching out and clasping her hands comfortingly. "Nothing's real to me. I feel as if I'm in the middle of some terrible dream." A bleak smile curved her lips. "I keep waiting for it to end, but it goes on and on. Here, come sit by me."

Varka used a corner of her scarf to blot her dripping tears. "Why has God allowed it?"

Tasia shook her head. "I don't know why any of this has happened. But it's His will, and we must accept it."

"I have endured many things in my life. But this ... I cannot!"

Gently Tasia shushed her. "Varka, we have little time. Tell me—did you deliver the letter to Uncle Kirill?"

"I placed it in his hands, just as you told me to do. I stood there while he read it, and held it to a candle flame afterward, until it was nothing but ashes. He began to cry, and said, 'Tell my niece that I will not fail her. I swear it on the memory of her father, my beloved brother Ivan.'"

"I knew Kirill would help me. Varka ... what about the other thing I asked of you?"

Slowly the servant reached inside the square woven pouch hanging across her sagging bosom and withdrew a tiny glass vial.

Tasia took the object in her hand, turning it so that the black liquid slid back and forth with an oily shimmer. She wondered if she could really make herself drink it. "Don't let them bury me," she said in a detached tone. "If I do wake up again, I don't want it to be in a coffin."

"My poor child. What if it is too strong a dose? What if it kills you?"

Tasia continued to stare at the vial. "Then justice would be served," she said bitterly. If she weren't such a coward, if she had faith in God's mercy, she would meet her death with dignity. She had prayed for hours in front of the holy icon in the cell's corner, begging silently for the strength to accept her fate. It had not come. She had thrown herself against an invisible wall of terror, again and again, battered and desperate for escape. All of St. Petersburg wanted her dead. A life for a life. Even her great fortune couldn't silence the howl of the mob.

She deserved their hatred. She had killed a man—at least, she supposed she had. Motive, opportunity, evidence ... everything at the murder trial had pointed to her. There had been no other suspects. During the long months of her imprisonment in this cell, where prayer had been her only link to sanity, no new information could be found to throw doubt on her guilt. Her execution would take place tomorrow morning.

But a ridiculous plan had come into Tasia's head, inspired by the passage in Job: "that thou wouldest hide me in the grave, that thou wouldest keep me secret ..." *Hide in the grave* ... If she could somehow find a way to assume the appearance of death, and escape ...

Tasia jiggled the contents of the vial, a mixture of poisons secretly obtained from a chemist in St. Petersburg. A feeling of unreality came over her.

"You remember everything we planned?" she asked.

Varka nodded unsteadily.

"All right." Tasia broke the wax seal in a decisive motion. Lifting the poison in the air, she feigned a toast. "To justice," she said, and downed the entire draught. She shuddered at the unbearable taste. Holding the palm of her hand to her mouth, she closed her eyes and waited until a tremendous wave of nausea subsided. "It is in God's hands now," she said, giving back the vial.

Varka bent her head and sobbed. "Oh, my lady—"

"Take care of my mother. Try to give her comfort." Tasia smoothed the servant's rough gray hair. "Go," she whispered. "Quickly, Varka." She leaned back on the pallet and tried to focus on the icon while Varka left. Suddenly she was very cold, and her ears were ringing. Frightened, she concentrated on breathing in and out. Her heart pounded in her chest with the force of a mallet. *"My lovers and my friends stand aloof . . . my kinsmen stand afar off . . ."* The Madonna's sorrowful face began to dissolve *". . . that thou wouldest hide me in the grave . . . keep me secret, until thy wrath be past . . ."* The words of a prayer froze on her lips. *Dear God, what is happening to me? Papa, help me . . .*

So this was what it was like to die, all feeling draining away, her body turning to stone. Life ebbed from her like the receding tide, and her memories drifted away, leaving her to sink into the gray world between death and life. *"On my eyelids is the shadow of death . . ."* *"Hide me in the grave . . ."*

* * *

For a long time she was aware of nothing until
the dreams began. There was a parade of images:
knives, pools of blood, crucifixes, and holy rel-
ics. She recognized the saints in her beloved
icons, Nikita, John, Lazarus half-wrapped in his
burial shroud, his solemn eyes staring into hers.
The images floated away, and she was a child
again. *It was summer at the Kapterev dacha in the
country. Sitting with her plump legs dangling from
the edge of a gilt chair, she ate ice cream from a golden
plate. "Papa, may I give the rest to Ghost?" she
asked, while a fluffy white puppy waited expectantly
nearby.*

*"Yes, if you're finished." A smile broke across her fa-
ther's bearded face. "Tasia, your mother thinks that perhaps we should name the dog something more
cheerful ... Snowdrop, or Sunshine—"*

*"But when she sleeps in the corner of my room at
night she looks like a ghost, Papa."*

*Her father laughed gently. "Then we'll call her what-
ever you wish, my clever one."*

*The scene changed, and Tasia found herself in the li-
brary of the Angelovsky Palace, filled with books and
gold-embossed leather. There was a sound behind her,
and she whirled to face her cousin Mikhail. He staggered toward her, his face twisted in a grimace. A knife
protruded from his throat, and a scarlet stream welled
over his gold brocade coat. Blood was spattered on
Tasia's hands and the front of her gown. Screaming in
horror, she turned and ran. She came to a church and
pounded on the massive wooden doors until they
opened. The church blazed with the light of a thousand
tapers, illuminating the smoke-darkened icons on the
walls. The faces of the saints were drawn with sorrow
as they looked down at her. The Trinity, the Blessed Virgin, St. John the Divine ... Falling to her knees, she*

touched her forehead to the stone floor and began to pray for deliverance.

"*Anastasia.*"

She looked up and beheld a darkly beautiful man standing before her. His hair was as black as coal, his eyes like blue fire. She shrank from him. He was the devil, coming to claim her life as forfeit for her sins. "I didn't mean to do it," she whimpered. "I didn't want to hurt anyone. Please, have mercy—"

He ignored her pleas and reached down for her. "No," she cried, but he lifted her in his arms and carried her away in the darkness. Then the hurtful arms vanished from around her, and he was gone. She reeled in a world of noise and brilliant color, her nerves shattering. A powerful force drew her through currents of ice and pain. Resisting, she tried to pull back, but she was dragged inexorably to the surface.

When Tasia opened her eyes, she recoiled from the light of a nearby lantern. She groaned in pain, and immediately the flame was turned low.

Kirill Kapterev's blurry face was above her, his voice a quiet rumble. "I thought the sleeping princess was just a folk tale. Instead I found her right here on my ship. Somewhere in the world there must be a handsome prince asking the moon where he may find his beloved."

"Uncle," she tried to say, but a shuddering sound came from her lips.

He smiled at her, though his broad forehead was webbed with lines of worry. "You're with the world again, little niece."

Tasia was comforted by his voice, so similar to her father's. He had the look of all the Kapterev men; a strong face with thick brows, high cheekbones, and a beard clipped to a precise point. But unlike her father, Kirill had a passionate love for the sea. In his youth he had served in the Russian fleet, and eventually established his own trading company. He owned vast shipyards and a string of commercial frigates. Several times a year he captained one of his ships from Russia to England and back again, transporting textiles and machinery. As a little girl, Tasia had thrilled to Kirill's occasional visits, for he always told her exciting tales, brought her gifts from foreign lands, and carried with him the salt-and-brine scent of the sea.

"I didn't believe in this resurrection of yours," Kirill said, "but I've seen it with my own eyes. I pried the lid off your coffin myself. You were as stiff and cold as a corpse. Now you're alive again." He paused and added dryly, "But perhaps I speak too soon. Come, let me help you sit up."

Tasia protested with a moan as he raised her shoulders and stuffed a pillow behind her. They were in a ship's stateroom, the walls paneled in mahogany, the portholes covered by embroidered velvet curtains. After pouring water from an enameled pitcher into a crystal glass, Kirill held it to her lips. Tasia tried to take a sip, but a spasm of nausea overcame her. Her face whitened, and she shook her head in refusal.

"All St. Petersburg was talking about your mysterious death in prison," Kirill said, trying to distract her. "Many officials wanted to examine your body—including the governor of the city and the minister of the interior, no less—but by that time the family had already collected it. Your servant Varka delivered you into my care and arranged the funeral before anyone realized what was happening. Little did the mourners know that the coffin being lowered into the ground was filled with bags of sand." He frowned regretfully. "Your poor mother is grieving, but we can never let her know you are still alive. The truth is, she wouldn't be able to keep herself from telling someone. It's a pity. I wish there were some other way, but . . ." He lifted his burly shoulders in a resigned shrug.

Tasia ached at the thought of her mother's sorrow. Everyone believed she was dead. It was a strange feeling, knowing that for those she had known and loved all her life, she had ceased to exist.

"You must try to walk a few steps," Kirill said.

She struggled to slide her legs to the side of the bed. Letting Kirill take most of her weight, she rose to her feet. Her joints ached, causing her eyes to flood with tears of pain. Kirill urged her to take a step. "We'll move around for a bit to waken your blood."

"Yes," she gasped, forcing herself to obey. It hurt to breathe, to be touched, to bear her own weight. She was cold—she had never been so cold in her life.

Kirill spoke quietly as he coaxed her to shuffle across the floor. His long arm was locked across her trembling body, lending her balance. "Your father must be scowling at me from heaven for allowing his only child to come to this. When I think of the last time I saw you . . ." Kirill shook his head. "You were dancing the mazurka at the Winter Palace. The tsar himself stopped to watch you. Such fire and beauty. Your feet touched the floor so lightly. Every man there wished to be your partner. It wasn't much more than a year ago . . . A lifetime, it seems."

She was hardly so agile now. Every step was agony, every breath a burst of cold fire in her lungs.

"A tricky enterprise, crossing the Baltic in spring," Kirill said. "Drift ice all around. We'll stop at Stockholm to load up with iron, and then it's off to London. You have someone there who'll provide refuge?" He had to repeat the question before she was able to answer.

"Ashbourne," Tasia gasped.

"Your mother's cousin? Hmm. I can't say I'm pleased to hear that. I don't think much of your mother's family. And I think even less of the English."

"Wh-why?"

"Imperialist snobs, not to mention hypocrites. Englishmen consider themselves the most civilized race on earth, when their true nature is coarse and quite cruel. Innocence doesn't last long there—remember that. Don't trust any of them." Kirill paused, as if realizing his assessment might not prove comforting to a young woman who was about to make a new life there. He struggled to think of something nice to say about the English. "On the other hand, they build very fine ships."

A wry smile pulled at Tasia's lips. She stopped walking and tightened her hand on his heavy arm. "*Spaséeba*," she whispered in thanks.

His face turned grim as he heard the heartfelt note in her voice. "*Nyet*, I don't deserve your gratitude, little niece. I should have done more for you. I should have killed Angelovsky myself, before he ever put his filthy hands on you. To think your foolish mother would betroth her daughter to such a man. Oh, I heard all the rumors about him ... his appearances in public dressed as a woman, and smoking opium for days at a time, and all his perversities—" He stopped at the sound of protest from Tasia. "Well, no need to speak of it now." He urged her forward again. "After our walk, I'll have the cabin boy bring a glass of tea. You must drink every drop."

Tasia made a croaking sound and nodded. She longed to rest, but the tortuous walk continued until Kirill was satisfied that it had been enough. Carefully he helped her ease into a chair. She sat like an arthritic old woman, folded in a miserable heap. Kirill covered her with a blanket. "Little firebird," he said in a kindly way, holding her hand for a moment.

"Papa . . ." she said in a muffled voice.

"*Dah*, I remember that he used to call you that. To Ivan you were all the light and beauty in the world. The firebird is the symbol of happiness." He smiled thoughtfully. "As the story goes, the firebird falls into deathlike sleep at sunset, and later awakens to new life." He brought a handful of objects to her, setting them on a nearby shelf where she could view them. "Your mother wanted these to be buried with you," he said gruffly. "You can keep them with you in England. They are little bits of your past, to help you remember."

"No."

"Take them," he insisted. "Someday you'll be glad to have them."

Tasia glanced at the keepsakes. Her throat tightened as she saw the filigree cross on a gold chain. Her grandmother, Galina Vasilievna, had worn it every day of her life. A small diamond was set in the center of the cross, surrounded by a mass of blood-colored rubies.

Next to the necklace was a fist-sized icon of the Madonna and Christ Child, their halos painted with gold. Tasia's eyes stung with tears as she saw the last object, a carved gold ring that had belonged to her father. Reaching for the ring, she closed her thin fingers around it.

Kirill smiled at her compassionately, reading the hopelessness in her eyes. "You're safe now," he murmured. "You're alive. Keep thinking of that—it might help."

Tasia stared after him as he left. Experimentally she ran her tongue across her cracked lips. She concentrated on bringing some moisture to her dry mouth. Oh, she was alive, but not safe. For the rest of her life she would be like a hunted animal, always wondering when the end would come. What kind of existence was that? *I'm alive*, she thought numbly, waiting for a spark of joy, relief, anything except the shadows that filled her entire being.

One

Alicia, Lady Ashbourne wrung her hands nervously. "Luke, I have wonderful news. We have found a governess for Emma. She's a splendid young woman; intelligent, beautifully mannered . . . perfect in every way. You must meet her at once and see for yourself."

Lucas, Lord Stokehurst looked up with an ironic smile. "So that's why you invited me here this afternoon. And I thought it was for my charming company."

For half an hour he had been plied with tea and small talk in the drawing room of the Ashbournes' Queen's Square estate. He had been close friends with Charles Ashbourne since their days at Eton. Charles was a sociable man who had the rare gift of always seeing the best in people—a gift that Luke did not share. Discovering that Luke would be in London for the day, Charles had invited him to take tea when his business was concluded. As soon as Luke entered the drawing room, he had known from the Ashbournes' expressions that they were going to ask a favor.

"She's perfect," Alicia repeated. "Isn't she, Charles?"

Charles agreed with enthusiasm. "I would say so, m'dear."

"Since you had such poor luck with the previous governess," Alicia continued, "I've kept an eye out for a suitable replacement. You know how fond I've always been of your daughter, and since she has no mother of her own . . ." She hesitated. "Oh, dear. I didn't mean to remind you of Mary."

Luke's dark face was expressionless. Several years had passed since the death of his wife, but it still hurt to hear her name. It would hurt until the day he died. "Go on," he said evenly. "Tell me about this paragon."

"Her name is Karen Billings. Although she has lived most of her life abroad, she recently decided to make her home in England. She's staying with us until we can find her suitable employment. In my opinion, she's mature enough to provide the discipline Emma needs, but also young enough to befriend the child. I'm certain that once you meet her, you'll see how right she is for the position."

"Fine." Luke finished his tea and shifted on the brocade settee, stretching his long legs. "Send her references to me. I'll look through them when I have time."

"I would, but . . . there's a little problem."

"Little problem," Luke repeated, lifting one dark brow.

"She has no references."

"*None?*"

A touch of color rose from the lace collar at Alicia's throat. "She prefers not to answer questions about her past. I'm afraid I can't tell you the reason. It's a very good reason, though. You must trust me on that point."

After a short silence, Luke began to laugh. He

was a handsome man in his mid-thirties, with black hair and vivid blue eyes. His face was more notable for its masculinity than its beauty, with a stern mouth and a nose that was well-shaped but a little too long. The smile he wore most often was that of a man who mocked his own importance. He had an air of cynical charm that others strove to copy. When he laughed, as he was doing now, the laughter never quite reached his eyes.

"Enough said, Alicia. I'm sure she's a fine governess. A treasure. We'll let some other family have the good fortune of employing her."

"Before you refuse, you must at least talk to her—"

"No," he said flatly. "Emma is all I have. I want the best for my daughter."

"Miss Billings *is* the best."

"She's your latest charity project," Luke countered sardonically.

"Charles," Alicia pleaded, and her husband joined in the debate.

"Stokehurst," he said mildly, "what harm would it do to meet the girl?"

"It would be a waste of time." There was no mistaking the finality in Luke's tone.

The Ashbournes exchanged a glance of dismay. Gathering her courage, Alicia approached him in a few halting footsteps. "Luke, for the sake of your daughter, won't you meet this woman? Emma is twelve years old ... on the verge of some rather wonderful and terrifying changes. She needs someone to help her understand herself and the world around her. You know I would never suggest someone who was unsuited for the position. And Miss Billings is such a *special* person. Let me run upstairs and fetch her. I promise it won't take long. Please."

Luke scowled, pulling his arm away from her hand. In light of her insistence, he couldn't very well refuse. "Bring her down before I change my mind."

"You darling man." Alicia hurried out of the room, the elaborate draperies of her skirts swishing behind her.

Charles went to pour him a brandy. "Thank you. It's kind of you to indulge my wife in this matter. I don't think you'll regret meeting Miss Billings."

"I'll meet her, but I won't hire her."

"You might change your mind."

"Not a chance in hell." Luke stood and made his way past a multitude of tables cluttered with handmade ornaments and posy vases. He joined his friend at the carved mahogany sideboard and accepted the brandy snifter. Gently he swirled the amber liquid and gave Charles a wry sideways smile. "What's going on, Charles?"

"I don't really know," came the uncomfortable reply. "Miss Billings is a complete stranger to me. She appeared on our doorstep a week ago. No belongings, no baggage, not a shilling as far as I can tell. Alicia welcomed her with open arms, and won't tell me a deuced thing about the girl. My guess is that she's a poor relation of Alicia's who encountered some sort of trouble. I wouldn't be surprised if her last employer forced his attentions on her. She's young and quite easy on the eye." Charles paused and added, "Prays a lot."

"Wonderful. Exactly what I had in mind when I said I wanted a governess for Emma."

Charles ignored the sarcasm. "There's something about her ..." he said thoughtfully. "I can't quite explain it. I'm convinced that she has lived through something extraordinary."

Luke's eyes narrowed. "What do you mean?"

Alicia reappeared before Charles could reply. She was followed by a wraithlike figure dressed in gray. "Lord Stokehurst, may I present Miss Karen Billings?"

Luke acknowledged her curtsy with a short nod. He wasn't going to make it easy for her. She might as well learn right now that no one would hire a woman with her lack of credentials. "Miss Billings, I'd like to make something clear—"

A pair of catlike eyes lifted to his. They were pale grayish-blue, like light shining through frosted glass. Her lashes were unusually heavy, framing her eyes with inky blackness. Suddenly Luke lost his train of thought. She waited patiently while he stared at her, as if this reaction was a common occurrence.

"Easy on the eye," as Charles had put it, was a massive understatement. Her beauty was riveting. The severity of her hairstyle, pulled back and pinned tightly at the nape of her neck, would have been unflattering to any other woman on earth. But it became her, revealing a face as delicate as porcelain sculpture. Her eyebrows were straight, dark slashes across her white skin. Her mouth, shaped in passionate, sad curves, was a wonder to behold. No man could look at that face and remain unaffected.

"My lord," she said, finally breaking the silence. "Thank you for taking the time to meet me."

Recovering himself, Luke gestured casually with his half-empty glass. "I never leave without finishing my brandy." Out of the corner of his eye he

saw Alicia frown at his rudeness. Miss Billings
watched him calmly. Her posture was perfect:
reedlike body held straight, chin lowered a respectful notch. Nevertheless, there was a spine-
tingling tension in the room, like the wariness of
two cats circling each other.

Luke took another swallow of brandy. "How old
are you?" he asked bluntly.

"Two and twenty, sir."

"Really." Luke gave her a skeptical glance, but
let the answer pass unchallenged. "And you claim
to be competent to teach my daughter?"

"I am well-versed in literature, history, mathe-
matics, and all the social aspects of a young lady's
education."

"What about music?"

"I play the pianoforte."

"And languages?"

"French . . . and some German."

Luke let the silence draw out while he pondered
the hint of strangeness in her accent. "And Russian," he finally said.

There was a flicker of surprise in her gaze.
"Also Russian," she admitted. "How did you
guess that, my lord?"

"You've lived there for some part of your life.
Your accent isn't quite perfect."

She inclined her head like a princess acknowl-
edging an impudent subject. Luke couldn't help
but be impressed with her bearing. His rapid vol-
ley of questions hadn't disconcerted her. Reluctantly he acknowledged that his daughter, with
her wild red hair and the manner of a cheerful
savage, could use a lesson or two in this steely decorum. "Have you been employed as a governess
before?"

"No, my lord."

"Then you have little experience with children."

"That is correct," she admitted. "But your daughter isn't precisely a child. Thirteen, as I understand it?"

"Twelve."

"A difficult age," she commented. "Not a child, not quite a woman."

"It's especially difficult for Emma. Her mother passed away a long time ago. There's been no one to show Emma how a proper young lady should behave. Over the past year she's been developing what the doctors call a nervous condition. She needs a mature, motherly figure to help her overcome it." Luke gave the words "mature" and "motherly" special emphasis. They were the last two words anyone would use to describe the fine-boned woman in front of him.

"Nervous condition?" she repeated softly.

Luke didn't want to talk to her any longer. He hadn't intended to discuss Emma's problems with a stranger. But as he met her clear gaze, he was compelled to go on, as if the words were being squeezed from his chest. "She cries easily. There are occasional tantrums. She's nearly a head taller than you, and she despairs at the fact that she hasn't finished growing yet. Lately it's been impossible to talk to her. She claims I wouldn't understand if she tried to explain her feelings, and God knows—" He broke off, realizing how much he had told her. It wasn't at all like him.

She filled the silence immediately. "My lord, I think that to call this a nervous condition is nonsense."

"Why do you say that?"

"When I was younger, I experienced something

similar to what you've described, as did my female cousins. It is normal behavior for a girl Emma's age."

Her quiet conviction almost convinced him she was right. Luke wanted desperately to believe it. He had gone through months of dire and mysterious warnings from physicians who had prescribed tonics that Emma refused to take, special diets she wouldn't follow. Worse, he had suffered the endless hand-wringing of his elderly mother and her gray-haired cronies, and the pangs of his own guilt for not having remarried. "You've failed her," his mother had said. "Every girl needs a mother. She'll grow up to be so impossible that no one will want her. She'll be a spinster, all because you never desired anyone but Mary."

"Miss Billings," he said brusquely, "I'm glad to hear your opinion that Emma's problems are not serious. However—"

"I didn't say they weren't serious, my lord. I said that they were normal."

She had breached the uncrossable line between employer and servant, talking to him as if they were equals. Luke scowled as he wondered if her insolence had been unconscious or deliberate.

The room was smothered in silence. Luke realized he had forgotten the Ashbournes were there until he saw Alicia fidgeting with the needlepoint pillows on the settee. Charles, meanwhile, appeared to have found something extraordinarily interesting to watch through the window. Luke looked back at Miss Billings. Having excelled for years at the art of staring people down, he waited for her to blush, stammer, erupt into tears. Instead she returned his stare, her eyes pale and piercing.

Finally her gaze dropped, traveling down the

length of his arm. Luke was accustomed to such glances from people ... some startled, some repelled. There was a gleaming silver hook in place of his left hand. The hand had been injured nine years ago, and amputated to save him from a life-threatening infection. Only his stubborn nature had been able to keep him from wallowing in fury and self-pity. If this was the lot that life had given him, he would do his best with it. He had become accustomed to it, made the thousands of adjustments in his life that it required. Many people found the hook threatening, a fact he didn't mind using to his advantage. He watched for Miss Billings's reaction, hoping he made her uncomfortable. She showed nothing except a detached interest that stunned him. No one looked at him that way. No one.

"My lord," she said gravely. "I have decided to accept the position. I will collect my belongings now."

She turned and walked away from him with a crisp rustle of gray muslin skirts. Alicia beamed at Luke before hurrying after her protegée.

Luke stared at the empty doorway with his mouth half-open. He slid a disbelieving glance to Charles. "She's decided to accept the position."

"Congratulations," Charles said tentatively.

A dark smile crossed Luke's face. "Call her back."

Charles looked at him in alarm. "Wait a moment, Stokehurst! I know what you're planning to do. You'll tear Miss Billings to shreds and have my wife in tears, and leave me to deal with the aftermath! But you must take Miss Billings for a few weeks until I can find another situation for her. As a friend, I ask you—"

"I'm no fool, Charles. Tell me the truth. Who is she, and why *must* I take her off your hands?"

Charles folded and unfolded his arms and paced around the room. It was rare to see him in such a state of agitation. "She's in . . . well, let's call it a difficult situation. The longer she stays with us, the more danger there is for her. I'd hoped you would take her this afternoon and keep her safely in the country for a while."

"She's hiding from someone, then. Why?"

"That's all I can tell you."

"What is her real name?"

"It's not important. Please don't ask."

"*Don't ask?* And you expect me to allow her around my daughter?"

"There'll be no danger for Emma," Charles said hastily. "Not one damned bit. Good Lord, knowing the way Alicia and I feel about your daughter, how could you think we would expose her to any harm?"

"At the moment I don't know what to think."

"Just for a few weeks," Charles begged. "Until I can find something else for her. Miss Billings really is qualified to be a governess. She won't harm Emma. She may even do her some good. Luke, I've always been able to count on you. I'm asking for your help."

Luke was about to refuse when he remembered the strange, searching look Miss Billings had given him. She was in trouble, yet she had decided to trust him. Why? And who was she? A runaway wife? A political refugee? He couldn't stand mysteries, couldn't leave them alone. He had the typical Englishman's passion for organizing and making sense of things. The urge ran too deep to be denied. There was no temptation greater than an unanswered question. "Damn," he said under his breath, and gave Charles a brief nod. "A month, no more. After that, you'll take her off my hands."

"Thank you."

"I'm doing you a favor, Charles," he said darkly. "Don't forget this."

Ashbourne's face creased in a grateful smile. "You wouldn't let me."

Tasia kept her gaze glued to the window as the carriage passed through the tidily plotted landscape. She thought of her native country, the endless miles of uncultivated land, the sky of smoky blue and gray. How different this was. For all its economic and military might, England was surprisingly small. Outside the crowded city, it was a land of fences and hedges and green meadows. The common people they passed on the road seemed more prosperous than the peasants in Russia. Their clothing was modern, no smocks or robes in sight. Their sturdy carts and animals were well-kept. The rural towns, with their wooden farm buildings and thatched cottages, were small and neat. But there were no wooden bathhouses here, as there were in every village in Russia. How in the world did these people stay clean?

There were no birch forests. The earth was brown instead of black. The air lacked the cool tang of the Baltic. Tasia searched for church spires, but there was a surprising lack of them. In Russia there were churches everywhere, even in the most remote areas. Gold onion domes poised on white towers would gleam on the horizon like lit candles, signaling the way for lost souls on their journeys. And the Russians loved bells, their musical

peals signaling the time for worship and the beginning and ending of festivals. She would miss
the sound of bells pealing in joyful cacophony. The
English did not seem like a bell-ringing sort of
people.

Thoughts of home began to make Tasia's chest
ache. It seemed much longer than a week since she
had arrived on her cousin Alicia's doorstep. Exhausted, drained of color, Tasia had managed only
a wan smile and a brief greeting of *"Zdráhstvuyti"*
before half-fainting in her arms. Although stunned
by her unexpected appearance, Alicia had taken
Tasia inside immediately. There was no question
that she would help her in every way possible.
Loyalty ran strong in their family, bred through
generations of Slavs whose violent history had
made them fiercely tribal. Although Alicia had
been brought to England while still a child, she
was full-blooded Russian.

"No one knows I'm alive," Tasia had told her.
"But if somehow they discover what has happened, they'll suspect I've taken refuge with relatives somewhere. I can't stay with you. I must
disappear."

Alicia hadn't needed to ask who "they" were.
The government authorities wouldn't go that far
in the pursuit of justice, being too busy with constant riots and political intrigue. But if Mikhail's
family suspected she had escaped, they wouldn't
rest until she was found. The Angelovskys were
powerful, and Mikhail's older brother Nikolas was
known to have a taste for revenge. "We must find
you a position as a governess," Alicia had said.
"No one takes notice of a governess, not even the
other servants. It's a singularly lonely position, but
quite anonymous. As a matter of fact, we have a

friend who might agree to hire you. A widower with one daughter."

Now that she had met Lord Stokehurst, Tasia wasn't certain what she thought of him. Usually it was easy for her to read a person's character, but Stokehurst was difficult. There had been no one like him in St. Petersburg. None of the long-bearded court officials, the self-important military officers, or the languid young aristocrats she had met had been so worldly, so Western. Tasia sensed a tremendous force of will beneath his cool exterior. He was a man who would turn ruthless to get what he wanted. She would rather have nothing to do with such a man, but she didn't have the luxury of choice.

She recalled the way he had tensed when she had seen the silver hook. She had not been repelled by it. Without that flaw he wouldn't have seemed quite human to her. But the air had turned crisp with challenge, and Tasia had known that Stokehurst would rather inspire fear than pity. How much effort it must take for him to camouflage all hint of vulnerability from others. And how much pride he had. It surrounded him like an invisible mantle.

During the ride to his country estate, Stokehurst kept the gleaming hook in full view, resting it casually on his thigh. Tasia suspected the ploy was deliberate, to see if she was unnerved by it. She doubted she was the first to be tested this way. And she *was* nervous, though it had nothing at all to do with the hook. She had never been alone with a man in her life.

But she was no longer a sheltered heiress destined to marry a prince and preside over palaces filled with servants. Now *she* was a servant, and the man sitting opposite was her master. She had always ridden in the family carriages, upholstered in mink, with gold trappings and rock-crystal doors, and interiors painted by French artists. This vehicle, luxurious though it was, could not compare. Grimly Tasia reflected that she had never drawn her own bath, or washed her own stockings. Her one useful skill was needlework. From the time she was a child she had possessed a little basket filled with needles, scissors, and colored silk thread, for her mother had believed that a girl should never be allowed to sit idly.

Tasia forced the thoughts from her mind, reminding herself that she must never look back. It did not matter that she had lost her life of privilege. Riches were nothing. All the Kapterev wealth had not been able to keep her father from dying, nor had it brought her comfort in times of loneliness. She wasn't afraid of poverty, or work, or hunger. She would accept whatever the future held. All went according to God's plan.

Wondering just what sort of woman he was taking back with him, Luke watched her with keen blue eyes. Every fold of her dress was perfectly arranged, every muscle still. She sat against the velvet upholstery as if she were posing for a portrait.

"Would you like to know how much I'll be paying you?" he asked abruptly.

She stared at her folded hands. "I trust you will provide an adequate salary, my lord."

"Five pounds a month should be acceptable." Luke was annoyed by her slight nod. The amount was well above the usual rate. Some sign of gratitude, or praise for his generosity, wouldn't be unwarranted. But there was nothing.

He didn't think Emma would like her. How could this fey creature find any common ground with his scapegrace daughter? She seemed to be lost in some inner world that held far more appeal than reality. "Miss Billings," he said tersely, "if you aren't able to fulfill the position to my satisfaction, I'll give you adequate time to find a new situation."

"That won't be necessary."

He snorted at her confidence. "You're very young. Someday you'll learn that life holds many surprises."

An odd smile flitted across her lips. "I have already made that discovery, my lord. 'Twist of fate' is how the English put it, yes?"

"I suppose it was a twist of fate that brought you to the Ashbournes?"

"Yes, my lord."

"How long have you been acquainted with them?"

The hint of a smile vanished. "Is it necessary that you ask questions, sir?"

Luke settled back in his seat and folded his arms comfortably. "I think I'm entitled to a few. Regardless of your dislike of questions, Miss Billings, the fact is that I've agreed to entrust you with my daughter's welfare."

Her forehead puckered as if she were trying to solve a riddle. "What would you like to know, my lord?"

"Are you a relative of Alicia's?"

"A distant cousin."

"Are you Russian by birth?"

She didn't move, her lashes lowered. It seemed as if she hadn't heard him. Then she nodded slightly.

"Married?"

Her gaze remained on her folded hands. "Why must you ask that?"

"I want to know if I should expect an enraged husband to appear on my doorstep someday."

"There is no husband," she said quietly.

"Why not? Even without money, your face is attraction enough to land a few decent offers."

"I prefer to remain alone."

He smiled wryly. "I prefer that myself. But you're far too young to resign yourself to a lifetime of solitude."

"I am twenty-two, sir."

"Like hell," he said softly. "You're barely older than Emma."

She glanced up at him then, her face lovely and severe. "Years don't really matter, do they? Some people never know more at sixty than they did at sixteen. Some children are aged by experience, and they know far more than the adults around them. Maturity isn't easy to measure."

Luke looked away, the glint of challenge fading. What had happened to her, and why was she alone? There must be someone—a father, a brother, a guardian—who had taken care of her. Why was there no one to protect her now?

He rubbed his fingertips over his left sleeve, feeling for the outline of the leather strap that bound the hook to his arm. Miss Karen Billings—whoever she was—made him restless. Silently he damned Charles. A month. A whole bloody month.

She was absorbed by the scenery outside the window as they neared the outskirts of Southgate. Originally an estate village, it had broadened into a bustling town with the largest marketplace in the county. It was bordered with lush meadows and creeks, and a forest of beech and oak. The handsome brick buildings that housed the corn exchange, the mill, and the grammar school had been designed by Luke's grandfather. He had also lent his talents to the church in the town center, an austere structure faceted with large stained-glass windows.

The outline of an impressive manor house rose on a broad hill that overlooked the land for miles around. Miss Billings glanced at Luke questioningly.

"That's Southgate Hall," he said. "Emma and I are the only Stokehursts in residence. My parents prefer to stay on our property in Shropshire. My sister married a Scotsman, and they live in Selkirk."

The carriage traveled up a winding road, through the gate of a massive wall that had originally protected a Norman fortress. Southgate Hall had been built on the remains of the original castle. The central section dated from the sixteenth century, while the rest had been added in modern times. With its romantic profusion of turrets and gables, and its soaring height, it was known as one of the most picturesque homes in England. Art students often visited to paint their own renditions of the distinctive house and the interplay of brick and glass across its east-facing front.

They stopped at the entrance, surmounted by trefoil moldings and a medallion bearing the family crest. After being helped from the carriage by footmen dressed in black livery, Tasia stared at the carved image over the door. It was a hawk, clutching a single rose in its talons.

She started as she felt a touch at her elbow, and

turned toward Lord Stokehurst. The sun was at
his back, casting his lean face in shadow. "Come
inside," he said, gesturing for her to precede him.
An elderly butler with a long chin and balding
head held the door open. Lord Stokehurst introduced them. "Seymour, this is Miss Billings, the
new governess."

Tasia was surprised at being presented to the
butler, instead of the other way around. Then
she remembered that she was no longer a lady, but
a servant of lower rank. Inferior was always presented to superior. A rueful smile crossed her lips,
and she dropped a quick curtsy to Seymour. They
entered a magnificent hall two stories high, with
an octagonal stone table in the center. A flood of
natural light shone through the solar windows up
above. Tasia's appreciation of the hall was interrupted by a shout that echoed off the walls.

"Papa!" A tall girl with gangly limbs and a mass
of wild red hair flew into the room.

Luke frowned as he saw his daughter rounding
the corner in pursuit of a large dog. Not quite full-
grown, the dog was a mixed breed with a liberal
dose of wolfhound. A few months ago Emma had
bought him from a peddler in the village. No one
at Southgate Hall, even those with a professed
love of animals, shared her appreciation for the
mutt. His coat was shaggy and coarse, a mixture
of brown and gray. He had small eyes, a huge
muzzle, and ridiculously long, flapping ears that
had inspired Emma to name him Samson. His
huge appetite was equaled only by his resistance
to any kind of training.

Catching sight of Luke, Samson rushed forward
with happy, deep-throated barks. But as he noticed
the presence of a stranger, he bared his teeth and

began to snarl. Drops of saliva splattered the floor. Emma clutched his collar and commanded him to be quiet, while he lunged to break free. "*Stop* it, Samson, you blasted beast! Be*have* yourself—"

Luke's deep voice undercut the din. "Emma, I told you not to bring him in the house." As he spoke, he automatically pulled Miss Billings's frail form behind him. The dog seemed intent on tearing her to bits.

"He won't hurt anyone," Emma shouted, struggling to keep hold of the dog. "He just makes a lot of noise!"

Luke was about to drag the dog away when he realized Miss Billings had slipped around him. Staring at the snarling animal with narrowed eyes, she began to speak in Russian. Her voice was soft and guttural, crackling like flame. Luke didn't understand a word of it, but the hair on the back of his neck stood straight. Her voice had a similar effect on Samson, who quieted and stared at the newcomer with wide eyes.

Suddenly the dog dropped to his stomach and crawled toward her. A whimpering appeal came from his throat, while his tail swept across the floor with violent wags. Miss Billings bent and patted his rough head gently. Rolling onto his back, Samson wriggled in ecstasy. Even after Miss Billings stood up, the slobbering giant remained at her feet.

Responding to a curt order from Luke, a footman rushed to take the dog outside. Samson lumbered away with great reluctance, his head held so low that his tongue and ears nearly dragged the ground.

Emma was the first to speak. "What did you say to him?"

Miss Billings's blue-gray eyes swept over the girl, and she smiled faintly. "I reminded him of his manners."

Warily Emma addressed the next question to her father. "Who is she?"

"Your governess."

Emma's jaw dropped. "My *what?* But Papa, you didn't tell me—"

"I didn't know myself," he said dryly.

Tasia's gaze swept over Stokehurst's daughter. Emma was a skinny, awkward girl just crossing the threshold of adolescence. Her curly hair was a carroty-red that would draw attention wherever she went. Tasia guessed that Emma was the victim of merciless teasing from other children. The hair would have been temptation enough, but she was also very tall—it was possible she would eventually reach six feet. Her shoulders slumped forward in an effort to conceal her height. The skirts of her frock were too short, and her nails were dirty. She had her father's beautiful sapphire eyes, but her lashes were auburn instead of black, and her face was spattered with golden freckles.

A tall, gray-haired woman approached them, her angular face wearing a no-nonsense expression. There was a huge ring of keys at her belt, the symbol of authority worn by every housekeeper.

"Mrs. Knaggs," Stokehurst said, "this is the new governess, Miss Billings."

The housekeeper's brows pinched together in a frown. "Indeed. A room must be prepared. I suppose the same as before?" Her tone implied that this latest governess would probably last no longer than the previous one.

"Whatever you think best, Mrs. Knaggs." Stokehurst strode to his daughter and kissed the top of her head. "I have work to do," he murmured. "We'll talk at supper."

Emma nodded, her gaze fastened on Tasia while Stokehurst left them without another word.

"Miss Billings," the housekeeper said briskly, "I shall direct someone to prepare a room for you. In the meantime you might like to sit with a cup of tea."

A cup of tea had never sounded so inviting. It had been a long day, and Tasia hadn't yet recovered her strength since leaving Russia. She was exhausted. But she shook her head. At the moment it was more important to give her attention to Emma. "Actually I would rather tour the house. Would you take me around, Emma?"

"Yes, Miss Billings," the girl said dutifully. "What would you like to see? There are forty bedrooms, and nearly as many sitting rooms. There are galleries, courtyards, the chapel ... It would take a full day to show you everything."

"For now, just show me what you think is important."

"Yes, Miss Billings."

As they wandered through the ground floor of the mansion, Tasia admired the beauty of the place. It was very different from the Ashbournes' fashionably cluttered Victiorian home with its heavy furniture. Southgate Hall was filled with clean white plasterwork and pale marble. Large glass windows and high ceilings made the rooms airy and bright. Most of the furniture was French, similar to what Tasia had been accustomed to in St. Petersburg.

At first Emma said very little, stealing frequent glances at Tasia. However, after they toured the music room and strolled through a long gallery filled with artwork, Emma's curiosity asserted itself. "How did Papa find you?" she asked. "He said nothing about bringing a governess for me today."

Tasia paused to examine a pastoral scene by Boucher. It was one of many modern French works in the gallery, all of them chosen with a good eye for light and color. She dragged her attention from the painting as she replied. "I was staying with your friends, the Ashbournes. They kindly recommended me to your father."

"I didn't like the last governess. She was very strict. She never wanted to talk about interesting things. Only books, books, books."

"But books are very interesting."

"I don't think so." They continued to walk along the gallery at a slow pace. Emma stared at her openly now, her blue eyes quizzical. "None of my friends has a governess like you."

"Oh?"

"You're young, and you have a strange way of talking. And you're very pretty."

"So are you," Tasia said softly.

Emma made a comical face. "*Me?* I'm a big, carrot-topped girl."

Tasia smiled. "I always wished to be tall, so that when I walked into a room, everyone would think I was a queen. Only women with your height can be truly elegant."

The girl blushed. "I've never heard that before."

"And your hair is lovely," Tasia continued. "Did you know that Cleopatra and the ladies of her court used to dye their hair with henna to make it red? It's quite a fortunate thing to have it naturally."

Emma made a skeptical sound as they turned a

corner. The next hallway was lined with glass windows that provided views of the gold and white ballroom. "Are you going to teach me how to behave like a lady?" she asked suddenly.

Tasia smiled, thinking that Emma had inherited her father's habit of springing blunt questions right in one's face. "It was mentioned to me that you required some advice on the subject," she admitted.

"I don't see why anyone should have to be a lady. All those blasted rules and manners ... I shan't be any good at it." She screwed up her face comically.

Sternly Tasia willed herself not to laugh. It was the first time in months that something had tickled her sense of humor. "It's not difficult. It's almost like a game. I think you'll do very well at it."

"I can't do anything well if I don't see a reason for it. Why does it matter if I eat with the wrong fork, as long as I am fed?"

"Do you want the philosophical reason, or the practical one?"

"Both."

"Most people believe that without proper etiquette, all civilization would crumble. First go the manners, then morality, and then we should come to an end just as the decadent Romans did. More importantly, if you make an obvious faux pas after you've come out in society, it will embarrass you and your father, and make it very difficult for you to attract the attentions of honorable young men."

"Oh." Emma stared at her with increasing interest. "Were the Romans really decadent? I thought all they did was have wars and build roads and make long speeches about government."

"Horrifyingly decadent," Tasia assured her. "We'll read about them tomorrow, if you like."

"All right." Emma flashed her a smile. "Let's go to the kitchen. I want you to meet Mrs. Plunkett, the cook. She's my favorite person in the house, after Papa."

They went through a narrow pantry with shelves of dry goods, and a pastry room outfitted with a marble table and every conceivable size of rolling pin. Emma took Tasia's arm and pulled her past several kitchen maids who regarded them curiously. "This is my new governess, and her name is Miss Billings," Emma announced without stopping.

The kitchen was very large and filled with servants busily preparing supper. There was a long wooden table at the center of the room, overshadowed by low-hanging pots, pans, and copper molds. A stout woman stood there wielding a large knife, showing one of the cook maids how to chop carrots properly. "Mind you don't cut them too thick—" She stopped and smiled broadly as she caught sight of Emma. "Ah, here's my Emma, and she's brought one of her little friends to visit."

"Mrs. Plunkett, this is Miss Billings," Emma said, propping a leg on the seat of a wooden chair. "She's my new governess."

"Bless my eyes," the cook exclaimed. "It's time we had a new face around here, and such a pretty one at that. But look at you—no wider than a broomstick." She reached for a platter heaped with pastries and pulled back the cloth that covered them. "Try one of these apple tarts, lamb, and tell me if the crust is too thick."

As she looked at her, Tasia understood Emma's affection for the cook. Mrs. Plunkett had apple-colored cheeks, merry brown eyes, and a warm, motherly presence. "Try it," the cook encouraged, and Tasia reached for a tart.

Emma followed suit, choosing the largest one on the platter. She bit deeply into the pastry. "Splendid," she said with her mouth full. She grinned at Tasia's reproving glance. "Oh, I know. It's not polite to talk while I'm eating. But I can do it so none of the food shows." She shoved it to the side of her cheek. "See?"

Tasia was about to explain why it still wasn't proper when she saw Emma wink at Mrs. Plunkett. She couldn't help laughing, in spite of her efforts to maintain an air of dignity. "Emma, I fear there may come a day when you accidentally spray crumbs over some important guest."

Emma's grin broadened. "That's it! I'll spit food all over Lady Harcourt the next time she comes to visit. Then we'll finally be rid of her. Can you imagine Papa's face?" Seeing Tasia's confusion, she explained. "Lady Harcourt is one of the women who want to marry Papa."

"One of them?" Tasia asked. "How many are there?"

"Oh, practically everyone wants him. During our weekend parties, I eavesdrop on some of the ladies. You would scarcely believe the things they say! Usually I don't understand half of it, but—"

"Thank the Lord for that," Mrs. Plunkett said heartily. "You know you shouldn't eavesdrop, Emma."

"Well, he's *my* father. I have a right to know who's scheming to catch him. And Lady Harcourt is trying very hard. Before you know it they'll be married and I'll be on my way to boarding school."

Mrs. Plunkett chuckled. "If your father were going to marry anyone, he'd have done it by now. There was no one for him but your mother, and I don't believe there ever will be."

Emma frowned thoughtfully. "I wish I remembered more about her. Miss Billings, would you like to see my mother's portrait? It's in one of the upstairs parlors. She used to take her tea there."

"Yes, I would like that," Tasia said, taking a bite of apple tart. She wasn't hungry, but she forced herself to eat.

"You'll be very happy here," the cook told her. "Lord Stokehurst provides a large housekeeping allowance, so nothing is rationed. We have all the butter we want, and ham every Sunday. And we've plenty of soap, eggs, and good tallow candles for our own use. When visitors come, we hear such stories from their servants. Some never have an egg in their lives! You're a lucky girl to be hired by Lord Stokehurst. But I expect you know that."

Tasia nodded automatically. She couldn't help wondering how her own servants in Russia had been treated. A wave of guilt came over her as she realized that she had never given a thought to the quality of their food or asked if they had enough to eat. Surely her mother was generous with them—but there was a possibility that Marie might be too self-absorbed to see to their needs. None of them would ever dare ask for anything.

All at once she realized that Emma and Mrs. Plunkett were looking at her strangely.

"Your hand is shaking," Emma said frankly. "Aren't you feeling well, Miss Billings?"

"You're very pale," the cook added, her plump face concerned.

Carefully Tasia set down her tart. "I am a little tired," she admitted.

"I'm sure your room is ready by now," Emma said. "If you'd like, I'll take you there. We can finish our tour tomorrow."

The cook wrapped the tart in a napkin and pressed it in Tasia's hands. "Take this, poor lamb. Later we'll send up a supper tray for you."

"How kind you are." Tasia smiled into her soft brown eyes. "Thank you, Mrs. Plunkett."

The cook stared after the young woman as she left with Emma. There was silence in the kitchen until the doors closed. All the kitchen maids began to talk eagerly.

"Did you see her eyes? They're just like a cat's."

"She's all bones. That dress was hanging off her."

"And the way she talks . . . some of the words are all fuzzy-like."

"I wish I talked like that," one of them said wistfully. "It sounds pretty."

Mrs. Plunkett chuckled and motioned for them to return to work. "Time for gossip later. Hannah, finish those carrots. And Polly, mind you keep stirring that sauce, or it will be nothing but lumps."

Luke and Emma sat alone at the linen-covered dining table. The blaze in the marble fireplace cast a warm glow over the Flemish tapestries and the marble carvings on the walls. A servant came to fill Emma's glass with water and Luke's with French wine. The butler uncovered dishes at the sideboard and ladled a fragrant broth with truffles into shallow bowls.

Luke regarded his daughter with a smile. "It always worries me when you look so pleased,

Emma. I hope you're not planning to torment the
new governess as you did the last one."

"Oh, not at all. She's much better than Miss
Cawley."

"Well," he said casually, "I suppose anyone
would be preferable to Miss Cawley."

Emma giggled. "That's true. But I like Miss Billings."

His eyebrows lifted. "You don't think she's too
serious?"

"Oh, no. I can tell that underneath she wants to
laugh."

Luke thought of Miss Billings's implacable face.
"Somehow I didn't have that impression of her,"
he muttered.

"Miss Billings is going to teach me all about etiquette and propriety, and everything. She says we
don't always have to study in the schoolroom upstairs. I can learn just as well if we take our books
outside and read under a tree. We're going to read
about the ancient Romans tomorrow, and after
that we're to speak nothing but French until supper. I'm just warning you, Papa, because if you ask
me something after four o'clock tomorrow, I shall
be *compelled* to reply in a language you don't understand."

He gave her a sardonic glance. "I speak French."

"*Used* to," Emma countered triumphantly. "Miss
Billings says if a language isn't practiced frequently, one loses it in no time at all."

Luke set down his spoon, wondering what kind
of an act the governess was putting on for his
daughter. Perhaps she was trying to befriend
Emma so that when it came time to leave, she
could use his daughter's feelings as a weapon
against him. He didn't like it. Karen Billings had

better watch her step carefully, or he would make her rue the day she was born. Only a month, he reminded himself, keeping his temper under tight rein. "Emma, don't become too attached to Miss Billings. She may not be with us for very long."

"Why not?"

"Any number of things could happen. She may not do an adequate job of teaching you. Or she may decide to accept another position." He took a sip of wine. "Just keep it in mind."

"But if I want her to stay, she will," Emma said stubbornly.

Luke didn't reply, only picked up his spoon and dipped it in his soup. After a minute, he changed the subject and began to tell her about a thoroughbred horse he was thinking of buying. Emma followed his lead, carefully avoiding any mention of the governess for the rest of the meal.

Tasia wandered about her room, a third-floor chamber with a charming round window. She was pleased by the thought that the sun would wake her each morning. The narrow bed was covered with fresh white linen and a simple quilted blanket. There was a mahogany washstand in the corner, with a chipped porcelain basin decorated in a flowered blackberry pattern. Near the window were a chair and table, and on the opposite wall a battered armoire with an oval mirror on the door. The room was small, but clean and private.

Her valise had been set by the bed. Carefully Tasia unpacked the hairbrush and the cakes of rose-scented soap that Alicia had given her. It was also because of Alicia that she owned two dresses: the gray one that she was wearing and a black muslin that she hung in the armoire. She wore her grandmother's gold cross under her clothes at all times. The ring from her father was knotted in a handkerchief and hidden at the back of the armoire beneath her personal linens.

Finally Tasia moved the wooden chair to the corner of the room. She stood her icon against the chair back, so that she could look at it when she was in bed. Lovingly her fingers traced the Madonna's tender face. This was her *krasnyi ugolok,* her "beautiful corner." All those of Russian Orthodox faith had such a place in their homes, where they could find peace at the beginning and end of each day.

Her thoughts were interrupted by a tap on the door. Opening it, Tasia came face to face with a housemaid a few years older than she. The girl wore a starched apron and a cap that covered most of her flaxen hair. Her features were attractive, but there was a hard look about her eyes. Her lips were compressed into a thin line. "I'm Nan," the girl said, handing her a cloth-covered tray. "Here's your supper. Set it outside the door when you're done. I'll come to collect it in a bit."

"Thank you," Tasia murmured, confused by the girl's attitude. She seemed angry about something, though Tasia had no idea why.

Enlightenment was soon in coming. "Mrs. Knaggs says I'm the one who must attend you when you want something. I didn't need the extra work. My knees already ache from going up and down the stairs all day. Now I'm to carry your kindling and cans of bathwater and your supper tray."

"I'm sorry. I won't require very much."

Nan sniffed contemptuously and turned on her heel, trudging back down the stairs.

Tasia brought the tray to her table, giving the icon a wry glance as she passed by it. "See what these English are like?" she murmured. The Madonna's face remained placid and long-suffering.

Gingerly Tasia lifted the cloth to see what was beneath. There were slices of duck, a dab of brown sauce, a white roll, and boiled vegetables. All of it was carefully arranged and garnished with violets. There was also a little glass cup filled with pasty white pudding. The same thing had been served at the Ashbournes' home. Blancmange, Alicia had called it. The English seemed fond of food with no flavor. Tasia picked up one of the violets and draped the cloth back over the dinner tray. She wasn't hungry. But if she were . . .

Oh, if only she could have a slice of dark Russian bread with butter, or salted mushrooms sopped in cream. Or some blinis, the delicate pancakes dripping with honey. Some familiar smell or taste, anything to remind her of the world from which she had come. The last few months of her life were a confusing whirl in her head. Everything had fallen through her fingers like sand. Now she had nothing to hold on to.

"I have myself," she said aloud, but her voice sounded strained. Absently she wandered across the room and stopped in front of the mirrored armoire. It had been a long time since she had looked at herself, other than taking swift glances to make certain her hair was neat and all her buttons were fastened.

Her face was very thin. The bones of her cheeks looked sharp and delicate. The roundness had gone from her neck, leaving lavender hollows to emerge from beneath her high collar. There was no color in her skin. Unconsciously Tasia clenched her fingers around the violet until its rich perfume spilled into the air. She didn't like seeing the fragile woman in the mirror, a stranger with all the confidence of a lost child. She wouldn't let herself be fragile. She would do whatever was necessary to regain her strength. Discarding the bruised flower, she strode to the table.

Picking up the dinner roll, she bit into it and began to chew. It nearly choked her, but she swallowed and forced herself to eat more. She would finish her supper. She would sleep all night without waking or dreaming ... and in the morning she would begin to make a new life for herself.

Two
❧ ❧

The servants' hall was filled with conversation. Smells of coffee, toasting bread, and frying meat wafted through the air. Quickly Tasia straightened her skirts and smoothed her hair. Wiping her face clean of expression, she pushed open the door. The long table in the center of the hall was crowded with people. They fell silent and stared at her. Looking for a familiar face, Tasia found Nan's unfriendly gaze upon her. The butler, Seymour, was busy in the corner ironing a newspaper. He didn't spare her a glance. Just as Tasia considered backing out of the room and fleeing, Mrs. Plunkett's cheerful face appeared before her.

"Good morning, Miss Billings! You're up and about early today. 'Tis a surprise to see you in the servants' hall."

"I gathered that," Tasia said with a faint smile.

"I'm almost done preparing your breakfast tray. Nan will bring it upstairs very soon. Do you take tea in the morning? Chocolate, maybe?"

"Might I eat down here with everyone else?"

The cook was perplexed. "Miss Billings, these are ordinary servants. You're the governess. You don't take your meals with us."

It must be a peculiarly English attitude. Her own governess hadn't lived in such isolation. "I'm supposed to eat alone?" Tasia asked in dismay.

"Aye, except the times when you're invited to eat with His Lordship and Miss Emma. That's how it's usually done." She chuckled at Tasia's expression. "Why, it's an *honor*, lamb, not a punishment!"

"I would consider it a greater honor to take my meals here with you."

"You would?" Every face in the hall was turned toward her now. Tasia steeled herself not to flinch as dozens of gazes raked over her. Flags of color burned high on her cheeks. Mrs. Plunkett regarded her for a moment, then shrugged. "I suppose there's no reason why you couldn't. But I warn you, we're a common lot." She winked as she added, "Some might even chew with their mouths open."

Tasia walked to the empty space at one of the long benches. "May I?" she murmured, and a few housemaids shifted to make room for her.

"What will you 'ave, miss?" one of them asked.

Tasia looked at the row of bowls and platters before her. "Some toast, please. And perhaps some of that sausage . . . and an egg . . . and one of those flat things . . ."

"Oatcakes," the maid said helpfully, passing the food to her.

One of the footmen down at the other end of the table grinned as he watched Tasia fill her plate. "She may look like a sparrow, but her appetite is horse-sized." There was a scattering of friendly laughter, and everyone began to eat and talk as before.

Tasia enjoyed the bustling warmth of the servants' hall, especially after the loneliness of the past months. It was nice to sit in the midst of a crowd. Although the food tasted strange to her, it was hot and filling.

Unfortunately her contentment was soon destroyed by Nan's unfriendly stare. The housemaid seemed determined to make her feel unwelcome. "Look at the way she cuts her food in little bites, all ladylike," Nan sneered. "And how she touches the napkin to her lips, just so. Everything is 'may I' and 'might I.' Well, I know 'zactly why she wants to sit with the lot of us. It does no good to put on airs when she's all by herself."

"*Nan*," one of the girls chided. "Don't be a cat."

"Let 'er alone, Nan," someone else said.

Nan quieted, but she continued to glare at Tasia.

Tasia choked down the last few mouthfuls of her breakfast, though it was suddenly like swallowing paste. She'd been hated and feared and sneered at for months by peasants who didn't know her, by cowardly peers who had abandoned her ... and now by a spiteful housemaid. Finally Tasia lifted her head to stare back at Nan, her eyes narrowing into slits. It was the same icy look she had given the prison guard in St. Petersburg, and it had the same withering effect on Nan. The housemaid flushed and looked away, her hands balled into fists. Only then did Tasia stand and leave the table, carrying her plate to the great wooden sink. "Good day," she murmured to no one in particular, and was answered by a chorus of friendly replies.

Slipping out to the hallway, Tasia came face to face with Mrs. Knaggs. The housekeeper seemed less forbidding than she had the night before. "Miss Billings, Emma is changing from her riding clothes. After breakfast she will be ready to begin her lessons at precisely eight o'clock."

"Does she ride every morning?" Tasia asked.

"Yes, with Lord Stokehurst."

"They seem very fond of each other," Tasia said.

Mrs. Knaggs glanced around the hall to make certain they were not being overheard. "Lord Stokehurst dotes on the child. He would give his life for her. He very nearly did, once."

An image of the silver hook appeared in Tasia's mind. Unconsciously she touched her own left wrist. "Is that how—"

"Oh, yes." Mrs. Knaggs had noticed the gesture. "A fire in London. Lord Stokehurst went right into the house before anyone could stop him. Every inch of the place was blazing. The people who saw him go in there believed he would never be seen alive again. But he came out with his wife over his shoulder and the child in his arms." The housekeeper tilted her head to the side, seeming to watch the movements of ghosts. "Lady Stokehurst didn't live to see the next morning. For days Lord Stokehurst was out of his head with grief, and pain from his wounds. The worst damage was done to the left arm—they say he pulled a burning wall apart with his bare hands to save his wife. The hand festered and poisoned his blood, till they had to choose between taking it off or letting him die. It was ironic, how kindly life had treated him until then, and to lose so much all at once . . . There's not many it wouldn't have broken. But the master is a strong man. Not long after it all happened, I asked if he would give Emma into the safekeeping of his sister, Lady Catherine. She would have taken the child for as long as necessary. 'No,' he said, 'the baby's all I have left of Mary. I could never give her away, not even for a day.'" Mrs. Knaggs paused and shook her head.

"I've let my mouth run away with me, haven't I? It hardly sets a good example for the others, to stand here with my tongue wagging."

There was an ache in Tasia's throat. It hardly seemed possible that the man Mrs. Knaggs had just described was the same cool, self-possessed aristocrat she had ridden with in the carriage yesterday. "Thank you for telling me about him," she managed to say. "Emma is fortunate to have a father who loves her so much."

"I would say so." Mrs. Knaggs stared at her curiously. "Miss Billings, if truth be known, you are not at all the kind of governess I expected His Lordship to hire. You're not from England, are you?"

"No, ma'am."

"You're already the subject of speculation around here. No one at Southgate Hall has any secrets worth telling—and it's clear you have a great many."

Not knowing how to reply, Tasia shrugged and smiled.

"Mrs. Plunkett is right," the housekeeper mused. "She says there is something about you that invites people to talk. Maybe it's just that you're so quiet."

"It's not intentional, ma'am. I take after my father's side of the family. They're all quiet, and they tend to brood. My mother is very talkative and charming. I always wished to be more like her."

"You do well enough," Mrs. Knaggs said with a smile. "I must be off now. Today is washday. There's no end of scrubbing, starching, and ironing to be done. Perhaps you would like to occupy yourself in the library or music room until Emma is ready."

"Yes, ma'am."

They parted company, and Tasia wandered through the mansion, searching for the music room. Her tour with Emma last night had been so brief, and she had been so tired, that she remembered nothing except the kitchen.

Purely by chance she stumbled onto the music room. It was circular in shape, fitted with curving mullioned windows. The pale blue walls, stenciled with gold fleurs-de-lis, rose to a ceiling painted with cherubs playing musical instruments. Seating herself at the shining piano, Tasia lifted the cover and tried a few chords. As she expected, the instrument was perfectly tuned.

Lightly her hands wandered over the keys, searching for something that would suit her mood. Like all St. Petersburg society, her family had a passion for everything French, especially music. She began to play a sprightly waltz. After a few bars, she stopped as another melody came into her mind, gently beckoning. She was thinking of a Chopin waltz, a haunting piece that seemed to ripple from the heart of the piano. Although she hadn't played it for a long time, she still remembered it fairly well. Closing her eyes, she went slowly at first, gaining confidence as the music overtook her, building in lush strains.

All at once something prompted her to open her eyes. The music stopped abruptly, locked inside her frozen hands.

Lord Stokehurst stood only a few yards away. There was a strange look on his face, as if he'd received a terrible shock.

"Why are you playing that?" he barked.

In her alarm, Tasia could barely find her voice. "I'm sorry if I've displeased you." Hastily she stood up and skirted around the bench, keeping it between them. "I won't touch the piano again. I only meant to practice a little—"

"Why that music?"

"Sir?" she asked in confusion. He was upset by the piece she had been playing. It must have some special significance to him. Suddenly she understood. The frantic pace of her heart began to ease. "Oh," she said softly. "It was her favorite, wasn't it?" She didn't mention Lady Stokehurst's name. There was no need. Stokehurst paled a few shades beneath his tan, and she knew she was right.

The blue eyes flashed dangerously. "Who told you?"

"No one."

"Then it was just a coincidence?" he sneered. "You just happened to sit there and play the one piece that—" He bit off the rest of the sentence. His cheek muscles flexed as he clenched his teeth. The force of his anger, held in such tenuous check, nearly caused her to back away.

"I don't know why I chose that one," she blurted out. "I . . . I just felt it."

"Felt it?"

"I-in the piano."

Silence. Stokehurst seemed to be torn between fury and amazement as he stared at her. Tasia wanted to take the words back, or explain more, anything to ease the crushing stillness. But she was paralyzed, knowing that whatever she did or said would only make things worse.

Finally Stokehurst turned and walked away with a muffled curse.

"I'm sorry," Tasia whispered. She continued to

stare at the doorway, realizing the scene had not gone unobserved. In his fury, Stokehurst hadn't noticed that his daughter had hidden herself just outside the door. One of Emma's eyes was visible as she peeked around the edge of the frame.

"Emma," Tasia murmured. The girl vanished, as silently as a cat.

Slowly Tasia eased herself back onto the piano seat. She thought of Stokehurst's face when she had been playing the waltz. He had watched her with a sort of agonized fascination. What memories had been stirred by the music? She didn't think many people had ever seen him that way. The marquess seemed like a man who prized his self-control. Perhaps he had convinced himself and everyone else that he had gone on with his life, but inside he was still grieving.

It was very different from her mother's attitude about her father's death. "You know your dear papa would want me to be happy," Marie had told her. "He is in heaven now, but I am still alive. Always remember the dead, but don't dwell on them. Your papa doesn't mind that I have gentlemen friends, and neither should you. Do you understand, Tasia?"

Tasia hadn't understood. She had resented the way her mother had recovered from Ivan's death with such apparent ease. Now she was beginning to regret the harsh judgments she had made about Marie's behavior. Perhaps Marie should have stayed in mourning longer, perhaps she was self-indulgent and shallow, perhaps she had too many gentlemen friends . . . but she had no hidden wounds, no festering grief. It was better to live fully rather than be haunted by the memory of what was lost.

* * *

Luke wasn't conscious of where he was going. He kept walking until he found himself in his bedroom. The massive bed, draped in ivory silk and poised on a rectangular platform, had never been shared by anyone except him and his wife. It was sacred territory. He would never allow another woman here. He and Mary had spent their first night together in that bed. A thousand nights together. He had held her when she was pregnant, had been at her side when she had given birth to Emma.

His head was filled with the waltz. The melody pounded in his brain until he groaned and sat on the edge of the platform. He clasped the side of his skull as if that would keep the memories from coming.

Difficult though it was, he had accepted Mary's death. He'd been out of mourning for a long time. He had family and friends, a daughter he loved, a beautiful mistress, a life that kept him too busy to dwell on the past. It was just the moments of loneliness he couldn't seem to conquer. He had been friends with Mary since childhood, long before they had fallen in love. He had always gone to her first, to share happiness or grief, to pour out his anger, to find comfort. When she died, he had lost his best friend as well as his wife. Only Mary had filled that place in his heart. Now it was painfully empty.

Half in a dream, he saw Mary seated at the piano, her hair blazing in a pool of sunlight from the window. The waltz had poured from her fingertips . . .

"Isn't it lovely?" Mary cooed, her hands dancing over the keys. "I'm getting much better at it."

"Yes, you are," he agreed, smiling against her brilliant red curls. "But you've been practicing that waltz for months, Mary Elizabeth. Are you ever going to play another one? Just for the sake of variety?"

"Not until this one is perfect."

"By now even the baby has it memorized," he complained. "And I'm beginning to hear it when I sleep at night."

"Poor man," she said lightly, continuing to play. "Don't you realize how fortunate you are that I've chosen such a divine piece to torment you with?"

Sliding his hand under her chin, Luke bent her head back and kissed her upside-down. "I'll think up some torments of my own," he warned.

She laughed against his mouth. "I'm sure you will, darling. But in the meantime, run along and let me practice. Read a book, puff on your pipe, shoot something with your gun . . . whatever it is men usually do in their leisure hours."

Luke slid his hands over her full breasts. "They usually prefer to make love to their wives."

"How bourgeois," she murmured, arching willingly against his palms. "You're supposed to go to your club and talk politics. Besides, it's the middle of the day."

He kissed the side of her neck. "I want to see you naked in the sunlight. Come to bed with me." Ignoring her protests, he lifted her in his arms, and she gave a surprised laugh.

"But my practicing—"

"Later."

"I may never accomplish anything great in my life," she said, "but after I go, they'll always be able to say 'My, she played that waltz to perfection.' " She stared over his shoulder at the abandoned piano as he carried her upstairs . . .

Remembering, Luke felt his mouth twist in a

bittersweet smile. "Mary," he whispered, "you did play it to perfection."

"My lord?" His valet's voice broke the spell. Luke started, and looked toward the mahogany bureau. Biddle was standing there with an armful of starched white shirts and cravats. A lean, small man in his forties, Biddle was never so happy as when he was putting things in order. "Did you say something, sir?" the valet asked.

Luke stared down at the patterned carpet, taking a deep breath. The ghostly echoes faded from his ears. He made his voice crisp. "Pack a change of clothes for me, Biddle. I'll be staying overnight in London."

The valet didn't blink. It was a request he had obeyed hundreds of times before. Everyone knew what it meant. Tonight a visit would be paid to Iris, Lady Harcourt.

Tasia was still sitting at the piano when Emma returned to the music room. The girl was dressed in a simple blue frock that matched her eyes. "I've had my breakfast," Emma said in a subdued tone. "I'm ready for my lessons now."

Tasia nodded matter-of-factly. "Let's choose some books from the library, then."

Emma wandered to the piano and touched a key. The single note hovered in the air. "You were playing my mother's waltz. I always wondered what it sounded like."

"You don't remember her playing it?"

"No, but Mrs. Knaggs told me that she was especially fond of one waltz. Papa never would tell me which one it was."

"I'm certain it is painful for him."

"Would you play it for me, Miss Billings?"

"I don't believe Lord Stokehurst would allow it."

"After he leaves. I heard Biddle—that's his valet—telling one of the footmen that Papa will be visiting his mistress tonight."

Tasia was startled by the child's frankness. "You know everything that goes on in this house, don't you?"

Her sympathetic tone caused Emma's eyes to fill with tears. "Yes, Miss Billings."

Tasia smiled, reaching for her hand and squeezing it. "I'll play it for you after he leaves. As many times as you want."

Emma sniffled, wiping her eyes with the back of her free hand. "I don't know why I cry so much. Papa doesn't like it."

"I know exactly why." Exerting a gentle pressure on her hand, Tasia tugged the child onto the bench beside her. "Sometimes when you're growing up, it seems as if your emotions fill you up inside, and no matter how you try, you can't hold them back."

"Yes," Emma said with a vigorous nod. "It's dreadful. They come spilling out at all the wrong times, and I feel like such a ninny-head."

"That's how everyone feels at your age."

"Even you? I can't imagine you crying, Miss Billings."

"Of course I did. In the years after my father died, I hardly did anything else. He was the most important person in the world to me. After he was gone, it seemed there was no one for me to talk to. I would burst into tears at the slightest provocation. Once I cried for an hour after stubbing my toe." Tasia smiled. "But eventually it passed, as it will with you."

"I hope so," Emma said, her tears drying. "Miss Billings ... were you very young when your father died?"

"I was about your age."

"Did they make you wear black crepe?"

"Yes, I wore mourning for a year and one month."

"Papa said I must never wear it. He wouldn't even allow it when my cousin Letty died, because it makes him sad to see me draped in black."

"That is very wise of him. It's very wearisome, being in mourning for someone." Tasia closed the piano and motioned for Emma to stand up with her. "The library," she said briskly. "We have work to do, *ma chère mademoiselle.*"

Iris, Lady Harcourt was standing in her bedroom before a full-length mirror. The glass had been placed there ostensibly so she could view herself after she was dressed, but had been used on occasion for more interesting purposes. She was dressed in a gold gown that flattered her peach-tinted skin and red hair. It had taken all day to prepare herself. She had soaked in a scented bath, dressed with the help of a lady's maid, and endured two hours of having her hair curled with heated tongs.

Luke, who had walked into Iris's elegant Cornwall terrace unannounced, stood with his shoulder braced against the side of the doorjamb. A half-smile curved his mouth as he watched her. Iris was the kind of woman he had always liked, a beautiful redhead full of warmth and relaxed charm. Her voluptuous body was always tightly corseted, her long legs concealed by the draped layers of her skirts. Her bountiful breasts were modestly covered, for there was no need to make an impressive display. The lushness of her bosom spoke for itself.

Suddenly realizing she was being observed, Iris turned with a start. Her ruddy brows inched up her forehead. "Darling. You were so quiet I didn't hear you. What are you doing here?"

"Surprise visit." Pushing off from the doorframe, Luke approached her lazily. "Hello," he murmured, and kissed her.

Iris pressed up against his mouth with a sigh of delight. Her arms climbed around his hard shoulders. "A surprise indeed," she said when their lips parted. "As you can see, I'm dressed for the evening. I'm going out." She shivered at the way his teeth closed gently on her neck. "Dinner party," she managed to say.

"Send your regrets."

"If I don't attend there'll be an odd number. And they're expecting me." She laughed as she felt Luke unfasten the top button of her gown. "Darling, no. What if I promise to leave early and hurry back to you? Will that satisfy you?"

"No." The second button slipped free. "You're not going at all."

Iris frowned at him, even as her breath quickened. "You're the most arrogant man I know. And you have a definite problem with compromise. I'm not saying you don't have your good points, darling . . . but we must work on your temperament."

Luke tangled his fingers in her upswept hair, ruining the elaborate pile of curls. "It's taken centuries of selective breeding to achieve a specimen like me. You should have seen the early Stokehursts. Nothing to brag about, believe me."

"Oh, I do," Iris purred. "I'll bet they were complete savages." Her eyes widened as he jerked her against his aroused body. His mouth toyed gently with hers, then sealed over it. Iris groaned softly, all thoughts of the dinner party dissolving. She pushed herself against him, eager for his possession. Luke was an experienced and generous lover, knowing how to bring her to the edge of insanity. He liked to tease, to make her beg, to leave her sore and exhausted and satisfied. "At least let me take my corset off," she whispered. "I nearly fainted the last time."

Luke smiled, a movement of bristle and warmth against her cheek. "That's because you stop breathing at the important moments." He finished the row of buttons, and the dress fell to a heavy heap on the floor. The sharp edge of his hook caught the tapes of her petticoats and the strings of her corset, until her sumptuous body burst from its tight bindings.

"You should have to wait like other men," Iris said with a shiver of excited laughter. "It isn't civilized to go around ripping off women's garments, like some ruthless pirate."

"You can rip mine off," he said diplomatically.

"Oh, how very generous. How very . . . very . . ." The rest of her words were smothered by his demanding kisses.

Hours later they lay entwined in the darkened bedroom, while a few lit candles touched the air with a soft glow. Iris stretched in contentment as Luke traced the rich curve of her waist and hip. "Darling," she murmured, rolling toward him. "I want to ask you something."

"Mm." Luke kept his eyes closed, letting his fingers drift across her skin.

"Why won't you marry me?"

Luke turned his head, giving her a thoughtful glance. Through all the years of their acquaintance, he'd never considered marrying Iris. They had separate lives, never needing each other in more than a superficial way. There was friendship, and passion, just enough to make everything pleasant.

"Don't you care for me?" Iris wheedled.

"Of course I care for you." He patted her round hip and stared into her eyes. "But I'm not going to marry anyone, Iris. You know that."

"We're very good together. There's not a soul in the world who would begrudge us this marriage. And no one would be surprised by it."

He shrugged uncomfortably, unable to deny it.

"Is it that you're reluctant to commit yourself only to me?" Iris propped herself up on one elbow. "I wouldn't keep you from going to other women's beds, if that was what you needed. I wouldn't take away your freedom."

Surprised, Luke sat up and scrubbed his fingers through his dark hair. "Freedom to have sex with women I care nothing about?" He looked down at her with a wry smile. "Thank you, but I've done that before. I didn't find it all that satisfying. No, I don't need that kind of freedom."

"My God. You were born to be *someone's* husband."

"Mary's," he said, nearly inaudibly.

Iris frowned, stroking the light pelt on his chest with her palm. "Why only her?"

Luke was silent for a moment, choosing his words with difficulty. "After she went, I realized ... part of me was gone forever. I don't have as much to give a woman as you seem to think. I wouldn't make a good husband. Not the kind I was for her."

"Darling, your version of being a poor husband would far surpass anyone else's best attempts. You were so young when you lost Mary. How can you claim you'll never love again? You're only thirty-four. You must want more children, a family—"

"I have Emma."

"Don't you think she'll want brothers and sisters?"

"No."

"Fine, then. I don't have my heart set on children."

"Iris," Luke said gently, "I'm not going to marry you or anyone else. I don't want more than what we already have. If this relationship is making you unhappy, if you need more than I can give you, I'll understand. There are men who would jump at the chance of marrying you, and God knows I don't want to stand in the way—"

"No." Iris gave an anxious laugh. "I'm just greedy, I suppose. I wouldn't mind sleeping with you every night, and living in your home, and having everyone know I'm yours. But that doesn't mean I'm unhappy with things as they are. Don't look guilty. You've made no promises. You've been very careful not to. If this is all I can have of you, it's still more than any other man has given me."

"That's not true," Luke said gruffly, wishing he could be what she wanted. He was uneasy at the thought of living with a woman who loved him, when he couldn't love her back. It would be a shadow marriage, a mockery of what he'd once had with Mary.

"It is true," Iris insisted. "I'm always honest with you, Luke."

He kissed her shoulder, keeping his face averted. "I know."

"Which is why I'm going to tell you something. You haven't let yourself fall in love with anyone since Mary. But someday you will. You won't be able to stop it from happening. And I wish it could be me."

Luke caught her hand, which had wandered down to the indentations of muscle below his rib cage. Gently he kissed the tips of her fingers. "If I could love anyone that way again, it would be you. You're a good woman, Iris."

Her mood changed from lovelorn to wanton, and she eased her sleek body over his. "I'll have to correct that impression. I'm really very naughty."

Luke laughed and rolled her over, straddling her voluptuous hips. He brushed his mouth over hers in a provocatively light kiss. "Let me please you tonight."

"You always do." Her breath caught in her throat as his hand traveled slowly down her body.

"I have something special in mind," he whispered, and for a long time after that she was too consumed with pleasure to reply.

It had been two weeks since Tasia's arrival at Southgate Hall, and she had found a place for herself amid the comfortable routines of the estate. It was a blessing to live in such a peaceful place, after the last traumatic months. She had been the focus of suspicion and condemnation for so long that she was grateful for the opportunity to fade into the background. And Alicia Ashbourne had been right—no one took notice of a governess. The servants were pleasant to her, but hardly inclined to welcome her into their group. And she was too far beneath Lord Stokehurst and his highborn guests, socially speaking, to merit their attention. She existed in an in-between world.

Not only was Tasia's position isolated, but she was unable to let down her extreme reserve with anyone except Emma. Perhaps spending three months in prison had given her this sense of being an outcast, of being separate from everyone. It was impossible for her to trust anyone, when she couldn't even trust herself. She was afraid of her own feelings, and most of all she was afraid to remember what she had done the night of Mikhail Angelovsky's death.

She experienced frequent nightmares about Mikhail, in which she had visions of blood and knives, and her ears rang with his taunting voice. Worse, there were odd moments in the day when she would have frightening flashes of memory. In the space of a second, she would see Mikhail's face, his hands, a glimpse of the room where he was killed ... and then with a hard blink, she would make the vision vanish. It made her as nervous as a cat, never knowing when something would trigger another image of her dead cousin.

Thank God for Emma, who was eager for all her time and attention. It was good to have someone to think about besides herself, someone whose problems and needs were more immediate than her own. The child was extremely isolated. Tasia felt that Emma needed the companionship of other girls, but there were no local landowners with children of a similar age.

Tasia and Emma spent six hours a day on lessons, everything from the theories of Homer to the proper use of a nail brush. Daily prayers were not overlooked, for Emma's faith had been learned in a scattered fashion from her father and the servants. Emma soaked up the varied curriculum with surprising quickness. She had an intuitive understanding of language, and a perceptiveness that surprised Tasia. There was little that escaped Emma. She had a boundless curiosity that drove her to investigate everyone and everything around her. Each bit of gossip on the estate was carefully ferreted out to be pondered and analyzed.

It was all Emma knew of the world, the circle of eighty people who spent their lives working like the parts of a great clock to keep the estate running. Forty were indoor servants, while the rest were employed in the stables, gardens, and mill house. Two were hired full-time just to clean windows. Most of the servants had been employed by the Stokehursts for years, and they rarely left. As Mrs. Plunkett had told Tasia, the staff at Southgate Hall was treated well. Even if they hadn't been, it would be difficult to find a new position. Work was scarce, and life very uncertain.

"Something's wrong with Nan," Emma told Tasia one day. They were sitting in the garden with a pile of books, drinking tall goblets of lemonade. "Have you noticed how strange she looks lately? Mrs. Knaggs says it's only that Nan has a touch of spring sickness, but I don't believe that. I think she's in love with Johnny."

"Who is Johnny?"

"One of the footmen. The tall one with the crooked nose. Every time she sees him, Nan sneaks off to a corner with him. Sometimes they talk and kiss, but most of the time she cries. I hope I never fall in love. No one ever seems happy when they're in love."

He said I'm to dismiss her in the morning and have her sent back to her village."

"Is anyone with her now?" Mrs. Plunkett asked.

"No, there's nothing to be done except let her stomach empty itself. She doesn't need help for that. Besides, none of the girls like her well enough to stay with her."

"And the young man?" Seymour asked, his long forehead creasing.

The housekeeper shook her head ruefully. "He disclaims any responsibility."

Tasia looked around the table in confusion. What did they all know that she didn't? "What is the matter with Nan?" she asked.

It was so rare for her to break in on a conversation that the others looked at her in surprise. Finally Mrs. Knaggs answered. "Didn't you hear? No, of course not, you've been with Emma all day. It's very distasteful. Nan has a follower."

"A follower?" Tasia was puzzled by the unfamiliar term. "Do you mean a lover?"

"Precisely." Mrs. Knaggs rolled her eyes and added uncomfortably, "And now there are . . . consequences."

"She's pregnant?" Tasia asked. A few eyebrows raised at her bluntness.

"Yes, and she's been hiding it from everyone. In an effort to solve the problem, she took a handful of special pills and drank a bottle of oil to get rid of the baby. She only succeeded in making herself ill, the poor little wretch. Thank God the baby wasn't harmed. Now Nan's going to be dismissed, and it's likely she'll end up in the streets." Mrs. Knaggs frowned and shook her head, as if it were too distasteful to discuss any further.

"At least she won't be troubling you no more, Miss Billings," the head housemaid said.

Tasia was filled with horror and sympathy. "No one is with her?"

"There's no need," Mrs. Knaggs said. "The doctor's seen her. I made certain Nan took the medicine he prescribed. Don't be concerned, my dear. Maybe Nan will learn a lesson. It's her own foolishness that brought her to this."

Tasia bent her head over a cup of tea, while the others continued the conversation. A few minutes later, she pretended to stifle a yawn. "Excuse me," she murmured. "It has been a busy day. I think I'll retire now."

It wasn't difficult to find Nan's room. The sounds of gasping and retching drifted into the hall from behind a closed door. Gingerly Tasia knocked and entered the room. It was even smaller than hers, with a single-paned window and walls covered with drab paper. She recoiled at the stench in the air. A crumpled figure writhed on the bed. "Get out of here," Nan's weak voice said, just before she bent over the metal basin and gagged.

"I came to see if I could help," Tasia said, striding to the window. She opened it a few inches, letting some fresh air blow inside. Turning back to the bed, she frowned as she saw that Nan was a ghastly shade of green.

"Go away," Nan moaned. "I'm going to die."

"No, you're not." Tasia went to the washstand. There was a pile of rags, all of them wet and dirty. Fumbling in her sleeve, she located one of her own handkerchiefs and dampened it with water from the pitcher.

Leaving the room, Tasia went to find Mrs. Knaggs. The housekeeper was giving instructions to a kitchen maid, who was clearing the dishes from the servants' table.

"You went to Nan," Mrs. Knaggs said as soon as she saw Tasia's face. "I rather thought you might."

"She's very ill," Tasia said gravely.

"There's no point in doing anything for her. She'll be gone soon."

Tasia was surprised by the housekeeper's callousness. "Ma'am, I don't see the harm in trying to make her more comfortable. Couldn't you direct one of the maids to help me carry a few supplies upstairs and change the bed?"

Mrs. Knaggs shook her head. "I've told the others they need have nothing to do with her."

"She's not a leper, Mrs. Knaggs. She's only pregnant."

"I don't want any of the girls to be exposed to the influence of promiscuity and immorality."

Tasia was tempted to answer sarcastically, but she bit her tongue to hold back the words. "Mrs. Knaggs," she said carefully, "isn't it the second great commandment to love thy neighbor as thyself? And when the Pharisees brought the adulteress to our Lord and asked Him if she should be stoned, didn't He say—"

"Yes, I know. 'He that is without sin among you, let him first cast a stone.' I daresay I'm as well-acquainted with the Bible as most people."

"Then surely you know the verse, 'Blessed are the merciful, for they shall obtain mercy'—"

"You are quite right, Miss Billings," the housekeeper interrupted hastily, apparently sensing that a sermon was approaching. "I'll have one of the maids bring up bed linens and fresh water right away."

Tasia smiled. "Thank you, ma'am. There's one more thing ... Do you happen to know if Lord Stokehurst will be returning tonight?"

"He'll be in London for the evening." Mrs. Knaggs looked at her meaningfully. "You understand."

"Yes, I do." The irony was not lost on Tasia. A man's philandering was winked at, accepted, even encouraged. Lord Stokehurst was free to have his pleasure. Even Johnny the footman wasn't being held responsible for the baby. Only Nan was paying the price.

Mrs. Knaggs stared at her speculatively. "Is there something you wish to speak to the master about, Miss Billings?"

"It can wait until morning."

"I'm certain you can't mean to speak to him about Nan's situation. The master has already made his decision on how it should be handled. No one ever questions his orders. Surely you wouldn't be foolish enough to displease him by bringing up the subject."

"Of course not," Tasia said. "Thank you, Mrs. Knaggs."

Returning too late to go on his usual morning ride with Emma, Luke closed himself in the library to attend to some work. Managing his three estates and other properties required an endless stream of correspondence with land agents, stewards, and lawyers. Between writing letters, he pored over account books and piles of receipts. The tedious atmosphere was underscored by the ticking of the mantel clock. In his concentration he hardly noticed the knock at the door. It came again, louder this time.

"Come in." Luke kept writing as someone entered the room. "I'm busy," he muttered. "Unless it's important, I don't want to be dist—" He broke off as he glanced at the intruder. It was Miss Billings.

So far their encounters had been brief and impersonal; chance meetings in the hall, a few words here and there about Emma. Luke had noticed that the governess avoided him whenever possible. She didn't seem to like being in the same room with him. No woman had ever been so cold to him, so unaware of him in every way.

As always, her face was pale and tense. Her figure was fragile, her waist so slender that he could have easily wrapped his hands around it. When she moved her head, the light slid over her ebony hair, making it gleam. She stared at him with those exotic eyes, looking like an underfed cat. After waking up next to Lady Harcourt's voluptuous cream-and-peaches warmth, Luke found the sight of the governess jarring.

He had no idea why Emma liked her so much. Yet Emma seemed happier than she had been in months. Luke was afraid his daughter was becoming attached to the governess. A pity, since Miss Billings would be leaving soon. The month was already half-over. Emma would just have to get used to someone else. It didn't matter how much good the governess did for his daughter, she still wasn't going to stay. Luke didn't trust her. She was sly, mysterious, haughty . . . all the qualities of a cat. He hated cats.

"What do you want?" he asked curtly.

"Sir, there is a matter I wish to discuss with you. It concerns one of the housemaids, Nan Pitfield."

Luke's eyes narrowed. This was something he hadn't expected. "The one who's been dismissed."

"Yes, my lord." Rosy color swept up her face, softening the parchment-white skin. "Everyone is aware of why she's being forced to leave. The young man who fathered the baby—one of your footmen, as I understand it—has abandoned all responsibility. I've come to ask you to give Nan a little money, to help her survive until she's able to work again. She comes from a poor family. It will be difficult for her to find employment anywhere, certainly nothing above five pounds a year—"

"Miss Billings," he interrupted, "Nan should have considered all of that before she decided to indulge herself in a backstairs romance."

"It wouldn't take very much to help her," the governess persisted. "A few pounds would make no difference to you—"

"I'm not going to reward a servant who hasn't done her job adequately."

"Nan works very hard, my lord—"

"I've made my decision. I suggest you turn your attention to what I'm paying you for, Miss Billings, and that's to give lessons to my daughter."

"And what kind of lesson are *you* teaching her, sir? What is Emma to think of your behavior? You're acting without a shred of compassion or mercy. Why must your servants be punished for having ordinary human needs? I don't approve of what Nan did, but neither can I blame her for trying to find some happiness. Nan was lonely, and she succumbed to a young man who said he loved her. Must she be made to suffer for it the rest of her life?"

"That's enough." His voice was unnaturally gentle.

"You care nothing about your servants," she continued recklessly. "Oh, you're willing to give them butter and candles—it's a small price to pay for having everyone think of you as the benevolent lord of the manor. But when it comes to really helping your servants, really caring for them, you can't be bothered. You'll just cast Nan out and forget all about her, while she'll starve, or become a prostitute—"

"Get out." As Luke shot to his feet, the tip of his hook slashed into the glossy surface of the desk, ruining the antique wood.

The governess didn't move. "Do you conduct your life so chastely that you are fit to judge her? If I'm not mistaken, you've just returned from a liaison of your own!"

"You're about to be dismissed with Nan."

"I don't care," she said passionately. "I would prefer to walk the streets myself than live under the same roof with such a heartless man—a hypocrite!"

All at once his temper exploded. Luke strode around his desk with a snarl, catching the front of her bodice in his large hand. She gave a whimper of fear. Luke shook her briefly, like a dog with a rat. His knuckles pressed hard against her sharp collarbone. "I don't know who the hell you were before you came here," he growled, "but you're a servant now. *My* servant. You obey me without question. My word is the last in all things. If you defy me again—" Suddenly Luke stopped. He didn't trust himself to speak further.

She refused to look away, though terror filled her eyes. Her breath fluttered against his chin, and her small hands came over his, plucking help-lessly. The word "no" came to her lips, soft shape without sound.

Luke breathed in uneven gushes of air. The urge to conquer, to dominate, was overwhelming. His blood sang with primitive masculine urges. She was very small, her weight dangling from his grip on her dress. He kept her off-balance, forcing her to lean into his hold. He could smell her skin: soap, salt, a trace of roses. He couldn't stop him-self from lowering his head, drinking in the scent. There was a responsive ache in his groin, his flesh filling with hot blood and sensation. All at once he wanted to shove her down to the desk and lift her skirts, and take her right there. He wanted to feel her stretched beneath him, her nails digging into his back, her body arching to take him deeper. He thought of her slim legs clamped around his waist . . . and he closed his eyes hard against the image.

"Please," she whispered. The ripple of her swal-low touched his knuckles.

Blindly Luke turned away, letting go of her with a shove. He kept his back to her, embarrassed by the swelling of his body, the flush on his face. "Get out," he said thickly.

He heard the swish of her skirts as she fled the room, the way she fumbled with the door handle. The door closed behind her with a forceful thump. Jerking the chair away from the desk, Luke sat down heavily and swiped at his face with his sleeve. "Christ," he muttered. One moment every-thing was normal, and the next the world had blown apart.

The tip of his forefinger rubbed over the deep scratch on the desk as he thought. Why had she bothered to plead for a disgraced housemaid? Why had she challenged him at the risk of losing her own position? Puzzled, he leaned back in his chair. It bothered him that he wanted to understand her. "Who are you?" he muttered. "Damn you, I'm going to find out."

Hurtling into her room, Tasia closed the door and threw her back against it. She panted hard, dizzy from running up the stairs so fast. There was no doubt she would be dismissed. She had been foolish. She deserved whatever happened. What right did she have to give the lord of the manor a dressing-down for his behavior? It was unreasonable, especially when she had never bothered to champion the causes of her own servants. She felt like the hypocrite she had accused him of being.

"Everything looks so different from belowstairs," she said aloud, and smiled grimly. She went to her little mirror, pulling the hairpins from her chignon and jabbing them back in more tightly. She had to calm herself. Soon it would be time to begin the daily lessons with Emma . . . if Lord Stokehurst didn't fire her the moment she reappeared.

There was something she had to do first. Searching in the armoire, she delved past her folded linens and closed her hand around a knotted handkerchief. She felt the hard lump of her father's gold ring. "Thank you, Papa," she whispered. "I'm going to put this to good use."

As Tasia appeared in the doorway of Nan's room, she saw that the girl was fully dressed and looking much better than she had the night before.

Surprise crossed Nan's face as she saw Tasia. "Miss Billings!"

"How do you feel today?"

Nan shrugged. "Fair. Though I can't hold anything in my belly 'cept a drop of tea. And my legs are weak." She gestured to a frayed hamper. "I'm almost finished with my packing."

"And the babe?"

Nan lowered her eyes. "It seems all right."

Tasia smiled slightly. "I came to say goodbye before you left."

"It's very kind of you, miss." Self-consciously Nan reached beneath her mattress and pulled out a small object. It was the icon. "Here she is." Reverently Nan traced the Madonna's face with her finger. "She belongs with you. I'm sorry I took her, Miss Billings. You were kindness itself, when you should've hated me."

Tasia received the icon without expression, though her heart gave an extra thump of gladness at having it back. "There is something I want to give you," she said, and handed Nan the knotted handkerchief. "You must sell it and keep the money it brings."

Frowning curiously, Nan untied the cloth. Her eyes widened as she saw the gold ring. "Oh, Miss Billings, you couldn't mean to give this to me!" She tried to hand it back, but Tasia refused.

"You'll need it for yourself and the baby."

Nan hesitated, staring down at the ring. "Where did you get it?"

A smile curved Tasia's lips. "Don't worry, I didn't steal it. The ring belonged to my father. I know he would approve. Please take it."

Nan closed her fingers over the object and began to sniffle. "Miss Billings, why are you doing this?"

There wasn't an easy answer to that. Tasia couldn't afford to be generous, not when her own resources were scarce. But it felt good to help Nan. For a few minutes at least, someone was staring at her with gratitude ... It made her feel strong and useful. And there was the baby. Tasia hated the thought of a tender new life being given such a cold welcome to the world: no father, no food, no home. A little extra money wouldn't solve anything, but it might give Nan some hope.

She realized Nan was waiting for a reply. "I know what it's like to be alone and in trouble."

Nan's gaze flitted down to her stomach. "You mean you—"

"Not that kind of trouble." Tasia laughed wryly. "But in a way it was just as serious."

Clutching the ring, Nan stepped forward and hugged her impulsively. "If it's a boy, I'll name him Billings!"

"Oh, my." Tasia's eyes sparkled with amusement. "You'd better shorten it to Billy."

"And if it's a girl, Karen. That's your first name, aye?"

Tasia smiled. "Call her Anna," she said gently. "I think that would be nice."

Emma seemed distracted during their morning lessons, only half-answering Tasia's questions. Samson was stretched out at their feet, turning up his furry stomach invitingly. He was quiet, seeming to understand the importance of remaining undetected by hostile housekeepers and irritable fathers. Occasionally Emma nudged his ribs with her toes, and he swiveled his big head around with a happy dog-grin, his tongue drooping down the side of his jaw.

"Miss Billings?" Emma asked, pausing in the middle of a paragraph about Roman military strategy. "Nan is going to have a baby, isn't she?"

Taken aback, Tasia wondered how the girl had found out so soon. "That isn't a proper subject for discussion, Emma."

"Why won't anyone explain it to me? Isn't it more important for me to know about real life than a lot of moldy history?"

"Perhaps when you're older someone will explain things to you, but in the meantime—"

"It happens when a man and a woman sleep in the same bed, doesn't it?" Emma's gaze was bright and perceptive. "That's what happened—Nan and Johnny slept together. And now a baby is coming. Miss Billings, why would Nan take a man into her bed if she knew a baby would happen afterward?"

"Emma," Tasia said softly, "you mustn't ask such questions of me. It's not my place to answer. I don't have your father's permission—"

"How will I ever find out? Is it some terrible secret that only grown-ups can understand?"

"No, it's not terrible." Tasia frowned and rubbed her temples. "It's only that ... it's very personal. There must be a woman that you trust and care for—your grandmother, perhaps—who will answer your questions."

"I trust you, Miss Billings. And it makes me very anxious to think about the things I don't know. When I was eight, my aunt saw me kissing one of the village boys, and she was very angry. She told me you can get a baby that way. Is that true?"

Tasia hesitated. "No, Emma."

"Why would she tell me something false? Was it wrong of me to kiss that boy?"

"I'm certain she thought you were too young to understand the truth. And no, it wasn't wrong. You were merely curious. There was no harm done."

"What if I want to kiss a boy now? Would that be wrong?"

"Well, not exactly, but . . ." Tasia smiled uncomfortably. "Emma, perhaps you should tell your father that you would like to talk to a woman about . . . certain matters. He'll find someone appropriate. I doubt he would approve of me being the one to answer your questions."

"Because you argued with him this morning about Nan." Emma began to coil a lock of blazing red hair around her finger, avoiding Tasia's gaze.

"Did you eavesdrop, Emma?" Tasia asked, her tone reproving.

"Everyone has been talking. No one *ever* argues with Papa. All the servants are surprised. They think you're very brave and foolish. They say you'll probably be dismissed. But don't worry about that, Miss Billings. I won't let Papa send you away."

Tasia smiled, touched by Emma's artless reassurance. She was an endearing child. It would be very easy to love her. "Thank you, Emma. But you and I must abide by your father's decisions, whatever they are. I made a mistake this morning by forcing my opinions on him. I was rude and ungrateful. If Lord Stokehurst chooses to dismiss me, it would be no more than what I deserve."

Emma scowled, suddenly looking like her father. She tapped her long foot against Samson's snout. Gently he opened his jaws and chewed her heel. "Papa will keep you here if I want you to stay. He feels guilty because I don't have a mother. Grandmama says that's why he has always spoiled me. She wants him to marry Lady Harcourt, but I hope he doesn't."

"Why?" Tasia asked softly.

"Lady Harcourt wants to take Papa away from me, and have him all to herself."

Tasia made a noncommittal sound. She was beginning to understand the fierce attachment between the Stokehursts, forged by the death of the woman they had both loved. The loss of Mary Stokehurst was an open wound for both of them. It seemed as if father and daughter used each other as an excuse to keep from reaching out to other people, and risk having their hearts broken again. It might be best for Emma to go to a place where she could make friends with girls her own age and find new outlets for her energy. Far better than to spend her time prowling around a country estate, spying on the servants.

Tasia gave Emma an enigmatic smile. "Perhaps we should finish this chapter and go for a walk. Some fresh air might clear the cobwebs away."

"You're not going to explain anything to me about Nan," Emma said with a resigned sigh, and dutifully returned her attention to the book.

There was no word from Lord Stokehurst all day. He remained in the library, conducting meetings with a parade of tenants and men from the village. "Farming practices," came Seymour's reply, when Tasia asked what the visitors had come to talk about. "The master is making improvements on the estate, to ensure that the tenants are working the land as productively as possible. Some of them are nearly medieval in their practices. The master is advising them about modern methods and giving them the opportunity to make complaints against the estate manager."

"That is very kind of him," Tasia murmured. In Russia, landowners were far removed from the business of the estate. They hired stewards to insulate them from concerns that were beneath their notice. Certainly she had never heard of peasants being given advice or help directly from the master's household.

"It is a practical policy," Seymour remarked. "The more His Lordship invests in his own estate, the more profitable it becomes for all concerned."

Tasia thought it very astute reasoning. "It is a good thing that His Lordship is not too proud to talk directly with the peasants. Where I come from, a man of his position would communicate with them only through a steward."

Suddenly there was a glint of amusement in Seymour's eyes. "In England they don't usually like to be called peasants. Better to say tenants."

"Tenants," she repeated obediently. "Thank you, Mr. Seymour."

The butler gave her one of his rare smiles and nodded as she walked away.

Evening approached, and there was still no word from Lord Stokehurst. Tasia thought he was deliberately making her wait, so that she would have ample time to worry about when she would be dismissed. For the first time she took supper alone in her room, to avoid the questions and curious gazes of the other servants. She ate slowly, her stare fixed on the darkening sky outside her window. All her muscles were tense as she wondered what would happen. Soon she would be banished from Southgate Hall. She would have to make plans. The thought of returning to Charles and Alicia was galling. But perhaps they wouldn't be surprised that she had failed in her first position. The Kapterevs had never been known for their humility. Silently she vowed that she would *choke* on her opinions before spouting them to her next employer.

An excited knock caused the door to rattle. "Miss Billings! Miss Billings!"

"Nan?" Tasia asked in surprise, recognizing the voice. "Come in."

The housemaid burst into the room, her eyes glowing and her cheeks pink. She hardly looked like herself. "Miss Billings, they said at the servants' hall that you were up here. I had to come and see you straightaway ..." She paused to recover her breath.

"I thought you would have left by now. Nan, you must have run all the way up the stairs. It's not good for you."

"Yes, but I wanted to tell you ..." Nan let out a burst of excited laughter. "I'm getting married!"

Tasia's eyes widened. "Married? To whom?"

"To Johnny! He proposed not ten minutes ago, an' asked me to forgive him for everything. Said he'd be as good a husband as he could be, an' I said that's enough for me! Now my baby will have a name, an' I'll have a proper husband!" Nan hugged herself in joyful excitement.

"But how? Why?"

"Johnny said that Lord Stokehurst had a talk with him this afternoon."

"Lord Stokehurst?" Tasia repeated, dazed.

"The master told Johnny that no man in his right mind wants to get married, but everyone must sooner or later, an' that a man should own up to his doings, an' if Johnny had gotten a girl with child, he should give 'em both his name. His Lordship even gave us some money to start with. We're leasing a plot of land to farm near the village. Isn't it a wonder? How can everything change so quick-like?"

"I don't know," Tasia said, recovering enough from her amazement to smile. "It is wonderful. I'm very happy for you, Nan."

"I came to give this back to you." She thrust the knotted handkerchief back at Tasia, weighted with the lump of the gold ring. "I didn't tell Johnny about it—he might've made me keep it. But you need it, Miss Billings. You're too kind for your own good."

"Are you sure you shouldn't keep it?"

"We'll be all right now, me an' the babe. We got someone to look after us now. Take it back, miss, please."

Tasia held her hand out, and the ring dropped into her palm. She closed her fist around it and hugged Nan tightly. "God be with you," she murmured.

"An' you, Miss Billings."

As Nan left the room, Tasia sat down on her bed, her thoughts whirling. Nothing had ever surprised her more than Lord Stokehurst's actions. She had never dreamed he might change his mind so abruptly. What had caused it? Why would he have taken it upon himself to talk Johnny into marrying Nan, and even sweetened the bargain with what amounted to a small dowry? She turned the matter around and around in her head, unable to think of what his motives might be.

The hour grew late. Tasia knew she wouldn't be

able to fall asleep tonight, not with all the questions that bothered her. Sighing, she set her supper tray outside the door and decided to visit the library. A long, dull book was just what she needed.

Making her way down the servants' stairs, Tasia moved through the hallways like a shadow. The household had settled for the evening. The routine was always the same. By now the last of the supper dishes had been washed, and the necessary kitchen utensils set out for Mrs. Plunkett for tomorrow morning. Biddle had polished the master's shoes and boots. Mrs. Knaggs was sitting with her mending basket, and perhaps writing a list of household supplies to be purchased. Most of the lamps in the hallways had been turned down, covering the house in shadows.

Finding the library, Tasia lit a lamp and turned the flame to a bright glow. The light played over the mahogany cabinets and shelves, and gleamed softly on the leather-lined walls. Tasia enjoyed the smell of books and leather, and the traces of smoke and brandy that lingered in the air. The library was a masculine sanctuary, used for discussion of business, politics, or highly private matters. There was a sense of intimacy and family history in the room. She browsed from one shelf to another, looking for something that would put her to sleep. Judiciously she selected an armload of books, examining each one.

"*The Aspects of Progressivism,*" she read aloud, and wrinkled her nose. "*Revolution and Reform in Modern Europe. The Wonders of British Expansionism.* Well, any one of these should do . . ."

A mocking voice came out of the shadows, startling her. "Back for the second round?"

Three
❧ ❧

The pile of books dropped from Tasia's hands. She gasped, whirling toward the voice. "*Oh . . .*"

Lord Stokehurst stood up from the large chair near the fireplace. He had been sitting in the dark with a drink, staring into the empty grate. Casually he set a half-finished glass of brandy on a bronze table, and approached her.

Tasia's heart pounded hard in her chest. "Wh-why didn't you let me know you were here?"

"I just did." Stokehurst had the appearance of a man who had spent all day at his desk. The turned-down collar of his shirt was smudged with ink, and the top buttons were undone, revealing a gleam of brown skin at the base of his throat. A few locks of black hair had fallen on his forehead, softening the hard angles of his face.

His deep blue eyes held an intimate curiosity that sent a shiver down Tasia's spine. Against her will she thought of what she had tried to put out of her mind all day . . . the moment during their argument when he had gripped the front of her dress in his fury. His aggressive maleness had terrified her. Along with her fear, however, had come a breathless feeling that hadn't left for a long time. She focused on the heap of books at her feet, hoping he wouldn't see the flush spreading on her face.

"You seem to have lost your composure," he said.

"Anyone would, h-having a man leap out of the shadows like that." Tasia swallowed hard, trying to steady herself. She owed him an apology. "My lord, Nan came to see me—"

"I don't want to talk about it," he interrupted curtly.

"But I misjudged you—"

"No, you didn't."

"I-I overstepped my bounds."

Stokehurst didn't argue with that, only stared at her with a mocking lift of his brows. He made her very nervous, standing there ... all darkness and devilish power spun into the shape of a man.

Tasia forced herself to go on. "It was kind of you to help Nan, my lord. She and the baby will be much better off und ..."

"Only if you consider a reluctant husband better than none. He doesn't want to marry her."

"But you convinced him that it was the right thing to do."

"That doesn't mean he won't make Nan pay for it in a hundred different ways." He shrugged. "At least the child won't be born a bastard."

Warily Tasia watched him through the screens of her lashes. "Sir ... do you intend to dismiss me?"

"I considered it." There was a deliberate silence before he continued. "But I've decided against it."

"Then I'm to stay on?"

"For the meantime."

Tasia was so relieved that her knees wobbled. "Thank you," she whispered. She crouched to gather the pile of books, sitting lightly on her heels.

To her dismay, Stokehurst came to help. He bent and tucked a couple of the heavy volumes beneath his left arm. They reached for a book at the same time, their fingers brushing. Startled by the touch of his warm hand, Tasia jerked back so sharply that her balance was lost. She fell back in an awkward heap on the floor. She was as stunned as she was humiliated. She was *never* clumsy. Her face burned at Stokehurst's quiet laughter.

Rising to his feet, Stokehurst replaced the books on the shelf and reached down for her. He pulled her up effortlessly, his powerful grip engulfing her hand up to her wrist. Although his hold was gentle, there was a hint of alarming strength in it. How easy it would be for him to snap her bones like matchsticks. Tasia stepped back from him quickly, smoothing her skirts and yanking the waist of her bodice to settle everything in place.

"Which book did you want?" Stokehurst asked, his blue eyes gleaming with amusement.

Blindly Tasia pulled one from the shelf, not bothering to read the title. She held it flat against her chest, as if it would shield her from his mockery. "This one will do."

"Very well. Goodnight, Miss Billings."

Although she had been dismissed, Tasia didn't move. "Sir," she said hesitantly, "if you have a moment, there is something I would like to talk to you about."

"Another downtrodden housemaid?" he asked in jeering apprehension.

"No, my lord. It's about Emma. She ... found out about Nan's situation. Naturally she has been asking questions. Sir, it occurred to me . . . Well, it reminded me . . . I asked Emma if anyone has ever talked to her about . . . You see, she's old enough to begin . . . She's of the age when girls . . . You understand."

Stokehurst shook his head, his alert gaze trained on her.

Tasia cleared her throat. "I'm referring to the time each month when women . . ." She stopped again. In her embarrassment, she wished she could drop through the floor. She had never said anything so intimate to any man.

"I see." His voice sounded strange. When Tasia risked another look at him, she saw a comical mixture of surprise and dismay on his face. "I hadn't thought about that," he muttered. "She's still a little girl."

"Twelve." Tasia twisted her fingers together. "Sir, I didn't . . . My mother neglected to explain to me . . . and then one day . . . I-I was very frightened. I would not wish for Emma to be so unprepared."

Stokehurst went to the bronze table, picking up his drink. "Neither would I." He downed the rest of the liquor in a single gulp.

"Then I have your permission to talk to her?"

Luke shook his head, gripping his empty glass. "I don't know." He hadn't wanted to accept the signs that Emma was getting older. The idea of his daughter beginning her monthly flow, developing a woman's body, a woman's emotions and desires . . . it was too soon. It made him uneasy. He'd never allowed himself to think about it before. Someone had to prepare Emma for the changes that would take place as she matured. But who? His sister was too far away, and his mother was as likely to tell Emma some nonsensical story as the truth. The duchess was a woman of refined sensibilities. She disapproved of Southgate Hall's French decor, considering all rococo curves and scalloped edges to be immoderately suggestive. She abhorred the sight of chair legs unconcealed by fringe. All things considered, she wasn't the best person to explain the workings of human anatomy to his daughter.

"How much do you plan to tell her?" he asked bluntly.

The governess blinked in surprise and strove for a matter-of-fact tone. "Only the things a young girl should know. If you don't wish for me to talk to her, my lord, then I think someone else should very soon."

Luke stared at her intently. Her concern for his daughter seemed genuine. She wouldn't have brought up the subject otherwise, not when it made her so uncomfortable. And Emma liked her. Why not have her do it?

"You may as well talk to her," he said, making up his mind. "Just don't start quoting Genesis while you're at it. Emma doesn't need the weight of a few thousand years' worth of biblical guilt added to her conscience."

Her lips pursed, and she answered in a prickly tone. "Of course, my lord."

"I assume all your information is correct?"

She nodded briefly, her face suffused with red.

Suddenly Luke smiled. She looked very young in her discomfort, flushed and struggling for composure. He couldn't help enjoying it. "How can you be certain?" he asked, prolonging the moment.

She refused to take the bait. "With your permission, my lord, I would like to retire for the evening."

"Not yet." Luke knew he was being arrogant, but he didn't care. He wanted her to stay. It had been a tedious day, and he was in need of some diversion. "Would you like a drink, Miss Billings? Some wine, perhaps?"

"No, thank you."

"Then stay here while I have some."

She shook her head. "I must decline your invitation, sir."

"It's not an invitation." Luke gestured to the chairs by the fireplace. "Sit down."

For a moment she didn't move. "It is very late," she murmured. Then she made her way to one of the chairs and perched on the edge of it. After placing the book on a side table, she knotted her hands in her lap.

Leisurely he refilled his glass. "Tell me what it's like to live in Russia."

She tensed in alarm. "I can't—"

"You've already admitted you came from there." Luke sat with his drink, stretching out his long legs. "You must be able to tell me *something* without revealing your precious secrets. Describe it for me."

She regarded him doubtfully, as if suspecting him of trying to trick her. "Russia makes one feel very small. The land is endless, and the sun is softer there than in England—it makes everything look a little gray. At this time of year in St. Petersburg, the sun never sets. White nights, they call them . . . Only the sky isn't white, it turns rose and violet, and stays that way from midnight to morning. That is when it is most beautiful, to see the black shapes of the buildings against the sky.

The tops of the churches are round, like this." She shaped an onion dome with her delicate hands. "Inside the churches, there are no statues allowed. Instead we have icons—religious paintings of Christ, the Apostles, the Virgin, the saints. Their faces are long and narrow and sad. It is a very spiritual look. The saints in the English church are too proud."

Luke conceded the point, recalling with amusement that the sculptures in his own chapel had a vaguely smug look.

"And there are no pews in Russian churches," she continued. "It is more respectful to the Lord to stand, even if the service lasts for hours. To Russians it is very important to be humble. The common people are modest and hardworking. When the winter lasts longer than expected, they tighten their belts, gather around the hearth, and make jokes and tell stories to take their minds off their empty stomachs. The Russian church teaches that God is always with us, and everything that happens, good or bad, is His will."

Luke was fascinated by the changes in her face. For the first time she had relaxed in his presence. Her tone was soft, and her eyes appeared more catlike than usual in the shadows. She kept on talking, but he didn't listen. He wondered what it would feel like to pull down her silky black hair and wind it around his wrist, holding her still for his kisses. Her body was so light, he would barely feel her weight in his lap. Yet for all her physical frailty, she had a steely will and a fearlessness that he admired. Even Mary hadn't dared to stand up to him in a temper.

"When things are very, very bad," she continued, "the Russian people have a saying: *Vsyo proidyot.* Everything will pass. My father used to say—" She stopped with a sharply indrawn breath.

From the expression in her eyes, it was clear that the subject of her father was an emotional one. "Tell me about him," Luke murmured.

Her eyes brightened with a sheen of tears. "He died a few years ago. He was a good, honorable man, the kind that people trusted to mediate their arguments. He had the ability to see all points of view. Since his death nothing has been the same." A bittersweet smile touched her lips. "Sometimes I want to talk to him very badly. I can't make myself believe that I never will again. It makes things worse, living so far away from home. Everything I knew of him is back there."

Luke watched her uneasily. An explosive emotion pressed upward beneath his calm surface, something too dangerous to analyze. After Mary's death, he had concentrated only on survival. Some needs could be satisfied. The rest he had locked away forever. That vault of loneliness and desire had never been threatened, until now. He should send the governess away for good, before it became worse. The argument over the pregnant housemaid had been the perfect excuse to dismiss her, Ashbournes be damned. But somehow he hadn't been able to do it.

He dragged a question from his taut throat. "Will you ever go back?"

"I . . ." She gave him a glance so wretched and lost that it made his breath stop. "I can't," she whispered.

In the next instant, she was gone, rushing from the library without taking the book she had come for.

Luke was afraid to follow her. He sat there in a paralysis of emotion and lust. Sinking low in his chair, he glared at the ceiling. God knew he wasn't a fool where women were concerned. He was the last man on earth likely to fall for a mysterious waif. She was too young, too foreign, too much the opposite of everything Mary had been.

At the thought of his wife, Luke stood up, his muscles unlocking. How could he betray Mary this way? He remembered the pleasure of sharing a bed with his wife, the way her warm body had snuggled against his in the night, the way she had kissed him awake each morning. It had always been comfortable between them. After she was gone, he had been driven by physical need to find other women, but it was never the same.

He had never dreamed he would want someone else. Not like this, with his self-control crumbling, his emotions in a revolution. The governess was becoming an obsession, and he couldn't seem to stop it from happening.

He didn't even know her real name.

With a self-mocking laugh, he reached for his brandy. "To you," he muttered, raising the glass to the chair she had occupied. "Whoever the hell you are."

Tasia reached her room and shut the door with a bang. She had run up three flights of stairs without stopping. Gasping for breath, she held her hand over a cramp in her side and leaned against the wall. She shouldn't have rushed out of the library, but if she had stayed, there was a good chance she would have burst into self-pitying tears. Talking about Russia had caused homesickness to well up inside her. She wanted to see her mother. She was desperate for familiar people and places. She wanted to hear her own language again, to have someone call her by her real name—

"*Tasia.*"

Her heart stopped. She looked around the empty room, startled. Had someone whispered her name? Out of the corner of her eye, she saw a flicker in the armoire mirror. All at once she was filled with fright. She wanted to run in panic, but some terrible force compelled her to take a step forward, and then another, while her staring eyes remained fixed on the mirror.

"*Tasia,*" she heard again, and she reeled in horror. She covered her mouth with her hand, gripping hard to stifle a scream.

Prince Mikhail Angelovsky stared back at her from the mirror, his eyes dark holes in his blood-smeared face. His bluish lips parted in a leering grin. "*Murderess.*"

Tasia was riveted by the ghastly sight. There was a strange buzzing in her ears. This wasn't real ... It was only a vision, something born of imagination and guilt. She closed her eyes briefly to make it go away, but when she opened them again, the image was still there. She lowered her hand and spoke through numb lips. "Misha," she faltered, "I didn't mean to kill you—"

"*It's on your hands.*"

Trembling, Tasia looked down and saw that her hands were drenched with blood. A choked cry escaped her. She clenched her fists and shut her eyes. "Leave me alone," she sobbed. "I won't listen. Leave me alone." She was too frightened to pray, to run, to do anything but stand there petrified. Slowly the humming noise faded from her ears. She opened her eyes again, staring at her hands. They were clean and white. The mirror was empty. Somehow she made her way to the bed and sat down, not bothering to blot the fresh tear streaks on her cheeks.

It took a long time to calm herself. When the terror faded, she had no strength left. Lying back on the bed, she stared up at the blurry, shadowed ceiling and used her sleeve to wipe her eyes. It didn't matter that she had no memory of killing Misha. The guilt weighed more heavily on her each day. She supposed there would be other visions, and probably nightmares. Her conscience wouldn't let her forget or ignore what she had done. The murder would always be with her. Her stomach seemed to flip over, and she groaned in quiet misery. "Stop it," she told herself fiercely. She couldn't torment herself with thoughts of Mikhail Angelovsky, or she would go insane.

The first day of May was clear and bright. The last bitter trace of winter had left the air, replaced by the verdant scent of springtime. Sprawled on the carpeted floor of an upstairs sitting room, Emma twirled her red hair into wild ringlets. She seemed appalled by her governess's matter-of-fact explanation of the menstrual cycle.

"Disgusting," Emma muttered. "Why is everything such a *bother* for women? Bloody rags, stomach cramps, counting the days each month . . . why don't men have to go through some of this?"

Tasia smiled. "They have their own burdens, I imagine. And it's not disgusting, Emma. It's the way God created us. In return for all the 'bother,' as you put it, we are blessed with the ability to give birth."

"And what a lark *that* is," Emma said sourly. "I can hardly wait to be blessed with labor pains."

"Someday you'll want your own children, and you won't mind all that."

A thoughtful frown appeared on Emma's face. "Once I begin my monthly bleeding, it means I'm old enough to have a baby?"

"Yes, if you share a bed with a man."

"Just sharing a bed will do it?"

"It's more complicated than that. You'll learn the rest later."

"I'd rather learn everything now, Miss Billings. I'm capable of imagining some pretty dreadful things."

"What happens between a man and woman in bed isn't dreadful. I've been told it can be quite pleasant."

"It must be," Emma said speculatively. "Or else those women wouldn't invite Papa into their beds." Her eyes widened with dismay. "Oh, Miss Billings, you don't think he's given babies to any of *them* do you?"

Tasia's face turned hot. "I don't think it is likely. There are ways to prevent babies from happening, if one is careful."

"Careful about what?"

As Tasia thought of various ways to sidestep the question, they were interrupted by a housemaid's appearance at the door. It was Molly, a buxom, dark-haired girl with a toothy smile. "Miss Emma," she said, "the master sent me to tell you that Lord and Lady Pendleton have arrived. He says for you to come downstairs at once."

"Drat!" Emma exclaimed, rushing to the window overlooking the front drive. "There they are, getting out of the carriage." She turned to Tasia and rolled her eyes. "Every year they insist on coming to watch the Maypole dance with Papa and me. Lady Pendleton says it's *so* entertaining to watch the 'rustics' celebrate. The crotchety old snob."

Tasia joined her at the window, gazing at the plump, middle-aged woman swathed in brocade. Lady Pendleton wore an imperious frown. "She does look rather haughty," she admitted.

"You'll have to go to the village with us, Miss Billings. I'll drop dead from boredom if you don't."

"It wouldn't be fitting, Emma." The last thing Tasia wanted was to take part in a noisy village festival. It was improper for a governess, who was supposed to maintain her dignity at all times, to be seen in such a setting. Besides, the thought of being in a large gathering made her nervous. The memory of the bloodthirsty crowd at her trial, the sea of accusing faces inside and outside the courtroom, was still too vivid in her mind. "I'm going to stay here," she said firmly.

Emma and Molly protested at the same time.

"But Papa gave all the servants time off to go down to the village."

"It's bad luck not to take part in May Day," Molly exclaimed. "You have to welcome summer with the rest of us. They've done it this way for a thousand years!"

Tasia smiled. "I'm certain summer will arrive whether I welcome it or not."

The housemaid shook her head impatiently. "You have to come tonight, at least. That's the most important part of it all."

"What happens tonight?"

Molly seemed to be stunned by her ignorance.

"The Maypole dance, o' course! And then two men dress in a horse suit and go through houses in the village. People join hands and follow the horse in a long line. It's good luck to have the parade pass through your house."

"Why a horse?" Tasia asked, entertained by the notion. "Why not a dog or a goat?"

"It's supposed to be a horse," Molly replied, looking offended. "It's *always* been a horse."

Emma began to giggle. "Wait until Papa hears. Miss Billings wants our May Day horse to be changed to a goat!" The sound of her laughter drifted down the hall as she left to join her father and the Pendletons.

"Emma, don't tell him that," Tasia called, but the child made no response. Sighing, Tasia looked back at Molly. "I'm *not* taking part in any spring-time celebrations. If I recall correctly, it's nothing more than a pagan rite—worshipping Druids and fairies, and such things."

"Don't you believe in fairies, Miss Billings?" Molly asked innocently. "You should. You're just the sort they like to carry off." She left with a snicker, while Tasia frowned after her.

The Stokehursts spent the afternoon observing the Maypole dance with the Pendletons. Most of the servants didn't show up for the cold dinner Mrs. Plunkett had prepared. They were all busy adorning themselves for the night's revelry. Tasia was certain that the springtime celebration was only an excuse to drink and cavort through the village. She wanted no part of it. Closing herself in her room, she settled by the open window and listened to the sound of drumbeats and chants float-ing up from the village. The night air was crisp with the scent of frost. She stared outside, imagining that the forest was filled with fairies, and that the flickering light of torches was the glow of their wings.

"Miss Billings!" The door to her room burst open. Three girls poured inside without waiting for an invitation. Bewildered, Tasia stared at Molly, Hannah, and Betsy. They were dressed identically, in white blouses, beribboned and flowered wreaths, and colored skirts. "Miss Billings," Molly said merrily, "we've come to take you to the village with us."

Tasia smothered a groan and shook her head. "Thank you, but I have nothing to wear. I'll stay here. Have a wonderful time, all of you."

"We brought some clothes." A collection of blouses and skirts dropped to her bed in a bright heap.

Hannah, a small, blond kitchen maid, smiled at her shyly. "Some of it's ours, and some of it's Miss Emma's. Keep what you like—they're all old things. Try the red skirt first, Miss Billings."

"I'm not going," Tasia said firmly.

The girls began to bully and coax her. "Miss Billings, you *must*. It's likely the only fun you'll have all year—"

"It's dark outside. No one will know it's you."

"Everyone is going. You can't stay here all by yourself!"

To Tasia's surprise, Mrs. Knaggs appeared at the doorway with an armload of flowers. The housekeeper's face was stern. "What is this I hear about Miss Billings going down to the village?"

Tasia was relieved that she finally had an ally. "Mrs. Knaggs, they are insisting that I accompany them, and you know how imprudent the idea is."

"Yes," Mrs. Knaggs said, and broke out into an

unexpected smile. "And if you *don't* go with them tonight, Miss Billings, I shall be very displeased. When you're an old woman like me, you can stay inside and watch through the window. For now you belong at the Maypole dance."

"But ... but ..." Tasia stuttered, "I don't believe in pagan rituals." Like all Russians, she had been brought up with a complex mixture of religion and superstition. It was proper to respect nature and all its powerful forces, but God was displeased by the worship of idols. Tree worshipping and any other May Day customs were definitely not acceptable.

"Don't do it because you believe in it," Molly said, laughing. "Do it for luck. For fun. Haven't you ever done something just for fun?"

Tasia longed to stay hidden in the privacy of her room. She tried a few different objections, but her excuses were batted away. "All right," she said reluctantly. "But I won't enjoy it."

The girls giggled and chattered, holding up articles of clothing while she undressed. "The red skirt," Hannah insisted, while Molly argued for the blue.

"She doesn't even need a corset," Betsy said, staring enviously at Tasia's slender, linen-clad form.

Molly helped to pull a drawstring blouse over Tasia's head. "Her titties aren't much bigger than Emma's," she said with a friendly laugh. "But don't worry, Miss Billings. A few more weeks of Mrs. Plunkett's puddings, an' you'll have a shape like mine."

"I don't think so," Tasia said doubtfully, glancing at Molly's ample bosom. She submitted, resigned to her fate, as they pulled the pins from her hair. The women exclaimed in admiration as her shining black hair fell to her hips.

"Oh, how pretty." Hannah sighed. "I wish mine looked like that." She went to the mirror and frowned at her own gold curls, tugging as if it might make them longer.

They plaited Tasia's hair with ribbons and flowers, and let it hang in a thick rope down her back. Standing back, the girls viewed the results with satisfaction.

"You're a lovely thing," Mrs. Knaggs said. "Every lad from the village will be trying to steal a kiss from you!"

"What?" Tasia asked in dismay, while the girls pulled her out of the room.

"It's a village custom," Molly said. "Sometimes the lads rush up and steal a kiss for luck. No harm in it."

"What if I don't want to be kissed?"

"You can run away, I s'pose ... but there's no need. If he's an ugly sort, it'll be over quick enough, and if he's a likely lad, you won't want to run!"

It was dark outside, a canopy of clouds covering the stars. The village was illuminated by torches and by lamps set in cottage windows. Drumbeats became louder and louder as they approached the green, tangling in a mixture of rhythms.

As Tasia had expected, wine played an important role in the celebration. Men and women were drinking from bottles and flasks, slaking their thirst between rounds of enthusiastic dancing. Linking hands, they circled the flower-wrapped Maypole and sang pagan songs about trees, the earth, and the moon. The sense of freedom and fun reminded Tasia of the Russian peasants' love of *voila*, the occasional chance to make mischief and have one's way, drink and break things, and be wild.

"Come on!" Molly cried, grabbing one of Tasia's hands, while Betsy took the other. They plunged into the circle and became part of it, singing an ancient ballad about a magic oak forest. "You don't have to sing, Miss Billings. Just make noise and keep your feet moving!"

That was easy enough. Tasia kept pace with the others, repeating the chants she heard, until the drumbeat was echoed by her own pounding heart. The circle broke as everyone paused to gulp more wine. Molly handed her a soggy wineskin. Awkwardly Tasia drank a stream of sweet red liquor. When the dance resumed, a handsome blond boy took Tasia's left hand. He smiled and joined in the song, crowing as loudly as the others.

Perhaps it was the wine, or the foolishness of the dance, but Tasia began to enjoy herself. All the women darted in the center of the circle, taking the wreaths from their hair and waving them high in the air. The scent of flowers mingled with sweat and wine, giving the air a peculiar earthy-sweet smell. Tasia circled the Maypole until the world reeled around her, the torch flames dancing like fireflies.

She broke outside the group of dancers and tried to catch her breath. The damp folds of her blouse clung to her, and she pulled at it repeatedly. In spite of the night's coolness, she was flushed and hot, exhilarated. Someone handed her a bottle, and she took a swallow of wine. "Thank you," she said, wiping a stray drop from the corner of her mouth. As she looked up, she realized the blond boy had given it to her. He took back the bottle and kissed her cheek before she had time to react.

"For luck," he said, and grinned as he turned back to the Maypole.

Tasia blinked in surprise, raising her hand to her cheek.

"The horse is 'ere!" a man shouted, and the crowd gave an enthusiastic roar.

"The horse, the horse!"

Tasia dissolved into laughter as she saw two lads in a ragged brown horse costume, one of them manfully wielding the great painted mask that served as its face. The horse's neck was encircled with a wreath of flowers, and a skirt swung around the legs beneath. A few showy kicks, and then the beast turned toward the village center, lumbering forward. The crowd followed him, clasping hands to form a long chain. Tasia was caught up in the line as they wound through the village like a giant serpent. The line passed through the first cottage, while the doors were held wide open for them. Rush mats had been spread on the floor to absorb the mud from hundreds of feet.

Emerging from the back of the cottage, Tasia let herself be pulled along. People paused at the side of the street to let the dancers pass, clapping in time to the ancient songs. A group of men stood by the buildings of the corn exchange, some of them openly fondling their female companions. An unseen obstruction caused the parade to slow. The dancers stomped their feet and sang as they waited.

Hearing catcalls, Tasia glanced at the boisterous men nearby. She was stunned to see Lord Stokehurst standing with them, his white teeth flashing as he grinned at their antics. What was he doing here? Tasia's muscles tensed as she prepared to run away before he could see her. But it was too late ... In that instant he turned and looked straight at her. His smile faded, and his throat rippled with a forceful swallow. His lips parted with a surprise that seemed to equal her own.

He was very disheveled, his vest open and his shirt unbuttoned at the throat. With the torch light casting golden gleams on his dark hair, he was the living image of a *bogadyr*, the hero of an old Russian tale. His blue eyes held hers, direct and devilish, as if he were contemplating something indecent.

The line began to move again, but Tasia's feet were leaden. All she could seem to do was stand there in a trance. The man behind her protested. "Come, lass, either pick up yer feet or step to the side!"

"I'm sorry," she said, hopping out of the way. Immediately her place in line vanished.

Before she could run away, Lord Stokehurst appeared in front of her. His fingers manacled her wrist, closing until her pulse throbbed hard against the pad of his thumb. "Come with me," he said. Bemused, Tasia followed with no thought of pulling back.

There were whistles from the group of men, and cheers from the dancers as the line glided toward the next house. All sound was muffled by Tasia's frantic heartbeat. Stokehurst's legs covered the ground in long strides, forcing her to match his pace with a hasty trot. He was angry, and with just cause. She shouldn't have made an exhibition of herself. She should have conducted herself with dignity, and stayed at the mansion. Now Stokehurst would tear her to shreds with a few words, and perhaps dismiss her on the spot.

He pulled her away from the well-lit houses, into a grove at the edge of the village green. Stopping in the shadow of a large tree, he released her wrist.

Tasia looked up at him, barely able to see his shadow-crossed face. "I shouldn't have been dancing," she said meekly.

"Why not? Tonight I gave everyone leave to do as they liked."

Her chagrin turned to surprise. "You aren't angry?"

He stepped closer, ignoring the question. "You look like a Gypsy, with your hair like that."

The remark, so unexpectedly personal, filled Tasia with confusion. Something about Stokehurst was very different from usual; some customary restraint had been removed. There was a new menace in his soft voice and his deliberate movements ... Suddenly she realized she was being hunted. She retreated in ever-deepening alarm, stumbling on a thick tree root. His hand closed over her shoulder to steady her. Even after she had found her balance, he didn't let go. The heat of his palm sank through her blouse. Stokehurst raised his other arm, and the tip of the steel hook dug into the tree bark, close to her ear. She was trapped. Exquisitely aware of the solid weight of his body, she shrank backward until the tree trunk was solid against her spine.

He was drunk, she thought wildly. He didn't realize what he was doing. "Sir ... you're not yourself. You have been drinking."

"So have you."

He was close enough for her to smell the sweet wine on his breath. Tasia drew her head back, pressing her skull hard against the tree. Briefly the glow of a distant passing torch cast Stokehurst's face in dull red, and then they were submerged in darkness once more.

His fingers caught beneath her chin, and she made a small sound, shrinking backward as much as possible. "No," she whispered on a faint, terrified breath.

"*No?*" he repeated. He sounded amused. "Then why did you come away with me?"

"I th-thought . . ." Tasia struggled for breath. "I thought you were angry. I thought you wanted to shout at me in private."

"And you'd prefer that to a kiss?"

"*Yes.*"

He laughed at her fervent reply, and his hand slid to the back of her neck, gripping the tense muscles. The heat of his skin startled her, made her shiver. A cold breeze surged around them, but Stokehurst was large and warm. In spite of her teeth-chattering alarm, Tasia was almost tempted to draw closer to him, into the refuge of his body.

"You're afraid of me," he murmured.

She nodded awkwardly.

"Is it this?" He moved, and the hook gleamed before her eyes, like a silver fish darting through water.

"No." She didn't know precisely what she was afraid of. A strange feeling had taken hold of her, all her senses quickening, everything becoming painfully vivid. His soft, hot mouth grazed the wisps of hair at her temple, sending a shock through her body. Her fists came up against his broad chest, pressing hard.

"What about a kiss for luck?" he suggested. "Somehow I think you could use some luck, Miss Billings."

A nervous laugh bubbled up, impossible to restrain. "I don't believe in luck. O-only prayer."

"Why not both? No, don't stiffen like that. I'm not going to hurt you."

She twitched in surprise as he leaned over her. "I must go," she said desperately, and made the mistake of trying to push past him. Stokehurst moved swiftly, catching her against his hard body. He wrapped her long braid around his hand once, twice, pulling her head back securely. His dark face was just above hers, his knuckles digging into her nape. Tasia closed her eyes. She felt a gentle kiss at the corner of her lips, and she gasped in response.

His hold on her tightened. He brushed another kiss on her closed lips, and another. Somehow she had expected violence, impatience ... anything but the soft, burning imprints of his mouth. His lips slid across her cheek to her ear, and then to her throat. The tip of his tongue touched the violent flutter of her pulse. Suddenly Tasia wanted to press against him and lose herself in the dark rush of excitement. But she had never surrendered her control to anyone. The very thought of it was enough to startle her back to sanity. "Don't," she said in a muffled voice, her hands coming to his dark hair. "*Please* don't!"

He lifted his head and looked down at her. "How sweet you are," he whispered. His hand fell from her hair, and he extracted one of the flowered sprigs that had been tucked in her braid.

With the backs of his fingers, he traced the fragile edge of her jaw.

"My lord . . ." she said unsteadily, and took a deep breath. "Sir, I hope . . . it's possible . . . that we could pretend this didn't happen?"

"If that's what you want." His thumb brushed the tip of her chin. The flowers he held sent a heady fragrance through the air.

She nodded awkwardly, clamping her teeth on her trembling lip. "It was the wine. And the dancing. I s-suppose anyone would have been carried away by all the excitement."

"Of course. Folk dancing can be pretty heady stuff."

Tasia flushed, aware that he was mocking her. But it didn't matter. An excuse had been made. "Good night," she said, pushing away from the tree. Her joints felt like rubber. "I must return to the mansion now."

"Not by yourself."

"I want to go alone," she said stubbornly.

There was a short silence, and then he laughed. "Fine. Don't blame me if you're accosted. But I suppose it's not likely to happen twice in one night."

Her footsteps were light and rapid, her slim form seeming to melt into the darkness.

Luke went to the spot where she had leaned, and braced his shoulder against the heavy trunk. Restlessly he dug his boot heel into the hard-packed earth. He had been gentle with her when he had wanted to be cruel, to bruise her lips with his, leave marks on her tender skin. The needs he thought had died long ago had been resurrected with a vengeance. He wanted to take her to his bed and keep her there for a week. Forever. Guilt pressed down on him. He was angry with her for setting his life askew, for making his memories of Mary more distant than ever before.

She would be gone soon. Not much longer, and the month would be over. Charles Ashbourne would find a new place for her. All he had to do was ignore her until time took care of everything. Turning, he lashed out in frustration, tearing off a chunk of bark. The hook left a narrow gash on the trunk. He began to walk with long strides, away from the lights and dancing, away from the celebration.

Tasia stood at her window, staring outside with wonder. Remembering the seeking warmth of his mouth, the gentleness and closely contained strength, she shivered. She had been alone for such a long time. It had been frightening and intensely sweet to be held in his arms. The comfort, the illusion of safety, had affected her deeply.

Slowly she raised her fingers to her lips. Stokehurst must have been amused by her ignorance. She had never been kissed before tonight, except for the halfhearted embrace she had shared with Mikhail Angelovsky just after their betrothal agreement.

Misha, as family and friends called him, had been a sublime mixture of beauty and overindulgence. He was sloppy in his personal habits, overdressed, and doused in heavy cologne, with his hair too long, his neck spotted with blemishes where he had neglected to wash. Most of the time his large gold eyes were vacant, owing to his surpassing love of the opium pipe.

Abruptly her mind was filled with voices. Tasia swayed slightly, feeling sick.

"Misha, I love you, a thousand times more than she ever could. She'll never be able to give you what you need."

"You jealous, wrinkled old fool," Mikhail replied. *"You know nothing about what I need."*

The voices faded, and Tasia frowned in bewilderment. Was it a memory, or something conjured by her imagination? She sat and buried her head in her hands, lost in the torment of her thoughts.

With the London Season drawing to a close, the *haut ton* began to close their town estates and withdraw to the country. Lord Stokehurst was giving one of the first house parties of the summer. The weekend of socializing and hunting would be attended by all the local families of note. Tasia hardly relished the idea of a weekend party, a looming threat to her privacy. On the other hand, the Ashbournes would be attending, a piece of welcome news. Tasia was excited about the prospect of seeing her cousin Alicia, the only fragile link to her past. She hoped they would be able to find a few minutes to talk together.

To no one's surprise, Iris, Lady Harcourt had been invited to act as hostess. "It was her idea," Mrs. Knaggs confided to the after-dinner group of upper servants. "Lady Harcourt wants the master and everyone else to see how well she fills the role. It's plain as pudding she wants to be lady of the manor."

Lady Harcourt arrived two days early, to ensure that everything was done to her satisfaction. From that moment on, the estate was in a ferment of activity. Massive flower arrangements were carted in, and musicians were heard practicing in the spare rooms. Lady Harcourt made a multitude of changes about Southgate Hall, everything from rearranging furniture to altering Mrs. Plunkett's menu. Tasia admired her diplomacy. In spite of Lady Harcourt's interference, she was so gracious that the grumbling among the staff was kept to a minimum.

Emma was openly displeased about the situation, even daring to argue with her father. Their voices rang through the entrance hall as they came from their morning ride.

"Papa, she's changing *everything!*"

"I've given her leave to do as she likes. Enough of this complaining, Emma."

"But you haven't even listened—"

"I said that was enough." Catching sight of Tasia, who had been waiting for Emma, he pushed his rebellious daughter forward. "Do something with her," he snapped, and strode away with a scowl. It was the first time he had spoken to her in days.

Wearing a scowl identical to her father's, Emma whirled to face Tasia. Her blue eyes flashed with fury. "He's an ogre!"

"I gather you were arguing about Lady Harcourt," Tasia said calmly.

Emma scowled. "I don't want it to look as though she belongs here when she doesn't! I hate it that she has the run of the house. And I *hate* the way she drapes herself around Papa, and the way her voice oozes treacle when she talks to him. It makes me positively ill."

"It's only for the weekend. You can certainly

bring yourself to act like a true lady, Emma, and treat her with politeness and respect."

"It's not just the weekend," Emma muttered. "She wants to marry him!" Suddenly her anger vanished, and she looked at Tasia with desperation. "Oh, Miss Billings, what if she does? I'll be stuck with her forever."

All at once Tasia found her arms filled with an ungainly twelve-year-old. She hugged Emma affectionately and smoothed her wild red hair. "I know it's not easy for you," she said. "But your father has been lonely since your mother died. You know that. The Bible says, 'Let every man have his own wife.' Would you rather that he never married again, and grew old alone?"

"Of course not," Emma said in a muffled voice. "But I want him to marry someone I like."

Tasia laughed. "My dear, I don't think you would ever approve of anyone he takes an interest in."

"Yes, I would!" Emma pulled away and frowned indignantly. "I know just the right person. She is young and pretty and intelligent, and would suit him to perfection."

"Who is that?"

"You!"

Taken aback, all Tasia could do was stare at her dumbly. "Emma," she finally managed to say, "you must forget that idea at once."

"Why?"

"To start with, men of your father's position don't marry governesses."

"Papa's not a snob. He wouldn't give a fig about that. Miss Billings, don't you think he is handsome?"

"I've never given his looks a thought. It's time for your lessons."

"Your cheeks are red," Emma said in triumph, her sudden glee undiminished by Tasia's warning glance. "You *do* like his looks!"

"Handsomeness—or beauty—is superficial."

"Papa is handsome on the inside too," Emma persisted. "I didn't really mean it when I called him an ogre. Miss Billings, perhaps you could be nicer to him, and smile sometimes. I just know you could make Papa fall in love with you, if you would only try!"

"I don't want anyone to fall in love with me," Tasia returned, spluttering with laughter at the child's outrageousness.

"Don't you like my father, Miss Billings?"

"I believe him to be an honorable man."

"Yes, but do you *like* him?"

"Emma, this is ridiculous. I don't know Lord Stokehurst well enough to like or dislike him."

"If you married him, you wouldn't have to work anymore. You would be a duchess someday. Wouldn't that make you happy? Don't you want to live with us forever?"

"Oh, Emma." Tasia smiled fondly. "You're very kind to think of my happiness. But there are many things you don't understand, and I'm afraid I can't explain them. I'll stay with you as long as I'm able. That's all I can promise."

Emma was about to reply when she noticed someone approaching. Her mouth snapped shut, and she regarded the auburn-haired woman with poorly veiled suspicion. "Lady Harcourt," she muttered.

The woman stopped in front of them. She was wearing a gown of dark red silk, draped to dis-

play her voluptuous figure to perfection. "Emma,"
she said lightly, "do introduce me to your companion."

Emma complied sullenly. "My governess, Miss
Billings."

Lady Harcourt acknowledged Tasia's curtsy
with a cool nod. "How odd. From the way Lord
Stokehurst described you, I assumed you were
middle-aged. You're just a child."

"Lady Harcourt," Tasia said, "if there is any way
that I—or Emma—may assist you in your prepara-
tions for the weekend, you have only to ask." She
gave the girl a meaningful look. "Isn't that so,
Emma?"

"Oh, yes," Emma said with a saccharine smile.

"Thank you," Lady Harcourt replied. "The best
help you could provide is to keep each other occupied, and out of the way of the guests."

"Certainly, ma'am. As a matter of fact, we're late
in beginning Emma's morning lessons."

"Keep out of the way?" Emma repeated in irri-
tation. "But it's *my* house—"

Her words were cut off as Tasia jerked her away
smartly, marching her toward the schoolroom. "I
think we'll begin with an essay on politeness,"
Tasia said under her breath.

"Why should I be polite to her, when she's not
polite to me?" Emma glanced at Tasia with grim
satisfaction. "She didn't seem to like you very
much, Miss Billings."

"I thought Lady Harcourt was very gracious,"
Tasia said evenly.

Emma stared at her closely. "I think you're just
as blue-blooded as she is, Miss Billings. Maybe
even more so. Mrs. Knaggs says that with your
skin and your bone structure, you could pass for a

member of the nobility. You can tell me who you really are. I'm very good at secrets. I think you must be someone extraordinary ... a princess in disguise ... or a foreign spy ... or maybe—"

Laughing, Tasia stopped and caught her shoulders, giving her a little shake for emphasis. "I'm your governess. That's all. I have no wish to be anything else."

Emma gave her a chiding glance. "That's silly," she said shortly. "You're much more than a governess. Anyone can see that."

The guests took an entire day to arrive, appearing at all hours. Servants were kept busy running up and down the stairs to ensure their comfort. The ladies secluded themselves for a while, later emerging in gowns of different hues, with draped and bustled skirts, and trimmings of lace and delicate embroidery. Wielding elaborate painted fans, the women gathered in the sitting rooms to gossip and partake of refreshments.

Tasia observed the activity and remembered doing the same thing herself in Russia, attending balls and parties with her family. How sheltered she had been, never thinking of the world beyond St. Petersburg. How many hours she had misspent. Even the time she had worshipped in church on her knees seemed like a waste in retrospect. It would have been better to do something practical for the poor, rather than just pray for them. Here in England she had become useful for the first time in her life, and she liked the feeling. Even if it were possible, she would never go back to the idle existence she had once led.

In the evening a magnificent supper of more than thirty dishes was given. The dining room was filled with long, linen-covered tables, the air fragrant with the scents of venison, salmon, goose, and puddings. Passing by the doorway, Tasia heard endless rounds of toasts being made, accompanied by bursts of good-natured laughter. She imagined how attractive Lady Harcourt must look, her hair glittering red and gold in the light of the chandeliers. And Lord Stokehurst, watching her with a mixture of pride and masculine pleasure, enjoying the success of the evening. Tasia smoothed the little frown from her forehead and went upstairs to share supper with Emma. It would be just the two of them tonight. Children were never invited to eat at formal dinners, and neither were governesses.

After the dinner was concluded, the guests separated for a brief time, the ladies in the drawing room with tea, the gentlemen remaining in the dining room with port and brandy. Eventually the guests rejoined in the summer parlor for entertainment. Emma begged Tasia to let her go downstairs and watch. "Lady Harcourt has invited a fortune-teller to come and make predictions about the future. Her name is Madame Miracle, and she's a clairvoyant, which is much better than an ordinary fortune-teller. Oh, Miss Billings, we have to go downstairs and see! What if she says something about Papa? Can't I sit quietly in a corner? I promise to behave myself. I'll be a perfect lady."

Tasia smiled. "I suppose we could watch for a while, as long as we remain inconspicuous. But don't expect too much of anyone named Madame Miracle, Emma. She sounds like an unemployed actress to me."

"I don't care. I want to hear what she says about everyone."

"Very well," Tasia said, regarding Emma's crumpled clothes with a critical eye. "But before we go, you might change into your dark blue dress and smooth your hair."

"It doesn't want to be smooth tonight," Emma said, pulling at her rebellious curls. "Every time I smash it down, it springs up worse than before."

Tasia laughed. "Then we'll tie a ribbon around it."

As she helped Emma to change clothes, Tasia worried silently about bringing the girl downstairs. After all, Lady Harcourt had asked them to stay away from the guests. Although there had been no specific instructions form Lord Stokehurst, he would probably agree with Lady Harcourt's wishes. But Emma had been an angel all day, studying quietly for hours and taking supper in the schoolroom without a word of protest. She deserved a reward for her good behavior, and surely no harm would come of it.

There was a handsome assemblage in the large parlor. Men and women sat in clusters on elegant French couches and chairs with curved backs. Subdued lamplight shed a mellow glow on the silk-covered walls and the sprays of delicate plasterwork. A cool breeze blew through the netting on the windows.

Catching sight of his daughter, Lord Stokehurst disengaged himself from a conversation and walked toward her. He was severely handsome in dark, tailored clothes and a silk waistcoat patterned in moss-green and charcoal. He reached his daughter and leaned down for a brief kiss. "I haven't seen you all day," he said. "I wondered where you were hiding."

"Lady Harcourt told us not to—" Emma began,

and stopped with a wince as Tasia discreetly poked her in the back. "We've been busy with my lessons, Papa."

"What did you learn today?"

"In the morning we studied deportment, and in the afternoon, German history. I've been so good all day that Miss Billings said I could watch Madame Miracle from the corner."

"Madame Miracle," Stokehurst said with a short laugh, "is a charlatan. You can sit with me at the front, Emma, but only if you promise not to believe a word she says."

"Thank you, Papa!" Emma beamed and went with him, pausing to glance over her shoulder. "You come too, Miss Billings!"

Tasia shook her head. "I'll stay back here."

She stared at the center of Stokehurst's broad back as he walked away with his daughter. A forlorn, uneasy feeling came over her. She wondered why he hadn't spared her a single glance. He had deliberately ignored her. Beneath his cool self-possession there had been something tightly reined and threatening.

Her thoughts were diverted as Lady Harcourt drew a black-garbed woman to the center of the room. "If I may have your attention, I would like to introduce our special guest for the evening. In London, Paris, and Venice, Madame Miracle is acknowledged as a clairvoyant with extraordinary powers. There is a rumor that she is frequently consulted by a certain member of our own royal family. Fortunately for us, she has graciously accepted my invitation to join our gathering this evening, and reveal her special gifts for our benefit."

A ripple of welcoming applause scattered

through the room. Tasia retreated to the back wall, her face expressionless.

Madame Miracle was a dark-haired woman in her forties, with kohl-rimmed eyes and rouged cheeks. A brilliant red and gold silk shawl was knotted around her shoulders. She wore jeweled rings on every finger and heavy bracelets that jangled on her wrists. Theatrically she passed an arm over a round table that had been draped with black scarves and weighted with lit candles. There were other objects on the table: a small bowl filled with colored stones, a deck of cards, and a few ornamental figurines.

"My friends," Madame Miracle began in a dramatic voice, "it is time to shed doubt and earthly limitations as we bid the spirits welcome. Tonight they will come to reveal the mirror to our souls. Prepare yourselves to discover the secrets of the future and the past."

As the woman continued to speak, Tasia became aware of a whisper nearby.

"Tasia."

A chill went down her spine, and she turned quickly. Alicia was standing behind her, wearing an irrepressible smile. Obeying her silent gesture, Tasia slipped through the doorway, and they hurried into the empty hall together. Smiling with relief and happiness, Tasia hugged her.

"Cousin," she exclaimed, "I'm so glad to see you."

Alicia stood back and grinned at her. "Tasia, you look wonderful! The past weeks have made quite a difference in you."

Tasia looked down at herself critically. "I haven't noticed any changes."

"The lines have gone from your face, and your figure has filled out a little."

"I've been eating. The food is very good here." Tasia made a face. "Except for the blancmange. They serve it all the time."

Alicia laughed with her. "You seem to be thriving on it. Tell me, Tasia, are you happy? Are you well?"

Tasia shrugged uncomfortably, tempted to confide about the vision of Mikhail in the mirror, and about her nightmares. But that was all the result of a guilty conscience. She would accomplish nothing by telling Alicia, except to worry her. "I'm as well as could be expected," she finally said.

A compassionate look came over Alicia's face. "Charles and I are your family, Tasia. We will do what we can to help you. I trust Lord Stokehurst has been kind?"

"He hasn't been *un*kind," Tasia said cautiously.

"Good." Alicia took her hands and pressed them hard. She glanced around the empty hall. "We'd better go back. There'll be a chance for us to talk later."

Tasia let a minute or two pass before easing back into the parlor. Her fine brows quirked in surprise as she saw that Emma was seated at the clairvoyant's table. In spite of her father's warnings, Emma appeared to be spellbound by Madame Miracle. "Do you see anything?" Emma asked eagerly.

A pattern of colored stones had been laid out on the table. Madame Miracle studied them closely. "Ah," she said, nodding over the stones as if the arrangement were of great significance. "It is all becoming clear. You were born with a rebellious spirit. You have strong emotions—perhaps too strong—but eventually all will come into balance. In time your gift for love will attract many people to you, all seeking to draw from your strength." She paused and took Emma's hands, closing her eyes to concentrate harder.

"What about my future?" Emma prompted.

"I see a husband. A man from a foreign country. He will bring conflict ... but with patience and forgiveness you will weave the opposing forces in your life into a circle of unity." She opened her eyes. "You will be blessed with many children. A happy future, indeed."

"What kind of foreigner will I marry?" Emma demanded. "French? German?"

"The spirits did not say."

Emma frowned. "Could you ask them?" she urged.

Madame Miracle released her hands and shrugged prosaically. "That is all."

"Drat," Emma muttered. "Now I'll have to wonder every time I meet a foreigner."

Stokehurst grinned and gestured for his daughter to return to him. "It's time for someone else to have a turn, sweet."

"Miss Billings," Emma said instantly. "I want to know what the spirits say about Miss Billings!"

Tasia blanched as Emma pointed to her. Seats creaked as everyone turned to look. Abruptly she was ripped from her privacy, becoming the object of strangers' eyes. More than two hundred people were staring at her. A cold sweat broke out all over her body. For a moment she was back in Russia, at the murder trial, people staring at her with rapacious curiosity. Panic swamped her. She shook her head, unable to make a sound.

Sinking deeper into the nightmare, she heard Lord Stokehurst's voice.

"Why not?" he asked softly. "Come here, Miss Billings."

Four
❧ ❧

Tasia shrank back against the wall. Murmurs rustled through the crowd. "Only the governess," came a loud whisper, while someone else asked, "Why bother with her?"

Stokehurst pinned Tasia with a calculating stare. "Don't you want to know what your future holds?"

"My future is of no consequence to anyone, sir," she said calmly, while her mind raced with worry. Stokehurst seemed to want to punish her for something. Why? What had she done to provoke him?

Emma glanced from her father to Tasia, her eager smile wavering as she apparently sensed that something was wrong. "It's quite fun, Miss Billings," she said uncertainly. "Won't you give it a try?"

All at once Alicia Ashbourne rose from her chair. Anxiety made her voice taut. "I would like to have *my* fortune told. Let's not waste time on someone who's unwilling."

"In good time, Lady Ashbourne," Stokehurst said smoothly. "First we'll let the spirits have a go at our mysterious governess."

Alicia sputtered objections as her husband Charles pulled her back to her seat. Rubbing her stiff hand between his, Charles tried to soothe her.

Iris Harcourt's face puckered in a frown. "Luke, there's no need to torment the child. If she doesn't want to, let her be."

Stokehurst seemed not to hear her. His hard gaze was riveted on Tasia. "Come, Miss Billings. Don't keep us all waiting."

"I would rather not—"

"I insist."

He intended to have his way, no matter how much of a scene it caused. There was no escape. Tasia moved forward as if she were walking to the guillotine.

"Don't be afraid, child," Madame Miracle said, waving her to the table. "Sit. Take the stones and warm them in your hand."

Squaring her shoulders, Tasia reached the table and sat down. She was cornered. There was nothing to do but confront the situation head-on. She scooped up a fistful of the stones and clenched them tightly. Everyone was watching her. She felt their stares like knife points on her skin.

"Now," Madame Miracle instructed, "let them drop through your fingers."

Opening her hand, Tasia let the stones fall to the table. They rattled on the cloth-covered surface, some bouncing on uneven edges and scattering widely.

Looking troubled, the woman shook her head. She gathered the stones into a pile and put them back into the bowl. "It would be better if you tried again."

"Why?" Tasia asked in a low tone, although she knew. It was a bad reading.

Madame Miracle shook her head and gestured for her to pick up the stones.

Once more Tasia dropped them to the table.

This time one of them teetered at the edge and fell to the carpet.

"Ah." The clairvoyant exhaled softly. "The pattern repeats itself. It is the shape of two brothers, death and sleep." She bent to retrieve the stone that had fallen. Rolling it between her fingers, she studied the markings closely. It was bloodred in color, speckled with black. Setting down the stone, she took Tasia's hands in a firm grip. "You have traveled far from your birthplace. You have been torn from your home and history." She paused, her painted brows knitting together. "Not long ago you touched the very wings of death."

Transfixed, Tasia made no sound. The candle flames seemed to turn red and purple at the edges.

"I see a distant land ... a city built on bones. It is surrounded by ancient forests. Wolves hide among the trees. I see piles of gold and amber ... palaces, land, servants ... all of it yours. I see you, wearing a gown of silk and a necklace of precious jewels."

Suddenly Lady Harcourt interrupted in a droll tone. "Miss Billings is only a governess, Madame. Pray tell, how has she achieved such a splendid future? Made a brilliant marriage, I suppose?"

"Not the future," Madame Miracle said. "I speak of the past."

The room was very quiet. Tasia's heart churned, and she tugged at her imprisoned hands. "I want to stop," she said hoarsely.

The clairvoyant's knotted fingers tightened, and a prickling heat began to build between their palms. Their joined hands twitched as if an electric current passed through them. "I see you in a room filled with gold and fine paintings and books. You are seeking someone. A shadow falls across your face. There is a young man with yellow eyes. Blood ... His blood is spilling to the floor. You call his name ... something like ... Michael ... *Michael*—" The woman screamed and jumped back, jerking away from Tasia's hands. Tasia remained sitting at the table, frozen in terror.

Madame Miracle staggered backward and held up her scarlet palms. It looked as if she had taken hold of a boiling kettle. "She burned me!" she cried, glaring fearfully at Tasia. "Witch!"

Tasia struggled from her chair, though her legs would hardly support her. "Fraud," she countered, her voice trembling. "I've heard enough of your ridiculous lies." Blindly she walked through the room, her head held high, though her bowels were wrenched with terror. She was desperate for a place to hide. *Oh God, what have I done?* Voices from the past swarmed through her mind.

"They should burn you—"

"My poor child."

"I didn't mean to do it."

"—burn you to ashes."

"God help me—"

"Witch!"

"No," she whimpered, breaking into a run, stumbling, fleeing from the howling demons that chased her.

The room erupted in excitement. Women snapped open their fans to stir the air and conceal their rapid-fire gossip. Guests milled around Madame Miracle with eager questions. Stone-faced, Luke strode out of the room in pursuit of the governess. As he reached the hallway, he felt a violent tug at his sleeve. He stopped and turned to face Alicia.

She was furious, her cheeks blazing crimson and her mouth tight.

"Not now," Luke said harshly.

"What is wrong with you?" Alicia demanded. She pulled him to the side of the grand staircase, where there was less chance of being overheard. "I should have Charles thrash you! How could you do that to my cousin? Putting her on vulgar display when you know all about her need for secrecy—"

"I know nothing about her. Except that I'm sick of the way she floats around the mansion with her martyred air and her tragic glances, brimming with deep, dark secrets. God only knows what effect it's having on my daughter. I've had enough."

Alicia drew herself up as tall as possible. "And so you decided to torture her in public! I never thought of you as cruel before. Well, I'm going to find Tasia and take her away with me at once. I wouldn't allow a stray dog to be subjected to your so-called hospitality, much less my cousin."

Luke's gaze shot to her face with searing intensity. "Tasia? Is that her name?"

Horror-struck, Alicia clapped her hand to her mouth. "Forget it," she gasped between her fingers. "Forget it at once. Just let me take her back to London. I promise you'll never have to set eyes on her again."

His jaw hardened. "She's not going anywhere."

Alicia faced him like a yapping terrier confronting a wolfhound. "You've interfered *quite* enough, thank you! You were only meant to be a temporary safeguard. Now you've put her in danger. Dragging her in front of all those people—it could well be a death sentence, and all because of your offended pride. I assured Tasia that you were trustworthy, and you proved me false. How does it feel to destroy someone's life on a whim?"

"You dragged me into this," Luke said through his teeth. "I'll be damned if I won't see it through. What do you mean, 'death sentence'? What the hell has she done?"

Alicia frowned and looked away. Just when Luke thought she would refuse to answer, her voice emerged reluctantly. "I don't know what she's done. I'm not even certain she knows."

Driven to new heights of frustration, Luke uttered a foul oath. "I'll find her. Go back to the others."

"And who will protect my cousin?" Alicia demanded.

"I will."

"A fine job you've done so far!"

Plowing through the melée, Emma reached Madame Miracle and Lady Harcourt. She stared at both of them with snapping blue eyes, her golden freckles standing out in sharp relief against her flushed skin.

"Emma," Lady Harcourt said rapidly, "a childish tantrum is the last thing anyone needs at the moment."

Emma ignored her, turning to Madame Miracle. "Why did you have to make sport of Miss Billings? She's done nothing to you."

The woman puffed up indignantly. "I would not abuse my gift in such a way! I revealed the truth exactly as the spirits showed it to me!"

Frowning, Emma folded her lanky arms. "I think you'd better leave now. I rang for our butler. Seymour will show you out. If you don't have a carriage of your own, one of ours will take you."

"Emma, dear," Lady Harcourt said in a cutting tone, "just because your high-strung governess has taken offense doesn't mean the rest of the guests shouldn't be entertained. This is a matter for adults, not children. Why don't you go to your room and amuse yourself with your books and dolls?"

Emma gave her a sly glance. "Very well. But I should hate for Madame to face my father when he returns. He has such a horrible temper. Who knows what might happen?" Grinning unpleasantly, Emma curled her finger into a hook, drew it across her own neck, and made a gurgling sound.

Madame Miracle turned pale and began to scoop up her belongings.

"Emma, don't make up horrid stories about your father," Iris hissed. "Go to your room. I won't tolerate your interference. I am the hostess, and I want Madame to stay."

Emma's devil-child expression vanished, replaced by mulish determination. "She made Miss Billings unhappy. I want her to leave. And it's *my* home, not yours."

"Ill-mannered brat!" Iris glanced around the room, seeming to take a hurried survey of the guests. "Where is your father?"

Emma shrugged innocently. "I have no idea."

Luke went to the small third-floor room, finding the door ajar. The air was thick, filled with stifling silence. A chair was overturned on the floor, a small wooden icon laying beside it. The governess ... Tasia ... stood at the window. Somehow she knew it was he. "My lord," she said tonelessly, without turning around.

Suddenly Luke realized that she wasn't angry,

or embarrassed, or even afraid. She was devastated. He had hurt her far more than he'd intended. Remorse swept over him, and the dark color of shame crept up his face. Uncomfortably he cleared his throat in the prelude to an apology.

"I came to see how you—" He stopped suddenly. Expressing concern at this point would sound like mockery, when he had been the cause of her pain.

She kept her back to him. Her voice was strained with the effort of sounding normal. "I'm fine, sir. I just need a few minutes alone. That woman was very strange, wasn't she? Forgive me for making a scene. If you would go, please ... and let me restore myself. I just need to be alone ..." She wound down like a mechanical toy, her words grinding into silence, her shoulders trembling. "Go ... please."

Luke reached her in a few swift strides and pulled her stiff body into his arms. "I'm sorry," he said against her hair. "I'm so damned sorry."

Tasia struggled against him, wedging her hands between them. As her face came close to his shoulder, she caught the traces of brandy and tobacco smoke that clung to his coat. It was a good, comfortingly masculine smell. She stopped pushing against him. He was very strong and warm, the steady beat of his heart filling her ear. No one had ever held her like this except her father, when she was a child frightened of the dark. Her throat clenched against a swell of tears.

"No one's going to hurt you." Gently he smoothed her hair. "I'll keep you safe. You have my word."

No one had ever offered to keep her safe. It had a strange and powerful effect on Tasia. Tears flooded her eyes, and she blinked furiously to keep them back. He was only saying those words in a misguided attempt to be kind. He didn't know what it meant, how much she needed. He didn't know how desperately alone she was. "You can't promise that," she said, her teeth chattering. "You don't understand."

"Make me understand." He sank his fingers into her tight chignon and pulled her head back, staring into her face. "Tell me what you're afraid of."

How could she? How could she admit that she was afraid of being caught and punished for her crimes, and most of all that she was afraid of herself? If he knew what she had done, what she was, he would hate her. Her mind lingered on that, his sneering contempt if he knew ... if he knew ... The stinging tears spilled over her cheeks, and she began to cry with a force that hurt. The harder she tried to stop, the worse it became. Stokehurst groaned and hauled her close, tucking her head against his chest.

Sobbing violently, she clutched her arms around his neck. He held her in a smothering grip, pressing words of comfort into her hair, her throat, his breath warm on her skin. He rocked her gently, until several minutes had passed and the fine linen of his shirt was sodden beneath her cheek. "Hush," he finally whispered. "You'll make yourself ill. Hush now." His palm rubbed warm circles across her shoulders and back. "Take a nice, long breath," he said, his jaw scraping against her temple. "Another."

"They c-called me a witch," she said wretchedly. "Before."

The stroke of his hand stopped, then resumed

its leisurely pace. He was quiet, giving her the time she needed.

Her words burst out in a shivering torrent. "Sometimes I would see things ... about people I knew. I-I could tell if an accident would happen ... or if someone was lying. I had dreams, and visions. Not very often, but ... I was always right. Word traveled all the way to Moscow. People s-said I was evil. Witchcraft was the only way they could explain it. They were afraid of me. Soon the fear turned into hatred. I was a danger to everyone." She shuddered and bit down on her lower lip, afraid of what else she might confess.

He cuddled her against his shoulder, making a soothing noise.

Gradually her hiccupping sobs faded to sniffles. She rested heavily against him. "I've made your shirt all wet," she said in a small voice.

He reached in his coat and found a handkerchief. "Here." As he held it to her nose, she blew with a childish gust that made him smile. "Better?" he asked gently. Tasia took the handkerchief from him and nodded, blotting her eyes. Now that the tears were over, an ache that had lodged in her chest for months was gone. Stokehurst tucked a loose lock of hair behind her ear, his thumb drifting over the soft lobe.

"You were angry with me tonight," Tasia said hoarsely. "Why?"

Luke was tempted to give her any one of a half-dozen meaningless replies that came to mind. But he owed her the truth. He traced the web of tear tracks on her cheek with his fingertip. "Because you're going to disappear someday, without ever having told me who you are or what kind of trouble you're in. You're more of a mystery with each day that passes. You're about as substantial as mist in the moonlight. It made me angry that I couldn't have something—someone—I wanted so badly. And so I tried to hurt you."

Tasia knew she should pull away from him. Her instincts told her that he wouldn't try to stop her. But she was mesmerized by the sweep of his fingertips along her skin. A pleasant ripple of sensation went through her.

Lightly he caught her jaw in his hand. "Tell me your real age," he said. "I want the truth."

She blinked in surprise. "I already told you—"

"What year were you born?" he insisted.

Tasia winced. "Eighteen fifty-two."

He was quiet for a moment. "Eighteen." The way he said it, the word sounded profane. "Eighteen."

Tasia felt the need to defend herself. "Actual years aren't important when one considers—"

"Spare me a repetition of the years-don't-really-matter speech. They matter a hell of a lot for what I've been thinking about." He let go of her jaw and shook his head, as if the day's events had been too much for him to deal with.

Unnerved by his silence, Tasia stirred against him. He seemed to have forgotten he was still holding her. "My lord," she said apprehensively, "I suppose you intend to dismiss me now?"

He scowled. "Do you have to ask that every time we have a conversation?"

"I thought that after what happened this evening you might—"

"No, I'm not going to dismiss you. But if you ask again, I'll personally boot you off the estate." He followed the surly statement with a kiss on her forehead, his mouth warm and light. Drawing his head back slowly, he looked into her eyes. "Do you feel all right now?"

Tasia was completely bewildered by his behavior. "I-I don't know." She moved away, though she longed to stay in his arms and hide from the world. "Thank you for the handkerchief. I'm sure you want it back."

He glanced at the wad of soggy linen she held out to him. "Keep it. And don't thank me. I was the reason you needed it in the first place."

"No," Tasia said softly. "You weren't the reason. I've held everything in for so many—" She stopped and folded her arms around herself. She turned toward the round window, where their images appeared in a rippled distortion. "Did you know the ancient Russians used to build their fortresses on top of hills? When the Tartar invaders attacked, the Russians would pour water over the hill, on all sides. In a very short time it would turn to ice, and no one could climb up. The siege would last as long as the ice and the supplies held out." She traced the curved edge of the window with her fingertip. "For a long time I've been alone in my fortress. No one can join me, and I can't leave. And sometimes . . . my provisions fail me." She glanced at him, her eyes luminous, like opals. "I think you understand that very well, sir."

Luke stared at her intently. She refused to look away, seeming calm—but there was a visible throbbing in her throat, just above the edge of her black silk collar. He touched the rapid pulse. "Go on," he murmured. "What else do you think you know about me?"

Suddenly the moment was shattered by a crisp voice.

"Ah, here you are!" Lady Harcourt stood at the

doorway, a fixed smile on her face. She spoke to Tasia, but her gaze went to Lord Stokehurst. "We've all been concerned about you, my dear."

"I'm fine," Tasia said, while Stokehurst's hand fell away from her.

"So I see. The evening turned out to be more dramatic than I expected. Madame Miracle has fled, and the guests are entertaining themselves with music. Fortunately we have some accomplished pianists present." Lady Harcourt gave her full attention to Stokehurst. "Your concern for the servants is admirable, darling, but it's time to return to our guests." Moving forward, she slipped her arm through his. As she tugged Stokehurst from the room, she paused to glance back at Tasia. "Miss Billings, your little spell—or whatever you care to call it—seems to have upset Emma. If you had done as I suggested and kept her away from the guests, none of this would have—" She stopped at a brief murmur from Stokehurst, and shrugged. "As you wish, darling."

Tasia clutched the handkerchief even more tightly. Her face was expressionless as she watched the pair leave. They were a handsome couple, both tall and magnificent. Stokehurst would be an ideal husband for Lady Harcourt. And it was clear that she wanted to marry him. A bleak feeling came over Tasia, and she set her teeth hard against the wobble of her jaw.

Moving slowly, she picked up the chair in her room, which had been knocked over in her stumbling haste. She restored the icon to its usual place. Her face felt hot and puffy. She touched her tender eyelids and winced at the sting.

"Oh, Miss Billings!" All of a sudden Emma rushed into the room, all flying curls and excited eyes. "Miss Billings, that horrible old witch is gone. I sent her away. Were any of the things she said true? Did you really live in a palace? Oh, you've been crying!" She threw her arms around Tasia. "Didn't my father find you?"

"He found me," Tasia said, and laughed unsteadily.

As they descended the stairs, Iris kept hold of Luke's arm and looked at him with simmering displeasure. "Well, your shy little governess managed to ruin the evening with her theatrics."

"I'd say your fortune-teller deserves all the credit."

"Madame Miracle only revealed what the spirits told her," Iris said defensively.

"I don't care if the spirits appeared in top hats and danced on the table. Madame Miracle should be shot." Luke's mouth hardened. "Right along with me. Between the two of us, we managed to make quite a spectacle of Miss Billings."

"Miss Billings made a spectacle of *herself*," Iris corrected. "And what happened tonight is proof that she is dreadfully immature, Luke. You must hire someone of a more suitable age to teach Emma. They're a pair of scheming children. I wasn't going to tell you, but I overheard the two of them the other day, plotting to get you to marry Miss Billings!"

"What?"

"They're hatching a plot. Emma wants you to marry the governess. It's rather adorable, but at the same time, it should make you think twice about the wisdom of hiring a naive girl just out of the schoolroom—"

"You're making too much of it," he said

brusquely. "While I don't doubt my daughter's enthusiasm for her governess, I can assure you that Miss Billings has no ambition to marry me."

"Being a man, you would be fooled by her facade. She's a conniving creature, and she's trying to manipulate the situation to her advantage."

Luke gave her an ironic glance. "First she's naive, then she's conniving. Which is it?"

Iris marshaled her dignity. "Obviously that's for you to decide."

"There's no need to be jealous."

"Isn't there? What about the scene I just witnessed? Are you going to deny that she means something to you? Would you have touched her like that even if she were a homely old hag? Oh, she's set a neat trap for you. A lovely, helpless girl, all alone in the world, staring up at you with those big gray eyes, asking you to play the white knight and rescue her from her dreary little life ... How could any man resist?"

"She hasn't asked for anything," he said, stopping on the stairs to face her. "And they're blue, not gray."

"Oh, yes," Iris sneered, bracing her hands on her hips. "The color of mist on the lake. Or maybe violets touched with morning frost. I'm sure you can come up with some lovely comparisons on your own. Why don't you go upstairs and write an ode? Don't give me that condescending look, as if I'm being unreasonable! I refuse to compete with some scrawny girl for your attentions. I don't play well in a crowded field, and in any case I deserve better than that."

"Are you working up to an ultimatum?"

"Never," Iris spat. "I wouldn't dream of making it that easy for you! You want me to make you choose, and then everything will be convenient. I'd sooner cut my tongue out. Just don't make the mistake of coming to my bed tonight, or any night, until you can convince me that you're not pretending I'm *her!*"

His gaze raked insolently over her voluptuous figure. "It's not likely I'd confuse the two of you. But in any case, you won't be bothered with my attentions tonight."

"Good!" Iris snapped, and sailed ahead without him, her skirts trailing grandly in her wake.

The rest of the evening was pure hell. Luke didn't ask or care if the guests were enjoying themselves. They had all assembled in the music room, partaking of refreshments while various members of the gathering volunteered to show off their skills at the piano. The group was buzzing with gossip beneath the strains of music being played.

Charles approached Luke, coming to stand with him at the back of the room. "Stokehurst," he muttered, "what the devil is going on?"

Luke shrugged defensively and set his jaw. "I apologized to Tasia for my behavior. You can reassure Alicia that everything is fine."

"I can't reassure her when I'm not convinced of it myself!" Charles sighed deeply. "Alicia and I would like Tasia to return to us. We'll find some other situation for her."

"That's not necessary."

"I believe it is. Good God, man, I asked you to keep her safe, to *hide* her . . . and you exposed her to your guests like some carnival attraction! It's only out of fear of drawing further attention to

Tasia that Alicia has refrained from taking her away this very evening."

A flush covered Luke's face. "It won't happen again. I want the girl to stay."

"Is that what *she* wants?"

Luke hesitated. "I think so."

Charles frowned at him. "I've known you for too many years, Stokehurst ... there's something you're keeping from me."

"I give you my word I'll protect Tasia. Tell Alicia that I regret what happened. Convince her that Tasia is better off staying here. I swear I'll protect her from now on."

Charles nodded. "Very well. You've never broken your word in the past—I'll have to trust that you won't start now."

Casually Charles walked away. Luke stood alone at the back of the room, feeling guilty and strangely confused. Everyone shot speculative gazes at him, except for Iris. She sat a few yards away, pointedly ignoring him. Luke was well-aware that if he had any desire to visit her bed that night, he would have to exert a considerable amount of charm, followed by an apology and the promise of a visit to the jeweler's. But he didn't want to make the effort. For the first time, the thought of sharing Iris's bed left him cold.

He was consumed with thoughts of Tasia. Whatever had happened in her past was bad, he had no doubt of that. She had experienced a lot—too much—in her short lifetime, and had survived it on her own. She was an eighteen-year-old girl, unwilling to ask for help, or trust anyone who might offer it. And he was too old for her, a man of thirty-four with a half-grown daughter. He wondered if she had ever given a thought, even a passing one, to the difference in their ages. Probably not. So far there had been no sign that she was attracted to him: no flirtatious glances, no lingering touches, no effort to prolong their brief conversations.

Come to think of it, he had never seen her smile. Certainly he hadn't given her reason to. For a man who was known as having a way with women, he had been remarkably *un*charming to her. An ass. And it was too late to retrace his steps and undo the damage. Trust was a fragile thing, built one careful piece at a time. With his actions tonight, he had destroyed any hope of gaining her confidence.

It shouldn't matter so much. The world was full of beautiful women, women of intelligence and charm. Without conceit Luke knew that many of them were readily available to him. But in all the years since Mary, no one had caught his interest as this girl did. Brooding in silence, Luke drank steadily, turning grim and unsociable. He ignored his responsibilities as host, and he didn't give a damn what anyone thought. Many of the faces he saw were the same faces he had seen at the parties he hosted with Mary at his side. Year after year the patterns repeated themselves, round and round like a spinning wheel.

He was thankful when the group finally broke for the evening, everyone heading off to cavort with their bed partners of choice. Biddle, the valet, was waiting in his room in case he needed assistance. Luke snapped at him to turn down the lamps and leave. Sitting in a chair, fully clothed, he lifted a bottle of wine to his mouth and took a deep swallow, abusing the subtle vintage.

"Mary," he muttered, as if by saying her name he could conjure her out of the shadows. The stillness of the room mocked him. He had held on to grief for a long time, until it had somehow dissolved on its own, leaving ... nothing. He thought the pain would be there forever. God, he would prefer that to this emptiness.

He had forgotten how to enjoy life. It had been easy in his boyhood—he and Mary had laughed all the time, relishing their youth, their hopes, blindly trusting in their shared future. They had faced everything together. Was it possible to find that with someone else?

"Not bloody likely," he muttered, raising the bottle again. He couldn't stand the prospect of more disillusionment, more pain, more shattered dreams. He didn't even want to try.

Sometime in the middle of the night, Luke set down the half-finished bottle and wandered out of his room. The moon was a huge disk in the sky, strewing white-gold light through the windows. He made his way through the quiet mansion, lured by the thought of cool breezes outside. He crossed a stone courtyard and went through an opening in the tall box hedges that bordered the garden.

Luke's feet crunched on the graveled walkway as he proceeded to a marble bench set in a patch of greenery. Hyacinths spread their heavy fragrance through the air, mingling with lilies and heliotrope planted in lush beds. He sat on the bench, sprawling his legs out comfortably. Then he was still, his attention caught by an ethereal shape moving among the hedges. He thought he was hallucinating. But there it was again, the elusive gleam of white.

"Who is it?" he asked aloud, his heart thumping. The movement stopped, and he heard a gasp.

A few soft footsteps, and then *she* appeared.

"Miss Billings," he said, a quizzical note in his voice.

She was dressed in the peasant costume she had worn the night he had kissed her, a simple skirt and a loose white blouse. Her hair was loose, streaming down to her hips. A light-colored shawl was draped over her head. "My lord," she said breathlessly.

He relaxed, shaking his head. "You looked like a ghost drifting through the garden."

"Do you believe in ghosts, sir?"

"No."

"Sometimes I think I'm being haunted."

"People do that to themselves. Usually people who have too much on their consciences." He gestured to the place on the bench beside him. After a brief hesitation, she accepted the silent invitation. Sitting on the end of the bench, she kept a prudent distance between them. They were both quiet, steeped in the sense of being outside time. The garden was a sanctuary from the rest of the world.

Tasia wondered why she hadn't been surprised to find him there. Her innate mysticism, sprung from a mixture of religion and Slavic blood, led her to accept the coincidence easily. They were both there because they were meant to be. It felt natural to sit with him, staring at the golden moon as if it had been hung for their private viewing.

He reached over to pull at her scarf, unable to resist the temptation, uncovering a river of shining dark hair that fell over her shoulders. "What's haunting you?" he asked.

Tasia bent her head, the smooth locks forming a glowing nimbus around her face.

"Don't you ever get tired of carrying all those secrets around?" He touched a lock of her hair, winding the delicate strands around his finger. "Why are you out here at this hour?"

"It was confining inside. I couldn't breathe. I wanted to be under the sky." She hesitated, sliding him a wary glance. "Why are *you* here?"

Letting go of her hair, he faced her in an easy move, straddling the bench. Tasia was sharply aware of his spread knees, the closeness of his powerful body. She perched on the edge of the bench like a small bird poised for flight. But he didn't reach for her, only gave her a steady look that made her blood rush. "You're not the only one who remembers something you'd like to forget," he said. "Some nights it keeps me awake."

Tasia understood at once. "Your wife."

Slowly he turned his wrist until moonlight struck off the silver hook. "It's like missing a hand. Sometimes I reach for something before I remember my hand is gone. Even after all the years that have passed."

"I heard about the way you brought your wife and Emma out of the fire." Tasia glanced at him shyly. "You were very brave."

His shoulders lifted in a dismissive shrug. "It had nothing to do with bravery. I didn't stop to think. I just went in after them."

"Some men would have worried about their own safety."

"I would have traded places with her. It's harder being the one left behind." He frowned. "Not only did I lose Mary ... I lost myself. I lost the way I was with her. And when the only thing left is a memory, and year by year the details are slipping away . . . you try to hold on all the more tightly. You can never let go long enough to reach for something else."

"Sometimes Emma asks me to play her waltz," Tasia said, staring out at the garden. It was filled with the soothing trill of crickets and the rustling of the miniature creatures that inhabited its fragrant corners. "She listens with her eyes closed, thinking about her mother. Mary—er, Lady Stokehurst—will always be a part of her. And you. I don't think there's anything wrong with that."

Aware of an annoying tickle on her skin, Tasia brushed at it absently and looked down. Her eyes widened as she saw a long-legged spider strolling delicately along her arm.

She jumped up with a frenzied yelp. After knocking the visitor off, she whacked her shirts vigorously, chattering in a stream of Russian. Stokehurst shot off the bench at her cry, his face startled. When he realized what it was, he sank back down, choking with laughter.

"It was only a spider," he finally said, still snickering. "In England we call that kind a harvestman. They don't bite."

Tasia switched back to English. "I hate *every* kind of spider!" She continued to brush wildly at her skirts, her sleeves, any place some uninvited guest might have settled.

"It's all right," Stokehurst's voice was thick with amusement. "He's gone now."

The statement didn't placate her. "Are there any more?"

He caught one of her wrists. "Stop hopping up and down, and let me look." His attentive gaze swept over her. "I think it's safe to say you've sent every living creature in the vicinity running for cover."

"Except for you."

"I don't scare easily. Come here, Miss Muffet." He pulled her wrist until she was back on the bench beside him. "You'd better sit close, in case he comes back."

"Who is Miss Muffet?"

"An important figure of English literature. I'm surprised an educated woman like you doesn't know about her." He slid an arm around her waist, pulling her close against him. The peasant blouse and skirt were lighter than her normal clothes, with no stays or pads to amplify her figure. Tasia felt the hard, smooth muscles of his chest, and the resounding rhythm of his heart. His linen shirt was warm where it lay against his skin.

"Let me go," she said in a low voice.

"And if I don't?"

"I'll scream."

The glimmer of his smile appeared briefly. "You've already done that."

Tasia didn't resist as he leaned over her, his head blocking the moonlight. She tensed, not in fear but in anticipation, her eyes closing. His mouth came to hers. The sweet, heavy pressure drew a quiver of pleasure up through her spine. Suddenly dizzy, she flattened her hands on the muscles of his shoulders. He held her more tightly, kissing her until all thoughts of sin and reason and self-preservation exploded in a burst of fire. And she kissed him back, so hard that her lips parted from the force of it.

Luke welcomed the opening, reaching for the inner depths of her mouth. He hadn't expected her fierceness, the response that rose up and closed

over him like tidal waters. Everything changed in
that potent flood. His illusion that he had any
choice at all where she was concerned had dissolved forever. She was as necessary as the blood
that fed his marrow. She filled the emptiness inside him, for some mysterious reason that his
heart comprehended when his mind could not. He
tried to gentle the kiss, turn it into something less
raw, less feverish, but she wouldn't let him. She
reached across the back of his shirt, clawing, desperate to feel the heat and hardness beneath the
thin fabric.

He moved, dragging her slender body across his
lap. She whimpered as their mouths slipped apart.
Luke stared at her, struck by her beauty, the
gleaming black tumble of hair, the ripe mouth, the
slant of her brows. And her body, light, supple,
elastic with youth. His hand left the taut line of
her waist, sliding to the loose neckline of her peasant blouse. The garment came from her shoulder
with a firm tug. She caught her breath sharply as
his hand slid into her blouse to find the tender
shape of her breast.

Anchoring her in his lap, he took her mouth
again, a long kiss that soon broke into a myriad of
shorter ones, luscious fragments of kisses, some
hard, some soft and seeking. He fondled her
breast, his warm fingers cupping the delicate
weight. Gently his thumb passed over the tip until
the nub of silk became exquisitely tight.

Tasia struggled to embrace him, twisting to
push closer. Her hands slid to his hair, the thick
locks that lured her fingers to sink deep and play
and tangle. Every sensation of her life, the deepest
pleasure and sharpest pain, dimmed in compari-
son to the satisfaction of being with him. He was

so powerful, so gentle. He was everything she had ever dreamed of.

But it had all been ruined, before they ever met. She had ruined it.

Tasia jerked back with a gasp. His eyes opened. Before she could look away, he saw the flash of anguish. Tasia wanted to leave him then, run from words and questions and demands for explanations that couldn't be given. His arms turned to steel. He anchored her against his chest, not letting her move.

"This can't lead to anything," she whispered.

His hand drifted over her long hair, gathering it in silken sheaves and letting it strain through his fingers. There was a brief rush in his lungs that sounded like laughter, but when he spoke, his voice was anything but amused. "If there had been a choice for either of us, we wouldn't have taken it this far. What makes you think anything can stop it now?"

She raised her face and glared at him miserably. "I can stop it by leaving. You want me to tell you everything, but I can't. I don't want you to know about me and the things I've done."

His wide mouth twitched with impatience. "Why? Do you think I'll be shocked? I'm hardly an idealistic boy, or a hypocrite. Good Lord, do you actually think your sins could be worse than mine?"

"I know they are," Tasia said bitterly. Whatever his sins were, she doubted that murder was among them.

"You're an arrogant little fool," he muttered.

"*Arrogant—*"

"No one's feelings count but your own. No one is affected but you. Well, you're wrong. It's not just you anymore. I'm part of this now—and I'll be damned if I'll slink away just because you've decided I don't fit in with your plans."

"*You're* the most arrogant person I've ever met in my life! An authority on matters you know nothing about!" Her temper, driven by the force of her Slavic blood, came rushing to the surface. She trembled with the urge to shout. Instead she spoke in a lethal undertone. "I don't care about your feelings. I don't want anything from you. Let me go! I will leave tomorrow. I can't stay after this. I'm not safe here anymore."

Her bones gave slightly, molded by the force of his hold. "So you can go on hiding, running, staying invisible, never letting anyone care ... Not much of a life, is it? More like a living death."

Tasia flinched. "It's all I can have."

"Is it? Or are you too much of a coward to try for something more?"

She writhed wildly. "I hate you," she gasped.

Luke controlled her without effort. "I want you. Enough to fight for you. And if you run from me, I'll find you." His lips parted in a savage smile. "By God, it feels good to want someone again. I wouldn't trade this for a fortune."

"I won't tell you anything," she said passionately. "I'll disappear, and in a month you'll forget all about me, and everything will be the same as before."

"You won't desert Emma. You know what it would do to her. She needs you." That was unfair of him, and they both knew it. "We both do," he added gruffly.

Tasia was outraged. "I know why Emma needs me ... but *you* ... All you want is f-fornication!"

He averted his face then. A muffled sound escaped him. For a triumphant moment Tasia thought that she had shamed him, and then she realized he was laughing. Infuriated, she began to struggle. He positioned her against his body. She felt the flat of his silver hook against the small of her back. Low beneath his hips, a hard ridge jutted with burning intimacy. Her breath came fast, and she felt a peculiar throb of excitement in the place where he pressed. She held very still.

His smiling mouth brushed over her hot cheek. "I won't deny it. Fornication ranks high on the list. But it's not the only thing I want from you."

"How dare you, when there is a woman waiting upstairs for you! Or have you already forgotten Lady Harcourt?"

"There are some things I have to resolve," he admitted.

"Indeed."

"Iris and I have no claim on each other. She's a good woman, with many qualities I respect and like. But there's no love on either side, and she would be the first to admit it."

"She wants to marry you," Tasia said accusingly.

He shrugged. "Well, friendship isn't a bad reason to marry. But it's not enough for me. Iris knows my opinion on the matter. I've made it clear on many occasions."

"Perhaps she thinks you'll change your mind."

An engaging smile appeared. "Stokehursts don't change their minds. We're very stubborn. In that regard, I'm the worst of the lot."

Suddenly Tasia found it hard to believe she was having such a conversation with him, here in the darkness, tangled in his arms. She had dared to criticize him, and he had allowed it freely. It was an alarming sign of how things had changed between them. Her thoughts must have been easy to read, for he laughed and loosened his hold. "I'll let you go for now," he said. "If we stay like this much longer, there's no telling what I may be driven to do."

Tasia wriggled out of his arms, but stayed on the bench and faced him. "I meant what I said about leaving. It must be soon. I have a . . . a feeling that trouble is coming."

Luke gave her a shrewd glance. "Where will you go?"

"To a place that no one will know about, not even the Ashbournes. I will find work. I'll be all right."

"You won't be able to hide," he said. "People will always notice you, no matter how you try to fade into the background. You couldn't change your looks and bearing if you tried for a hundred years. Besides, you weren't meant for that kind of life."

"I don't have any choice."

He took her hand carefully. "Yes, you do. Would it be so terrible to come out of your fortress?"

Tasia shook her head, the locks of her hair moving in a sinuous curve over her shoulders. "It's not safe."

"What if I'm there to help you?" Slowly he turned her hand over, his thumb dipping into her palm.

The temptation to believe him was overwhelming. Tasia was horrified that her common sense was so easily defeated. A few kisses in the moonlight, and suddenly she was considering entrusting her safety, her very life, to a man she scarcely knew. "What would you want in return?" she asked unsteadily.

"I thought you were supposed to be perceptive. Use your intuition . . . or whatever you call it." He leaned over and kissed her, his mouth so deeply stirring that Tasia had no thought of pulling away. Helplessly she answered him, openmouthed and enthralled. She had never understood sensuality before, one body speaking to another with skin and taste and movement. She felt his hand sliding through her hair, fingers coming to grip her scalp and pull her head closer. The sensation of being held steady, gently ravaged, was so exciting that she began to shake. Wanting more, she pressed against him with an awkward surge. He gathered her close and pulled his head back, his breath pelting hard on her face. "Damn," he whispered. "You don't make anything easy, do you?"

Blindly she searched for his mouth, luring him with glancing kisses. She touched the edge of his lower lip with her tongue, and he groaned and gave her what she wanted, catching her mouth with full, greedy possession. Luke let it go on for too long, until his body was hard and ready to explode. Somehow he found the presence of mind to call a stop to it. "Go," he said thickly, shoving her away. "Now, while I can still let you."

She pulled up the sagging neckline of her blouse, staring at him with the eyes of a sorceress. Carefully she rose to her feet, her figure wraithlike amid the streaks of shadow and light. After a fierce glance at her, Luke focused on the ground. He waited for several minutes, staying motionless long after the sound of her footsteps had faded.

He tried to comprehend what had happened. If his problem had been the absence of feeling before, it was now the reverse. Too much feeling, too fast, and with it came all the potential for pain he had avoided for so long. A rough laugh escaped him. "Welcome back to the living," he told himself grimly. There was no choice but to take the chance he'd been given, and see it through to the end.

On Saturday evening, the results of Lady Harcourt's planning were spectacular. The gold and white ballroom was filled with huge flower arrangements. Blossoms were reflected into infinity by the huge mirrors lining the walls. The musicians were as talented as any Tasia had ever heard, filling the air with heavenly waltzes. Together she and Emma peered into the ballroom from one of the windows in the adjoining gallery. People were dancing, smiling, flirting, admiring each other, all of them aware of what a splendid scene it was.

"Wonderful," Emma said, awestruck.

Tasia nodded in agreement, staring at the profusion of beautiful gowns. Hungrily she took in every detail. English styles were different from those in St. Petersburg, or perhaps it was just that she hadn't given a thought to fashion for so long that it had changed without her noticing.

Necklines were square-cut and shockingly low, covered with transparent gauze or filmy netting in a sham display of modesty. Bustles were smaller—in some cases gone completely—and the skirts were tightly molded over the thighs. How was it possible for the women to dance in such narrow gowns? There was no room for the legs to move. Somehow the ladies managed it, looping their long trains over their gloved wrists and gliding smoothly in their partners' arms.

Tasia glanced down at her own dress, plain black silk buttoned up to the neck. Underneath she wore thick stockings and sturdy black shoes that fastened over the ankles. She was ashamed to admit it to herself, but seeing the women in their finery caused her a pang of jealousy. Once she had owned gowns far more beautiful than any she saw here ... the white satin with just a hint of pink, the ice-blue silk that had flattered her eyes, the delectable lavender *crepe de chine*. She had worn diamond pins in her hair, and ropes of rubies and pearls around her waist. What would Lord Stokehurst say if he saw her dressed like that? She imagined his blue eyes gleaming with admiration as they traveled over her body—

"*Stop it*," she muttered, trying to banish the vain thoughts. " 'Wisdom is more precious than rubies.' " When that didn't work, she struggled to recall other helpful verses. " 'Better is the poor that walketh in his uprightness.' 'Favor is deceitful and beauty is vain—' "

"Miss Billings?" Emma interrupted, staring at her quizzically. "Why are you talking to yourself?"

Tasia sighed. "I'm reminding myself of some important things. Here, one of your curls is escaping. Hold still." She reached out to tuck Emma's rebellious locks back into place.

"Does it look all right now?"

"Perfect." Tasia stood back and smiled in satisfaction. She and one of her housemaids had spent an hour on Emma's hair, pulling it in a loose sweep from her face, braiding the thick curls and pinning the ends underneath. Emma wore an ankle-length dress of pale green satin and white lace, trimmed at the waist with a dark green sash. After a laborious search, the gardener had brought what he declared to be the finest roses he had ever produced, with lush pink blossoms and an intoxicating fragrance. Mrs. Knaggs had helped to pin one at Emma's shoulder, one in her hair, and one at the waist of her dress. By the time they finished, Emma had glowed with pleasure, claiming she felt like a princess.

Emma's blue eyes sparkled as she hunted for a glimpse of her father through the window. "Papa said he would come here after he opened the ball with Lady Harcourt. He promised that next year I can have a children's ball, right here, while the adults dance in the big room."

A new voice entered the conversation. "It won't be long before you're in the big room with the rest of us."

Emma whirled around at her father's approach and posed extravagantly. "Look at me, Papa!"

Luke grinned, stopping to admire her. "My God. You're beautiful, Emma. You've turned into a young lady. A fine thing to do to your poor old father." He reached out and caught her close for a moment. "You look like your mother tonight," he murmured.

"Do I?" Emma asked, beaming. "Good."

Tasia watched Stokehurst with his daughter. She steeled her spine against a sudden tremor as she remembered the moonlight on his black hair, and the warmth of his mouth. His body was elegant and powerful in the tailored black coat and white waistcoat. As if he sensed her keen interest, he glanced at her. Hastily Tasia looked away, a blush rising from her high collar.

"Good evening, Miss Billings," he said blandly.

She didn't need to look at him to know there was a mocking gleam in his eyes. "My lord," she replied under her breath.

Emma was in no mood to dally. "I've been waiting for *hours* to dance with you, Papa!"

He laughed at his daughter's impatience. "You have? Well, I'm going to waltz you back and forth until you complain about your aching feet."

"Never," Emma exclaimed. She placed one hand on his leather-bound wrist, just below the flashing hook, and rested the other on his shoulder. At first he whirled her in a vigorous romp, making Emma laugh. Then they settled into a smooth, graceful waltz. Stokehurst had obviously seen to it that his daughter had lessons, and had practiced with her.

A smile twitched at Tasia's lips, and she withdrew to the doorway, enjoying the sight.

"They're a remarkable pair, aren't they?" came Lady Harcourt's soft voice.

Tasia gave a start. Lady Harcourt was standing a few feet away. She wore a gown of pale yellow satin covered with tiny gold beads. The scooped neckline showed a hint of her deep cleavage, while the waist came to a scalloped point low on her hips. Several diamond and topaz combs glittered in her auburn hair, holding her loose braided chignon in place. Most spectacular of all was the necklace around her throat, a web of jeweled flowers with diamonds in the center.

"Good evening, Lady Harcourt," Tasia murmured. "The ball seems to be a great success."

"I haven't sought you out in order to talk about the ball. I'm sure you know exactly what I intend to say."

Tasia shook her head. "I'm sure I don't, my lady."

"Fine, then." Iris fidgeted with the tassel that hung from her fan. "I don't mind being blunt. I've always believed in approaching a problem directly."

"My lady, I would never wish to cause you the slightest problem."

"Well, you have." Iris stepped closer, staring at the distant figures of the Stokehursts as they waltzed at the far end of the gallery. "You *are* the problem, Miss Billings. Ultimately your presence here will bring pain and trouble for everyone: me, Emma, and especially Luke."

Dismayed, Tasia stared at her without blinking. "I don't see how that's possible."

"You're distracting Luke. You're leading him away from the thing that would bring him true happiness—companionship with one of his own kind. I understand him. I've known him for years, you see. I knew him back when Mary was alive. The relationship they shared was special—and I can give him something very close to that. I'm actually a rather nice woman, Miss Billings, in spite of what you may think."

"What do you want me to do?"

"I'm asking you to leave, for his sake. If you give a fig about him, you'll do as I ask. Leave Southgate Hall, and don't look back. I'll reward you well for it. Perhaps you would like to have this necklace I'm wearing." Iris lifted the fall of jewels away from her skin, making them sparkle. "You never thought to have such riches, did you? Every gem is real. You'll be comfortable for the rest of your life with the money it will bring. You could buy a little cottage in the country, even hire a cook maid for yourself."

"I don't want your jewelry," Tasia said, mortified.

The wheedling note left Iris's voice. "You're an

intelligent girl, I see. You want more, and you've decided that Emma is the key. Gain the affection of his daughter, and that will lead Luke to a romantic interest in you. You may be right. But don't fool yourself into thinking the affair will last longer than a matter of weeks. Your youth may hold his attention for a little while, but you don't have what it takes to keep him."

"What makes you so certain?" Tasia was appalled to hear herself ask. Instantly she bit her lip. The words had rushed out before she could stop them.

"Ah," Iris said softly. "Now the truth is out. You do want him. And you actually harbor hopes of keeping him. It should annoy me . . . but instead I pity you."

The words were derisive, but Tasia sensed the deep unhappiness beneath them. Her heart softened with sympathy. This woman had known Lord Stokehurst intimately, had thrilled to his kisses and his smiles, had spun dreams of becoming his wife, and now she was fighting for the chance to keep him. Tasia tried to think of words to reassure her. After all, Lady Harcourt wanted her to do what she was already planning to do—leave. She couldn't stay even if she wanted to. "Lady Harcourt, please believe you have nothing to fear. I won't—"

"*Fear?*" Iris said defensively. "Of course I don't *fear* you—a governess with no dowry, no family, and no figure to speak of!"

"I'm trying to explain—"

"Don't waste your long-suffering gaze on me, child. I've said my piece. All I ask is that you think about it." Before Tasia could say another word, Iris walked away. She stepped through the doorway, her gown shimmering. "What a splendid sight the two of you make," she called with a wide smile. "Emma, you dance like an angel. My lord, after this waltz you must return to the ball with me. You are the host, after all."

The dancing was interrupted by a midnight feast that lasted for two hours, followed by more music, more waltzes, more of everything, until the night waned and the horizon began to glow with the approach of the morning sun. Sated and drunk, the crowd dispersed, the floors creaking as scores of sore feet trod across them in search of soft beds. The guests slept for most of the day, taking breakfast in the afternoon. Some left early Sunday evening, while others preferred to travel on Monday. Iris was one of the Sunday departures. She had come to Luke's room to inform him, barging in while he dressed.

"I'm leaving for London within the hour," she said, watching as Biddle fastened the right cuff of Luke's shirt.

Raising his brows at her quiet intensity, Luke shrugged into a claret-colored coat. He took his time about replying, first glancing at the selection of narrow cravats Biddle displayed, then deciding not to wear one. He ordered the valet out of the room and turned to Iris. "Why so soon?" he asked evenly. "You seemed to enjoy yourself last evening."

"I refuse to spend another night waiting in vain for the sound of your footsteps! Why didn't you come to me after the ball?"

"You banished me from your bed, remember?"

"I told you not to visit me if you couldn't get that Billings girl out of your head. It's clear that you can't. Every time you look at me, you wish I was she. It's been going on for weeks. I'm trying to fight it, but I don't know how!"

Iris held her breath as she saw Luke's expression change, the remoteness fading. For a moment she tensed with impossible hope. Then his regretful voice doused the flicker of happiness. "Iris, there's something I should tell you—"

"Not now," she said grimly, backing away. "Not now." She left with determined strides, her hands clenched.

Dutifully Luke attended the after-dinner gathering, making conversation, smiling at light quips, applauding as several guests performed skits, recited poetry, and did their best at the piano. His impatience grew, finding outlet only in the monotonous tapping of his foot. When he couldn't bear to sit still any longer, he excused himself with a quiet murmur.

He wandered through the house with the appearance of aimlessness. He wanted no one and nothing but her, even if it was just to sit in silence and stare at her. It was a hunger he had never known before. She was the only one in his life who saw him, and *knew* him, for who and what he was.

Iris thought she understood him. Most women prided themselves on thinking they had superior knowledge of the male mind, and therefore could manipulate men to their advantage. But Iris had never known what it was like to have her life destroyed, and what it took to rebuild; the pain and rage, the will to survive . . . and the isolation it imposed. Tasia understood all too well. That was the bond between them, the basis for unspoken but mutual respect, the inner recognition that had tormented him since the first moment they met. They were exactly alike, in the only way that mattered.

As he walked along a first-floor hallway, Mrs. Knaggs passed with an armload of fresh linen. The housekeeper paused to nod respectfully. "Good evening, my lord."

"Mrs. Knaggs, where is—"

"Upstairs, sir. With Emma, in the green sitting room."

Luke frowned. "How did you know what I was going to ask?"

The housekeeper smiled smugly. "After all these years working for the Stokehursts? There's hardly anything that Seymour, Biddle, and I *don't* know, my lord."

Luke gave her a warning glance, and she went on her way, unruffled as usual.

The sitting room was cozy and well-lit, a little more cluttered and fringed and cushioned than the other parlors in the house. He heard Emma's animated voice as she read aloud from a novel. Tasia was curled at the end of a brocade settee, one slender arm draped across its curving back. She changed position as she saw him, straightening a little and drawing her arm into her lap. The top two buttons of her gown were undone, showing a glimpse of her white throat. Lamplight cast a golden gleam over her skin and gilded her hair. Emma threw her father a quick grin and kept on reading.

Luke sat in a nearby chair and stared at Tasia. Beautiful, troubled, stubborn woman. He wanted her, every inch of her body, every secretive turn of her thoughts. He wanted to wake up in the morning and find her arms around him. He wanted to keep her safe, until she lost the haunted look in her eyes. She stared back at him, her forehead touched with a questioning frown.

You've never smiled at me, he thought fiercely. *Not once.*

It seemed as if she read his mind. A curve touched her lips, sweet and wry, as if he had provoked it in spite of her wish to hold it back.

It felt strange to Luke, being forced to depend on someone for the first time. He couldn't break down her defenses; she would only resist him more. The only way to gain what he wanted was to let down his own defenses and encourage her to do the same. It would require more patience than he possessed. But somehow he would manage it, no matter what it cost. Nothing was too much to ask, no price too dear, if only she would love him.

Five

❧ ❧

With the weekend party concluded, the last few guests departed on Mondy. Luke was free in the afternoon to go to Iris's London terrace. It was time to end their arrangement, and he knew Iris must be aware of it by now. There was only one woman he wanted, and everything he had to give was for her alone. Perhaps Iris would be disappointed at first, but she would recover quickly. In addition to a well-managed fortune, Iris had a circle of devoted friends—and there were at least a dozen men who were ready to flatter and console her. Luke had no doubt that she would do very well without him.

Iris welcomed him into her bedroom with a sensuous kiss, her body covered in only a few scraps of black silk. Before Luke was able to explain why he had come, she erupted into a prepared speech without allowing him a chance to break in.

"I'll give you a few weeks to amuse yourself with her," Iris said briskly. "When you tire of her, you can come back to me. We need never mention her again. Didn't I promise to give you all the freedom you wanted? I don't want you to feel one bit guilty. Men need variety. I understand that. There is nothing that needs to be forgiven. As long as I know you'll come back—"

"No," Luke interrupted, his voice coming out too harshly. He checked it and took a deep breath.

Her hands moved in a helpless flutter. "What is it?" she asked plaintively. "There's a look on your face I've never seen before. What's wrong?"

"I don't want you to wait for me. I'm not coming back."

Iris gave a frantic little laugh. "But why should we throw away everything for some temporary indulgence? Don't be fooled by appearances, darling. She's a pretty, waiflike thing who seems to need you ... Well, just because I'm not all skin and bones doesn't mean I don't need you every bit as much! And when you tire of her—"

"I'm in love with her."

An astonished silence settled over the room. Iris's throat worked frantically. She looked away to hide her expression. "That's not something you would say lightly," she finally said. "I suppose Miss Billings is pleased with herself."

"I haven't told her. She's not ready for it."

Iris sneered with sudden outrage. "Dainty, frail creature that she is, she'd probably faint dead away. God, the irony of it—that a full-blooded man like you would fall for a pale little nothing like *her*—"

"She's not as frail as you seem to think." In a flash Luke remembered Tasia in the garden, the sweet hunger of her mouth beneath his, the scratch of her nails over his shirt ... His blood quickened in response, and he paced across the room like a caged wolf.

"Why her?" Iris demanded, following him. "Is it because Emma likes her? Is it her youth?"

"It doesn't matter why," he said curtly.

"Of course it does!" Iris stopped in the center of

the room and began to sniffle. "If she hadn't come along and bewitched you, we would still be together. I need to know why her and not me! I want to understand what I did wrong!"

Sighing, Luke reached out and drew her against him. He felt a pang of guilt mingled with affection. They had known each other for a long time, first as friends, then as lovers. She deserved far more than he'd been able to give her. "You did nothing wrong," he said.

Iris rested her chin on his shoulder and sniffled more loudly. "Then why are you leaving me? How cruel you are!"

"I don't mean to be," he said softly. "I'll always care about you."

Iris jerked away with a wrathful glare. "The most useless words in the English language are 'I care'! I'd rather you didn't care at all, and then I could hate you. But you care just a little ... and not enough. Damn you! Why does she have to be beautiful and young? I can't even gossip about her with my friends. Anything I say will make me appear to be a jealous old hag."

Luke smiled at the petulant droop of her lips. "Never."

Iris strode to the gold-framed mirror and began to arrange her hair, fluffing the auburn tendrils around her face. "Are you going to marry her?"

Ruefully he wished that everything were that simple. "If she'll have me."

Iris sniffed in disdain. "I don't think there's much doubt of that, darling. She'll never have another chance to snare a man like you."

Luke walked up behind her, reaching over her shoulder to catch her agitated hand in his. Their eyes caught in the mirror. "Thank you," he said quietly.

"For what?" There was a quaver in her voice.

"For being so generous, and beautiful. For taking away the loneliness so many nights. I don't regret a single one of them. I hope you don't." He squeezed her fingers hard before letting go.

"Luke ..." Iris turned to him with emotion-filled eyes. "Promise me if something goes wrong ... if you decide you've made a mistake ... then promise you'll come back to me."

Luke leaned over and kissed her forehead gently. "Goodbye," he whispered.

Iris nodded, a tear sliding down her cheek. As he left the room, she turned away, closing her eyes against the sight of him walking out of her life.

Luke reached the front entrance of Southgate Hall just as the sun was setting. He had ridden the black Arabian stallion hard from Iris's town house, finding respite in the rush of wind past his ears and the racing of the ground beneath them. He was streaked with dust and sweat, his muscles filled with the pleasant burn of exertion. Dismounting, he gave the reins to the waiting footman. "Make certain he's cooled off well," he said as the servant led the horse toward the stables.

"My lord." Seymour stood in the doorway, wearing an expression of mild concern that, coming from a butler, heralded disaster. "My lord, the Ashbournes—"

"Papa!" Emma appeared in a wild flurry, hurling herself down the front steps and into his arms. "Papa, I'm so glad you're here! Something's dreadfully wrong—Lord and Lady Ashbourne are here. They've been talking with Miss Billings in the library for at least an hour."

Luke was stunned. The Ashbournes had left Southgate Hall only this morning. Something was definitely out of order if they had returned so quickly. "What did they say?"

"I haven't heard a word, but they looked very peculiar when they arrived, and it's been so quiet. Please, you must go in there and make certain Miss Billings is all right!"

Luke tightened his arms, crushing her briefly. "I'll take care of it. Go up to your room, and don't worry." He pulled back and gave her a warning glance. "No listening at the keyhole, Emma."

She laughed guiltily. "How else am I supposed to know what goes on around here?"

He put his arm around her shoulder, walking her into the entrance hall. "You should be too busy with your own interests to spend your time worrying over adults, sweet."

"I am very busy. I have the horses, and Samson, and my books, and Miss Billings—Papa, you won't let anyone take Miss Billings away, will you?"

"No," he murmured, kissing her head. "Go to bed, sweetheart."

Dutifully Emma scampered away, and Luke went to the library. The heavy doors were closed, but the sound of quiet murmurs filtered through. His jaw hardened, and he shoved into the room without a hint of warning. The Ashbournes were seated in heavy leather chairs, while Tasia huddled in a corner of the low-backed settee.

Charles's face was wreathed in worry. "Stokehurst," he said in dismay, "we thought you were—"

"Out for the evening?" Luke said pleasantly. "I had a change of plans. Tell me what brings you to visit."

"Bad news from abroad, I'm afraid," Charles said, striving for a light tone. "We've been convincing Miss Billings to come away with us. The month is almost over, Luke, and I always keep my promises." Seeing Tasia's sudden wary confusion, he explained. "Lord Stokehurst agreed to take you on for precisely a month, during which time I would find you a new situation."

"I've changed my mind," Luke said, staring at Tasia. She was white and still, her hands resting in a little knot on her lap. "Miss Billings isn't leaving Southgate Hall." He went to the built-in mahogany sideboard and reached for a crystal decanter. He poured a healthy splash of brandy into a snifter and brought it to Tasia.

Slowly her fingers unfolded, and she took the glass in her palms. Luke reached down and lifted her chin, forcing her to look into his eyes. She gave him a fixed stare, her thoughts hidden behind a mask.

"Tell me what's happened," he said gently.

Charles was the one to reply. "It's best for all concerned if you don't know, Luke. Just let us leave with no questions asked—"

"You can leave," Luke assured him. "But Miss Billings stays."

Charles sighed in exasperation. "I've heard that tone many times before, Luke, and I know what it signifies—"

"It doesn't matter now," Tasia interrupted. She drained the brandy, closing her eyes as the smooth fire slid down her throat. Her pale, bright gaze returned to Luke, and she gave him a shaky smile. "You won't want me to stay, after you know."

Luke reached for the empty brandy snifter. "Another?" he asked brusquely, and she nodded.

He went to refill the glass. Tasia waited until his back was turned before she spoke in a strained voice. "I am Lady Anastasia Ivanovna Kaptereva. Last winter in St. Petersburg I was convicted of murdering my cousin, Prince Mikhail Angelovsky." She paused as she saw him tense, the muscles of his back locking. "I escaped from prison, and came to England to avoid execution."

Tasia hadn't intended to prolong the story, but she found herself describing her life in St. Petersburg after her father's death. Somehow she forgot that she was speaking and others were listening. The past rushed over her, and she saw it as if it were all happening again. She saw her mother, Marie Petrovna, swathed in lynx fur, her arms and throat adorned with jewels the size of robin's eggs. And the men who swarmed around her in eager hordes, at parties on the royal yacht, during visits to the opera and theater, at lengthy midnight suppers.

Tasia remembered her first *bal blanc*, where aristocratic girls were presented as the choicest offerings of the Russian nobility. She had worn a white silk gown, her waist cinched by a girdle of rubies and pink pearls. Men had pursued her, each of them with an eye on the fortune she would inherit someday. But of all the suitors who showed interest, the most notable was Prince Mikhail Angelovsky.

"Mikhail was an animal," Tasia said with sudden intensity. "When he was sober, he was vicious.

The only time he was tolerable was when he inhaled enough opium smoke to put himself in a stupor. He was seldom without his pipe. He also drank quite a lot." She hesitated, and a blush spread over her face. "Mikhail didn't like women at all. Everyone knew how he was, but his family turned a blind eye to it. When I turned seventeen, the Angelovskys approached my mother. An agreement was made. They decided I would become Mikhail's wife. It was common knowledge that I didn't want the marriage. I begged my mother, my family, the priest, anyone who might listen, not to force me to marry him. But they all said it would be good for the family, keeping two large fortunes closely linked. And the Angelovskys hoped that marriage might reform Mikhail."

"And your mother? What was her opinion?"

At the sound of Stokehurst's voice, Tasia looked at him for the first time. He was beside her on the settee, his face inscrutable. She held the empty brandy snifter in a tight grip, until the fragile glass threatened to splinter. Carefully Stokehurst pried it from her fingers and set it aside.

"My mother wanted me to be married," Tasia said, staring into his alert blue eyes. "She didn't like it when the men who came to visit her began to show interest in me. I look very much the way she did in her youth—it made her uncomfortable. She told me that it was my duty to marry for the benefit of the family, and afterward I could fall in and out of love with whomever I wanted. She said I would be very happy as the wife of an Angelovsky, especially . . . one who preferred boys."

Stokehurst snorted derisively. "Why?"

"She said that Mikhail wouldn't bother me with

his attentions, and I would be free to do as I liked." At Stokehurst's scathing glance, Tasia shrugged helplessly. "If you knew my mother, you would understand how she is."

"I understand exactly," he said, his mouth twisting. "Go on with the story."

"As a last resort, I decided to visit Mikhail in secret, and beg him to help me. I thought I might be able to reason with him. There was a chance he would listen. So I ... I went to see him." Tasia stopped then. Words tumbled inside her, fragmenting, jamming in her throat until she couldn't speak at all. Feeling a trickle of cold sweat on her temple, she reached up and wiped her forehead with the back of her hand. It always happened when she tried to remember ... She was filled with panic, suffocated with it.

"What happened?" Stokehurst asked softly.

She shook her head, breathing in uneven bursts, unable to get enough air.

"Tasia." His hand covered hers in a hurtful grip. "Tell me the rest."

Somehow she forced the words out through her chattering teeth. "I don't know. I went to him, I think ... but I don't remember. I was found in the Angelovsky Palace with a knife in my hand ... and Mikhail's body ... The servants were screaming, and his throat ... blood ... Oh God, it was everywhere." Tasia held on to his hand with both of hers, feeling as if a dark pit were opening beneath her, and he was the only thing that kept her from falling. She wanted to fling herself against him, and press deep into the smell of horses and sweat and brandy, and feel his arms around her. Instead she quenched the urge and stayed where she was, staring at him desperately while hot tears splashed from her eyes. He was strangely calm, as steady as a rock, watching her without any sign of shock or horror.

"There were no witnesses to the actual murder?" he asked.

"No, just the servants who found me afterward."

"There was no proof, then. You can't be certain that you did it." Luke turned to Charles with a quizzical glance. "There has to be more. They couldn't convict her solely on circumstantial evidence."

Charles shook his head ruefully. "I'm afraid their system of justice is nothing like ours. The Russian authorities can define a crime any way they choose, withhold any case from the regular courts, imprison a man indefinitely on the mere suspicion that he's committed a crime. They don't require proof or even evidence to convict someone."

"I must have done it," Tasia sobbed. "I dream about it all the time. I wake up wondering if I'm remembering or imagining. S-sometimes I think I'm going mad. I did hate Mikhail. I spent weeks in a prison cell thinking about that, knowing I deserved to be executed. The thought is as bad as the deed, don't you see? I prayed for acceptance, for humility, until my knees were bruised from the floor, but it didn't work . . . I still wanted to *live* . . . I couldn't stop myself from wanting it."

"What happened then?" Luke asked, lacing his fingers through hers.

"I took a sleeping draught in prison, to make everyone think I was dead. They filled the coffin with sand, and there was a funeral, while I . . . I was brought to England by my Uncle Kirill. But there were rumors that I was still alive. Government officials decided to have my body exhumed, to settle the matter. When they discovered that the coffin was empty, they realized I had escaped. That was why Uncle Kirill sent a message to the Ashbournes."

"Who is looking for you?"

Tasia was silent, gazing down at their linked hands.

Charles rearranged himself in a more comfortable position in his chair. The creases on his face had relaxed, as if he were relieved at being able to confide the whole story to someone. Even as a schoolboy, Charles had hated to keep secrets. He wasn't very good at it. Everything showed on his face. "It's a rather complicated question," Charles said to Luke. "The imperial government has so many secret divisions and special sections of law enforcement that no one really knows who's responsible for what. I've read Kirill's letter a dozen times, trying to make sense of everything. It seems that Tasia has not only committed a civil offense, she has now broken the criminal code by undermining respect for the sovereign authority—a political crime punishable by death. The imperial government doesn't care about justice. It cares about the appearance of order. Until Tasia is executed in a public display, the enemies of the tsar will use her as a means to ridicule the crown, the corps of gendarmes, the ministry of the interior—"

"And you think they would actually follow Tasia here and bring her back to Russia?" Luke interrupted. "Just to make a point?"

"No, they wouldn't go that far," Tasia said in a low voice. "As long as I remain in exile, I'm safe from them. The problem is Nikolas." Luke watched her blot her wet cheeks with her sleeve, and the childlike gesture wrung his heart. He waited silently for her to go on, although he was simmering with impatience. "Nikolas is Mikhail's older brother," she continued dully. "The Angelovskys want revenge for Mikhail's death. Nikolas is looking for me. He'll find me if it takes the rest of his life."

Suddenly the compassion on Luke's face was stamped out by arrogant confidence. If all they were concerned about was Nikolas Angelovsky, that was a problem easily solved. "If he does, I'll send him straight back to Russia."

"Just like that," Tasia said with a frown.

Luke smiled slightly, envisioning some pampered prince in satin knee breeches. "There's nothing to worry about."

"If you knew Nikolas, you would understand the cause for concern." Tasia pulled her hand away and withdrew to the corner of the settee. "I have to leave, before you make everything worse. You would never understand someone like Prince Angelovsky, or what lengths he would go to. Now that Nicholas knows I'm alive, it's only a matter of time until he finds me. He doesn't have the choice to stop, even if he wanted to. Everything he is, blood, history, family, compels him to make me pay for what I did to his brother. He is a powerful, dangerous man." As Luke tried to speak, she forestalled him with a stilted gesture and turned to Charles and Alicia. "Thank you for everything you've done, but you mustn't involve yourselves any further. I will find a new place by myself."

"Tasia, you can't disappear without letting us

know where you're going," Alicia cried. "Please let us help you!"

Tasia stood and smiled with loving regret. "You've been wonderful to me, cousin. You've helped me as much as anyone could have. Now I have to manage on my own. *Spaséeba.*" Her expression was shuttered as she glanced at Luke, but he sensed her fatigue, her need for comfort ... He saw the price she had already paid for survival. Words seemed to fail her, and she turned away abruptly.

The men stood in unison as she left the room. Luke began to follow her, but he was stopped by Alicia's voice.

"Let her go."

Luke swung around with a scowl. He was exasperated, angry, eager to do battle. "Did I miss something?" he inquired acidly. "Angelovsky is only a man. He can be dealt with. There's no reason to let fear of him ruin the rest of her life."

"He's barely human," Alicia said. "Prince Nikolas and I are third cousins. I know quite a bit about the Angelovskys. Would you like to hear what kind of people they are?"

"Tell me everything," Luke muttered, staring at the empty doorway.

"The Angelovskys are complete Slavophiles. They hate everyone who isn't Russian. Their family is connected to the royal house by marriage. They are among the wealthiest landholders in Russia, with property scattered over a dozen provinces. I'd guess they own approximately two million acres or more. Nikolas's father, Prince Dmitri Sergeyevich, murdered his first wife because she was barren. Then he married a peasant girl from Minsk. She bore him seven children; five girls and two sons. The children were beautiful, exotic . . . and primitive. None of them has spent a minute of their lives bothering about abstract things like principles or ethics or honor. They act on instinct. I've heard that Nikolas is just like the Old Prince, very brutal and cunning. If a wrong is done to him, he'll repay it a hundredfold. Tasia is right—he doesn't have the choice of whether to seek revenge. In Russia they have a saying: 'Another's tears are like water.' It suits the Angelovskys to perfection. There's no mercy in their nature." Alicia turned to Charles's protective embrace with a miserable sigh. "Nothing will stop Prince Nikolas."

Luke watched the two of them coldly. "I can. And I will."

"You don't owe anything to Tasia, or to us," she said in a muffled voice.

"I've had too much taken from me." An odd blue-white glitter came into his eyes. "Now that I finally have a chance at some happiness, I'll be damned if I let some bloodthirsty Russian bastard meddle with it."

Charles wore the same look of bewilderment as his wife. "Happiness," he echoed. "What are you saying? That you have some sort of personal feeling for the girl? A few days ago you were dangling her before your guests like a bit of live bait on a hook—" He stopped at Luke's darkly sullen look, and continued in a more diplomatic tone. "It's no great surprise that you're attracted to her. She's a beautiful girl. But please, you must try to put her interests above your own. She's vulnerable and frightened."

"And you think it's in her best interest to let her fend for herself?" Luke sneered. "No friends, no family, no one to help her—for God's sake, am I the only one who's thinking clearly?"

Alicia pulled away from her husband. "She's better off on her own than putting herself at the mercy of someone who will take advantage of her."

Charles stared in dismay, lifting his hands as if he yearned to clamp them over her mouth. "Darling, you know Luke is not that kind of man. I'm sure he has the best intentions."

"Does he?" Alicia gave Luke a challenging stare. "What exactly *are* your intentions?"

Luke responded with his old sardonic smile. "That's between me and your cousin. I'd like to work out some sort of arrangement that will suit her. If she and I can't come to an agreement, she'll leave. At this point you don't have much say in the matter, do you?"

"I don't know you at all anymore," Alicia snapped. "I thought Tasia would be safe with you, because you were the man least likely to cause trouble. You've never interfered in peoples' lives before. I wish to heaven you hadn't started now! What has happened to you?"

Luke kept his mouth shut, retreating behind a wall of cold pride. He was amazed that they didn't understand, that they couldn't see. When he had sat holding Tasia's hand and listening to the misery she had gone through, his emotions had filled the room. He loved her. He was terrified that she would vanish and leave him just as she had left everything else in her life. He couldn't allow that, for her sake and certainly for his own. He wanted to take action, but there was so much that needed to be explained and understood. If only he could think clearly, unfettered by the pangs of need and love that made everything so difficult to sort out.

The Ashbournes were staring at him, Alicia with displeasure, Charles with the perception of an old, familiar friend. Charles was no fool. Taking his wife firmly in tow, he gave Luke a half-amused, half-understanding glance. "It will be all right," Charles said quietly, although it wasn't clear to whom he was speaking. "Everyone will do what they must, and things will settle into place."

"That's what you always say," Alicia complained.

Charles smiled complacently. "And I'm always right, aren't I? Come, darling ... we're of no use to either of them now."

From her window Tasia had watched the Ashbournes' carriage leave. After hanging up her gray dress and brushing it with mechanical precision, she started to pack. She arranged her belongings in neat piles. The light from a single candle flame sent deep shadows stretching across the room. All light from the village below was extinguished. Even the moon and stars were covered with a murky haze.

Although she was dressed only in her thin shift, her skin was moist with perspiration. A breeze from the window chilled her for a moment, and she rubbed her palms over the goosebumps on her upper arms. She was trying not to think, or feel. She didn't want anything to break through the layer of ice that surrounded her.

It was over, this brief foray into the life of Lucas Stokehurst, and she was glad to end it. Things had become complicated. She could never afford to lean on someone else. She had only herself. She wondered how she should leave, how to tell Emma goodbye, without having to face Stokehurst again. He would make it impossible. It wouldn't matter if he were kind or cruel. Either way would hurt too much to bear.

Quiet footsteps—a man's footsteps—approached her door. Tasia turned, her arms still crossed over her chest, her eyes dilating into pools of blackness. *No . . . go away*, her mind cried, but her lips moved in a silent spasm. The door opened and closed with a click of the latch.

Stokehurst was in the room with her, his gaze lingering on her bare legs and arms and the exposed length of her neck. It was clear what he had come for. He wore a dressing robe opened far enough to show the clean line of his collarbone and the curved edge of muscle. His skin gleamed like freshly cast bronze. With one glance Tasia saw that he wasn't wearing the hook, that there was a mixture of love and desire on his face. He didn't say a word, nor did he intend to.

A frantic sound rose from her throat, but there was nothing she could say that he didn't already know. The awareness of all her fears and needs was there in his gaze, and still he came closer, his shoulders blocking out the candleglow, his body all darkness and heat as he took her against him.

Tasia hesitated and then threw her arms around him, holding on with all her strength. She was rigid in his embrace, breathing, waiting, her heart pounding brutally fast. His aroused body pressed close, sheltering her as if they stood together in a raging storm. He bent to cover her trembling lips with his own. It was not the way a man should kiss a virgin, no gentleness, no allowance made for innocence. He searched deeply with aggressive surges of his tongue. Closing his hand over her shift, he bunched the thin fabric in his palm and pulled it to her waist.

Luke tugged her naked hips against him, his fingers spreading over the velvety white curve of her bottom. Tasia gasped and reached her arms around his neck, her skin warming instantly at his touch. Her failing soul came to life as he covered her face with warm kisses. Groping over his shoulders, she found the edge of his robe, and pushed beneath to find the hard slope of his back. He responded to her touch with a groan of anguished passion and pulled her shift down until it dropped in a tangled ring on the floor.

He removed his robe, taking Tasia down to the narrow bed with him. His dark head lowered over her body. She felt his mouth on her breast, in tender bites, teasing licks, and when she began to gasp from the torment, he fastened his lips over her nipple and rubbed softly with his tongue.

Tasia felt a quiver of something like pain starting low in her stomach and shooting to the secret place between her thighs. He kissed her other breast, cupping underneath it with hot, gentle fingers, and she lifted herself against him in panting confusion. The ache inside her was maddening. She wanted to feel the entire length of his body on hers, wanted him to crush her with his weight. Wrapping her arms around his long muscled back, she tried to pull him closer. He resisted, staring down at her intently, his hand drifting over her stomach toward the froth of curls no one had ever touched before.

He reached down to a place that was swollen and acutely tender, and she gave a muffled cry as he touched her. His fingertips slid through a patch of slickness, exploring, delicately shaping, working into the soft entrance to her body. He kissed her lips, whispering her name, pressing love words into her damp skin. Tasia relaxed into a state of euphoric pleasure, accepting everything, too absorbed in sensation to mind the intimacy.

She felt him pushing her legs apart, making a cradle of her open thighs. His weight lowered, heralding a heavy pressure at her most vulnerable part. His eyes were staring into hers, and she felt herself drowning in the pools of dark blue. More pressure, burning ... a contained force that tore and impaled her. She moaned sharply at the sudden pain. He pushed deeper, taking full possession of her. Then he was still, except for the rough motion of his breathing.

Shaken, Tasia lifted her slim hands to his face, trying wordlessly to communicate her awe at the dark beauty of his body joined to hers. He turned his mouth to her palm, catching her fragile skin with a biting kiss. His hips nudged deeply against hers, and she rolled upward in instinctive response. His slow rhythm filled her. All discomfort was forgotten as he began an exquisite destruction of her senses, until she twisted in mindless excitement beneath him. Their bodies tangled and merged, evoking a deep pleasure that crossed not only physical but spiritual boundaries. Tasia was lost in a bright rush of sensation, her lips parting with a soundless cry.

Soon afterward Luke gained his own release. There was a tremor in his arms as he held her tightly, astonished and replete in every part of his being. He watched over her as she slept. The candle stub burned out, leaving nothing but a trace of smoke in the air and a congealing pool of wax in the dish. His eyes adjusted to the darkness, enough to make out the edge of her profile and the dainty tip of one breast. She was soft and light against him, sleeping in the crook of his arm with utter trust. The ebony trails of her hair streamed over everything: their bodies, the pillow, the mattress. Carefully he gathered the silken locks into a dark river over her shoulder.

The touch of his hand disturbed her dreams, and she yawned and straightened her limbs in a trembling stretch, reminding him of a kitten with flattened ears. A few sleepy blinks, and she was awake, staring at him in wonder.

Luke smiled, holding her still as she made a sudden move to roll away. "You're safe," he murmured.

Her body tensed, and he heard the sound of her hard swallow. Finally she broke the silence. "Shouldn't you worry about your own safety? I might hurt you."

He kissed her forehead. "The only way you could do that is to leave."

Tasia turned her face away. "My life has been filled with such ugliness ... I don't want it to touch you, or Emma. And it would, if I remained here. There would be danger, and unhappiness ..." She quivered with a frustrated laugh. "My God, you found out tonight that I murdered someone—you can't ignore something like that! It won't go away!"

"Do you think you did it?" he asked quietly.

Tasia sat up and held the sheet to her breasts, staring at him in the darkness. "I've tried a thousand times to remember what happened that night, but I can't. My heart starts to pound, and I feel sick, and ... I'm afraid to know."

Luke sat up also, a shadowy presence close beside her. "I don't believe you killed him. I don't think it's in you. And wanting to kill someone is *not* the same as doing it, or else most of the population would be guilty of murder."

"What if I did? What if I'm guilty of stabbing a man in the throat because I hated him? I see it in my dreams, over and over again. Some nights I'm afraid to go to sleep."

Luke reached out and slid his fingers over the smooth curve of her shoulder. "Then I'll watch over your sleep," he whispered. "And I'll give you better things to dream about." His touch moved downward until he found the crisp edge of linen clasped over her chest. Nudging the sheet lower, he ran his thumb in a gentle circle over her breast, awakening the velvety tip to a throbbing point. He heard her breath catch, felt the shiver that went through her. "I'm not sorry he's dead," he said hoarsely. "I'm not sorry you're here with me now. And I won't let you leave me."

"How can you act as though my past doesn't matter?"

"Because it doesn't. Not to me. I'd gladly take your sins upon my own soul, and burn for them, if that was the price for being with you." She sensed rather than saw the mocking curl of his mouth. "What does that say about my character?"

"That you're a rutting fool," Tasia said miserably.

Luke had the audacity to laugh. "And worse." He slid his arm around her back and pulled her close, ignoring her protest as the sheet slipped away. He leaned his forehead on hers. Suddenly his amusement changed to soft-voiced ferocity. "I wish I could be perfect for you. But I'm not. I've sinned a thousand different ways. I'm bad-tempered and self-centered, and I've been assured by friends and enemies alike that I'm an arrogant know-all. I'm too old for you, and in case you hadn't noticed, I'm missing a hand." His jaw flexed with a faint smile. "Considering all that, I can accept you and your blighted past with no reservations."

"It's not about you, or your faults," she said heatedly, trying to twist away. His grip tightened, and they fell sideways on the bed in a heap. "A-and your reasoning doesn't work. Just because we're both flawed doesn't mean we belong together!"

"It means we'll understand each other. It means we'll enjoy ourselves a hell of a lot."

"I don't ... call this ... enjoyment," she grunted, trying to throw off his weight, gasping at the tangle of sheets and naked skin she had found herself in.

"It takes some getting used to," Luke said in her ear, jerking the white linen away from their bodies. "The first time is always the worst for a woman. You'll like it more later on."

Tasia had liked it far too much already, but she was hardly going to flatter him by telling him so. "I couldn't stay here even if I wanted to," she said breathlessly. "Prince Nikolas will find me. It's only a matter of time—"

"I'll be at your side when he does. We'll deal with him together."

"Nikolas doesn't negotiate or compromise. He'll accept nothing but your full cooperation in sending me back to Russia."

"I'll send him to hell first."

"You *are* an arrogant know-all!" she whispered

sharply, squirming beneath him. "I won't stay. I *can't.*"

"Hold still, we'll end up on the floor. This bed is too small." He crouched on top of her and wedged his knees between hers. Tasia flailed helplessly in an effort to throw him off, until she felt the hard silken pressure of him against her belly, and the seeking tug of his mouth at her breast. She went still with a gasp, while her skin turned hot and her nerves shot urgent messages through her body. His large hand clasped her throat as if he held a flower stem, then moved to the fragile curves of her ribs. "Did I hurt you before?" he whispered, tracing the shape of her bones, the soft dip of her stomach.

"A little," she said breathlessly. It was wrong to allow this ... immoral ... but somehow she couldn't seem to make herself care. These were her last hours with him, and all she wanted was to lose herself in his arms once more.

His mouth was at her ear, his teeth gently seizing the tiny lobe. His voice was nothing but a puff of warmth. "It won't hurt this time. I'll be careful."

And he was ruthless in his restraint, every movement slow and easy. She groaned at the languid path of his mouth sweeping across her skin, the combination of wet tongue and scraping bristle that made her weak with craving. He whispered against her stomach, words she couldn't hear, only feel. His dark face lowered, and his mouth pressed to the moist patch of curls in brief sojourn that made her body jerk fearfully. She writhed at the tender stroke of his tongue.

"No, *no*—"

He stopped immediately and levered himself upward, pulling her against his chest with a comforting murmur. Trembling, she linked her arms around him, her fists digging into the sleek hardness of his back.

"I'm sorry," Luke whispered, breathing roughly in her hair. "You're so sweet ... so beautiful ... I didn't mean to frighten you." His hand slid between her thighs, his fingers circling the place where all feeling gathered. Tasia closed her eyes and choked back a whimper, giving herself entirely into his care. He touched her as if he owned her, playing on her senses with devastating skill.

But the mastery wasn't one-sided. Soon she discovered that her novice touch had the power to excite him just as deeply. She smoothed both palms over his long muscled back, down to the springy fur on his legs. The textures of his body, hard, rough, large-boned, were exquisitely different from her own. He pushed against the touch of her hands and settled over her with a growl.

Her thighs spread in eager welcome, a wanton invitation he accepted at once. But as he entered her, it was slow, gradual, causing only a flash of pain. Tasia lifted herself upward in greedy demand, and Luke laughed softly, as if she were a child trying to gorge on sweets. Moving in deep nudges, he pressed inside her, barely thrusting at all. She made an impatient sound in her throat, struggling closer to him, wanting more, more—

"Not yet, Tasia," he murmured. "Not for a long time." And in spite of her demands and outright pleading, he made her wait, until the world had spun away and there was only the slow, regular plunge of him within her. Every nerve, impulse, cell, focused on attaining the satisfaction he held just out of her reach. She had no energy left to cry out when he finally allowed her release. With a soft moan, she shuddered violently, her face buried in his sweat-slick shoulder. He was similarly quiet in his climax, his breath hissing through his teeth, every muscle clenched. Relaxing, he fell asleep at once, curling his hand into the sheaf of her hair. Tasia crawled halfway over him and closed her eyes, too tired for worries or nightmares or memories, grateful for the temporary peace he had afforded her.

Tasia woke later than she had intended. The sun was halfway up the sky, the sounds of breakfast rising from the servants' hall. To her relief, Stokehurst had left in the night while she slept. She could not bear to face him now. He and Emma were out on their morning ride. By the time they returned, she would be gone. After dressing and completing her morning ablutions in a hurry, she sat down to write a letter.

My Dear Emma,

Forgive me for leaving without telling you goodbye in person. I wish I could stay longer, to see what a wonderful young woman you will become. I am so very proud of you. Perhaps someday you will understand why it was better for everyone that I left when I did. I give you my love, and hope you will remember me fondly.

Adieu—
Miss Billings

Carefully Tasia folded the square of parchment and sealed it with a few drops of wax. She blew out the flame, set down the stick of wax, and left the note in her room with Emma's name on it. It was the best way for all of them. She was relieved that her departure would be free of confrontations and awkward goodbyes. But there was a strange uneasiness lodged in her heart. Why had Stokehurst chosen to disappear without a word? Why was he letting her go like this? She had thought he might make one last effort to convince her to stay. He wouldn't give up something he wanted without a battle, and if he had spoken the truth about wanting her. . .

But perhaps he didn't want her anymore. Maybe one night had been enough for him. Maybe now his curiosity was satisfied.

The thought depressed Tasia. Her chest ached. Of course he had no further use for her. She had been adequate amusement for a few hours in the darkness. Now he would go back to Lady Harcourt, a woman with enough sensuality and experience to match his own.

Tasia wanted to weep, but instead she lifted her chin resolutely and carried her bags downstairs. There was a pleasantly acrid tea smell in the air. The carpets in the corridors were being cleaned. First the pile was scattered with dry tea leaves, and then it was painstakingly brushed by a battalion of housemaids. Mrs. Knaggs was busy supervising the activity, walking back and forth in a rustle of starched white apron. Tasia found her in one of the second-floor hallways, carrying a can of melted beeswax.

"Ma'am—"

"Ah, Miss Billings!" The housekeeper was flushed with exertion. She paused as Tasia came to her. "There aren't enough hours in the day to keep such a big place clean," she commented, gesturing with the small can. "Carpets are trouble enough, but the wood floors are even worse."

"Ma'am, I've come to tell you—"

"I already know. The master informed me this morning that you would be leaving us."

Tasia was taken aback by the matter-of-fact statement. "He did?"

"Yes, and he ordered one of the carriages to be readied, to take you wherever you want to go."

Rather than protest her departure, it seemed that Stokehurst was trying to make it as convenient as possible. "How kind of him," Tasia said dully.

"I hope you have a pleasant journey," Mrs. Knaggs said, her tone brisk, as if Tasia was merely going to the market for the day.

"You haven't asked why I'm leaving so suddenly."

"I daresay your reasons are your own business, Miss Billings."

Tasia cleared her throat uncomfortably. "About my month's wages, I was hoping—"

"Oh, yes." All at once Mrs. Knaggs looked mildly embarrassed. "The master seemed to feel that since you haven't stayed the entire month, you aren't entitled to the wages he promised."

Tasia turned red with surprise and rage. "It's only a few days short of a month! Do you mean to tell me he won't hand over a shilling of what he owes me?"

The housekeeper looked away. "I'm afraid so."

The bastard! The stingy, contemptible, smug, unscrupulous bastard. He was trying to punish her for not doing what he wanted. Tasia struggled for composure and finally spoke in a strained voice. "All right. I can get along without it. Goodbye, Mrs. Knaggs, and please tell Mrs.

Plunkett and Biddle and the others that I wish
them well—"

"Of course." The housekeeper reached out and
patted her shoulder in a friendly gesture. "We've
all become quite fond of you, my dear. Goodbye.
I must hurry with this wax—miles of floors to be
polished . . ."

Tasia watched the housekeeper stride away. She
was disconcerted by Mrs. Knaggs's breezy farewell, having expected something a little more
heartfelt. Maybe the rumor had already gotten out
that Stokehurst had spent the night in her room.
There were no secrets at Southgate Hall. That must
be the reason for the housekeeper's offhand
manner—she wanted Tasia to leave quickly, and
good riddance.

Humiliated, Tasia slunk to the entrance hall,
wanting nothing more than to be far away from
Southgate. Seymour, the butler, treated her with
the same friendly politeness as always, but she
couldn't meet his eyes as she asked for the carriage to be brought around. She wondered if he
too suspected what she had done with Lord
Stokehurst the night before. Perhaps it was written
on her face. Surely anyone could look at her and
see the loss of innocence. She was a fallen woman,
with yet another sin to add to her list.

"What destination shall I tell the driver, miss?"
Seymour asked diffidently.

"Amersham, please." It was a village on the
coach road with many old inns. Her plan was to
stay there for the night, sell her grandmother's little gold cross for as much as she could get, and
then hire a local man to convey her to the west of
England. She knew there were numerous rural

towns and ancient villages there, where she would be able to hide and assume the anonymous life of a dairymaid or houseservant.

Efficiently the footmen loaded the bags into the gleaming laquered carriage and helped her inside. "Thank you," Tasia murmured, flinching as the door clicked into place. She stuck her head out the window for another look at Seymour.

The butler's lips parted in a restrained smile. "Farewell, Miss Billings, and good luck." For Seymour, it was a rare burst of emotion.

"The same to you," Tasia said brightly, and then withdrew into the carriage, fighting back tears as the wheels rolled away from Southgate Hall.

Several minutes passed before Tasia realized they were traveling in the wrong direction. It began as a vague suspicion, which she tried to reason away. After all, she was hardly familiar with the landscape of England, and her only knowledge of Amersham was that it was located somewhere to the west of Southgate. But then the carriage turned off the main road, onto a narrow, heavily wooded path studded with a few ancient bits of gravel. Unless they were taking a shortcut through a forest, they were definitely not going to Amersham. Anxiously Tasia knocked on the roof for the driver's attention. Whistling cheerfully, he ignored her. They went deeper into the woods, passing a small unplowed meadow and a pond. Finally they came to a stop at a two-story cottage that was half-buried in ivy.

Stunned, Tasia emerged from the carriage, while the driver unloaded her belongings. "What are we doing here?" she asked. The driver gave her an impudent smile and gestured to the doorway, where a tall, dark form had appeared.

Luke's smiling blue eyes met hers, and he spoke in a gently chiding tone. "You didn't really think I'd let you go, did you?"

Six

Tasia clamped her mouth shut, while rage flooded her. Whatever else she had lost, she still had the power to make decisions for herself. No one was going to take it from her. Did he think he could trick her, manipulate her, and she would fall into his arms with a grateful sigh? It was beyond arrogance.

The carriage rolled away down the wooded lane, leaving her stranded with Stokehurst. Most women would probably consider it extremely good fortune. Stokehurst looked particularly dashing that morning, dressed in fawn trousers and a loose white shirt, his black hair disheveled. He was quiet, staring at her with apparent fascination and something else she couldn't quite understand.

Finally Tasia thought of what to say. She made her tone as cold and calm as possible. "This is how it will be when Nikolas Angelovsky finds me. He'll allow me no choice, and he'll justify himself however he wishes. You are just like him. Neither of you lets anything stand in the way of what you want."

To her satisfaction, a scowl appeared on Stokehurst's face. He folded his arms across his chest, watching as Tasia approached the front of the cottage.

The dwelling was decorated with terra-cotta

panels and bricks molded with the same hawk-and-rose motif she had seen at Southgate Hall. The initial "W" was woven into the pattern at regular intervals. Over two centuries of weathering had caused the designs to fade, but they were still distinguishable. The house had been lovingly cared for. Sections of ancient timber had been replaced with new wood, and the clay filling was freshly whitewashed. Had she not been so confused and angry, Tasia would have taken pleasure in the fairy-tale cottage, whose touches of crumbling age gave it an air of romantic decay.

"William, Lord Stokehurst," Luke said, watching her trace the faded initials by the door. "An ancestor of mine. He had the cottage built for his mistress in the sixteenth century, to keep her close to Southgate Hall."

"Why bring me here?" Tasia asked stonily. "Are you planning to keep me as your mistress?"

He seemed to give the matter great attention. Tasia realized he was considering the best way to handle her, which stirred her wrath even more. She didn't want to be handled or pacified. She wanted him to leave her alone.

"I want some time with you," he said bluntly. "With all that's happened in the last few days, we haven't really talked."

"We've *never* really talked."

He inclined his head in agreement. "Now we can."

Tasia made an infuriated sound and strode away from the door as if it were the gate to hell. She went to the side of the cottage, to a shaded paddock where a black stallion nibbled on a clump of hay. The horse's ears pricked, and he turned his head to the side, eyeing her with inter-

est. Hearing Stokehurst's footsteps behind her,
Tasia whirled to face him with her fists clenched.
"Take me to the village!"

"No," he said softly, holding her gaze.

"Then I'll walk."

"Tasia." He came closer and wrapped his hand
over her fist. "Stay here with me, just for a day or
two." His fingers tightened as she tried to pull
away. "I won't make any demands on you. I won't
touch you at all, if you don't want me to. Just talk
to me. You're in no immediate danger of Angelovsky finding you, certainly not here. Tasia . . .
there's no need for you to go on running for the
rest of your life. We can find another way, a better
one, if you'll trust me."

"Why?" she asked, her anger fading a little. The
softness of his tone affected her oddly. He had
never spoken to her like this before, with quiet, intense appeal. "Why should I trust you?"

He opened his mouth to say something, then
appeared to think better of it and kept silent. Staring at her, he brought her fist to his chest. His
heart was beating very fast. Slowly Tasia's fingers
unfurled, pressing over the driving thump.

Because I love you, Luke yearned to say. *I love you
more than anything in my life except Emma. You don't
have to give me anything. You don't have to love me
back. I just want to help you. All I want is for you to
be safe.* But she wasn't ready for those words. She
would be frightened, or scornful, and throw them
back at him. He hadn't reached the age of thirty-
four without developing a reasonably good sense
of timing. Strategically he hid behind a mocking
smile.

"Because I'm all you've got," he said, "except
for the Ashbournes. If I were you, I'd take help

where I could find it. There's not exactly a queue forming."

Tasia snatched her hand away and glared at him. She said something in Russian—decidedly not a compliment—and went into the cottage. The door closed with a slam.

Luke let out a sigh of relief. She wasn't happy to be there ... but she would stay.

As the day progressed, Tasia changed to her peasant blouse and skirt and left her hair to hang in a long braid down her back. There was no one to see her except Stokehurst, and she might as well be comfortable. Truth be told, the cottage was not a bad place to be held captive. She went from room to room, discovering treasures in every corner: rare books, engravings, and miniatures of haughty dark-haired people who could only be Stokehurst ancestors.

Everything in the house was worn and comfortable, the walls covered with faded tapestries and rich oil paintings, the furniture splendidly heavy and old. So cozy and private ... It was not difficult to imagine William, Lord Stokehurst visiting his mistress here, shutting out the rest of the world to seek pleasure in his lover's arms.

After investigating the underground wine vault and pantry, Tasia went outside to stroll around the pond, the paddock, and the vegetable plot. She wasn't exactly certain where Stokehurst was, but she sensed that he was aware of her movements. Fortunately he had the wisdom to let her wander alone and cool her temper.

In the afternoon she watched him exercise the stallion, training him to pivot on his haunches. Stokehurst was patient as he worked with the animal. The stallion, with its supple legs and elegant movements, reminded her of a dancer. For the most part he was well-mannered, but there were moments of rebellion for which he was disciplined by being halted for several seconds.

"He hates to be kept still," Luke said, noticing Tasia's presence during one of these periods. "Like any two-year-old." They proceeded with a walk and executed a perfect half-turn. Silently Tasia admired the sight of a skilled rider on a sensitive horse. Stokehurst guided the animal with the expert pressure of his legs, maintaining the rhythm of the walk as they pivoted a full turn. Having completed the trick with each hoof in proper sequence, the horse was rewarded with generous praise.

Luke dismounted and led the horse to the wooden railing where Tasia stood.

"Constantine, meet Lady Anastasia."

Tasia reached out to touch the horse's velvety nose. Constantine delicately investigated her empty hand. Suddenly he lowered his head to push at her shoulder, forcing her back a step or two. Tasia laughed in surprise. "What does he want?"

Luke scowled at the horse and muttered a reprimand, and then a rueful grin pulled at the corner of his mouth. "Emma spoils him with sugar lumps. Now he demands them. It's a hard habit to break."

"Greedy boy," Tasia cooed, stroking the horse's neck. Constantine turned his head to the side, to watch her out of one bright eye.

Smiling, Tasia glanced up at Stokehurst. His breath came fast from exertion, and his tanned face and throat glistened with sweat. The white shirt clung to his skin, following the curve of hard muscle. He was so masculine and natural, very different from the men she had known in Russian court life. They had been smothered in buttons, perfume, and pomade, all passion concealed by artifice.

Suddenly Tasia thought of a court ball she had attended, and the hussars and noblemen who had danced attendance on her. The Winter Palace, a building of more than a thousand rooms filled with priceless treasures, had blazed with light that defied the frosty darkness outside. The galleries had been lined with officers in full dress uniform. The air had been scented with heated perfume carried in small silver dishes by the imperial retainers. If Tasia closed her eyes, she could still recall the sweetly exotic fragrance. Women and men alike had been covered with jewels that blazed beneath the light of the golden chandeliers. Her own mother, Marie, had been acclaimed as one of the most beautiful women there, her smooth dark hair confined in a net of gold thread and diamonds, her snowy bosom half-exposed by her low-cut gown, her throat concealed by ropes of pearls and emeralds.

Tasia had danced beneath her chaperone's watchful eye, then picked daintily at a plate heaped with golden and black caviar, stuffed quail eggs, and buttery wisps of pastry. The Russian nobility lived with a splendor unequaled by anyone else in the world. She had taken it all for granted. Now that life was gone, and she was dressed in peasant clothes and standing in a paddock. Another world away. And she was experiencing a feeling perilously close to happiness.

"You're thinking of your old life," Stokehurst

said, surprising her with his perceptiveness. "You must miss it."

Tasia shook her head. "I don't, actually. Those days are interesting to remember, but ... now I see that I didn't belong there. I don't know where I would belong, even if I had the freedom to choose."

"Tasia ..."

She glanced up and found him staring at her with an absorbed look that made her insides tighten in sudden awareness. The silence seemed to hold them suspended in anticipation. Tasia struggled for a way to break it. "I'm hungry. I saw some food in the pantry ..." She backed from the paddock railing.

"Mrs. Plunkett sent along a cold supper. Chicken, bread, fruit—"

"Did Mrs. Plunkett know about this?"

Suddenly he wore an expression of pure innocence. "Know about what?"

"That I would be here with you!" Tasia regarded him with narrow-eyed suspicion. "She did! I can see it in your face. Everyone at Southgate Hall must have known I was going to be kidnapped today. And Emma? What have you told her?"

"She knows," he admitted, having the grace to look sheepish.

It was not a pleasant feeling to be the victim of a conspiracy, no matter how well-intentioned. Tasia stiffened with stung pride and walked off without another word.

She was still fuming as she busied herself with unpacking the food and setting it on a table in the common room. Mrs. Plunkett had prepared a feast of roasted meats, salads, fruit and cheese, and a small cake filled with custard. The sun had begun to descend in the sky, casting pinkish-golden light through the half-shuttered windows. After washing and changing, Luke went to the downstairs vault and brought back two bottles of wine. Tasia ignored him and unwrapped a crusty loaf of bread from a linen napkin.

Seeming unperturbed by her silence, Luke sat in a chair and applied himself to opening the wine, holding it between his knees while he uncorked it. "Steadier this way," he said, noticing Tasia's curious glance. "I could hold it in the crook of my arm—but I've lost a few good bottles that way." He gave her an ingratiating, boyish smile that caused some of her reserve to melt.

"Who looks after the place and tends the garden?" she asked.

"A caretaker who lives over the hill."

"Does anyone ever stay here?"

He shook his head. "It doesn't make sense to maintain a house that no one uses, but I've never been able to bring myself to close it. I like the idea of keeping a hideaway."

"Have you brought other women here?"

"No."

"Did you ever bring her?" This time Tasia's voice was soft. They both knew she was referring to Mary.

Luke was silent for a long moment, then gave a short nod.

Tasia wasn't certain how she felt about that ... flattered, perhaps, and uneasy. She was beginning to understand that she meant something to him, something important, and the knowledge was disturbing on a deep level.

"I'm sorry I deceived you." Luke aimed for a casual tone but didn't quite reach it. "I didn't know how else to get you here."

Tasia found a long wax taper in the drawer of a worn sideboard. She lit it from a wall sconce and then moved about the room, lighting candles until the air was golden. "You could have tried inviting me."

"Would you have accepted?"

"I don't know. I suppose it would have depended on how you asked." She pursed her lips and delicately blew out the taper, and looked at him through a veil of smoke.

Slowly Luke stood up and came to her. His eyes were filled with seduction, his smile an invitation to wickedness. "Miss Billings ... I beg you not to leave. There's a place I'd like to take you to. A cottage hidden deep in the woods. We could stay there, just the two of us, and shut out the rest of the world for as long as you want ... a day, a month ... forever."

"And what would we do there, just the two of us?"

"Sleep by day, and wake when the stars come out. Drink wine ... share secrets ... dance in the moonlight ..."

"With no music?"

He bent to her ear with a confidential whisper. "There's music in the forest. But most people never hear it. They don't know how to listen."

Tasia closed her eyes briefly. He carried a tantalizing mixture of smells, soap and water, damp hair, a touch of starched linen. "Are you offering to teach me?" she asked faintly.

"Actually, I was hoping you would teach me."

She drew back, staring into his eyes. Suddenly they laughed together, for no reason Tasia could fathom, except that all at once the moment was filled with delight.

"I'll consider it," she said, moving to a chair, and he seated her obligingly.

"Wine?"

Tasia nudged her empty glass forward in reply. He joined her at the table and poured the wine, and they raised a silent toast. The pale golden vintage was mellow and slightly sweet. Tasia nodded in answer to Luke's questioning glance, and lifted the glass to her lips again. Her drinking had always been limited to a few sips of wine here and there, always supervised by her mother and various chaperones. She relished the freedom of being able to have as much as she wanted.

They consumed the meal at a leisurely pace, while the sky darkened outside and shadows crept into the corners of the cottage. Luke devoted himself to being charming. He watched with amusement as she kept holding out the wineglass for more, and warned that she would have a headache in the morning.

"I don't care," Tasia replied, downing more of the delicious beverage. "It's the best wine I've ever tasted."

Luke laughed. "And it gets better with every glass. Sip it slowly, sweet. Being a gentleman, I won't be able to take advantage of you if you're drunk."

"Why not? Drunk or sober, the results are the same, aren't they?" She tilted her head back, letting the sweet liquid slide down her throat. "Besides, you're not that much of a gentleman."

He gave her a narrow-eyed glance and made a lunge for her across the table. Tasia sprang up with a giggle, barely managing to avoid him. The room tipped, and she concentrated on keeping her balance. When she found her feet, she picked up her glass and wandered away aimlessly. She knew she was drinking too much, but she had a glowing feeling of well-being, and she didn't want it to stop.

"Who's that?" She gestured toward a portrait of a fair-haired woman on the wall. A few drops of wine sloshed over the rim of the glass. Frowning in dismay, Tasia applied herself to drinking the rest before she spilled any more.

"My mother." Luke joined her in front of the portrait and plucked the wine from her hand. "Don't gulp it, sweet, you'll make yourself dizzy."

Tasia was already dizzy. He was so steady and solid ... She leaned back against him, squinting at the painting. A handsome woman, the duchess, but there was an utter lack of softness in her face, and a compressed thinness to her lips. And her eyes, so keen and cold. "You don't favor her very much," Tasia said. "Except for the nose."

Luke laughed. "She has a strong will, my mother. She hasn't softened a bit with age. Very quick-minded, too. She's always sworn she would never outlive her wits. So far she's kept an iron grip on them."

"What is your father like?"

"An old scoundrel, with an insatiable passion for women. God knows why he married someone like my mother. To her, any display of emotion— even laughter—is undignified. My father claims that she never let him into her bed except the few times it took to produce offspring. They had three children who died in infancy before my sister and I were born. As the years passed, my mother turned more and more to the church, leaving my father free to chase women to his heart's content."

"Did they ever love each other?" Tasia asked absently.

His chest lifted with a thoughtful sigh. "I don't know. All I remember is a sort of polite tolerance they had for each other."

"How sad."

He shrugged. "They chose it for themselves. For their own reasons, neither of them approve of marrying for love—which is ironic, since both their children did."

Tasia settled more comfortably against him, enjoying the feel of firm muscle at her back. "Your sister loves her husband?"

"Yes, Catherine married a stubborn Scot with a temper to match hers. They spend half the time shouting at each other and the rest in bed."

The last few words seemed to hang in the air. Remembering the night before, the languorous hours in bed with him, Tasia felt her face burn. She took a shallow breath, and then another, and blindly sought her wineglass. "I'm thirsty—" She turned and half-collided with him, her balance precarious. He slid a steady arm behind her back. Suddenly Tasia gasped as she felt a splash of liquid on her shoulder. "You spilled it on me," she exclaimed, fumbling at her peasant blouse.

"Did I?" he asked softly. "Here, let me see." His head bent, and she felt his warm mouth on her skin, right where the wine had spilled.

Confused, Tasia thought that they must be sinking—the floor was coming closer—and then she realized that Luke was lowering her to the carpet. Before she could object, she felt another small splash, and tiny rivulets that chased down to her belly. "You did it again!"

With a contrite murmur, he set the glass aside and pulled gently at the drawstring of her blouse. The damp garment slipped from her shoulders. There was a tug at her waistband, and her skirt inched down her hips. Tasia stared at herself in confusion. "Oh, dear," she said, perplexed by the way her clothes seemed to be falling off. But Stokehurst was smiling at her as if it were a perfectly natural thing. He leaned forward to her exposed chest and licked the side of her breast, and then the shallow curve beneath, picking up sweet drops of wine with his tongue. Tasia quivered in agitation, knowing she should make him stop. But his mouth felt so warm and tickling and nice. Her head wobbled on her neck, and she slid her arms around his shoulders to steady herself. "I must be drunk," she said thickly. "I've never been drunk before, but I always thought it would feel like this. All that wine . . . Oh, I must be! Am I?"

"Just a little." He dragged the skirt away from her body. She relaxed on the floor and kicked her legs to help him, sighing in relief as the cumbersome fabric was removed. With her legs free, she felt so light, unburdened . . . and then he was pulling off her other garments, one by one.

"You're taking advantage," she said sternly, and rolled to her side with a giggle. He lay down and faced her. She couldn't stop herself from touching his lips with her fingers, tracing the smiling curve. "Are you seducing me?"

He nodded, stroking back a skein of hair that had dropped over her chin.

"I'm sure I shouldn't want you to. Oh, my head is spinning." Tasia closed her eyes, and she felt his mouth on hers, warm and intense, making the blood dance in her veins. He was right above her, so handsome and tempting that she reached up for him.

"Help me with my shirt," he muttered.

What a splendid idea ... She wanted to feel his hard chest, and the shirt was in the way. Willingly she struggled with the line of tiny carved buttons, but they didn't want to let go. Grasping handfuls of fine linen, she yanked until there was a satisfying ripping, popping sound, and the shirt was hanging open. Pleased with her accomplishment, she stared at his long, bare torso and his candlelit face. His eyes were the color of the sea, pure, with no hint of green or gray. "How can your eyes be so blue?" Carefully she touched his face. "Beautiful blue ... so beautiful."

His thick lashes lowered. "God help me, Tasia. If you leave, you'll take my heart with you."

Tasia wanted to reply, but he kissed her until the words went skittering far out of reach. Hazily she focused on the sight of his hand closed around the wineglass once more, tilting it to let the contents spill over the brim. She couldn't think why he would be pouring wine on her, but he told her not to move, and she lay still in dreamy bewilderment as there were more cool trickles, splashes of golden liquid flowing over her body and between her thighs. She couldn't help squirming at the odd sensation, and then she felt his mouth skimming along the wet trail down her middle, scooping up tiny puddles with his tongue. She giggled and trembled as he found the wine-filled hollow of her navel. Gently he absorbed every drop, nuzzling across her skin with his parted lips, pausing to make hot swirls with his tongue.

Tasia fell silent, transfixed by the peculiar game he was playing, and by the prickling pleasure that seemed to cover every inch of her body. He pushed her thighs apart with his hand, and she opened compliantly, her will replaced by submissiveness. Everything centered on the movement of his mouth, the tantalizing pressure that traveled lower, brushing over crisp wine-soaked curls. Lightly his fingers combed through the soft thatch, making way for the sliding touch of his tongue. An acute throbbing began in the place he kissed, and she felt her body twitch in reaction. His tongue arrowed to the most sensitive place of all and lingered, until she gave a plaintive sigh and lifted upward into the tickling stimulation, whispering feverishly, *"Yes please yes right there . . ."* and the pleasure came in an ever-rising tide, a force barely contained in flesh. With a high-pitched cry she reached down to his dark head, pulling him closer. The exquisite convulsions drew out and lengthened, gradually fading to warm ripples.

Drugged with the aftermath of pleasure, Tasia stretched contentedly as his body moved over hers. She wrapped herself around his muscled body and reached down to touch him, her fingers curving around his hard length. He groaned and pushed upward, sliding gently into her swollen depths, and she closed around him in welcome. Tasia whimpered and locked her arms around his hard back, wanting to bear more of him, trying to bring his body heavy and smothering over her.

He resisted, keeping his weight poised above her. "I don't want to crush you," he murmured. "You're so small and light . . . as if your bones were hollow like a bird's." Tenderly his fingers traced the lines of her ribs, and he kissed her breasts and the ivory smoothness between them. "But when I feel the passion in you ... the way you fight to pull me nearer ... I come close to losing control, and it's all I can do to keep from hurting you."

"Don't hold back," she urged breathlessly, arching upward into each long thrust. "I won't break."

But nothing would alter his restraint, not the demanding clasp of her hands on his back and buttocks, not even the clench of her teeth on his shoulder. The sweet rush of forgetfulness came over them both, driving away coherent thought, making them one for a moment of rapture.

They spent the next few hours in a huge oak bed with massive carved bedposts and acres of blue curtains. Their exertions made Tasia hungry, and Luke obligingly joined her in a raid on the pantry. After they indulged in fruit, cheese, and cake, they crawled back into bed once more, Tasia hooked her toes at the edge of the mattress and stretched as long as possible, still coming a few feet short of reaching the other side. "It's too big," she complained, rolling over on the white linen sheets to smile at Luke. "I keep getting lost."

He laughed and scooped her into his arms. "I'll keep finding you."

Curving her arms around his neck, Tasia sat up in his lap, bringing their faces close together. "I like being decadent," she said artlessly. "No wonder so many women choose to be mistresses."

"Is that what you are now?" he asked, kissing the side of her throat.

Disconcerted, she looked at his dark face and blushed. "I-I wasn't presuming to take Lady Harcourt's place."

"Iris and I aren't involved any longer. That's why I went to London yesterday, to break things off between us."

Tasia's brows quirked in wary surprise. "Why?"

"Iris wanted more than I could give her, and I was selfish enough to keep her much longer than I should have. Now she's free to marry any one of several suitors who have been after her for years. I don't think it will take her long."

"And what about you?" Tasia began to crawl from his lap. "Will you want a new mistress to replace her?"

Luke locked his arm around her waist, keeping her still. "I don't like to sleep alone," he admitted frankly. "I suppose I could find another Iris and fall back into my usual fornicating ways."

The thought caused a stab of jealousy. Tasia frowned and kept silent, knowing she had no right to make objections.

Luke grinned, reading her thoughts. "But then," he said softly, "there's the question of what to do about you."

"I can take care of myself."

"I know that. But would you be willing to take care of someone else as well? And let them care for you in turn?"

Tasia shook her head, while her heart began to hammer. "I don't know what you mean."

"It's time for us to talk." His dark blue eyes were riveted on hers. He took a deep breath. "Tasia . . . I want you to be a part of my life, and Emma's. I want you to stay with me. But if you do, it can't be any other way than as my wife."

Tasia struggled away from him and snatched up a sheet to cover herself. She kept her head bent, unable to look at him as he went on.

"I never thought I could be a good husband to anyone but Mary. I never wanted to try with anyone else, until you came along." Luke touched the naked curve of her back, stroking her rigid spine with his knuckles. "I know you aren't certain of your feelings for me. If there were time, if things were different, I'd court you with all the patience I could wring from my soul. Instead I'm asking you to take a blind leap and trust in me."

For one moment Tasia could imagine what it would be like, sharing his home, his life, waking beside him every morning . . . but the vision slipped away, leaving her with a hollow ache. "If I were a different person I would say yes," she said miserably.

"If you were a different person, I wouldn't want you."

"We don't even know each other."

"I'd say the last twenty-four hours have been a fairly good start."

"I can only explain the same things over and over again," she said in a raw voice, "and you won't listen. I've done something even God can't forgive. Somehow, someday, I'll have to pay for it. Retribution is coming. Since I'm too much of a coward to face it, I'll keep running until it catches up with me."

"So Nikolas Angelovsky is serving as some instrument of divine justice? I don't think so. I think God has better means of punishing sinners than sending half-crazed Russian princes to do His will. And until you remember something, or come up with some kind of proof, I won't accept that you killed anyone. I'd feel that way even if I weren't in love with you. What in hell has made you so eager to take the blame for a crime you may not have committed?"

"You love me?" Tasia repeated, pushing aside her tangled hair to stare at him in amazement.

Luke scowled, hardly presenting the image of a besotted lover. "What do you think I've been trying to say?"

She gave a dazed laugh. "You have quite a way of working up to it."

His voice was gruff, as if he were embarrassed by his declaration. "Believe me, you weren't the most likely candidate. I've had women throwing themselves at me for years—some of them with damned fine prospects."

"I had excellent prospects in Russia," she informed him. "Land, a fortune, palaces—"

"So Madame Miracle wasn't far off the mark."

"No, indeed."

His mouth twisted. "I wouldn't care if you were a woodcutter's daughter. I'd prefer it, actually."

"So would I," she said after a moment.

They didn't look at each other. There was a bleak silence, a period of assessment during which they each considered the next step. Somewhere in the middle of their bickering, he had proposed, and she had refused. But it wasn't over yet.

Tasia felt like weeping. She didn't dare. He would comfort her then, and there was no point in clinging to each other when they would soon be parted forever. She gathered the sheet more tightly to her breasts.

"Luke," she said softly. It was the first time she had ever used his name, and he gave a slight start. "If you are ready to love again, and take a wife, you can find someone far more appropriate than

I. You would be best off with someone similar to Mary."

She meant it as a benediction and well-intentioned advice, but instead he looked at her keenly. "Is that what this is about? If I'd wanted a substitute for Mary, I could have found one years ago. But I wouldn't expect my second marriage to be an imitation of the first. I wouldn't want that at all."

Tasia shrugged in an offhand manner. "You might say that now, but if you married me, you would be disappointed. Not at first, perhaps, but after a while—"

" 'Disappointed,' " Luke repeated incredulously. "Why in hell . . . No, don't explain. Let me think for a minute." As she tried to speak, he raised his hand in a gesture for silence. It was important that there should be no misunderstandings on this subject. He struggled for a way to make it all clear for her, but the task seemed impossible. She was still young enough to think of the world in terms of absolutes, unaware of the infinite ways time could change everything.

"I was still a boy when I married Mary," he said, choosing his words with care. "I never knew what life was like without her. We went from being playmates to childhood sweethearts to friends, and finally to husband and wife. We never *fell* in love, we just . . . comfortably drifted into it. I won't belittle her memory by pretending it wasn't genuine. She and I cared about each other, and we had a hell of a good time . . . and she gave me a child whom I cherish. But when she died, I became a different man. I have different needs now. And you—" He reached for Tasia's hand and gripped it hard, staring at her downbent head.

"You've given my life a kind of passion and magic I've never known before. I know that we belong together. How many people on earth ever find their soul mates? They spend their lifetimes looking, and it never happens. But somehow, by some God-given miracle, you and I are here together—" He paused, and his voice turned scratchy. "We have a chance. You know what I want. I can't force you to stay. The choice is yours."

"I don't have a choice," Tasia cried, her eyes blurring with tears. "It's because I care for you and Emma that I must leave."

"You're lying to yourself. You'll use every excuse you can think of, rather than risk being hurt. You're afraid to love someone."

"What if the reason has nothing to do with me?" she snapped. "What if it's you? Maybe you're such an arrogant, self-centered, deceitful man that I don't want your love!"

Luke colored with fury. "Is that the reason?"

Tasia gave him a half-pleading, half-enraged glance. He was making her say things that would hurt them both. If only he would accept her decision. If only he wouldn't be so stubborn. "Please don't make it so difficult."

"Damn you ... I'm going to make it impossible." He dragged her beneath him, smothering her startled cry with a demanding kiss. He lifted his head and looked down at her. "I need you," he said, breathing hard. His hand was unsteady as it moved tenderly over her small breast. "I need you in so many ways. I can't lose you, Tasia."

Before she could answer, he kissed her again, until her thoughts vanished and her blood raced with exhilarating desire. She moved beneath him in eager invitation, brushing her soft curls against his swollen length, making him tremble with passion.

He thrust easily into her slick passage, finding her wet and ready for his intrusion. She gasped and clenched all her muscles around him, her small hands gripping his shoulders with desperate strength. She breathed hotly against his skin, and pressed her face to his chest so hard that he felt the edge of her teeth. Luke held her tightly and groaned as he felt the spasms of her climax all around him, drawing him deeper, until he reached the same exquisite release.

As soon as Tasia regained her breath, she rolled away and left the bed. Her knees trembled beneath her. She scooped up a silk robe from the floor, a man's robe that was far too big for her. Wrapping it around herself, she glanced back at Luke. His expression was inscrutable.

"Did I hurt you?" he asked quietly.

She shook her head in confusion. "No, but . . . I want to be alone for a while. I need to think."

"Tasia—"

"Please, don't follow me."

She heard him curse softly as she left the room. Making her way outside, she picked up the hem of the robe to keep it from trailing in the dirt.

It was the middle of the night, the sky velvety black and scattered with stars. The pond was calm and glassy, reflecting the sky overhead until it seemed that the water too was filled with stars. Tasia wandered closer to the edge. A clump of rushes stirred as a pair of frogs hopped away, prudently deciding to change their location. Tasia stomped her bare feet to frighten away any other creatures. She hiked up the robe and sat on the damp ground, dangling her toes into the cool water. Only then did she let herself think.

A passionate man, the marquess of Stokehurst ... and more at the mercy of his own emotions than he would have wanted anyone to know. He had been rough in his urgency, but he hadn't hurt her. Lifting her legs, Tasia hugged them to her chest and rested her chin on her knees. Desperately she wished there was someone to tell her what to do.

She went over the details of their conversation, word by word. Was it true, what he had said? Was she so afraid of being hurt that she would never be able to give her heart to anyone? She thought of the people she had loved in her life: her mother and father, Uncle Kirill, and her nanny Varka. She had lost them all. Yes, she was afraid. There was precious little left of her heart to lose.

She remembered her childhood, how anxious and alone she had been after her father had died. Her mother had been affectionate, but Marie's most important concern was and always would be herself. Some essentially childish element in Marie's nature would always prevent her from being able to fully love anyone else. As a little girl, Tasia hadn't understood that. She had believed herself unworthy of love. All her resentment and rebellion had been turned inward, against herself. And the way the church had of encouraging people to accept suffering and turn it to martyrdom ... well, that hadn't influenced her for the better. Not a pleasant feeling, being a martyr. And so far it hadn't proved to be very profitable.

Did she deserve a chance at happiness? Did she owe it to herself? She wasn't certain of the answer. But what, if anything, did she owe to Luke? He was a worldly, intelligent man, fully aware of the choices he made and their consequences. He wanted to marry her because he believed it would be good between them. If he had that much faith, then surely she could come up with some of her own.

He said he loved her. Tasia was overwhelmed by the thought. She couldn't think of any reason why he would love her, when she came to him needing so much, with so little to give. But if he felt even a fraction of the pleasure that she felt in his company, perhaps it was enough.

She clasped her hands and closed her eyes fiercely tight, and prayed. *Dear Lord, I don't deserve this . . . I'm afraid to hope . . . but I can't help it. I want to stay.*

"I want to stay," she said aloud, and realized she had her answer.

Luke slept on his back, his face turned to the side. He was pulled from a fathomless slumber by a stroke on his bare shoulder and a whisper in his ear. "Wake up, my lord." Thinking it was a dream, he turned away with a grumble. "Come with me," Tasia insisted, tugging at the sheet that covered him.

He yawned and muttered irritably. "Where?"

"Outside."

"Whatever it is, can't we do it inside?"

Her brief laugh tickled his neck as she struggled to pull him to an upright position. "You need clothes for what I have in mind."

Still more asleep than awake, Luke dressed in a minimum of clothes and left his feet bare. He gave her a quizzical frown as she applied herself to buttoning his shirt. She didn't quite look at him, but there was an air of eagerness about her. Taking his arm, she urged him to leave the cottage with her. The long hem of the silk robe trailed regally behind her as they went outside. A cool breeze helped to clear away some of Luke's sleepiness.

Tasia slipped her hand in his. "Come," she said, using all her weight to drag him forward.

He wanted to ask what in hell she was doing, but she was so intent on tugging him along that he kept silent and followed. They skirted the edge of the pond and headed to the woods, walking across a carpet of prickly resined needles and leaves.

Luke winced as he stepped on a sharp pebble. "Almost there?" he asked.

"Almost."

She didn't stop until they were surrounded by trees. The air was sweetly scented with moss, pine, and earth. A few points of stars winked through the tangled branches overhead, piercing the blackness of the forest. Luke was surprised—astonished—when Tasia turned to link her arms around his waist. She stood very still, leaning against him.

"Tasia, what—"

"Shhh." She pressed her mouth to his chest. "Listen."

They were both quiet. Gradually Luke became aware of the sounds around them: the hoot of an owl, the soft chirps and wing flapping of birds. The trill of crickets, the crackling, moaning sway of tree trunks. And rising above everything, the endless sighing of the wind through bowers of leaves. The trees stood with boughs entangled, like a congregation holding hands during a solemn hymn. The forest music soared to the sky and mingled there with other eternal rhythms.

Luke wrapped his arms around her and rested his chin on her hair. He felt her smile against his chest, and suddenly he was filled with love, drunk on it. Tasia tried to pull back a little, and he resisted, needing to keep her close.

"I want to give you something," she said, straining away until he loosened his hold. She fumbled for his hand, and he realized she was cupping something in her palm. "Here." She was slightly breathless. Her fingers opened, and he saw the bright gleam of gold against her skin. It was a heavy, masculine ring with some indiscernible engraving on the surface. "It belonged to my father. It's all I have left of him, except for my memories." As Luke remained motionless, she tried it on his smallest finger. It fit perfectly. "There," she said in satisfaction. "He always wore it on his index finger, but he wasn't nearly as large as you."

Luke turned his hand, admiring the simple but exotic design. Then he looked at her upturned face, trying to conceal his dread. "Is this to say goodbye?" he asked hoarsely.

"No . . ." Her voice shook a little. Her eyes were as bright as moonstones as she returned his steady gaze. "It's to say I'm yours. In every way . . . for the rest of my days."

He was frozen for a split second. All at once he kissed her hard and clutched her so brutally that she thought her bones might break. She didn't complain, however, only laughed in wild, unfamiliar joy until she had no more breath left.

"You'll be my wife," he said with savage delight, lifting his mouth from hers.

"It won't be easy," she warned, though she was smiling. "You'll probably want to divorce me."

"You always expect the worst," Luke accused, holding her tightly.

"I wouldn't be Russian if I didn't." Her hands searched busily over his back, as if she couldn't keep them still.

Luke laughed. "Just what I deserve. A woman who's even more of a pessimist than I am."

"No, you deserve better than me ... so much better ..."

He stopped her mouth with a ferocious kiss. "Never say that again," he warned, when their lips finally parted. "I love you too much to listen to such nonsense."

"Yes, sir," she said meekly.

"That's better." He examined the ring she had given him. "Something's inscribed on this. What does it say?"

Tasia shrugged. "Oh, it's just a sentiment that my father liked—"

"Tell me."

She hesitated. "It says, 'Love is a golden vessel, it bends but never breaks.' "

Luke was very still. Then he kissed her again, gently this time. "We'll be all right, you and I," he whispered. "I promise."

They held back from returning to the world immediately, deciding they could steal one more day together. Tasia was grateful for the reprieve. A promise had been made, but a sense of newness, even unease, still existed between them.

Tasia had never before talked to a man without having to guard her words. Luke knew about her past, her darkest secrets. Instead of making judgments, he defended her against her own doubts and self-accusation. He demanded the freedom of her body and her thoughts, and gave the same of himself. It was difficult for Tasia to adjust to the intimacy of it. Difficult, but not at all unpleasant, she decided drowsily, as she woke in his arms in a pool of afternoon sunlight. Opening her eyes, she found Luke watching her. How long had he been awake, guarding over her dreams?

"I can't believe it's really me, here in bed with you," she murmured. "Am I dreaming? Am I really so far away from home?"

"No, you're not dreaming. But you are home now." Luke eased the sheet down to her waist and slid his hand over her breast. The gold ring, warm from his skin, pressed lightly against the side of the shallow curve.

"My Uncle Kirill wouldn't approve of you. He doesn't like the English."

"Your Uncle Kirill doesn't have to marry me. Besides, he would approve of me wholeheartedly if he knew how well I'm going to take care of you." Idly he traced around her breast, where pearl-white skin edged soft pink. "I may not own a palace, my lady, but I'll keep you fed and sheltered. And I'll see to it that you're too busy to notice your humble surroundings."

"Southgate Hall isn't what anyone would call humble," Tasia said wryly. "But I would be happy living in a cottage like this, as long as you're here."

"And there's nothing else you want?"

"Well . . ." She slid him a provocative glance from beneath her lashes. "I would like some pretty dresses to wear," she admitted, and he laughed.

"Whatever you want. Rooms full of dresses. A

king's ransom of jewels." He stripped the sheet away, admiring her slender white legs and feet. "Ostrich-skin shoes, silk stockings, ropes of pearls for your waist, and a fan of peacock feathers for your wrist."

"Is that all?" she asked, laughing at the gaudy array he had described.

"White orchids for your hair," he said after a moment's consideration.

"You'd make a spectacle of me."

"But this is the way I prefer you—wearing nothing at all."

"I prefer it also." Tasia rolled on top of him, surprising them both with her boldness. "You're very nice to share a bed with," she said, propping her elbows on his chest. She paused before adding self-consciously, "I didn't expect to like it so much."

Luke's hand wandered over the smooth curve of her backside. "What did you expect?" he asked, amused.

"I thought it would be much more pleasant for a man than a woman. Certainly I didn't expect you to touch me the way you did, and ..." She lowered her gaze to his chest, and a bright wash of color swept over her face. "I didn't think there would be so much ... moving."

"Moving," Luke repeated softly. "You mean when I'm inside you?" She gave a small nod, and his chest went taut beneath her as he repressed a laugh. "Didn't anyone explain it to you?"

"Oh, after my engagement my mother admitted to me that a man and a woman 'joined,' but she never mentioned that anything happened afterward ... you know, all the moving and the ..."

"Climax?" he supplied gravely, as she foundered in abashed silence.

Tasia nodded, turning scarlet.

"Well, we could try it without so much moving," he mused.

"No!"

He lifted her chin and looked into her eyes. "Then you're satisfied with the way we've been doing it so far?"

"Oh, yes," she said earnestly, her blush remaining as he laughed in delight.

Rolling over, Luke trapped her between his elbows and settled his weight on her. "So am I." He captured her lips with a lingering kiss. "More than I've ever been in my life."

Tasia wrapped her arms around his neck, feeling her pulse quicken. "I would never want to share a bed with anyone else," she said, when he lifted his head. "When I was betrothed to Mikhail, it was all I could think about, having to let him touch me."

Luke's expression changed, turning watchful and tender. "And you were afraid?"

She looked up at him with remembered distress. "There was a constant knot of dread in my stomach. Most of the time Mikhail seemed as indifferent to me as he was to all other women. But sometimes ... he would stare at me with those strange yellow eyes, and he would ask me questions I couldn't answer. He said I reminded him of a hothouse flower, and that I knew nothing of the world or of men. He said it would please him to experiment with me. I had a fair idea what he meant, and it terrified me." She paused as she saw the anger passing over Luke's face. "Is it wrong for me to talk about him?"

"No," he soothed, kissing the space between her

brows and her forehead until the lines of worry eased. "I want to share all your memories, even the bad ones."

Tasia raised a slim hand to his face, caressing his lean cheek. "Sometimes you surprise me. You can be so kind and understanding ... but then I remember how you were about Nan Pitfield."

"The pregnant housemaid?" Luke smiled ruefully. "I can be an ass at times, as you well know. But you don't seem to have any hesitation about telling me. Most people don't dare stand up to me that way. When you came to the library and scolded me about Nan, I wanted to throttle you."

Tasia smiled, remembering his fury. "I thought you would."

He turned his lips into her palm. "But as I saw the way you were bristling with challenge, and felt your heart pounding against my hand, I wanted you so badly I couldn't bear it."

"Did you?" She laughed in surprise. "I had no idea."

"And later on I considered what you'd said. Much as I hated to admit it, you were right." His mouth took on a self-mocking curve. "It's not easy keeping all my vices in check. Occasionally I need someone to point out when I'm being a stubborn fool."

"I can do that," Tasia said helpfully.

"Good." He shifted positions, pulling her closer. "There'll be other arguments. I'll be arrogant and pigheaded, and you'll take me to task for it. We'll probably have some royal rows. But don't ever doubt that I love you."

All too soon their idyll came to an end, and they faced the necessity of returning to Southgate Hall.

"Couldn't we have another day?" Tasia asked wistfully as they strolled through a cool green meadow.

Luke shook his head. "I wish we could. But we've stayed away long enough. I have responsibilities—including a wedding to arrange. As far as I'm concerned, we're already married in the eyes of God. But I'd like to be married in the eyes of the courts as well."

Tasia frowned. "I'm going to be married, and my family doesn't know. By now they're aware that I'm alive, but they have no idea where I am. I wish there was some way I could assure them I'm safe and happy."

"No. That would make it easy for Nikolas Angelovsky to find you."

"I wasn't asking for your permission," Tasia said, annoyed by his refusal. "I only made an idle comment."

"Well, put the idea out of your head," he said brusquely. "I don't intend to spend the rest of my life waiting for Angelovsky to appear on my doorstep—but until I can think of something better, you'll keep your identity secret, and you won't communicate with your family."

Tasia pulled her hand from his. "You needn't speak to me as if I were one of your servants. Or is that the way an English husband addresses his wife?"

"I'm only concerned for your safety," Luke said mildly, his arrogance vanishing in an instant. He looked as innocent as a lamb—but Tasia wasn't fooled. He might try to conceal his domineering qualities now, but once they were married she would legally be his property, much as his horse was. It wouldn't be easy to manage him. But she was looking forward to the challenge.

The first thing Luke and Tasia did when they returned to Southgate Hall was find Emma and tell her they were to be married. As soon as she saw the two of them standing together, with Luke's arm around Tasia's waist, Emma seemed to understand everything in a flash.

Tasia had hoped Emma would be pleased by the news—in fact, she was fairly certain Emma would be very happy—but Emma's wild excitement far exceeded her expectations. The girl scampered back and forth across the great hall with boisterous screams, hugging anyone who crossed her path. Samson went into a similar paroxysm of joy, erupting into deep-throated barks as he bounded after Emma. "I knew you would come back," Emma cried, nearly knocking Tasia to the floor. "I knew you would tell Papa yes! He saw me the morning before you both left, and he told me that you were going to marry him, even though you didn't know it yet."

"He did?" Tasia gave Luke a shaming glance, her dark brows lowering over her pale eyes.

Luke pretended not to notice her silent rebuke, concentrating his own glare at Samson. The dog was rolling enthusiastically on the floor, scattering hair across the Aubusson carpet. "Why is it that every time I leave, I return to find this damned animal in the house?"

"Samson isn't an animal, he's part of the family," Emma said defensively, and added on a gleeful note. "And now so is Miss Billings! Will we have to find a new governess now? I won't like anyone else half so well."

"Yes, we'll have to find a new one. Miss Billings can't be Lady Stokehurst and your governess at the same time." He glanced at Tasia, as if judging how much activity she could withstand. "She'd drop from exhaustion within a week."

Although there was no sexual implication in his words, Tasia blushed, recalling how tired she had been after two nights of his lovemaking. Luke grinned as if he knew what she was thinking. "Now that you're no longer in my employ, Miss Billings, you'd better have Mrs. Knaggs show you to one of the guest rooms."

"My old room is perfectly fine," Tasia murmured.

"Not for my bride-to-be."

"But I don't want—"

"Emma," Luke interrupted, "choose a guest room for Miss Billings, and tell Seymour where her belongings are to be carried. And inform the housekeeper to have another place set at the table tonight. From now on Miss Billings will be taking her meals with us."

"Yes, Papa!" Emma scampered away with Samson at her heels.

Left alone with Luke, Tasia frowned at him. "I hope you don't plan to visit me tonight," she whispered sharply, knowing that was exactly what he intended.

He smiled at her, his blue eyes wicked. "I told you I don't like to sleep alone."

"I've never heard of such an indecent arrangement!" She resisted as he slid his arm around her waist and pulled her against him. "My lord! One of the servants will see—"

"Even if we keep to our own beds, everyone will assume we're together. We may as well enjoy ourselves. As long as we're discreet, no one will think the worse of us."

"*I* would." Tasia stiffened with genuine outrage. "I-I will not fornicate with you while we're under the same roof as your innocent daughter! I would be the greatest of hypocrites if I ever attempted to give her moral instruction after that."

"The horse is already out, Tasia. Too late to close the stable door."

"Well, the *bedroom* door *will* be closed," she said firmly. "Until we are married."

Luke's expression turned stony as he realized she would not budge. They exchanged a challenging glare. Abruptly Luke turned and walked away, his broad back tense beneath his shirt.

"Where are you going?" Tasia asked, half-afraid he would change his mind about everything.

"To arrange a wedding," came his muffled growl. "A damned quick one."

Seven
❧ ❧

Tasia saw very little of Luke for the next few days. He spent nearly every waking moment arranging for the private wedding to be held in the estate chapel, and in the evenings he returned to Southgate Hall to inform Tasia of his progress. She was never quite certain what his mood would be, for Luke was alternately tender and aggressive with her. Sometimes he would hold her as if she were made of fragile porcelain, wooing her with soft love words. But he was just as likely to pin her to the nearest wall and behave like a sailor on shore leave with the first available streetwalker.

"I'm coming to your room tonight," he said after one particularly heated episode, when he had yanked her into a dark corner and kissed her for five minutes.

"I'll lock the door."

"I'll break it down." His knee pushed between her thighs, delving between the layers of her skirts. He fastened his mouth to hers, thrusting his tongue deep, and she writhed against him in growing pleasure. His breath struck her cheek in hot bursts. "Tasia," he groaned, sliding his mouth to the tender hollow beneath her ear, "I want you. I want you so much I ache." He grabbed her wrist and pulled it low between their bodies, molding her hand around the hard ridge of his loins. Tasia lost all count of the sweltering minutes that passed as she stood there returning his kisses, feeling him throb intimately against her palm.

"We must stop," she gasped. "This isn't right. You're not being fair."

"Tonight," he insisted, pulling roughly at the buttons of her high-necked gown.

Tasia tore herself away from him, wobbling a little as she discovered that her knees had turned to jelly. "You will *not* come to my room," she said stubbornly. "I would never forgive you."

Luke's frustrated passion found vent in an explosion of temper. "Dammit, there's no difference in being together now or two days from now!"

"Except we'll be married then."

"You were willing enough to share my bed before."

"That was different. I thought I would never see you again. Now I'm going to make a place for myself in this household, and I will not lose the respect of the servants and your daughter by behaving like a strumpet." Her voice was quiet but firm, allowing no possibility that she would change her mind.

Luke was willing to try. In the short silence that followed, his approach softened from angry demand to wily coaxing. "Sweetheart, everyone here respects and adores you. Especially me. I need you. I can't help being impatient to hold you. All I want is to make you happy, to please you . . ."

Tasia watched him suspiciously as he drew closer. All at once he made a grab for her. She evaded him neatly, skittering out of his reach.

"Damnation!" His curse echoed in the hall as she hurried away.

"Don't you dare follow me," she said hastily,

vowing not only to lock her door but also to wedge a chair against it.

The next morning Luke approached her in the breakfast room. Tasia removed her attention from the landscaped scenery outside the arched windows and gave him a tentative smile. She remained sitting at the round oak table as he came to her. Luke motioned away a maid who was engaged in clearing the dishes.

"Good morning," he said, looking into Tasia's upturned face. Once again he was the self-possessed aristocrat, his passion safely banked, his expression implacable. "May I join you?" Before she could answer, he pulled out a chair and sat beside her. "I have to leave for London in a few minutes, but first there are two questions I want to ask you."

She matched his businesslike tone. "Very well, my lord."

"Does it meet with your approval if I ask the Ashbournes to witness the ceremony?"

Tasia nodded. "I would like that very much."

"Good. The other thing I need to know is . . ." Luke hesitated and reached out to her knee, toying with a fold of her skirt. His intent blue eyes met hers.

"Yes?" Tasia prompted softly.

"It's about the wedding ring. I wondered . . . if something like this would be acceptable." As he spoke, he opened his hand.

Tasia's eyes widened at the sight of the heavy gold band in his palm. Carefully she reached for it, holding it up to examine the pattern of roses and leaves carved on the glinting surface. The gold held the warmth of his skin.

"It's a family ring," he said. "No one's worn it for generations." Luke watched as she rolled the ring between her delicate fingers, contemplating the golden circle. She brushed her fingertip over the carved roses. "To the English," he said, "the rose is a symbol of secrecy. Long ago a host would hang a rose over his table to ensure that everything said beneath it would be kept private."

Suddenly Tasia had a fleeting image of a man and a woman in bed, the woman's long fingers outstretched as the ring slid past her knuckle. The man was dark-haired and bearded . . . and his eyes were blue. The vision faded, and Tasia knew who the lovers were. She looked at Luke with wry amusement. "Your ancestor William gave this to his mistress, didn't he?"

A smile softened the stern line of his mouth. "They say he loved her from the moment they met until the day he died." His caressing gaze swept over her. "I'll understand if you'd prefer something else, maybe with precious stones. This ring is old-fashioned—"

"No, I want this one." Tasia closed her hand over the ring. "It's perfect."

"I hoped you'd feel that way." Luke leaned over, resting his arm on the back of her chair. Their faces were very close. "Forgive me for last night. It's not easy, having you so close and not being able to take you to bed."

Tasia's lashes lowered. "It's not easy for me either." Feeling a rush of warmth and attraction, she inched nearer to him, her lips parted invitingly. She hadn't slept at all well after their skirmish last night. Alone in the darkness of her bedroom, she had craved his restless kisses and the warmth of his body next to hers.

Luke smiled and pulled his head back just before her mouth could brush his. "No, you little tease. You'll only start something you won't let me finish." He stood and pried the ring from her hand, brandishing it threateningly. "But after I put this on your finger, I'll have you whenever I want—and propriety be damned."

The guest room Emma had chosen for Tasia was one of the prettiest in Southgate Hall, with a sleigh-shaped bed draped in peach silk brocade and thick golden tassels. Emma sprawled on the carpet with a plate of pastries she had stolen from the kitchen, alternately feeding Samson and herself. The dog lazed beside her, licking his lips after gobbling each offering.

Tasia sat in a chair with a basket of mending, stitching the torn cuff of a man's shirt. She couldn't help laughing at the sight of Emma and Samson's sugar-dusted faces. "Should you be feeding him so many sweets?" she asked. "I'm sure it isn't good for him—or you, for that matter."

"I can't help being hungry. The taller I get, the more there is to fill up." Emma crossed her long, skinny legs and sighed. "I'll never stop growing. I hope the foreigner I'm going to marry will be a tall man. It would be dreadful to look *down* at one's husband all the time."

"Whatever his height, he'll be just right for you," Tasia said.

Emma continued to leaf through the pages of a ladies' magazine, poring over descriptions of the most recent fashion designs for autumn gowns. "Bronze will be all the rage this year," she said, holding up the book for Tasia to see. "Miss Billings, you must have a walking dress made exactly like this one, with the scalloped edges and the bows on the wrists. And little bronze boots to match!"

"I'm not certain bronze is a flattering color for me."

"Oh, it would be," Emma said earnestly. "Besides, *anything* would be a pleasant change after wearing nothing but black and gray."

Tasia laughed. "I'm very fond of pink," she said dreamily. "The shade so pale that it's almost white. There's nothing more beautiful than pink pearls."

The comment produced a rapid flipping of the pages. "I saw something toward the back ... an evening gown that would be *perfect* in that shade—" Suddenly Emma stopped, looking at her with wide eyes.

"What is it?" Tasia asked.

"I just thought ... what shall I call you now? You won't be Miss Billings anymore. And calling you Stepmother is horrid. But you're not old enough to be my mother, and I don't think it would be right to call you that ... would it?"

Tasia set aside her mending, understanding the reason for the child's concern. "No," she said gently. "Mary is still your mother, and will always be, even though she's in heaven. Your father won't ever forget her, and neither will you. I'll be your father's new wife, but I won't replace her. She has her own place, just as I'll have mine."

Emma nodded, seeming reassured. She came to sit by the chair, making a tent of her pointed knees and her skirt. Her flashing blue eyes, so like her father's, met Tasia's. "Sometimes when I'm alone, I think she might be taking a peek at me from behind a cloud. Do you think it's possible that people watch over us from heaven?"

"Yes, I do," Tasia said, treating the question seriously. "If heaven is a place of perfect peace, then certainly they must be able to. I imagine your mother would be very unhappy indeed if she couldn't see for herself that you were all right."

"I think she knows you're with Papa and me. I think she's glad, Miss Billings. Maybe she even helped you to find us. She wouldn't want Papa to be lonely anymore." Emma hesitated as Tasia turned her face away. "Miss Billings? Have I made you angry?"

Tasia looked back with a wavering smile. "No, you've brought tears to my eyes," she said, dabbing at her face with a sleeve. She leaned close to kiss the top of Emma's red head. "I have something to tell you, Emma. My name isn't really Miss Billings."

Emma looked at her consideringly. "I know. It's Tasia."

"How did you find out?" Tasia asked in astonishment.

"The other night after supper I heard Papa call you that, just as I was leaving the room. And I wasn't surprised, because I've always thought you were more than a governess. You can tell me the truth now—who are you, really?"

Tasia smiled ruefully as she stared into the girl's face. Emma's blue eyes were alight with curiosity. "My real name is Anastasia Kaptereva," she admitted. "I was born in Russia. I had to leave my home and come to England because of some trouble I was involved in."

"Did you do something wrong?" Emma asked incredulously.

"I don't know," came Tasia's soft reply. "As strange as it sounds, I don't remember much about it. I'd rather not tell you any details. All I can say is that it was a terrible time in my life . . . but your father has convinced me that I should try to put it behind me, and look only to the future."

Emma's long-fingered hand crept over hers. "Can I help you somehow?"

"You already have." Tasia turned her palm and squeezed the girl's hand affectionately. "You and your father have taken me into your family. It's the most wonderful thing anyone could have done for me."

Emma smiled at her. "I still don't know what to call you."

"What about *Belle-mère?*" Tasia suggested. "That's how the French say Stepmother."

"*Belle* means pretty, doesn't it?" Emma asked with a pleased expression. "Yes, that's a perfect name."

"If only there had been time to have a proper wedding gown made," Alicia lamented, helping Tasia put the finishing touches on her appearance. "You should have a fresh new gown of your own, not another old one of mine." They had altered an ivory summer dress from Alicia's wardrobe, but the fit wasn't as perfect as it might have been. "At least you'll be married in white."

"In this case, white is questionable," Tasia said. "It would be more fitting if I wore a red dress. Scarlet red."

"I'll choose to ignore that remark." Busily Alicia fastened white roses on the thick braided coils at Tasia's nape. "Don't feel guilty, dear, if you, er, forgot yourself with Luke. Most women would, if they were alone with him for more than five minutes. He's an irresistible man ... unless one happens to be married to Charles, of course." Alicia pretended not to notice Tasia's blush, and continued to talk lightly. "It's strange, but I didn't like Luke at all when I first met him."

"You didn't?" Tasia said in surprise.

"I suppose I was jealous of the way Charles worshipped him. Everyone in their circle repeated the clever things Stokehurst said, and talked about his latest escapades. None of them liked to make a move without asking his opinion first, even when they were deciding which girls to court! When I finally met him, all I could think was, 'What a spoiled, self-centered young man. What in heaven's name do they all see in him?' "

Tasia laughed. "What caused you to change your mind?"

"I realized what a good husband he was to Mary. Remarkable, really. With her, Luke was considerate, tender—all the things that men are usually afraid to be, thinking they might appear weak in front of others. And he never looked at another woman, no matter how they threw themselves at him. I came to see the strength of character beneath Luke's arrogance. And then there was the accident ..." Alicia shook her head in wonder. "Losing Mary, and being maimed for life ... he had every right to be bitter and self-pitying. Oh, how Charles dreaded visiting him that first time! 'Stokehurst will never be the same,' Charles told me, just before he went to Luke's sickbed. 'I don't think I can bear to see what's left of him.' But Luke had become more of a man, rather than less of one. He told Charles that he didn't plan to waste time feeling sorry for himself, and he wanted no one's pity. He intended to honor Mary's memory by giving Emma a happy life, and teaching her that outward flaws didn't matter, because only the inside of a person's heart is important. Charles came home with tears in his eyes, and said he admired Lord Stokehurst more than any man he'd ever known."

"Why are you telling me this?" Tasia asked, her voice husky.

"I suppose I'm trying to say that I approve of what you're doing, Tasia. I don't believe you'll ever regret marrying Stokehurst."

Uncomfortably Tasia turned to check her hair in the mirror. She avoided the sight of her own tear-brightened eyes. "Until recently all I've allowed myself to think about are the Angelovskys, and the dreadful thing I may have done. I don't know what my feelings are about Lord Stokehurst. I can't put them into words yet. But I do know that I've begun to turn to him in a way I've never turned to anyone."

"That's a promising beginning, I think." Alicia stood back to look at Tasia. "Lovely," she pronounced.

Tasia reached back to touch the flowers in her hair. "How many are there?"

"Four."

"Could you pin on another, please?"

"There's not room, I'm afraid."

"Then you must take one away. I'll wear either three or five."

"But why? . . . Oh, yes, how could I have forgotten?" Alicia smiled as she recalled the Russian tradition. "An odd number of flowers for the living, an even number for the dead." She glanced at the large arrangement of blossoms that Tasia would carry into the chapel. "Must I count your bouquet for you?"

Tasia smiled and picked up the mass of flowers, regarding it speculatively. "There's no time for that. We'll have to assume it's the correct number."

"Thank God," Alicia said in a heartfelt tone.

Despite the solemnity of the occasion, Tasia wanted to laugh at the sight of Samson waiting patiently by the door of the estate chapel. The dog's leash had been affixed to one of the back pews to ensure his noninterference in the wedding ceremony. His ears flapped and twitched as he watched the small gathering in the front of the chapel. Affected by the reverent atmosphere, he behaved with unusual dignity, only lapsing occasionally to paw and snort at the wreath of white flowers Emma had fastened around his collar.

The aloof faces of carved saints looked down from the walls. The chapel was small and slightly musty, candlelight warming the smooth stone and dark wood with its yellow glow. Tasia had a feeling of detachment as she stood next to Luke, with Emma at her right and the Ashbournes on his left. She repeated the vows in a voice that didn't seem to be her own.

How simple and astonishingly intimate this was, compared to the grand two-hour ceremony she would have had to endure in St. Petersburg. If she had married Mikhail Angelovsky, there would have been at least a thousand guests, and an Orthodox bishop to perform the rites. She would have been swathed in white brocade, silver fur, and a silver crown that complemented Mikhail's gold one. There would have been a procession around the altar, and the Angelovskys would have insisted that Mikhail carry the ancient Russian symbol of husbandly authority, a silver whip. And she would have been forced to kneel and kiss the hem of his ceremonial robe, in the ultimate gesture of subservience. Instead she had left it all behind, in a trail of blood and deception. Now she was in a foreign country, exchanging marriage vows with a stranger.

Luke held her hand firmly and spoke the words that would bind her to him until death. She looked into his clear blue eyes, her detachment vanishing. The last threads to the past were severed as she took another's name as her own and felt his ring slide onto her finger. Tasia knew an instant of panic just before he bent and fitted his mouth over hers. It was not a gentle kiss, but a brief, hard one. *You're mine now*, was his unspoken message. *Now and forever . . . and nothing will part us.*

The servants' hall rang with cheers as Lord and Lady Stokehurst appeared in the doorway. Luke had given the servants the next day off and supplied enough wine and food for an all-night celebration. People had come up from the village to play instruments and take part in the gathering. A crowd rushed around the newlyweds, offering congratulations. Tasia was touched by their warmth.

"Bless you, my lady!" the maids cried. "Bless you an' the master both!"

"There never was a prettier bride," Mrs. Plunkett exclaimed with tears in her eyes.

"The happiest day in Southgate Hall," Mrs. Knaggs said emphatically.

Mr. Orrie Shipton, the town mayor, raised a toast. His chubby face flushed with self-importance as he lifted a glass of wine high in the air. "To the marchioness of Stokehurst—may her gentle kindness grace this home for many years to come—and may she fill Southgate Hall with many children!"

To the delight of the gathering, Luke laughed and bent to kiss his blushing bride. No one could hear what he murmured in her ear, but the words caused her cheeks to flame even brighter.

After a few minutes Tasia left in the company of Mrs. Knaggs and Lady Ashbourne, while Luke lingered and accepted the hearty congratulations coming from every direction. Charles stayed at his side, beaming as if he were personally responsible for the entire situation.

"I knew you would do the right thing," Charles said *sotto voce,* seizing Luke's hand and shaking it enthusiastically. "I knew you weren't the rutting scoundrel Alicia claimed you were. I defended you on every point. When Alicia called you a lecherous, interfering swine who was stuffed on your own conceit, I said she was putting it much too harshly. And when she said you were overbearing and heartless, I told her it simply wasn't true. And when she began to rant about your swelled head and your selfishness—"

"Thank you, Charles," Luke interrupted dryly. "It's nice to know I was so well-defended."

"By God, this is a happy day, Stokehurst!" Charles exclaimed, and gestured to the merry gathering. "Who could have predicted this would happen when I introduced Tasia to you? Who would have thought Emma would take such a liking to her, or that you would come to love her? I must congratulate myself on—"

"I never told you I loved her," Luke said, staring at him quizzically.

"Afraid it's obvious, old man. Knowing how you feel about marriage, I was certain you wouldn't propose unless you loved her. And I haven't seen you so lighthearted since our days at Eton." Charles chortled into his cup of wine. "But I won't envy you, Stokehurst, when London society gets its first glimpse of her. You'll have to work hard to keep other men away from your wife. I can't decide whether you'll have more problems with the young bucks or the old rakes. Tasia has the kind of feminine mystery that most Englishwomen lack, and that combination of black hair and white skin—"

"I know," Luke said shortly, frowning in annoyance. Charles was right. Tasia's youth, beauty, and delicious trace of foreignness would make her a fantasy creature in many mens' eyes. Luke wasn't used to feeling jealous, and he didn't like it. For an instant he remembered how it had been with Mary, how comfortable and easy everything was. There had been no heart pangs with her, no jealousy, nothing but the familiarity of old friends.

Charles gave him an astute glance. "It's certainly not the same, is it?" he remarked with the deliberate blandness he always used to mask words of importance. "I confess I wouldn't know how to begin again, especially with a young wife. The things you've already experienced, Tasia knows nothing about. She has years' worth of mistakes, lessons to learn . . . and yet, to see the world through her eyes is rather like seeing it again for the first time. I rather envy you that." Charles smiled at Luke's arrested expression. "What is that quote? 'Though youth gave us love and roses, age still leaves us friends and wine . . .' " He raised his glass in a toast. "My advice is to enjoy your second taste of youth, Stokehurst. And leave the wine to me."

The lamps were turned discreetly low as Luke entered the bedroom. Tasia was alone, waiting for him with her hands clasped at her midriff. She was dressed in a linen nightgown trimmed with lace, her hair falling in a cloud of curls down her back. She was so beautiful, so fresh and innocent. Luke caught a glimpse of the gold band on her finger, and the knowledge of all that it signified was overwhelming. He had never wanted to care about a woman like this, had actually feared it, but now that all was said and done, he was glad. He had never felt such happiness, and with it came the curious relief of being unguarded, humble, human.

"Lady Stokehurst," he whispered, pulling her against his robe-covered chest. "You look like an angel in white."

"Cousin Alicia gave this to me." She fingered the sleeve of the gown, staring at him with luminous cat-eyes.

"Beautiful," he murmured.

Tasia wore a little frown. "My lord, I wish to discuss something important with you."

"Oh?" Luke toyed with her long curls as he waited for her to continue.

She rested a supplicating hand on his chest. "I expected that we would share the same room tonight. But I thought that you should be made aware of my instructions to Mrs. Knaggs that beginning tomorrow we will occupy separate bedrooms."

Luke's only visible reaction was a slight quirk of the eyebrows. They had never discussed sleeping arrangements. He had thought there would be no question that they would share the same bed. "I didn't marry you in order to sleep apart from you," he replied.

"Naturally you will have the right to visit my bed whenever you feel the inclination, my lord." Tasia smiled shyly. "My parents had this kind of arrangement, as do the Ashbournes. It's only proper. Alicia says that it's very common in England."

Luke contemplated her silently. No doubt there was a variety of marriage manuals and ladies' magazines that recommended separate beds as a feature of a respectable home. He didn't care about anyone's arrangement but his. He'd be damned if he spent one minute sleeping apart from Tasia merely to satisfy someone else's notion of a proper marriage.

He tightened his arm around her back. "Tasia, I will want you every night—and I don't much care for the idea of 'visiting' my wife. Don't you think it would be more convenient if we shared this room?"

"It's not a question of convenience," she said earnestly. "If we have only one room, people will know that we occupy the same bed every single night."

"God, no," he said, looking appalled. He scooped her up in his arms, carried her to the raised bed, and dropped her onto the wide expanse of ivory silk.

Tasia frowned at his sarcasm. "My lord, I'm trying to explain about propriety—"

"I'm listening."

But he wasn't, really. His hand played over her body, sliding from her hip to her breast until her explanation became all muddled. He bent over her breasts, licking through the bodice of her gown as he searched for a taste of skin beneath the rough screen of lace. Finding the hardened peak of one nipple, he bit lightly, and then stroked the damp lace with his tongue. Tasia gasped and fell silent.

"Go on," Luke murmured, peeling the gown away from her breast. His breath fell hotly on her naked skin. "Tell me about propriety."

She only moaned and reached for him, pulling his head closer. Smiling, he kissed the velvety tip and opened his mouth, drawing her tender flesh gently between his teeth. The idea of separate rooms was abandoned, as Luke gave her a thorough demonstration of why they would require only one room and one bed.

Tasia had married Luke with the expectation of finding peace. The past year had been so tumultuous that all she wanted now was a quiet, orderly life. She soon found out that Luke had different plans in mind. He began by taking her to London, despite her objections to leaving Emma. "My parents will be coming to stay with Emma," Luke said, lounging on the bed as he watched Tasia comb out her long hair. "She understands that newlyweds require some time alone to get used to each other. Besides, Emma likes nothing better than to bait my mother."

"She'll be up to mischief," Tasia warned, frowning at the thought of Emma left to run wild, with only the servants and two elderly grandparents to restrain her.

Luke smiled at her prim reflection in the mirror. "So will we."

Tasia was enchanted by the Stokehurst house in London, an Italianate villa situated on the Thames River. The house had three round towers with cone-shaped roofs. It was surrounded on three sides with picturesque shaded loggias. There were several indoor fountains adorned with antique tiles or marble sculpture. The previous owner had liked the sound of splashing water so much that he had wanted to hear it from every hall in the house.

"It doesn't look lived in," Tasia remarked as they strolled from room to room. In spite of the villa's elegance, it was bereft of knickknacks or any items of a personal nature. "One would never guess whose house this is."

"I bought this place after the other one burned," Luke said. "Emma and I lived here for a while. I suppose I should have hired someone to decorate it."

"Why didn't you live at Southgate Hall?"

He shrugged. "Too many memories. At night I kept waking up and expecting ..."

"To find Mary beside you?" she asked softly, when he didn't finish.

Luke stopped in the middle of a circular marble hall and turned her to face him. "Does it bother you when I mention her?"

Tasia reached up to brush the hair off his forehead, her slim fingers combing through the dark locks. The tender lines of her mouth curved in a smile. "Of course not. Mary was an important part of your past. I only count myself fortunate that now I'm the one who sleeps next to you at night."

Luke's eyes were dark, fathomless blue as he

stared at her. He traced the delicate tip of her chin with his thumb and forefinger, lifting her face. "I'm going to make you very happy," he whispered.

"I am—" Tasia began, but his fingers stilled the movement of her lips.

"Not yet. Not nearly enough."

He spent the first two weeks showing her London, from the original site of Roman occupation to the areas of Mayfair, Westminster, and St. James. They rode thoroughbreds through the lush acres of Hyde Park and visited Covent Garden, where they walked under the glass-canopied market rows and paused to watch a Punch-and-Judy show. Tasia smiled slightly at the antics of two puppets battering each other, but she didn't share the uproarious laughter of the crowd around her. The English had a strange sense of humor, finding a great amusement in pointless violence that seemed at odds with their civilized nature. Bored with the show, she tugged at Luke's arm to urge him closer to vendor stalls filled with flowers and fruit, and others laden with toys.

"It's like the Gostinny Dvor!" she exclaimed, and laughed at his quizzical glance. "A merchants' place in St. Petersburg, where everything is displayed in rows. This is very similar—except there are no icon stalls."

Luke smiled at the way she shook her head, as if a marketplace without icons was hardly worth visiting. "Do you need more than one icon?" he asked.

"Oh, one can never have too many of them. Icons are good for prayer, and they bring blessings and good luck. Some people carry an icon in their pockets all the time." She frowned a little. "I wish you had one. It never hurts to have extra good luck."

"I have you for that," he murmured, his fingers closing around hers.

They visited several shops on Regent Street, and a dressmaker's on Bond. The designer, Mr. Maitland Hodding, was a small, neat Englishman. Tasia liked the sense of economy in his designs, knowing that simplicity suited her far more than masses of ruffles and bows. She found it impossible to contain her excitement as she was seated in a gilt chair near tables piled high with books and fabric samples.

"I've always worn French gowns before," Tasia said, an idle comment that brought an emphatic response.

"French fashion," Mr. Hodding said scornfully, as he sorted through a sheaf of sketches to show her. "They raise the hemline and lower the décolletage, add a few flounces, and dye the whole of it a garish shade of magenta ... and for *this* thousands of Englishwomen sigh and dream of owning a gown from Paris! But you, Lady Stokehurst, will be a vision of elegance in the gowns we will create for you. You'll disdain to wear a Parisian fashion ever again." He beamed at her and lowered his voice, as if they were a pair of conspirators. "I expect you'll be so dazzling that Lord Stokehurst won't even notice the cost."

Tasia glanced at her husband, who was seated in a velvet chair. Two showroom assistants were seeing to Luke's comfort. One of them insisted on bringing him tea, while the other dedicated herself to stirring until ever grain of sugar was dissolved. Disliking the way the girls hovered over him, Tasia gave him a frown, which he answered with a helpless shrug.

It had not been lost on Tasia that other women were excited by her husband's dark handsomeness. At a small soirée the Ashbournes had given, she had seen how female guests of all ages had fluttered and giggled whenever Luke was near, and had stared at him with unblinking eyes. At first it had amused Tasia, but then she had begun to simmer like a pot on the stove. It didn't matter that Luke did nothing to encourage them. She hated the sight of the eager women milling around her husband, and she had an urge to rush over to him and shove them all away.

Alicia had appeared at her side, sliding a sisterly arm around her shoulders. "You're staring daggers at my guests, Tasia. I invited you here to make friends. This is not the way to go about it."

"They would like to lure him away from me," Tasia had said darkly, watching the group.

"Perhaps. But they've all had their chances for years, and he's never given any of them a thought." Alicia had smiled. "Don't think he isn't aware of your reaction, little cousin. Luke isn't above trying to make you jealous."

"Jealous!" Tasia echoed, indignant and surprised. "I'm not—" But she stopped, realizing that was exactly the reason for the hot, riled sensation in her chest. It was the first time she had ever felt that he belonged to her. For the rest of the evening she had glued herself possessively to Luke's side, giving cool nods to every woman who so much as glanced in their direction.

Recalling the episode, Tasia decided it was high time to have some new gowns so striking and beautiful that Luke wouldn't be able to take his eyes from her. She interrupted Mr. Hodding's display of sketches, resting her hand lightly on his arm. "These are all very lovely," she said. "Clearly you are a gifted designer."

Maitland Hodding pinkened with pleasure at the compliment, staring into her cat-shaped eyes as if mesmerized. "It will be my great honor to do justice to your beauty, Lady Stokehurst."

"I don't wish to copy anyone else, Mr. Hodding. I would like your help in creating a unique style for myself. Something more exotic than what I've seen in these sketches so far."

Excited by the idea, Hodding motioned for an assistant to bring a fresh sketchbook. They conferred for a long time, drinking countless cups of tea. Luke soon tired of the delicately perfumed atmosphere of the shop and the tedious details of fabric and design. He drew Tasia aside for a private conversation. "Will you be all right if I leave for a while?" he asked quietly.

"Oh, certainly," she replied. "We'll be busy for hours yet."

"You won't be afraid?"

Tasia was touched by his concern for her safety. Luke understood how afraid she was of being found by Nikolas. He saw to it that she was never left alone in public. Their home was well-protected by fences and locks, and the servants had been given thorough instructions concerning any strangers who might come to the villa's gates. On the occasions when Tasia wished to pay a call to someone, she was accompanied by two footmen and an armed driver. Most important, she continued to maintain her ruse as Karen Billings. Everyone except Emma and the Ashbournes believed her to be a former governess who had been fortunate enough to marry a Stokehurst. Tasia knew that after these precautions, it would be unreason-

able for her to worry about Nikolas Angelovsky . . . and yet the secret fear was always in the
back of her mind.

She looked up at her husband with a smile. "I'll
be perfectly safe here. Go, and don't worry about
me."

Luke bent to kiss her forehead. "I'll be back
soon."

After Tasia and Mr. Hodding had come to several mutually satisfactory agreements, they found
themselves half-buried in a mountain of silk, velvet, merino, and poplin. Mr. Hodding paused to
regard Tasia with frank admiration. "Lady Stokehurst, I have little doubt that when you wear these
designs, every woman in London will want to em-
ulate you."

Tasia smiled as he helped her to her feet. It had
been so long since she had worn a beautiful dress.
She would dearly love to burn the black gown she
was wearing. "Mr. Hodding," she asked, "is there
a day dress already made in the shop that I might
take away with me this afternoon?"

He looked at her thoughtfully. "I suppose I
could manage something along the lines of a simple blouse and skirt."

"I would be very grateful," Tasia said.

One of the female assistants, a petite blond
named Gaby, brought Tasia to a back room lined
with ornately framed mirrors that multiplied her
reflection into infinity. She helped Tasia change
into a wine-red skirt and a high-necked white
blouse with a fall of snowy lace down the front.
There was an ivory jacket-bodice that fit over the
blouse, its long hem forming a slim overskirt. De-
lighted, Tasia fingered the delicate embroidery of
pink flowers and green leaves around the sleeves

of the jacket. "It's lovely," she exclaimed. "Please have this put on my account."

Gaby stared at her admiringly. "There's not many who have the figure for it. Only a woman as slender as you could wear it well. But the waist of the skirt is too loose. If you'll wait, my lady, I'll bring a needle and stitch it, in the twitch of a cat's tail." She left Tasia alone in the room and closed the door behind her.

Tasia swished the skirts and turned in a circle, admiring the flowing red fabric. She could see herself from every angle in the parade of mirrors around her. The ensemble was jaunty and stylish, far more sophisticated than the girlish dresses she had worn in Russia. She wondered what Luke would say when he saw her, and laughed excitedly at the thought. Pausing in the middle of the room, she fluffed the lace of the blouse and smoothed the ivory silk jacket in feminine preening.

A shadow moved behind her. Tasia's smile faded as a chill swept over her skin. She stood there surrounded by reflections within reflections, flags of red and ivory, dozens of wide, staring eyes. Her own eyes. A dark form moved in and out of the images, coming closer. It couldn't be real ... but suddenly she was frightened. Her ears rang with a high-pitched tone. She was paralyzed, trapped inside the kaleidoscope, while her lungs labored to draw in enough air ... not enough air ...

There was a touch at her elbow. A man turned her to face him. She stared into Mikhail Angelovsky's grinning death-face, his yellow eyes locked with hers. Blood streamed from his throat and lips as he mouthed her name. *"Tasia ..."*

She gave a sharp cry and twisted in his hold. Somewhere in the careening room, there was a third presence. They formed a macabre triangle of death, the three of them trapped in a room of red and gold, the scene repeating over and over ... Tasia covered her face with her hands. "No," she whimpered. "Go away, *go away*—"

"Look at me, Tasia."

It was her husband's voice she heard. Her body gave a jerk, as if she had been touched by an electric current. Trembling, she looked up at him. The noise in her ears receded.

Luke was there, holding her. His face was pale beneath its bronze tan, his eyes piercing blue. She kept her gaze on him, terrified that if she looked away he might disappear, and Misha would come back. She must be going mad. She had mistaken her husband for a ghost. All at once the thought struck her as funny, and she began to laugh helplessly, the sound spilling from her lips. Luke didn't share her amusement. He continued to stare at her with a serious expression that made her realize how unbalanced she must seem. Somehow she managed to stop laughing. She used her sleeve to wipe the stray tears from her eyes.

"I remembered Mikhail," she said hoarsely. "It happened all over again. I saw everything. There was a knife in his throat, a-and blood gushing, and he wouldn't go away, he was holding me—"

Luke murmured quietly and tried to bring her close against his body, but she resisted. "Th-there was another man in the room," she said. "Someone else was there. I didn't remember it until now."

He stared at her intently. "Who? A servant? A friend of Mikhail's?"

Tasia gave a frantic shake of her head. "I don't know. But he was there during all of it. He was *part* of it, I'm sure—" She broke off as the door opened.

Gaby stood there with a confused expression. "My lady?" the girl asked. "I thought I heard a scream."

"I'm afraid I startled my wife," Luke said. "Allow us a few minutes of privacy."

"Yes, my lord." Abashed, Gaby withdrew with a murmured apology.

Luke returned his gaze to Tasia. "Do you remember what he looked like, this other man?"

"I-I'm not sure." Tasia bit her lip, trying to control her emotions. "I don't want to think about him—"

"Was he old or young? Dark or fair? Try to remember."

Closing her eyes, Tasia took a shivering breath and struggled to make the shadowy image clear in her mind. "Old . . . and tall. I'm not sure about anything else." She felt cold and sick, to the marrow of her bones. "I can't do this," she whispered.

"All right." Luke folded her against his broad chest and bent his head over hers. "Don't be afraid," he murmured. "No harm will come of knowing the truth, no matter what it is."

"If I'm guilty—"

"I don't care what you've done."

"But I care." Her voice was muffled in his coat. "I'll never escape it. I'll never be able to live with myself, knowing—"

"Hush." Luke hugged her so tightly she could hardly breathe. "Whatever happened in that room with Angelovsky . . . someday you'll remember it all, every detail, and then you're going to let it go. I'll be there to help you."

"But you won't be able to stop Nikolas—"

"I'll deal with Nikolas. I'll make everything all right."

Tasia tried to tell him that he couldn't, it wasn't possible, but he crushed his mouth on hers, his kiss hard, deep, a determined invasion. She didn't fight him. She relaxed into his hold, her arms lifting to encircle his neck. Luke's mouth gentled at the gesture of willingness, and the kiss ripened into exquisite tenderness. Tasia was flushed and aroused by the time he lifted his head. His mouth touched the edge of her ear and the pale curve of her neck above the white lace collar. Half-opening her eyes, Tasia caught sight of them standing together, her red-and-cream form locked against his dark one. She twitched in reaction.

"I should like to leave this room," she said, her voice unsteady. "All these mirrors . . ."

"You don't like mirrors?" he asked.

"Not this many."

Luke glanced at their surroundings with a wry smile. "I rather like seeing twenty of you at once." As he looked back at her face and read the signs of strain, his expression became unfathomable. "We'll go home now," he said.

Yes, she wanted to find a dark room and crawl into bed, and pull the covers over her head, and not think or feel. But she wouldn't let herself. She wouldn't indulge the guilt, the fear—or lunacy— whatever it was that inspired the macabre vision of Mikhail. "I would like to continue shopping," she said.

"I think you've had enough excitement for one day."

"You promised we would visit Harrods this afternoon." Tasia pushed her lower lip into a small pout, knowing it would distract him. As she had intended, he was charmed into agreeing.

"Anything," he said, kissing her cheek. "Whatever pleases you."

Tasia recovered her good spirits as they went to see the accumulation of wares at Harrods, the well-known department store on Brompton Road. Every time she stopped to admire something—a clock, a tray, a tiny hat adorned with bird-of-paradise feathers, a painted tin of comfits that Emma would like—Luke would gesture for a waiting attendant to have it packaged and sent to the carriage.

Tasia refused when he urged her to purchase yet another item she fancied. "We've bought too much already."

Luke was amused. "I didn't think the heiress to a great fortune would be so afraid of spending money."

"I couldn't buy anything without my mother's permission. And she didn't like to walk on public streets—she said it made her feet ache. She had the merchants and jewelers come to the palace with their goods. I've never been shopping like this."

Luke laughed and toyed with the frill of lace at her throat. The nearby attendant cleared his throat and pointedly looked away from the display of intimacy. "Spend as much as you like, sweet," Luke murmured. "You have a long way to go before you come close to costing what a mistress does."

Tasia hoped no one had overheard him. "My lord," she whispered reprovingly, and he grinned.

"You have no idea what your presence in my bed is worth. I advise you to take advantage of it."

She was torn between the urge to end the improper conversation at once and the desire to prolong it. The feel of his strong arm around her waist and his breath on her skin was irresistible. She stared into his smiling eyes, uncertain of how to react to his teasing. "Why did you want me as a wife and not a mistress?" she asked.

The quality of his smile changed, and his voice was very soft. "Would you like me to take you home and show you?"

Tasia stayed silent, imprisoned by his direct stare. She wasn't aware that she had gripped his arm until her hand slipped a little, feeling the edge of leather binding beneath his shirtsleeve. Suddenly all she could think about was being in bed with him, his mouth on her skin, the sensations he could coax from her body with such ease.

Seeing the answer in her eyes, Luke turned to the store attendant, who was hovering a few feet away. "I believe our shopping is concluded for now," he said blandly. "Lady Stokehurst has a touch of fatigue."

Even without having had experience of other men, Tasia knew that her husband was a superb lover. The way he used his touch, his body, his kisses, could be shaded with infinite meaning. There were nights when the hours of lovemaking blended into a slow-moving dream, sensations spilling over her in an endless flow. He cuddled, kissed, soothed her until she purred with the pleasure of being possessed by him. But often Luke liked to play in bed, aggressive rough-and-tumble games that left her breathless with laughter. Tasia was amazed at the way he could provoke her. Even as a child, she had been quiet and well-behaved. Luke stripped away her inhibitions, encouraging—no, demanding—that she respond to him in a way that defied all her old ideas of propriety.

Tasia wished it were possible to need Luke only a little. She tried to keep her feelings contained, but they flourished in unruly profusion. The attention he paid her, the conversations, smiles, the ready comfort, were like an addictive drug. He asked for very little in return. Guiltily she thought that she should say that she loved him, but somehow the words wouldn't come. It seemed as if the key to her destruction lay in that unspoken sentence. She could give only so much of herself, and then she drew back in fear, for reasons she couldn't explain even to herself.

"I've never been spoiled like this before," she told him one afternoon as they relaxed in the high-walled garden of the villa. "I'm sure it's wrong of me to let you."

The full heat of summer was almost upon them. They reclined in the shade of towering box and bay hedges, and a graceful spreading oak. Honeysuckle and thornless climbing roses spread their perfume through the air. Tasia toyed with a single rose, drawing the blossom along the edge of Luke's jaw.

He lay with his head pillowed in her lap. Idly he propped up one knee and swung it. "I don't see that spoiling has done you any great harm." He glanced up at her face, reaching to stroke the velvety curve of her cheek. "You're more beautiful than ever."

Tasia smiled and bent over his head, touching her nose to his. "Because of you."

"Is it?" His hand slid around the back of her neck, bringing her closer. They exchanged a long, savoring kiss before she replied.

"Russians have a word for the arrival of spring: *ottepel*. It is used to describe awakening. That's how I feel."

"Really." His eyes were bright with interest. "Show me what's been awakened."

"No," she squeaked, dropping the rose as he fondled her lustfully.

"I want to know exactly which part," he insisted, pulling her down to the grass until she was stretched beneath him. Casually he drew his hand down her body, ignoring her giggling protests that someone might see.

During the three weeks they had spent in London, Luke had gathered a thousand images of Tasia in his mind, but none so enchanting as this moment, as she struggled to climb on top of him in a wrestling match. Luke much preferred his wife's vigorous romping to her previous wan gracefulness. Her body had lost its spare, thin appearance, and there was a new roundness to her neck and face and limbs. Her breasts were still small, but softer and fuller. Her skirts rode up to her knees as she straddled his hips, hands braced on his shoulders for balance. She perched on him triumphantly. Luke flexed his shoulders slightly, making her aware of the sinewy power beneath her hands, reminding her that she was on top only because he allowed it.

"I want to ask you something," she said.

"Ask away."

"Promise me that before you refuse, you'll let

me say all I want. And that you'll try to listen with an open mind."

"Ask," he growled, feigning impatience.

Tasia took a deep breath. "I want to write to my mother," she said bluntly. "I need to assure her that I'm safe and happy, for my peace of mind as well as hers. I know that she worries about me. It can't be good for her health. And I think about her every day. I won't write anything that will betray my situation—no names or places mentioned. But it is absolutely necessary that I do this. You must understand how much it means to me."

Luke was silent for a moment. "I understand," he said tonelessly.

Her eyes sparkled with gladness. "Then you'll permit me to write to her?"

"No."

Before he could explain why, Tasia swung off him and gave him a sullen, determined stare. "I wasn't requesting your permission, I was trying to be courteous. It's not your decision to make. It's *my* mother, and *my* safety that's at stake."

"And you're *my* wife."

"I have always decided on the risks that are necessary to take. Now you're trying to deny me something I need desperately to do!"

"You know what I told you about contacting your family. You're aware of the reasons why."

"We can trust my mother not to mention this to anyone."

"Can we?" he asked evenly. "Then why didn't you trust her enough to tell her that your death was faked? Why did Kirill insist on keeping it secret from her?"

Tasia was quiet, glaring at him. She couldn't argue with his point. But the curb on her indepen-

dence was infuriating. She needed to establish
some fragile link to the world she had left. At
times she almost felt as if she didn't exist, cut off
as she was from everything she had been and
known and done. It was as if her old self had truly
died. No one could truly understand her confusion, the feelings of happiness and loss that coex-
isted inside her. Her husband was sympathetic but
unyielding. His decision was the final one.

"You can't stop me from doing as I please," she
said rebelliously. "Unless you plan to guard me
every minute of the day."

A warning glint entered his eyes. "I won't play
the role of prison guard," he agreed softly. "Neither will I be cast as a tyrant. I'm your husband,
with the right—and the responsibility—to protect
you."

Tasia knew that her burst of temper was unfair,
but she couldn't stop herself from defying him
further. "I could have this marriage annulled!"
Suddenly she found her wrist seized in a firm
grip, and she was hauled close against a masculine
body that was tense with anger.

"You took a vow before God to be my wife," he
said through his teeth. "That means more to you
than any laws ever written. You couldn't break a
spiritual covenant any more than you could kill a
man in cold blood."

"If you believe that, then you know nothing
about me," Tasia replied, her eyes blazing. She
yanked at her wrist, pulling hard until he released
her. Hurriedly she left him in the garden and retreated to the sanctuary of the villa.

Eight

They didn't exchange a word at supper. They ate alone in a dining room filled with yellow Italian marble, delicately carved Venetian furniture, and a sixteenth-century ceiling painted with mythological figures. Although the food was delicious as usual, Tasia could barely swallow a mouthful. The silence stretched her nerves thin.

Usually this was her favorite time of day. Luke would entertain her with stories of places he had been and people he had met. He coaxed her to tell him about her life in Russia. Sometimes they debated various issues in a rapid-fire fashion, and sometimes they flirted and engaged in bits of nonsense. One evening Tasia had sat in his lap for most of the meal, and taught him the Russian words for the morsels she fed him.

"*Yah'blahkah*," she had said, carefully guiding a bit of fruit to his mouth. "That is apple. *Greebi'* is the word for mushrooms. And this is *ri'bbah*. Fish." She had laughed at his pronunciation, and shook her head. "You English always make the 'R' so far back in your throat—as if you are growling. Say it against your teeth . . . *ri'bbah*."

"*Ri'bbah*," he said obediently, eliciting another laugh from her.

"Here, perhaps some wine will loosen your tongue." She lifted a glass of white wine to his lips. "This is *vino' byeh'lahyeh*. Make the words against your teeth. To speak Russian well, you have to spit a little. And keep your mouth round . . ." She had tried to shape his lips with her fingers as he spoke, and then they both dissolved in laughter, until she nearly fell out of his lap.

"Tell me the word for *kiss*," he said, gathering her against his chest.

"*Pahtsyeloo'eey*." She had wrapped her arms around his neck and pressed her mouth to his.

Tasia wished for one of those lighthearted evenings now. Several hours had passed since the argument she had instigated earlier. She knew she hadn't been fair. She wasn't even certain what had caused her flare of temper. An apology hovered on her lips, but pride kept her from saying anything. Meanwhile, her loving husband had disappeared, and in his place was an indifferent stranger, coldly unconcerned with the lack of conversation.

Tasia's misery grew with every minute. She drank three glasses of red wine in an effort to dull her discomfort. Finally she excused herself to totter alone up to their bedroom. After dismissing the maid, she pulled off her clothes and left them in a heap on the floor, then crawled naked into bed. The wine had made her groggy. She slept heavily, barely stirring in the middle of the night when she felt Luke's weight lower to the mattress.

Dreams consumed her in a thick red-black fog. *She was in a church, surrounded by burning candles, her nostrils filled with incense smoke. She couldn't breathe. Sinking to the ground, clutching at her throat, she raised her eyes to the rows of gilded icons. Please, please help me . . . Their pitying faces blurred, and she felt herself lifted, placed inside a narrow box. Clutching at the sides of the box, she tried to pull herself out.*

Nikolas Angelovsky's golden face was above her. He watched her with flat yellow wolf-eyes, while his teeth bared in an evil grin. "You'll never get out," he sneered, and slammed the lid on the coffin. A pounding noise began as he drove in nails to seal her inside. Tasia sobbed and thrashed, and somehow found the voice to scream.

"Luke! Luke—"

He shook her awake, bending over her writhing body. "I'm here," he said repeatedly, while she clutched at him and breathed in choking gasps. "I'm here, Tasia."

"Help me—"

"You're all right. You're safe."

The nightmare was slow to leave her. Shaking wildly, Tasia buried her sweat-blotched face in his neck. She had never felt so foolish and cowardly. "Nikolas," she managed to say. "He sh-shut me in a coffin. I-I couldn't get out."

Luke sat up and cradled her against his broad chest, rocking her as if she were a child. She couldn't see him in the darkness, but his arms were hard around her, and his low voice was close to her ear. "It was just a dream," he murmured. "Nikolas is far away, and you're safe in my arms."

"He's going to find me. He'll take me back there."

Luke continued to rock her slowly. "My sweet little girl," he whispered. "No one's going to take you away from me."

Tasia tried to gulp back her tears. "I'm s-so sorry about today. I don't know why I said those things—"

"Hush. It's all over now."

Suddenly she erupted into giggling sobs. "I'll go

crazy if I have another nightmare like that. I can't stop it from coming back. I'm afraid to sleep."

Holding her close, Luke whispered against her hair, endearments, meaningless phrases to comfort her. His muscled shoulder was tense beneath her wet cheek. Tasia gave a shuddering sigh and breathed in the scent of his skin. His hand was resting on her side, his thumb touching the outer curve of her breast. "Don't let go," she whimpered, turning to him with her body, her entire being, wanting him with a depth of hunger that frightened her.

"Never." He kissed her, his tongue skillfully exploring her mouth. At the same time, his hand moved over the soft rise of her breast. He allowed her no words, no time to think as he pulled her from the nightmare and replaced it with a dream of exquisite fire. His fingers skimmed the surface of her breast and pulled lightly at her nipple, worrying the tender flesh until it gathered to a point. Covering the bit of textured silk with his mouth, he used wet flicks of his tongue to stimulate her. Tasia's head fell back as liquid rushes of feeling washed over her, and she was bathed in the healing warmth of desire.

He pushed her down on the bed, flat on her back. Tasia lay in trembling submission, waiting for his touch, his warmth to cover her. There was nothing but stillness. Her eyes opened as she strained to find him in the darkness. "Please . . ." Blindly she reached for him, her groping hands finding only empty air.

She felt his mouth on her stomach, kissing and licking in a slow path from one hipbone to the other. Her muscles tightened, and she groaned his name. He was unmoved by her urgency. Brushing away her importuning hands, he feasted on her body as a gourmet savoring exotic cuisine. A swirling lick over her breast, a teasing bite at her waist, a string of kisses along her inner thigh. Driven to wanton shamelessness, she writhed and opened her legs wide. He laughed softly and slid his fingers into the tender opening of her body. She gasped as she felt his touch slip easily inside her, stroking deeply, probing with knowing gentleness.

His breath burned the silken hollow of her groin. He rubbed his mouth and nose into the mat of delicate hair, reaching with his tongue, dragging it deep through the fragrant softness. Using his mouth and his fingers, he teased her to the brink of fulfillment, drawing away just before she could climax.

Tasia gave a high-pitched moan, arching in frantic welcome as he swung over her and positioned himself between her thighs. He entered her in a smooth, hard glide. She convulsed at once with a scream of pleasure. He continued to move at a measured pace, sweat beading on his skin as he fought for control. She wrapped her arms around his neck, lost to everything but the feel of him pushing hard within the succulent depths of her body. The tide of sensation approached again, and she tensed beneath him while stinging tears slipped from her eyes. "I love you," she sobbed against his taut throat.

He deepened his thrusts, nudging against her womb, and she shuddered in ecstasy. Her body tightened around him, making it impossible for him to contain his passion. He joined her in a soul-wrenching climax, groaning at the wholesale shattering of his nerves. They stayed locked together, breathing hard, twining around each other in fierce reluctance to let the intimacy end.

"I love you," she said again, when she had the strength to speak. She buried her head against his chest. "I was afraid to say it before."

He smoothed her long hair in a gentle, repeated motion. "Why did you now?"

"I can't live that way any longer, being afraid of what's in my heart. And I don't want there to be secrets between us."

Luke pressed his lips to her forehead, and she could feel that he was smiling. "No secrets," he whispered. "No lies, no fear ... no past."

"If it all ends tomorrow, at least we've had this," she said, drugged with sleepy pleasure. "It's more than most people ever have. It should be enough."

"A lifetime wouldn't be enough." Luke kept her wrapped close, her hair spilling over him in dark rivers of silk, her sleek limbs tangled with his, her warm breath on his shoulder. He felt the mingling of fragility and resilience within her. Although he was not a religious man, a silent prayer resounded through him. *Thank you, God, thank you for leading her to me ...* How he had come to merit her presence in his life was a question better left uncontemplated. He wouldn't tempt fate by wondering.

During the month they had been apart, Emma seemed to have grown taller. She came into the London villa, red curls flying, and launched herself at Tasia with a peal of laughter. *"Belle-mère! I've missed you and Papa so much!"*

"I've missed you too," Tasia said, hugging her tightly. "How is Samson?"

"We had to leave him in the country." Emma pulled back and made a face. "He cried dreadfully. It took two servants to keep him from running after the carriage. He kept howling like this—" She demonstrated a mournful dog wail, making Tasia laugh. "But I told him it wouldn't be long before we all returned."

"Have you been keeping up with your lessons?"

"No. Grandmother never makes me study, except the times she tells me to 'go along and read a big book.' And Grandfather is always busy paying calls to his friends, or lurking in corners trying to pinch the housemaids."

"Oh, dear." Still smiling, Tasia walked with Emma to the front of the entrance hall, where the duchess had paused for a private word with Luke.

Her Grace, the Duchess of Kingston, was an imposing woman, tall and slender, with brilliant silver hair and dark, hawklike eyes. She was dressed in pearl-gray and plum silk, and a remarkable straw hat with a high "flower-pot" crown. There were two dead stuffed birds perched on the sloping brim of the hat.

"She killed them herself," Emma said in a deadpan tone, and grinned at Tasia's wide-eyed glance.

Luke stood with his mother, listening attentively as she gave him a detailed account of Emma's behavior for the past month. "She would be more at home living in the woods with wild creatures than under a civilized roof," the duchess proclaimed. "Fortunately I have a calming influence on Emma. She always benefits from the time she spends with me. You'll find she is much improved since you saw her last."

"How gratifying," Luke said, giving his approaching daughter a wink. "Where is Father?"

The duchess frowned. "Away on some romantic peccadillo. He snaps up silly young girls like an old cat hunting baby birds. You should be pleased by his absence. Otherwise he would be busy chasing your new bride round the villa."

Luke grinned and kissed his mother's wrinkled cheek. "Nothing that tying him to a heavy chair wouldn't solve."

"You should have suggested that years ago," the duchess replied sourly, appearing to store the idea for future consideration. She raised her voice and turned toward Tasia and Emma, who waited tactfully nearby. "I came to see what kind of woman could manage to bring my son to the altar. I would not have thought it possible after so many years."

Luke watched with pride as Tasia stepped forward to greet the duchess. "Your Grace," she said softly, and dropped in a supple curtsy. The duchess looked at Luke, making no effort to hide her surprise. Whatever his mother had expected, it was not a young woman with such royal bearing.

Tasia looked particularly beautiful that day, her dark hair swept in a chignon fastened with diamond-studded hairpins, her white throat gleaming through a scarf of blue gauze. Her gown was a close-fitting blue sheath, molded to her slender waist and hips. The skirts were drawn back to a small pleated bustle and draped to the floor in a slight train. Aside from the hairpins, the only jewelry she wore was her gold wedding band and a cross on a gold chain around her neck.

Luke tried to see her through his mother's eyes. Tasia had a quiet self-possession that was uncommon to anyone outside a convent. And there was a sweet solemnity in her eyes, the look of a child at evening prayers. How she could keep that look of innocence in spite of his corruptive influence was a mystery to Luke. But his mother would definitely approve, in spite of the fact that she still believed Tasia to be a mere governess.

"Welcome to the family," the duchess said to Tasia. "Although one must observe that you entered it under curious circumstances."

"Your Grace?" Tasia said, pretending not to understand.

The duchess frowned impatiently. "There is gossip in every corner of England concerning your mysterious appearance, and your precipitous marriage to my son. So precipitous, in fact, that the duke and I were not even invited."

Luke interrupted hastily. "We decided to keep the ceremony private, Mother."

"So it seems," came the frosty reply.

Tasia winced, remembering her brief conversation with Luke over the question of inviting his parents, ending with his flat statement that they would only bring interference and unwanted questions to the ceremony. Her slight movement caused the gold cross to swing on its long chain, attracting the older woman's interest.

"What an unusual piece," the duchess remarked. "May I see it?" Receiving Tasia's nod of permission, she lifted the ornament in her gnarled fingers. The filigree cross had been designed in the Kievan Russian style, with many tiers of thin gold thread and tiny gold drops to give it texture. The center was inset with a cluster of blood-colored rubies and a small, perfect diamond. "I've never seen such workmanship," the duchess said, carefully releasing the necklace.

"It belonged to my grandmother," Tasia replied. "From the time of her baptism until her death, she always wore a cross around her neck. This was her favorite." Obeying a sudden impulse, she removed the necklace. She took the duchess's heavily veined hand in her own soft one and pressed the cross into her palm. "I would like you to have it, ma'am."

The duchess was clearly startled by the gesture. "I have no wish to rob you of your keepsakes, child."

"Please," Tasia said earnestly. "You've given me a gift more precious than anything in the world . . . your son. I should like to give you a token in return."

The duchess looked from the gold cross in her hand to Luke, as if debating their respective worth. "There may come a day when you'll decide you've been shortchanged," she said dryly. "Nevertheless, I accept your gift. You may place the cross around my neck, child." She cracked a smile as Tasia fastened the chain. "I approve of my son's choice," she said. "You remind me of myself when I was a young wife. I will lecture Luke later about being a respectful and sympathetic husband."

"He treats me very well," Tasia assured her, glancing impishly at her husband. Luke appeared to be dumbfounded by his mother's comments. Sternly Tasia held back a smile. "Your Grace, would you allow me to walk with you to the lavender suite? I took the liberty of having it prepared for you."

"Yes, indeed. I do have a fondness for those rooms. Lavender is flattering to my complexion."

The two women walked away arm-in-arm, while Emma and Luke watched in openmouthed silence. Emma was the first to speak. "She made Grandmother like her. Grandmother doesn't like *anyone*."

"I know." Suddenly Luke laughed. "She may

be a witch after all, Emma. But don't tell her I said so."

The next few days passed in a pleasant fashion, although Tasia was dismayed by the amount of time Luke was gone. When he returned late every evening, his clothes reeking of cigar smoke, his breath tainted with port, he offered only cryptic explanations of the business meetings he had been obliged to attend. "Only men are present at these meetings?" Tasia had asked suspiciously, helping him off with his boots as he sat on the bed.

"Old, gray-haired men with big bellies and yellow teeth."

Tasia examined his shirt collar closely. "That's a relief. I should hate to start examining your clothes for traces of perfume and rouge every night."

Slightly drunk, and happy to be alone with her, Luke pulled her on top of him. "Feel free to examine everything," he invited, burying his nose and mouth in her sweet-scented hair. "Nothing to hide. Look here, in fact . . . and here . . ." He rolled and crawled amorously over his giggling wife.

In the daytime Tasia was usually busy with the duchess and Emma as the three of them shopped for house furnishings and paid calls to acquaintances. The duchess had undertaken to introduce Tasia to her most favored friends, old society lionesses who were charmed by Tasia's inflexible good manners. Such a modest, gently bred girl, they exclaimed approvingly. So different from the frivolous modern misses who knew nothing of how to employ a needle and thimble, and often didn't bother with gloves or curtsying. Tasia's decorum pleased the old ladies to no end, causing them to declare that their faith in the future of civilized society had been restored.

The duchess spent the afternoons resting in her room while Tasia oversaw Emma's lessons. To Tasia's delight, Emma had started writing a play. "I'm going to be a stage actress," Emma informed her. "Imagine me, treading the boards at the Theatre Royal ... I would make the most splendid Lady Macbeth ever!" She demonstrated her thespian talents by performing the sleepwalking scene from Macbeth with an enthusiasm that sent the duchess reaching for her smelling salts.

Upon receiving an invitation for a party to be given by Lady Walford in honor of her daughter's birthday, Emma declared violently that nothing short of an apocalypse would make her attend. "I'll be the tallest one there! I'll be taller than all the boys! And someone will say something about the color of my hair, and I'll be obliged to hit them in the nose, and there'll be a terrible scene. I'm *not going.*"

Luke's fatherly talk with Emma failed to make any impression on her. He looked perplexed and vaguely harassed as Tasia questioned him about the conversation. "She doesn't want to attend," he said shortly. "Forcing her to go will only make her miserable."

Tasia sighed. "I don't think you understand, my lord—"

"You're right," he said darkly. "In spite of my best efforts I stopped understanding Emma when she reached the age of seven. You handle her."

"Yes, Luke," she said, restraining a wry smile. Luke was a devoted father, but when Emma's problems could not be solved with presents and kisses, he seemed at a loss about what to do.

Tasia went to Emma's room and tapped gently on the closed door. When there was no response, she pushed the door open and looked inside. Emma was sprawled on the floor, sorting through her doll collection. There was a mutinous expression on her face.

"I suppose you're going to say you want me to go to the party," Emma muttered.

"Yes." Tasia sat beside her, her skirts billowing and settling in a shimmering green pool. "It's an excellent opportunity for you to make friends with some girls your age."

"I don't need friends. I have you and Papa, and everyone at Southgate Hall, and Samson—"

"And we all adore you," Tasia said, smiling. "But that's not enough, Emma. I know from experience. I grew up every bit as sheltered as you've been—more so—and I never had friends my age. I don't want you to be as lonely as I was."

Emma scowled. "I don't know how to talk to them."

"All you need is some practice."

"Papa said he wouldn't insist that I go if I didn't want to."

"*I* insist," Tasia said quietly. She saw the flash of surprise on the girl's face, and continued before Emma had a chance to respond. "We'll have a new dress made for you. I saw a beautiful color of silk in Mr. Hodding's shop, the shade of a ripe peach. It would be perfect with your hair."

Emma was shaking her head. "Belle-mère, I can't—"

"Just try," Tasia coaxed. "What's the worst that could happen?"

"I'll have a dreadful time."

"I think you could survive one dreadful evening. Besides . . . you may even enjoy yourself."

Emma groaned theatrically and occupied herself with rearranging the row of dolls. Tasia smiled, knowing her silence meant she would attend the party.

Luke sighed in relief as he closed the bedroom door, shutting out the rest of the world. He had spent yet another full day in meetings with bankers, lawyers, and businessmen. The endless haggling had tired and annoyed him. Not only did he serve on the boards of a railway company and a brewery, but he had reluctantly accepted a directorship at an insurance office.

He disliked the world of finance, preferring the role of gentleman landowner that had been passed down through his family for generations. He was not inspired by stocks and shares. He took satisfaction in plowed fields, growing crops, and a good harvest. But it was no longer possible to survive on agricultural rents alone. For the sake of his tenants as well as his family, he had invested in urban properties, factories, and railway stock, which brought in enough money to allow him to keep the rents low and make improvements on Stokehurst land.

The old gentry had mocked Luke for succumbing to the vulgar mercantile pursuit of wealth, but he had seen their estates shrink, their rent rolls plummet, and their tenants go bankrupt. Society was transforming rapidly, the aristocratic way of life crumbling as industrialists rose to prominence. Many a noble family who had once possessed unthinkable wealth had become penniless, because they wouldn't react to the changes around them.

Luke wouldn't let that happen to the people who depended on him. His land would never turn to overgrown weed. And his daughter would never be obliged to marry someone for his wealth. With all that in mind, becoming a businessman— unappealing as it was—seemed a small price to pay.

Luke smiled at the sight of his wife dressed in a modest white nightgown with white lace at the throat. Tasia's beautiful hair was loose and flowing, shining in the lamplight. She sat in bed with a book in her lap. "You were missed at supper," she said.

There was something different in her voice, a note of tension. He wondered if she was angry at having seen so little of him lately. "I wish I'd been here," he replied. "Instead I passed the time with a group of men who spent the evening arguing over the price of wheat and the comparative merits of their stockbrokers."

"And what did you all conclude?"

"That the old order is vanishing, as well as the concept of farming for profit." Luke frowned pensively, shrugging out of his coat. "I won't have the kind of life my father and grandfather had. Certainly not their leisure. My father has spent his life pursuing women, hunting, and shooting, and occasionally dabbling in politics. He thinks my involvement in trade and industry is tarnishing the family honor."

Tasia left the bed and came to help him with his clothes. She unbuttoned his shirt as he spoke. "But you are doing it for the good of the family, yes?" Spreading his shirt wide, she pressed a kiss to the hard, smooth surface of his chest.

"Yes." Luke smiled and tangled his fingers in

her hair, tilting her head back. "And I resent every minute I have to spend away from you."

Tasia slid her arms around his lean waist. "So do I."

"Is that what's bothering you?" he asked. "That I've been gone so much of the time lately?"

"Nothing is bothering me. Everything is absolutely fine."

"No lies," he reminded her quietly, and she blushed.

"There is something I've been concerned about ..." Her throat worked as she sought the right words. "I'm late," she said, her face bathed in hot color.

Luke shook his head, puzzled. "Late for what?"

"My ... monthly time," she said with difficulty. "It should have come a week ago. I've always been ... irregular that way, but still ... it's never been this long. It's nothing, I'm certain. I really don't think it's a ... a ..."

"Baby?" he suggested softly.

"It's too soon for that. I don't feel any different, and I'm certain I would feel something if it were *that*."

He was quiet, stroking her hair, fondling the curve of her ear.

"Would you mind?" Tasia asked in a small voice.

Luke stared at her until she was dizzy from the blue intensity of his eyes. "It would be the greatest joy of my life." He leaned his forehead on hers. "Whatever happens, we'll face it together. All right?"

She nodded. "You want a baby, then?"

His brow furrowed as he contemplated the question. "I haven't thought about it very much," he admitted. "I never expected to have any children except Emma. The idea of another ..." He paused and smiled crookedly. "Half me, half you ... yes, I want that. But I would prefer to have more time alone with you before we start having children. You're hardly more than a child yourself. I'd like to give you the chance to be young and carefree—something you've missed until now. I want to make up for the hell you've been through. I want to make you happy."

Tasia nestled against him. "Take me to bed," she said, her voice muffled. "That would make me very happy."

He arched his brows in surprise. "Why, Lady Stokehurst ... this is the first advance you've ever made to me. I'm fairly overwhelmed."

Busily she occupied herself with unfastening his trousers. "Not *too* overwhelmed, I hope."

He laughed. "Just don't complain when I keep you awake all night."

"I wouldn't dream of it," she whispered as his mouth came over hers.

"What a pity Papa doesn't smoke," Emma remarked, inspecting the objects poised inside a glass-covered shelf. "That's the handsomest cigarette case I've ever seen."

"I am glad he doesn't," Tasia said. "I've always regarded tobacco as a disagreeable substance."

Alicia, who had agreed to join them at Harrods for an afternoon shopping expedition, met them at the shelf. "I wish Charles had never taken up the habit. Still, it *is* an elegant case ..."

The engraved silver cigarette case was inlaid with gold and set with topaz stones. As the three women stared at it with appraising interest, a store attendant sped toward them. The waxed ends of his mustache twitching with eagerness as he reached them.

"Would the ladies care for a closer look?" he inquired diffidently.

Tasia shook her head. "I wish to purchase a birthday gift for my husband ... but not that."

"Perhaps he would appreciate gold mustache scissors and comb in a leather case?"

"He's clean-shaven, I'm afraid."

"An umbrella? One with an ivory or silver handle?"

Tasia shook her head. "Too practical."

"A box of Italian-made handkerchiefs?"

"Too impersonal."

"A bottle of French cologne?"

"Too smelly," Emma interrupted.

Tasia laughed at the attendant's perturbed expression. "Perhaps we'll continue to browse," she said. "I'm certain we'll find *something* appropriate, sooner or later."

"Yes, madam." Disappointed, the attendant left in pursuit of other customers.

Alicia gravitated toward a table laden with beaded handbags, baskets of gauzy embroidered scarves, and rectangular boxes of gloves. Tasia wandered in the opposite direction, drawn by the sight of a painted rocking horse. It was positioned on the floor, beside a row of handsome carved cradles. Carefully she nudged the horse with her foot, causing it to rock gently. A small, private smile touched her lips. With each day that passed, she was becoming more certain that she was pregnant. She imagined what their children would look like, tall, black-haired, and blue-eyed ...

"Belle-mère?" Emma said, having followed her

and noticed the child's toy. "Now that you are sleeping in Papa's bed, are you going to have a baby?"

"Someday, I expect." Tasia rested a light hand on Emma's shoulder. "Would you like to have a brother or sister?"

"Yes," the girl said readily. "Especially a brother. As long as I could help choose the perfect name for him."

Tasia smiled. "What sort of name?"

"Something special. Leopold, maybe. Or Quinton. Do you like those?"

"Oh, they're quite grand," Tasia said, picking up a small rattle and jiggling it experimentally.

"Perhaps Gideon . . ." Emma mused, circling the table. "Or Montgomery . . . yes, Montgomery . . ."

While Emma continued to ponder names, Tasia's smile faded. A strange, cold, sick feeling came over her, and she touched her fingers to the table to steady herself. She was disoriented. The taste of fear filtered through her mouth. *What is it, what's wrong—*"

Her head jerked up. Across the room she saw her nightmare vision, the image that would never leave her. *Mikhail* . . . yet it was not Mikhail. The man she had murdered had been pale and dark-haired, and this one was tawny and tanned and lethal . . . but there were the same eyes . . . flat yellow wolf-eyes. Mesmerized, Tasia watched the golden figure by the entrance of the store, handsome and as inexorable as the angel of death. He was no specter, no dream.

Prince Nikolas Angelovsky had come for her.

How bizarre, to see him in a department store, while they were surrounded by clerks and attendants and hordes of women. He was dressed in somber dark clothes that should have camouflaged his foreignness but only served to accentuate it. He was the most cruelly beautiful creature she had ever seen in her life, with golden skin and sun streaks in his brown hair, a chiseled face, and the body of a tiger magically transformed into a human.

The baby rattle shook in Tasia's trembling hand. She placed it gently on the felt-covered table. It hurt to smile, causing needles of pain in her frozen cheeks, but Tasia managed it. "Emma," she said softly, "if I'm not mistaken, you need new gloves."

"Yes, Samson stole my last ones and chewed them to rags. He never can resist fresh white gloves."

"Why don't you ask Lady Ashbourne to help you pick out a new pair?"

"All right."

As Emma left her, Tasia looked up again. Nikolas had vanished. Her gaze swept the room in a swift inventory. There was no sign of him. Her pulse raced at a sickening speed. She skirted the edge of the room with swift strides. Crossing the food hall, she passed rows of iced fish and hanging meats, stacks of grocers' wares, pyramids of jars, boxes of comfits and foreign delicacies. People were turning to look at her. Tasia realized she was breathing with a harsh, sobbing sound. She clamped her mouth shut, her nostrils flaring, her face drained of blood.

Emma is safe with Alicia, she reassured herself. *All I have to do is to elude Nikolas and find refuge somewhere, and send for Luke* ... She left the food hall and hurried through the draper's shop, toward the side exit. Once she was outside, she would blend into the crowded street. Even Nikolas, with his predator's instinct, wouldn't be able to find her in that bustling mass of humanity.

Tasia slipped outside into the fetid air of London on a summer day. Before her foot touched the pavement, she felt a brutal arm close around her middle with the impact of a blow, squeezing until she felt her spine flex from the pressure. At the same time, a large gloved hand covered the lower half of her face. Quietly, efficiently, two men ushered her along the side street to a waiting carriage. Nikolas was standing there with the calm of a satiated tiger. He was a young man, not yet twenty-five, but all traces of youth and kindness had vanished a long time ago, if indeed he had ever possessed those qualities. His eyes were as round and shiny as golden saucers ... emotionless ... sterile.

"*Zdráhstvuyti*, little cousin," Nikolas murmured. "You look well." He reached out and caught a tear that trembled on her lashes and fingered it as if it were some precious elixir. "You could have made it much more difficult for me, you know. You could have hidden in the country as a peasant girl. It might have taken years for me to locate you. Instead you became the fodder for gossip all over London—the mysterious foreign governess who married a wealthy marquess. After hearing a few of the stories, I knew it could only be you." He subjected her silk-clad form to a contemptuous glance. "Apparently your taste for luxury is stronger than your common sense." Gently he lifted her white-knuckled fist, surveying the thick gold band on her finger. "What is your husband like? Some rich old man with a yen for young flesh, I suppose. Someone should tell him what a dangerous child you are."

Nikolas gestured for the cossacks to shove her inside the carriage, but not before he saw the flicker of alarm in Tasia's eyes. Spinning around, he narrowly avoiding the whistling swing of an ivory umbrella handle. The knob missed his head and struck his shoulder with bruising force. Acting swiftly, he yanked away the makeshift weapon and seized the gangly young girl who had used it. She opened her wide mouth to scream.

"Make a sound and I'll have her neck broken in an instant," he said.

The girl fell silent, staring at him with blazing blue eyes. She was flushed with fury and fear. The contrast between her scorching pink face and fiery hair—the color of rare red amber—was enchanting.

"Another dangerous child," Nikolas said with a quiet laugh, holding her lanky, flat-chested body against his.

One of the cossacks addressed him in Russian. "Your Highness—"

"It's all right," he said curtly, answering in kind. "Get into the carriage with the woman."

The child he held spoke in a hoarse voice. "Let my stepmother go, you bastard!"

"I'm afraid I can't, my charming little beast. Where did you learn such bad words?"

The girl tried to wrench away from him. "Where are you taking her?"

"To Russia, where she'll be made to pay the price for her crimes." Nikolas grinned and released her, watching her stagger back a few steps. "Goodbye, little girl. And thank you—it's been a long time since anyone has made me smile."

She turned and ran wildly into the store. Nikolas stood watching her for a moment before he went to the carriage, climbed in, and signaled the driver to leave.

Charles Ashbourne sat on the library settee with his wife weeping against his shoulder. Emma occupied a leather chair, hugging her knees to her chest. She was quiet and pale with grief. Luke stood by the window, his gaze fixed on the river view. Having been summoned from a meeting of the Northern Briton Railway Company board with a succinct message that he was needed at home, he had raced to the villa to find the Ashbournes there with Emma. His daughter had been nearly hysterical. Tasia was nowhere in sight.

Prompted by Charles, Alicia had explained to the best of her knowledge what had happened. "I left her for a moment to look at the silk scarves," she faltered, "and suddenly she and Emma were gone. And then Emma came running in, screaming about some Russian man with yellow eyes who had taken Tasia into his carriage—I can't think of how he found her, except that he must have been following me—dear heaven, we'll never see her again!" She broke down and cried, while Charles patted her back and tried to calm her.

Except for her weeping, everything was quiet. Luke turned to look at the Ashbournes. He was trembling all over, with rage and a hint of madness that made everyone in the room cringe in anticipation of an explosion. But he remained wordless and white-faced. Unconsciously he traced his fingers over the wicked curve of the silver hook, as if it were a weapon about to be put to use.

Unable to bear the silence, Charles spoke nervously. "What now, Stokehurst? I suppose we could attempt some sort of negotiation through government channels—after all, we have an ambassador in St. Petersburg, and perhaps an envoy could be sent to appeal—"

"I don't need a damned envoy," Luke said, striding to the open doorway. "*Biddle!*" His voice echoed through the house like a peal of thunder.

The valet appeared in a flash. "Yes, my lord?"

"Make an appointment for me to meet with the foreign minister this afternoon. Tell him it's urgent."

"My lord, what if he refuses—"

"Tell him I'll find him no matter where he goes. He may as well make an appointment."

"Anything else, my lord?"

"Yes. Book passage for two to St. Petersburg. If there isn't a ship scheduled to depart within the next twenty-four hours, charter one."

"Sir, may I ask who will be accompanying you?"

"You."

"But my lord," the valet spluttered, "I couldn't *possibly*—"

"Go. When you're finished with everything else, you can start packing for me."

Biddle obeyed, muttering under his breath and shaking his head violently.

Charles approached Luke with quiet concern. "What can I do?"

"Take care of Emma while I'm gone."

"Of course."

Luke glanced at his daughter, and his face softened at the sight of her tear-swollen eyes. He crossed the room and sat beside her, drawing her close as she broke into renewed sobs.

"Oh, Papa," she said miserably, "I didn't know what to do—I just f-followed Belle-mère, and when I saw what was happening, I should have run for help, but I didn't stop to th-think—"

"It's all right." Luke gave her a crushing hug. "You couldn't have stopped it, no matter what you did. It's my fault, and no one else's. I should have done a better job of protecting you both."

"Why did that man want her? Who is she? Has she done something wrong? I don't understand anything that's happened—"

"I know you don't," he murmured. "She's done nothing wrong. But she's been unjustly blamed for a man's death, and there are people in Russia who want to punish her. The man you saw today is taking her back there."

"Are you going to bring her home again?"

"Yes," he murmured. "Don't doubt it for a second, Emma." His voice was soft, but his expression was cold and grim. "Prince Nikolas Angelovsky hasn't begun to realize what he's done. No one takes what is mine."

The ship *Eastern Light* was a small, serviceable merchantman, laden with English wheat, fine porcelain, and textiles. The weather was calm. All signs promised that the ship would make a good run, perhaps no longer than a week. As captain of the vessel, Nikolas preferred to spend most of his time on deck, making certain the crew's duties were performed with the same exacting precision that he attended to his. It was no rich man's conceit, Nikolas's decision to command the ship. He possessed excellent navigational skills, and the brutal, decisive nature of a born leader. He charted a familiar course across the North Sea, heading east to the Baltic, and through the mouth of the Neva River, where St. Petersburg sprawled in stony majesty.

At the end of the first day at sea, Nikolas went to the cabin where he kept Tasia locked in solitude. Even the cabin boy had been forbidden to speak to her, should she happen to call through the door.

Tasia, who had been reclining on the narrow bed, sat up with a start as he entered the room. She was wearing the same clothes she had been captured in, a suit made of amber silk and trimmed with black velvet ribbon. Since Nikolas had apprehended her in London, she hadn't said a word or shed a single tear. She supposed she was in a state of shock, now that the thing she had dreaded most had finally happened. It was difficult to make herself understand that the past had reclaimed her with such chilling ease. She stared at Nikolas in wary silence, taking in every move as he closed the door.

His face was wooden, except for the contemptuous curl at the corners of his mouth. "You're wondering what I want from you now, little cousin. You're about to find out."

Casually Nikolas strode to the brass-banded trunk against the wall. The well-oiled hinges made no sound as he lifted the lid. Tasia scooted backward on the bed, wedging her back against the paneled wall. She was tense, the silk beneath her arms turning moist with sweat. Confused, she watched him pull a wad of cloth from the trunk.

Nikolas approached her with the object clutched in his fist. "Recognize this?"

Tasia shook her head. He unfolded the garment and held it up. A cry was torn from her throat. She sat rigidly against the wall, her gaze riveted on the white tunic that Mikhail had worn the night of his death. It was designed in the traditional Russian style of the boyars, with a high gold-embroidered collar and long, wide sleeves. Ugly brown and black stains covered the front of the tunic ... the residue of Mikhail's blood.

"I've been saving it for this occasion," Nikolas said softly. "I want you to tell me exactly what happened the night my brother died ... his last words, the look on his face ... everything. You owe it to me."

"I don't remember," she said, her voice breaking.

"Then have a closer look. Perhaps this will jar your memory."

"Nikolas, please—"

"Look at it."

Tasia stared at the blood-crusted garment, the contents of her stomach pushing upward. She tried to hold down her gorge, but it seemed that the sickening-sweet smell of fresh blood was in her nostrils, the air was warm and rank around her ... and the objects in the room began to revolve in a steady whirl. "I'm going to be sick," she said thickly, her mouth filling with a sour taste. "Take it away ..."

"Tell me what happened to Misha." He held it even closer, until the dried brown stains filled her vision. She moaned and held her hand over her mouth, gagging. Suddenly he shoved a basin beneath her bowed head, and she vomited in violent spasms. Tears streamed from her eyes. Blindly she accepted a linen towel he handed her, and dried her face.

She looked up again and recoiled in horror as she saw that Nikolas was putting on the tunic, the garment straining over his shoulders, the death-pattern spread down his front. It had been a waterfall of bright red when Misha had worn the tunic, the knife protruding from his throat, his eyes bulging with pain and fear as he staggered toward her, reaching out for her—

"*Nooooo*—" she screamed, flailing with her stiff arms as Nikolas came nearer, a nightmare come to life—*stayawaystayaway*—her screams shot through the room, and her head was filled with a brilliant light, exploding, suddenly eclipsed by merciful darkness. The memory came back in a devastating flood. "*Misha*," she sobbed, and fell slowly into the endless black pit, where there was no speech, no sight, no sound, nothing but the pieces of her shattered soul.

Nine
❦ ❦

Nikolas was waiting by the bed when Tasia returned to consciousness. He had removed the stained tunic. In spite of his air of cold calmness, he was sweating from some strong emotion, perhaps anxiety or anger. The black shirt clung damply to his golden skin. He wanted so badly to know, she thought with an unwarranted flicker of pity. Was he motivated by grief for his dead brother, or merely a desire for justice?

Dazed, Tasia stared at him and licked her dry lips. "I'll tell you what happened that night," she said hoarsely. "Every detail. But first I need some water."

Nikolas poured her a glass of water and brought it to her without a word. He sat on the bed, watching as she levered herself to an upright position. She drank thirstily.

Tasia hardly knew how to begin. The memory had come to her in full-bodied strength, and with it all the emotions she had felt that night. But finally knowing the truth, being able to tell someone, filled her with relief.

"I didn't want the engagement with Misha," she said. "From everything I knew and heard of him, he was a strange, tormented man who played with people as a child plays with dolls. I didn't hate him as much as I feared him. Everyone was pleased by the engagement, telling me I would be a good influence on him." She laughed bitterly. "I think they had somehow convinced themselves that I might be able to tempt him into liking women. Shallow, stupid people! Even in my innocence I knew that a man who desired boys was never going to want me in his bed. At best I would have been a front for Mikhail, to give him the image of a properly married man. At worst, I would have been an object of perverted amusement for him, someone to hurt and degrade. He would have given me to other men, and made me do unnatural things no human being should do—"

"You don't know that for certain."

"Yes, I do," she said softly. "And so do you." When Nikolas didn't answer, she finished her water and continued. "I came to the conclusion that I was trapped. My own mother insisted on the marriage. It was strange, but the only one I could turn to for help was Misha himself. I considered it for several days. Finally I decided that I had nothing to lose by talking to him. There was a chance he would listen. There was something childlike about Misha—at times he seemed like a little boy wanting attention. And he had moments of capriciousness. I thought I might be able to convince him to release me from the engagement. A few words from him could have changed my fate so easily . . . so I went to him one night, to plead with him in private."

Tasia set the empty glass aside and twisted her fingers into a knot. Her eyes fixed on the woolen blanket that was folded in a rectangle and draped over the end of the bed. Staring steadily at the blanket, she spoke in a dreamlike manner.

"The palace was nearly empty. Only a skeleton

staff was there to attend to Misha's needs. I wore a shawl over my hair, and pulled it low to hide my face. The front door was unlocked. I entered without knocking or ringing the bell. Some of the servants saw me wandering through the palace, but they didn't try to stop me. I was very nervous. I remember hoping that Misha hadn't smoked so much opium that he would be insensible. At first I couldn't find him. I went upstairs and went from room to room. It was very messy. There was a smell in the air, like smoke and bad wine and rotting food. There were piles of furs and silk pillows on the floors, and half-eaten meals, and strange objects that Misha must have used for ... well, I didn't know what they were for. Nor did I care to."

Tasia's hands unclenched, and she made a fluttering motion, as if to pull something from her hair. "It was very warm in the house. I took off the shawl ..." Her fingers went to her throat and pressed to her throbbing pulse. "I called his name once or twice ... 'Misha, where are you?' ... but no one answered. I thought perhaps he might be in the library, sitting with his pipe. I walked to the end of the hall. Voices ... two voices were arguing loudly, passionately, and a man was crying ..."

The memory swept over her, and Tasia lost awareness of speaking.

"Misha, I love you, a thousand times more than she ever could. She'll never be able to give you what you need."

"You jealous, wrinkled old fool," Mikhail replied. *"You know nothing about what I need."*

"I won't share you with anyone, especially not a spoiled girl."

Mikhail's voice was silky, amused, taunting. *"Does it*

bother you to think of her in my bed? That fresh young body, all that innocence waiting to be corrupted ..."

"Misha, don't torment me like this!"

"I don't want you anymore. Leave now, and never come back. The sight of you tires me. In fact, it makes me sick."

"No, you're my life, you're everything—"

"I'm sick of your sniveling and whining and your pathetic attempts at lovemaking. I'd rather do it with a dog. Now get out of here."

The other man howled in agony, screaming and sobbing. There was a cry of surprise, a scuffle, violent sounds ...

"I was terrified," Tasia said, trying to steady her voice. The taste of tears was fresh on her lips, stinging the cracked surface. "But I couldn't stop myself from going into the room. I wasn't thinking, I had no idea what had happened. The other man was standing there like a wax statue. Mikhail was staggering away from him. Then Misha saw me, and started to make his way to me. There was so much blood, and the knife was sticking out of his throat, and he reached for me, staring ... as if he were begging for my help. I froze in place. I couldn't seem to make my feet move, and then ... Misha fell on top of me ... and everything went black. When I woke, the letter-knife was in my hand, sticky with blood. The other man made it look as if I had killed Mikhail, but I didn't." She gave an incredulous, tear-blurred laugh. "All these months I thought I had murdered a man. I suffered the most agonizing guilt, and no amount of prayer, fasting, or repentance could absolve it ... but I *didn't do it.*"

"What is the name of the man who killed Misha?" Nikolas asked softly.

"Samvel Ignatyich, Count Shurikovsky. I know without a doubt. I met him once at the Winter Palace."

Nikolas showed no reaction. He stood and regarded her with those unnerving eyes. Slowly he walked away.

As he reached the door, Tasia spoke. "You don't believe me?"

"No."

Tasia considered that for a moment. "It doesn't matter. I know the truth now."

Nikolas turned and smiled with contempt. "Count Shurikovsky is a respected man and a devoted husband, who happens to be the companion-favorite of the tsar. For years Shurikovsky has been the tsar's closest confidant and most trusted adviser, and the strongest supporter of his reforms. Without Shurikovsky's influence, the serfs of all the Russias would never have been liberated nine years ago. On top of all that, he's just been appointed governor of St. Petersburg. I find it charming that you chose to name Shurikovsky as my brother's lover and murderer. Why not say it was the tsar himself?"

"The truth is the truth," she said simply.

"As any Russian knows, the truth has many sides," he sneered, leaving the cabin.

It made sense that Biddle liked ships. On a ship everything was scrubbed clean and organized and lashed down. Luke realized with a touch of sour amusement that his valet's passion for keeping all things in their rightful places was perfectly appropriate on a ship—necessary, in fact—whereas it was an annoyance everywhere else. For his part, Luke had no special fondness for the ocean, and this journey was the most miserable one he had ever undertaken.

Luke paced between his cabin and the deck of the schooner, seldom stopping for long at either place. He couldn't relax, couldn't sit or stand still. He ate reluctantly and talked only when it was imperative. By turns morose and enraged, Luke entertained himself with thoughts of what he was going to do to Nikolas Angelovsky when he found him. He was terrified for Tasia's safety, and he was overwhelmed with self-hatred. He had failed her. He was supposed to be her protector. Through his lack of foresight, she had been stolen away with consummate ease.

The possibility of losing Tasia wasn't something he let himself think about, except at night when his dreams betrayed him. After Mary had died, he had been able to go on with some semblance of a normal life. He couldn't this time. Losing Tasia would break him permanently. He would have no love, no kindness to offer anyone, not even his daughter.

One night Luke stood at the stern of the ship for hours, staring at the wide, foam-ruffled wake it left in its path. It was late, and the sky was starless, a dull pewter shade with darker clouds streaked across. The sound of the waves was rhythmic and soothing. He remembered the night he had held Tasia and listened to the forest music with her, one of the ridiculous, sublime moments that only lovers would understand ... and suddenly he felt her with him so intensely that he half-expected to turn and see her there. He looked down at the gold ring that had belonged to her father, and the memory of her voice was sweet in his ears . . . "It says, '*Love is a golden vessel, it bends but never breaks.*' "

And his reply . . . "*We'll be all right, you and I.*"

His hand clenched into a fist. "I'm coming for you," he said, his rough voice mingling with the wind. "I'll find you soon, Tasia."

Ten
❧ ❧

St. Petersburg, Russia

As soon as the anchors were let go from the cat-heads and the ship was moored at the wharf, Luke and Biddle went ashore. There was a marketplace near the St. Petersburg Admiralty and shipyards. Luke made his way toward the main thorough-fare, while Biddle followed carrying their bags. They strode into the middle of a scene more for-eign than any Luke had experienced before. Build-ings, walls, and doors were painted with vivid colors that gave the area a circuslike atmosphere. The merchants wore long red or blue tunics, while the women wore flowered headscarves. Everyone seemed to be singing. Vendors called out musical descriptions of their wares, pedestrians hummed or sang as they meandered down the street—it gave Luke a discomforting feeling of conspicuous-ness, as if he had inadvertently wandered onto an opera stage.

Luke smelled fish everywhere. In addition to the strong scent that drifted from the ocean and the fish rafts on the Neva River, the market was filled with every conceivable kind of catch. Salmon, pike, eel, perch, and huge sturgeon reposed in crates stuffed with melting ice. A half-dozen shades of caviar were sold in large casks. Tiny translucent fish were bought by the shovelful and carried away in sacks and buckets. In the heat, their odor was so rank that any self-respecting English cat would have turned its nose up at them. "*Znitki*," one of the merchants explained, grinning at Luke's obvious repulsion.

The color and confusion of St. Petersburg were common to any large city—except that here it was more colorful and more confused than any place he'd been in his life. The streets were congested with people, animals, and vehicles. The river and canals were cluttered with boats of all sizes. There were churches of every denomination, ringing bells in a noisy cacophony. After ten minutes Luke gave up all attempts to make sense of it. He didn't intend to stay in St. Petersburg long enough to know anything more about it than he already did. All he wanted was to retrieve his wife, and never set eyes on Russia again.

Biddle, however, was not so easily daunted. He set about subduing the city, with an umbrella tucked firmly beneath one arm and a copy of the *British Traveler's Handbook for Russia* in the other hand. They wandered through the marketplace, past a row of stalls filled with a profusion of exotic flowers. A chattering tea seller came up to them, bearing a leather case filled with glasses and a pitcher full of brown liquid he called *kvas*, and thick slices of ginger cake. At Luke's curt nod, Biddle purchased two glasses of the stuff, and some cake. *Kvas* turned out to be a mild rye beer flavored with honey. Strange, but not unpleasant, Luke thought, finishing the drink.

The faces of the Russians interested him. Most of them were fair, with elegant features and blue eyes, but many had a more exotic Eastern appearance; broad faces and beautiful slanted eyes. Tasia's looks were a combination of both, melded into delicate and exquisite harmony. At the thought of his wife, his throat became tight, and the agonized fury that had been with him ever since her abduction began to build.

"Sir?" Biddle questioned nervously, apparently alarmed by his expression. "Was the beverage not to your liking?"

"The Kurkov Palace," Luke muttered. That was where the English ambassador was lodged. It was all he could bring himself to say.

"Right away, my lord." Gamely Biddle wandered to the streetside and began gesturing with his umbrella. "I will attempt to hire a hack. The book says these are called something like, er, *drozhki*, and not to be disturbed if the driver carries on a conversation with the horse. They talk to their horses here."

They rented a tiny open carriage and told the driver to take them to the English embassy. In accord with Biddle's prediction, the driver kept up a running dialogue with his horse, named Osip. The vehicle moved through the city at an unholy pace, like every other contraption on the streets. Often the driver screamed to warn pedestrians of their approach. Twice they nearly mowed down people crossing the road. Whether it was in a rickety cart or a fine lacquered carriage, Russians drove exceptionally fast.

St. Petersburg was a city of stone, water, and bridges. Even Luke, with his predisposition to hate everything about the place, had to admit it was beautiful. According to Biddle's recitation from the *British Traveler's Handbook*, St. Petersburg had been willed into existence a little more than a century and a half ago by the desire of Peter the Great to bring Western culture to Russia. Peter had succeeded magnificently. Some parts of the city seemed almost more European than Europe itself. The carriage passed astonishing rows of sumptuous palaces set along the granite embankments of the river. There were lions everywhere, made of stone, bronze, and iron, placed to guard bridges and buildings with their frozen grimaces.

The English ambassador, Lord Bramwell, was lodged at the handsome Kurkov Palace. It was located on eastern Nevsky Prospekt, the central street of the city. The carriage stopped in front of the building, a classical structure with pediments and tall white columns. Luke climbed out and strode up the wide marble steps, leaving Biddle to struggle with the bags and pay the driver. Two huge cossacks dressed in scarlet tunics and high black boots guarded the doors of the palace.

"I've come to see Lord Bramwell," Luke said brusquely.

The cossacks conferred with each other. One of them answered in broken English. "Is not possible," he said with a threatening stare.

"Why?"

"Lord Bramvell giving banquet for governor of city. Come later. Tomorrow. Next veek, maybe."

Luke glanced at Biddle in dismay. "Did you hear that? We're late for the banquet—" As he spoke, he turned and drove his fist deep into the cossack's stomach, causing him to double over. A blow to the back of the neck sent the man to a crumpled heap on the stairs. The other guard started for Luke, but froze with a gasp as Luke brandished his left arm. Luke smiled with patent menace, fully aware of the silver hook's shock value. "Come on," he invited softly.

The cossack shook his head swiftly, staring at the hook. He backed away and eased down the stairs.

"Sir, I've never seen you like this," Biddle murmured, looking at Luke in concern.

"You've seen me hit a man before."

"Yes, but you didn't seem to *enjoy* it quite so much—"

"I'm just getting started," Luke muttered, and pushed open the front doors.

The palace was filled with ivy, magnolias, and orchids. There were miles of polished wooden floors, with inlaid patterns of contrasting colors that gave them the appearance of Persian carpets. Liveried servants were positioned at every corner, standing as still as statues. Not a single pair of eyes lifted to Luke's face. "Where is Lord Bramwell?" he asked one of them. When that failed to provoke a response, he repeated impatiently, "Bramwell."

Timidly the servant pointed down one of the shining halls. "Bramvell."

"Sir," came Biddle's worried voice behind him. Biddle detested scenes, and he clearly sensed that one was imminent. "Perhaps I should wait in the entrance hall with the bags?"

"Yes, stay here," Luke replied, going in search of Lord Bramwell's banquet.

Biddle retreated to the entrance hall with obvious relief. "Thank you, my lord!"

Columns covered with gold and semiprecious stones lines the halls. The sounds of many conversations held in French—the language of diplomacy—poured from an open set of double doors decorated in a mosaic of gold tile and blue lapis. The sounds of a delicate stringed instrument, a zither or something similar, provided background music. Luke walked into the banquet hall, where at least two hundred foreign officials were seated at a long bronze table.

Servants dressed in gold and velvet paused in the act of pouring chilled champagne. The table was laden with meats, sweetbreads, cold salads, pies and dumplings, sour cream and caviar. Giant silver bowls filled with pickled mushrooms or salted cucumber were placed at measured intervals, in addition to enameled dishes of mustard and salt. A roasted peacock, feathers carefully spread in a brilliant fan, served as the centerpiece.

The distinguished guests fell silent at Luke's unexpected intrusion. The music stopped.

Luke recognized the ambassadorial insignias of Denmark, Poland, Austria, France, Germany, Sweden. He spared a brief glance at the guest of honor, who was seated at the head of the table. The governor was a lean, gray-haired man with aristocratic bone structure and dark, slanted Tartar eyes. His chest was laden with gold medals and jeweled buttons.

Noticing that the English ambassador was seated at the governor's right hand, Luke reached him in a few purposeful strides.

"Lord Bramwell," he said, while all gazes turned to him.

The ambassador was plump and pink-faced, with porcine features and a pair of beady eyes staring out from beneath two sparse eyebrows. "I am Bramwell," he said haughtily. "This interruption is most irregular—"

"I must speak with you."

Soldiers on sentry duty came forward to apprehend Luke. He swiveled to face them with a menacing stare.

"No, it's all right," Lord Bramwell said with imperious calm, holding up his pudgy hands to keep the sentries at bay. "This fellow has obviously gone to a great deal of trouble to see me. We'll let him speak. In spite of his lapse of manners, he has the appearance of a gentleman."

Luke introduced himself. "Lucas, Lord Stokehurst."

Bramwell regarded him thoughtfully. "Stokehurst ... Stokehurst ... if I'm not mistaken, you're the unfortunate husband of Anastasia Ivanovna Kaptereva."

Whispers flew around the table.

"Yes, I'm the husband," Luke said grimly. "I've come to discuss my wife's situation with you. If you'd care to conduct this in private—"

"No, no ... that won't be necessary." Bramwell gave Luke a patronizing smile and glanced at his guests as if to convey the difficulty of reasoning with a madman. "Regretfully, Lord Stokehurst, there's nothing I can do. It is my understanding that a date has already been set for your wife's hanging."

Luke had expected that the government would act quickly, but to actually hear the words "your wife's hanging" was like a kick in the stomach. It was hard to keep from leaping on the ambassador and ripping his throat out. Somehow he managed to keep his voice cold and steady. "I have a list of official actions I want you to take on my wife's behalf. You have the power to delay the execution."

"No, Lord Stokehurst, I cannot. In the first place, I am not disposed to risk my name and position in defense of a woman of questionable character. Moreover, I have no power to act until I receive instruction from my superiors in the foreign office in London. Now kindly remove your person from this gathering." Bramwell smiled smugly, settling back to his plate, clearly relishing the use of his power.

Gently Luke picked up the plate of exquisitely arranged food, sniffing appreciatively. He tossed it to the floor. The costly Sèvres plate fell with a splintering crash, sending shards of priceless china and clumps of food everywhere.

The room was silent. No one dared move or speak. Luke reached inside his coat. "Hmm ... I seem to recall ... ah, yes. Here we are." He slammed a thin folded sheaf of documents on the table in front of Bramwell. Several guests jumped at the sound. "Papers from the foreign minister in London, with detailed orders concerning the diplomatic actions you're to take in this matter. And if you don't convince your Russian counterparts that this is going to turn into an ugly international incident ..." The gleaming arc of his hook slid over Bramwell's shoulder. "... I might lose my temper," he finished softly. "We wouldn't want that."

Evidently the ambassador agreed. "I'll do everything I can to help you," he said hastily.

"Good." Luke smiled at him. "Let's go have a talk in private now."

"Certainly, my lord." Bramwell pushed back from the table and tried to assume the expression of genial host. "Please, everyone—Your Excellency—continue in my absence."

Governor Shurikovsky nodded regally. There was no sound until the nervous ambassador had

left the room with the large, sullen Englishman.
Then the assemblage burst into excited chatters.

Luke followed Bramwell into a small, private
drawing room. They closed the glass-paneled
door. "I imagine you have many questions," the
ambassador said, regarding Luke with a mixture
of dislike and fear.

"Just one for now. Where the hell is my wife?"

"You must understand. Public sentiment having
been aroused against her, and threats coming from
all quarters, there would be a great deal of risk in
keeping her at the official prison. And then, of
course, there is the matter of her previous
escape—"

"Where is she?" Luke growled.

"A pr-prominent citizen of St. Petersburg has
graciously offered to keep her in confinement at
his private residence while the state provides all
necessary security arrangements."

" 'Prominent citizen'?" Luke stared at him in furious disbelief. "Angelovsky," he said hoarsely. At
Bramwell's bobbing nod, he couldn't hold back an
explosion any longer. "Goddamned corrupt imperialist bastards—they've given her into Angelovsky's keeping? What next? Are they going to
accept his gracious offer to officially execute her
and save them the trouble? Is this a civilized country or something out of the Dark Ages? By God,
I'm going to kill someone soon—"

"My lord, please calm yourself!" the ambassador exclaimed, backing away from him. "I'm not
responsible for any of this!"

The blue eyes turned demonic. "If you don't do
everything in your power—and then some—to get

my wife out of this unholy mess, I'll grind your bones into powder beneath my heels."

"Lord St-Stokehurst, I *assure* you—" Bramwell began, but Luke was already leaving.

Walking with quick, ground-covering strides, Luke nearly bumped into a pair of men passing through the hall. He recognized the tall gray-haired one as the man who had been seated at the head of the table. His young companion was evidently an aide, dressed in an immaculate imperial uniform.

"Governor Shurikovsky," Bramwell said anxiously, "I hope you have not been too displeased by the interruption of our banquet."

Shurikovsky's slanted eyes fastened on Luke. "I wanted to see the Englishman."

Luke was silent, though his muscles tensed with challenge. God knew why the governor wanted to have a look at him. He felt an instinctive dislike for the man, whose eyes were as hard and dark as pebbles.

The aide spoke impudently, while the two men stared at each other. "What a strange tale this is! Prince Mikhail Angelovsky is murdered, the young woman who is responsible 'dies' in prison, several months later she is brought back to Russia very much alive, and now there is an English husband who wants to take her away again."

"You will not succeed," Shurikovsky said to Luke, his voice thin. "I speak for the government when I say that someone will pay for Angelovsky's death. Atonement must be made."

"Not by my wife," Luke replied softly. "Not in this life."

Before another word could be said, Luke was

gone in an instant, heading like a fast-moving storm to the Angelovsky Palace.

The Angelovsky residence was even more magnificent than the Kurkov Palace. The doors were decorated with gold, and the windows were bordered with strips of engraved silver. Works by painters such as Gainsborough and Van Dyck were framed in gold and precious gems. Chandeliers of crystal and enamel gave the impression of glittering floral arrangements hanging from the ceiling. Luke was privately astonished by the opulence around him. The queen of England didn't live in this kind of splendor. Or with this kind of security. Uniformed chevaliers, cossacks, and Circassian officers were everywhere, lining the entrance hall, the marble staircase, and every doorway.

To Luke's surprise, his demand to be taken to Prince Angelovsky was obeyed quickly and without question. Biddle was more than happy to be left waiting in the entrance hall, and Luke was led to a downstairs gentleman's room filled with tobacco smoke. The walls were covered with a collection of antique broadswords, rapiers, and Slavic axes with wickedly curved blades. In the center of the room was a turntable laden with decanters of liquor. A group of officers and aristocrats lounged in the room, sitting, standing, smoking, and talking. They all stared at the newcomer.

One of them disengaged himself from the group and stepped forward. He said something in Russian, saw that Luke didn't understand, and switched to lightly accented English. "What do you want?"

It had to be Angelovsky. He was younger than

Luke had expected, a man in his early twenties. He had startling yellow-gold eyes, a face of stark masculine beauty, and the exotic animallike quality Alicia Ashbourne had described. Luke had never wanted to kill someone so badly. A tremor of bloodlust went through him, but somehow he controlled it.

"I want to see my wife," he managed to say.

Angelovsky looked startled for a moment. He stared at Luke closely. "Stokehurst? Somehow I thought you'd be an old man." The corner of his mouth twitched with insolent amusement. "Welcome to Russia, cousin."

Luke was silent, clenching his teeth until his jaw trembled.

Seeing the faint movement, Nikolas mistook it for awe, perhaps even fear. He smiled into Luke's expressionless face. "You've wasted your time. The prisoner isn't allowed visitors. Take my advice—go back to your country and get a new wife."

He was taken by surprise as Luke moved with blinding speed, shoving him against the wall and snarling at him like a rabid wolf. The sharp point of the silver hook pressed into his chest until a drop of blood welled from the nick it had made.

Luke's voice was a scraping whisper. "Let me see her . . . or I'll use this to dig your heart out."

Nikolas stared at him for a moment, and then bared his teeth in a feral laugh of approval. "You have balls of stone, to threaten me in my own house, in a room full of weapons and soldiers! Very well, you may visit Anastasia. No harm will come of it. She'll still be mine when you leave. Now, if you please . . ." He glanced down at the spreading bloodstain on his shirt. Luke dislodged the stinging point of the hook and lowered his arm.

Taking a linen napkin, Nikolas pressed it to the sore spot on his chest. Still smiling, he spoke to a soldier. "Motka Yuriyevich, show my new cousin to the prisoner's quarters. And don't get too close—he may bite."

There were a few appreciative chuckles, for the Russians admired nothing more than brute force coupled with a strong will. To find that combination in an Englishman tickled their sense of humor.

Tasia's suite consisted of a small antechamber and a bedroom, both luxuriously furnished. She reclined on a sofa framed with lacy Russian woodcarving. Although she had not been allowed visitors, she had received a few tear-blotched, loving notes from her mother, Marie. Nikolas had allowed Marie to send a few of Tasia's old gowns from the Kapterev Palace. Tasia wore one of them now, a girlishly styled violet silk with a full skirt, puffed sleeves, and white lace trimming. Dully she sorted through a pile of French novels. So far her attempts at reading hadn't gone well. She found herself going over the same pages a dozen times.

She heard a key turning in the lock. The door opened and closed. Knowing it was one of the servants with an afternoon meal tray, Tasia kept her gaze on the book. "Put it on the table next to the window," she said in Russian.

Her order was met with silence. She looked up with a coldly questioning frown . . . and stared into a pair of smiling blue eyes. Her husband spoke in a rough voice. "I told you I didn't plan to sleep apart from you."

Tasia gave a cry of disbelief and flew across the room, flinging herself against him.

Luke laughed and caught her in the air, locking one arm around her narrow waist. Lowering her feet to the floor, he buried his face in the curve of her neck and shoulder. "God, I've missed you," he muttered, while she wriggled and tried to crawl closer.

"Luke, Luke . . . Oh, you came for me! Are you really here? No, it must be a dream!" Tasia slid her hands behind his head and pulled his mouth down, kissing him with violent passion. She reveled in his familiar smell, his taste, the solid strength of his body.

Somehow he managed to tear his mouth from hers. "We have to talk," he muttered.

"Yes . . . yes . . ." Tasia wrapped her arms around his neck and they kissed again, deep, yearning, heedlessly absorbed in each other. He pushed her against the wall, twisting his mouth over hers. Their tongues touched, played, slid hotly, while his fingers spread over her breast and molded the tender shape. Tasia nuzzled into the side of his neck, licking at the touch of salt on his skin. He groaned softly, urging her against the wall with the pressure of his aroused body.

"Are you all right?" he managed to ask, after smothering her with a brutally hard kiss.

She nodded and smiled unsteadily. "How is Emma? I've been so worried—"

"She wants you to come home as soon as possible."

"Oh, if only . . ." Tasia began with aching long- ing, but suddenly she jumped in excitement and clutched his shirt collar in her fists. "Luke, I re- membered everything on the ship! I know what happened to Mikhail! I didn't do *anything*. I stumbled on the scene at the worst possible moment, and I saw the real murderer. It wasn't me!"

His eyes narrowed. "Who did it?"

"Count Samvel Shurikovsky. He and Mikhail were lovers."

"Shurikovsky," Luke repeated, stunned. "The governor? I just saw him!"

"But how—"

"Never mind, just tell me everything."

Tasia related the story of all she had seen and heard the night of the murder, while Luke listened intently. His hand slid between the wall and her spine, keeping her pressed close to him. "But Nikolas doesn't believe me," she finished. "He *wants* me to be guilty, and he won't hear any evidence to the contrary. Count Shurikovsky is a very important man—the companion-favorite of the tsar. I'm certain that the servants knew he was in the palace that night, but they were afraid to say anything. Perhaps they were threatened or bribed to keep silent."

Luke was quiet, keeping his thoughts to himself. Tasia found it hard to believe he was actually there in St. Petersburg. The knowledge that he had followed her caused a burst of love and heat in her chest. She nestled against him with a sound of pleasure, and his arms tightened.

"Have you been eating?" he asked, kissing the edge of her temple where silken wisps of hair had escaped her pinned braids.

"Oh, yes, I have a very good appetite. They've sent up all my favorites: cabbage soup, blini with caviar, and the most wonderful mushrooms in cream. And big bowls of *kasha*."

"I won't ask what *kasha* is," Luke said wryly. He

surveyed her face, gently touching the dark circles beneath her eyes as if he could make them disappear. "You haven't gotten much rest."

Tasia shook her head. "They'll never let me go," she said softly. "I don't think there's anything you can do, Luke."

"There's a great deal I can do," he corrected gruffly. "I'm going to leave for a little while. Try to sleep until I come back."

"No," she said, clutching at him. "Don't leave yet . . . or I'll think I just imagined you. Hold me."

Luke enfolded her in a hard embrace. "My love," he said, his breath warm in the hollow beneath her ear. "My sweet, precious wife. Don't you know I would fight the world for you?"

She laughed shakily. "I think you may have to."

"The day of our wedding, I calculated the number of nights I was going to have with you. At least ten thousand. A week's worth has been stolen from me. Nothing is going to keep us apart for the rest."

"Don't . . ." Her fingertips came to his mouth. "You're tempting fate."

"I'll tell you what your fate is." Luke pulled back and stared into her eyes. "Nine thousand, nine hundred and ninety-three nights spent in my arms. And I'll have them, Lady Stokehurst, no matter what it takes."

Sitting on the carpeted steps with one leg propped up, Nikolas watched as Luke approached. "Now you've seen that she's being treated well. Food, books, furniture—"

"It's still a prison," Luke said coldly.

"Did Tasia tell you her story about Samvel

lgnatyich?" Nikolas smiled at Luke's blank look, and added, "Count Shurikovsky."

Pausing at the top of the steps, Luke looked down at him. "She told me you've decided not to believe her."

"There was never any relationship between Shurikovsky and Misha."

"Have you questioned Shurikovsky?" Luke asked.

"That would accomplish nothing, except to discredit me. It is a desperate lie that Tasia concocted in order to make us all look like fools."

"Then why wouldn't she come out with this story in court, during the trial? She didn't lie then. She's not lying now. But you'd rather send an innocent woman to her death than face an unpleasant truth."

"You dare mention the word 'truth'?" Nikolas's voice was suddenly thick. He stood and faced Luke squarely. He was just as tall as Luke, but with a far different build. Luke had a broad-shouldered, muscular body, whereas Nikolas was wiry, flexible, catlike. "I'd like to shove it back down your throat," Nikolas said. "Go question Shurikovsky with my blessing. I want to see your face when you realize what your wife has done."

Luke turned to leave.

"Wait," Nikolas muttered. "Don't try to see Shurikovsky now. Go tonight. After the sun sets. It is the Russian way to do these things privately, you understand?"

"I understand. Russians like to do everything in secrecy."

"We prefer the word 'discretion,'" Nikolas said mildly. "A virtue you don't seem to possess, cousin. I will go with you tonight. Shurikovsky doesn't speak any English. You'll need someone to translate."

Luke gave a harsh laugh. "You're the last person I'd take with me."

"You're a fool if you think I've persecuted your wife for personal reasons. If I could be proved wrong—if I came across evidence that Tasia has been unjustly accused—I would kiss the hem of her gown and beg her forgiveness. All I want is for my brother's murderer to be punished."

"You want a scapegoat," Luke said caustically. "You don't care who it is, as long as someone's blood is spilled in exchange for Mikhail's."

Nikolas's shoulders stiffened, but he showed no reaction. "I will go with you this evening, Stoke-hurst, to expose Tasia's lies and remove all doubt that she killed Misha."

Luke spent the afternoon harassing Lord Bram-well and his secretary until they began to write an official list of complaints about the mistreatment and illegal imprisonment of the wife of an English citizen. At sunset Luke returned to the Angelov-sky Palace. Nikolas greeted him while casually munching on an apple. The fruit was unusual, with pure white flesh and a translucent emerald skin. Nikolas smiled as he noticed Luke's interest. "A Russian glass-apple," he said, pulling one from his pocket. "I'm quite partial to them. Would you care to try one?"

Although he hadn't eaten all day, Luke shook his head.

Nikolas laughed. "The English are so proud," he mocked. "You are hungry, but you will not take food from my hand. It's only an apple, cousin." He tossed it toward Luke.

Luke caught it easily. "I'm not your cousin." He took a bite of the crisp, sugar-sweet fruit.

"But you are. Tasia is the granddaughter of my father's cousin. And now you are connected by marriage. Russians are very aware of all family ties, no matter how distant."

"Aware, but not loyal to them," Luke sneered.

"Murder does tend to put a damper on family relationships."

Exchanging a glance of mutual loathing, they went to the gleaming black carriage outside. The ride to Shurikovsky's home was excruciating, the silence infused with violent undertones. The streets were quiet. Warm light glowed from the windows of the homes and palaces they passed.

"Most likely Shurikovsky is with the tsar this evening," Nikolas said. At Luke's silence, he continued casually. "They are very close, almost like brothers. When the tsar goes to his country palace, *Tsarskoe Selo,* he always insists that Shurikovsky is part of the royal entourage. The governor is a man of great power and cunning."

"You respect him?"

"No, certainly not. Shurikovsky would kneel on the floor and bark like a dog if it would please the tsar."

"What do you know of his relationships?"

"There are none outside his marriage. Some men are driven by the desires of the flesh, but Shurikovsky isn't one of them. His appetite is for political power."

"You can't be that naive," Luke said.

"The circle of the Russian court is very small. It is impossible to keep secrets. If Shurikovsky had a taste for boys, everyone would know. There has never been a word. Not a whisper. And my brother always boasted about his conquests, in spite of the family's efforts to keep him quiet. Misha never mentioned or hinted to anyone that he even knew Shurikovsky. There was no relationship between them."

"So Mikhail was a family embarrassment," Luke mused. "How badly did the Angelovskys want to keep him quiet?"

For the first time, there was a flicker of emotion in the golden eyes. "Don't," Nikolas said in a low voice. "Don't even suggest it, or I'll . . ."

"You'll kill me?" Luke suggested, arching a dark brow. "I imagine you're capable of murder—family ties notwithstanding."

Nikolas kept his mouth closed, glaring at him. Hatred seethed in the air. Finally they reached Shurikovsky's residence, a two-story wooden manor house located on the Neva. There were two guards at the gilded and carved door. "*Dvornik*," Nikolas said, swinging out of the carriage. "Harmless watchmen. Before you begin to carve them up like roasted grouse, let me speak to them." Luke followed Nikolas from the carriage and watched as he exchanged a few words with the men and slipped them a handful of money. They were quickly and discreetly admitted entrance.

After speaking to an approaching manservant, Nikolas gestured for Luke to come with him along a hallway lined with gold brocade hangings. "None of the family is at home. Countess Shurikovsky is in the country. The governor is expected to return later this evening."

"And in the meanwhile?"

"We wait. And drink. Are you a drinking man, Stokehurst?"

"Not particularly."

"Russians have a saying, 'Not to drink is not to live.' "

They went to the library, designed in the European style with tall bookcases, mahogany furniture, and leather chairs. A servant brought glasses and a tray of chilled, frosted bottles. "The vodka is infused with different flavors," Nikolas said, pouring some amber liquid into a glass. He pointed to the array of bottles. "Birch bud, wood ash, pepper, lemon—"

"I'll take the birch," Luke said.

At Nikolas's request, the servant returned with another tray, piled with sardines, bread and butter, and caviar. Nikolas settled back in his chair with an air of contentment, holding his vodka in one hand and a sliver of dark bread piled with black caviar in the other. He finished both in short order and refilled his glass. The yellow eyes regarded Luke intently. Suddenly he gestured to the hook on Luke's left arm. "How did that happen?" he asked, sipping his second vodka more slowly.

"I was injured in a fire."

"Ah." The syllable expressed neither sympathy nor surprise. Nikolas continued to stare at him assessingly. "Why did you marry Tasia? Were you hoping to claim some of her fortune?"

"I have no need of her money," Luke said coldly.

"Then why? As an obligation to your friends the Ashbournes?"

"No." Luke tilted his head and swallowed the rest of his vodka. The drink was smooth and cold at first, but afterward came a stinging rush of heat that burned his nose and throat.

"For love, then," Nikolas said. Surprisingly, there was no mockery in his voice. "Of course.

You've never met anyone like Anastasia Ivanovna before, have you?"

"No," Luke admitted gruffly.

"That is because Tasia was brought up according to the old Russian tradition of *terem*. She was hidden in the country, away from all men except her father and a few close relatives. Very sheltered. Like a bird in a golden cage. It was common to do this a few generations ago, but rare in these days. After Tasia's first *bal blanc*, every man in St. Petersburg wanted her. Strange, quiet, beautiful girl. It was rumored that she was a witch. I could almost believe it myself, looking into those eyes. All the men feared and desired her. Except me." Nikolas paused to refill Luke's glass. "I wanted her for my brother."

"Why?"

"Misha needed someone to take care of him and understand the demons inside him. He needed a wife who was wellborn, intuitive, intelligent, capable of great endurance, and above all, a woman whose sense of duty would make her stay with him in spite of his abuse. I saw all those qualities in Tasia."

Luke glared at him. "Did you consider that instead of helping Mikhail, she might have been destroyed by him?"

"Of course. But that didn't matter, as long as there was a chance of saving Misha."

"He got what he deserved," Luke said with a grim smile, tossing back more of the vodka.

"And now so will Tasia."

Luke stared at the Russian, hatred uncoiling inside him. If anything happened to Tasia, he would make Angelovsky pay. They were both quiet, letting the vodka work its numbing effect on the senses. It was the only thing that kept Luke from leaping on the Russian prince and ripping his throat out.

Quietly a servant came to the library and addressed Nikolas in muffled tones. A conversation ensued, until finally Nikolas waved the servant away. He turned to Luke with a frown. "He says Shurikovsky has returned, but he is ill." He shrugged. "Too much to drink. Do you still want to speak with the governor tonight?"

Luke stood up. "Where is he?"

"In his bedchamber, preparing to retire." Nikolas rolled his eyes as he saw the determination on Luke's face. "All right, we'll go to him. With any luck he'll be too drunk to remember anything afterward. Only five minutes, understand? After that we leave."

They went upstairs to a lavish suite of rooms. Shurikovsky was seated on the edge of the bed, waiting passively as a servant undressed him. The governor looked completely different from the polished, self-possessed man who had presided over his own banquet earlier in the day. The gray hair was sticking out in untidy spikes. The keen eyes were now hazy and shot with red. Through the opening of his unbuttoned shirt, the drooping muscles of his chest were visible. The reek of wine and smoke was strong in the air, drifting from his sagging body.

"I don't know why I'm doing this," Nikolas whispered sharply, as he walked into the room. He raised his voice. "Governor Shurikovsky . . . Your Excellency . . ." He paused and spoke brusquely to the startled servant. "Get out."

Requiring no further prompting, the servant darted from the room. He brushed past Luke without a word. Luke stayed in the shadows by the door. Instinct kept him from moving forward. He sensed that his presence was better left undetected for the moment. A strange scene unfolded before him, one that he struggled to understand in spite of the language barrier.

"Your Excellency, I apologize for disturbing you," Nikolas said in Russian, walking to the slumped figure at the edge of the bed. "I'll be brief, and then leave you to your rest. There is something I would like to ask you, sir, concerning the death of my brother, Mikhail Dmitriyevich. Your Excellency, do you recall every making the acquaintance of—"

"Misha," the gray-haired man said thickly, staring up at the golden-eyed man before him. Miraculously he seemed to come to life. His shoulders straightened. His face glowed as if he beheld a wondrous vision. The dark eyes glistened with tears. "Oh, my beautiful boy, my lovely cub, how you've haunted me! I knew you'd come back, darling Misha."

Nikolas froze, his expression turning blank. "What?" he whispered.

Shurikovsky's thin fingers went to the hem of Nikolas's coat, tugging urgently. Slowly Nikolas obeyed the silent command, sinking to his knees before the seated man. His yellow eyes didn't move from Shurikovsky's face. He stayed absolutely still as the governor's trembling hand moved in a caress over his golden-brown hair. Shurikovsky's lean face contorted with loving agony. "My beautiful Misha, I didn't want to hurt you. You made me so upset with your talk of leaving me. But you're here now, *lyubezny*, that's all that matters."

From the doorway, Luke saw the tremor that went through Nikolas Angelovsky's body. Luke frowned in bewilderment.

"What did you do?" Nikolas whispered, his eyes locked with Shurikovsky's.

The governor smiled with ecstasy and madness. "Darling boy ... you'll never leave me, will you? All the sweetness of heaven is in your arms. And you need me too ... that's why you came back to your Samvel." Tenderly he traced the taut line of Nikolas's cheek. "I was destroyed at the thought of losing you. No one understands ... No one loves to the depth that we do. When you mocked me so cruelly, I went crazy, and I took the letter-knife on the table into my hand ... All I could think of was that I had to stop your words, your terrible laughter." He began to croon gently. "Wicked, lovely boy ... all's forgiven now. We'll add it to our other secrets ... my dearest love ..." He bent down intently.

Nikolas jerked away before Shurikovsky's lips touched his. He rose to his feet, breathing through his clenched teeth, shivers rippling through his body. Bewildered, gray-faced, Nikolas shook his head. Suddenly he moved like a startled cat, fleeing the room. The governor collapsed on the bed with uncontrollable sobs.

Luke followed Nikolas in the headlong dash from the house. "Angelovsky," he growled. "Damn you ... tell me what happened!"

Nikolas stopped as soon as he reached the fresh air outside. He paused, staggered forward a few steps to the side of the street, and stood there with his face averted. He struggled to catch his breath.

"What did he say?" Luke demanded. "For God's sake—"

"He confessed," Nikolas managed to say.

"An old man's drunken ramblings," Luke said, though his heart was pounding.

Nikolas shook his head, still hiding his face. "No. He killed Misha. There is no doubt."

Luke closed his eyes in relief. "Thank God," he whispered.

Alerted to their presence, the coachman urged the Angelovsky carriage forward and stopped. Nikolas was oblivious to everything, occupied with his inner chaos. "I don't believe it. It was easier to think that Tasia was guilty ... so much easier."

"Now we'll go to the police," Luke said.

Nikolas laughed bitterly. "You understand nothing about Russia! Perhaps in England it is different, but here no one in the government is ever guilty of anything. Especially a man who is close to the tsar. Too many things—reforms, policies— hinge on Shurikovsky's influence. If he falls, so will all the others who have attached themselves to him. You make a single noise about Shurikovsky, and you'll end up floating in the Neva with your throat slit. There is no justice here. I'd stake my life on the fact that someone else knew about the governor's affair with Misha. I'll bet the minister of the interior was aware of it—he's made a career out of using others' dirty little secrets for his own advantage. But it was easier for everyone involved to mishandle the investigation and trial, and sacrifice Tasia for the 'greater good.' "

Luke was outraged. "If you think I'll let my wife be executed in order to pacify your stinking government officials—"

"At the moment I can't think." Nikolas gave

him a baleful glance. His color was returning, and he seemed to be breathing easier.

"I'm getting Tasia out of this godforsaken country as soon as possible."

Nikolas nodded jerkily. "On that we agree."

Luke gave him a cynical smile. "Forgive me if I find this sudden turnaround hard to accept. A few minutes ago you were ready to execute her yourself."

"From the beginning all I've wanted was the truth."

"You could have looked a little harder for it."

"How brilliant at hindsight you English are," Nikolas sneered. "You always do the right thing the right way, don't you? All your bloodless rules and laws and documents ... You respect nothing unless it's been made over in your image. You think only the English are civilized, and everyone else is a barbarian."

"Of course this experience will convince me otherwise," Luke said sarcastically.

Nikolas sighed and scratched his head, ruffling the sun-streaked locks. "Tasia's life here is finished. I can't change that. But I'll help you to return her safely to England. It's my fault she's in danger now."

"And Shurikovsky?" Luke murmured.

Nikolas glanced at the nearby driver and dropped his voice to a whisper. "I'll take care of him. I'll have my justice."

Luke stared at the vengeful young man and shook his head. "You can't murder him in cold blood."

"It's the only way for it to be done. And I'm the one to do it."

"The governor is obviously crumbling under the

weight of his guilt. He'll finish himself off soon
enough. Why not let time take care of it?"

"Could you stand by and do nothing if your
brother had been murdered?"

"I don't have a brother."

"Your little red-haired daughter, then. Wouldn't
you seek revenge, if there was no other way for
her murder to be punished?"

Luke stiffened and kept silent.

"Perhaps you believe a self-indulgent parasite
like Misha isn't worth all this trouble," Nikolas
said softly. "You think he was no great loss to anyone. You may be right. But I'll never forget that
once he was an innocent child. I want you to understand something—Misha was not to blame for
the way he was. Our mother was a stupid peasant
woman whose only skill was breeding children.
Our father was a monster. He . . ." Nikolas swallowed audibly and continued without emotion.
"Sometimes I would find my brother in a dark
corner, or a closet, crying and bleeding. Everyone
knew he was an object of my father's lust. I don't
know why he chose to molest Misha and not me.
No one dared to interfere. Once I tried to confront
my father, and he didn't stop beating me until I
was senseless. It's not a pleasant thing, to be at the
mercy of a man who has none. Finally I was old
enough to . . . convince my father to stay away
from Misha. But by then it was too late. My
brother was destroyed before he ever had a chance
at a decent life." Nikolas's mouth twisted in a thin
smile. "And so was I."

Luke stared down the grand, melancholy street,
at the foreign silhouette of an onion dome, at the
buildings standing in a stalwart line along the
river. He had never felt so uncomfortable, so out

of place ... so English. This beautiful, complex country would ruthlessly bend a man to her will whether he was proud or humble, rich or poor. "Mikhail's past—and his death—are no concern of mine," he said tonelessly. "I don't care what you choose to do about it. All I want is to take my wife back to England."

Tasia slept peacefully in her room. She had done as Luke had asked and lay down to rest as soon as he had left her. For the first time in days she was able to relax. Everything was out of her hands now. Luke had found her, and he was somewhere in the city, doing what he could for her. No matter what happened now, her conscience was clear. All self-doubt and blame were gone. She lay on her back, floating amid quiet dreams, her hair spread over the pillow.

Her sleep was interrupted all at once as a large hand slid over her mouth to stifle her cry of surprise. A masculine voice rasped against her ear. "I have some unfinished business with you."

Eleven
❧ ❧

Tasia's eyes flew open, and she blinked at the shadowed face above her. Realizing it was her husband, she relaxed beneath him, though her heart drummed rapidly. His hand lifted.

"Luke—"

"Shhh . . ." His mouth covered hers in a searching kiss.

"How did you get in here?" she gasped, twisting her mouth free. "Colonel Radkov told me the security was being tightened, and I could have no more visitors—"

"Nikolas countermanded his orders. We're locked in together for the night."

"But why would Nikolas—"

"Later. I've got to have you now."

His crushing weight came over her, and all questions dissolved in a rush of excitement. It seemed like months since she had been with him, and it felt so good, his weight lowering over the bedclothes to hold her in place, his mouth hot and plundering. Tasia moaned in her throat and struggled to free herself from the confining sheets. He continued to kiss her, licking, teasing, sealing his lips over hers. Through the layers of his clothes and the linen sheets, she felt the shape of him rising hard and urgent against her. She pressed upward in demanding undulations, pleading for his possession.

Luke lifted himself to pull at the bedclothes, revealing her slender upper body covered in a thin chemise. He dragged his parted lips over her exposed skin and followed the edge of cambric as she pulled it down with her trembling hands. His head moved over her bared breasts, finding the soft peaks, sucking with gentle tugs of his mouth.

They strained together, undressing, touching, striving to press skin against skin. Luke was half-clothed, his shirt gaping open, one leg still encased in his trousers, when he entered her with a hard thrust. Tasia gasped at the twinge of pain, her body yielding to the relentless male force. He kissed her throat, her jaw, waiting until she had adjusted to him, and then he pressed deeper within her, making her groan with pleasure. Her hands moved over the backs of his shoulders and gripped the muscled surface.

He rolled over, his hand firm on her back. Tasia straddled his hips and braced herself on his long body. She sought the perfect angle, pressing all her weight on the luscious point of their joining. She rose and pushed down again, pleasured by the gliding heat within her. Obligingly he followed the rhythm she set, his eyes a sapphire gleam in the darkness as he watched her.

She squirmed on top of him, riding the steady movement, taking fierce delight in having all his strength and power captured beneath her, caught fast between her thighs. She slowed the pace, tormenting him and herself, while each driving thrust pushed her closer to the edge of ultimate sensation. Suddenly it overtook her in a blaze of sweet agony. She tensed and trembled, desperately biting her lips to hold back a whimper. Luke clamped his hand around the back of her neck to pull her head down, muffling her cry with his lips. He buried his sound of fulfillment in her mouth as he pushed upward in one last surge. Drained and satisfied, he relaxed in a sprawl, while Tasia lay heavily on his chest.

After a while she stretched with a dreamy sigh and removed her chemise and the rest of Luke's clothes. He lay there like a spoiled sultan accepting the ministrations of a favored concubine.

"You don't know how much I've missed this," Tasia said, tossing his shirt to the floor. She lowered herself to his chest again, lightly dragging the tips of her breasts over the hard, bare surface.

Luke grinned and began to play with her long hair. "I have some idea." He drew the feathery ends of her hair over his chest and neck, then tickled her shoulder. "You're getting very good at it. I think I'd better take you back to England with me. A talent like yours shouldn't be wasted."

"I agree," she said wistfully, pressing her lips to his warm skin. "Let's go right away."

"Tomorrow night," Luke replied, turning serious. Before she was able to reply, he told her about everything that had happened, and the plan he and Nikolas had conceived on the ride back to the Angelovsky Palace.

Tasia listened in silence, trying to sort through a confusing mixture of emotions. She felt relief and hope that perhaps there was a chance for her to continue the life she had begun with Luke in England. But more than anything, she was filled with a sense of injustice at what had been taken from her.

"I'll be glad to leave Russia," she said bitterly. "I

was sorry to go the first time, but not now. It's my country, my home ... but all I've ever seen was the beautiful facade. I never realized how everything was rotting underneath. How many people have been sacrificed for the 'greater good'? There's no future here. They say we are all children of the tsar. They call him Batushka, father of all the Russias, a benevolent parent who loves and protects us as God does. It's all a lie, a fairy tale invented to make it easy for a greedy few to take advantage of the many. The tsar and his ministers, and all the families like mine and the Angelovskys ... they don't care about Russia. They just want to make certain that nothing threatens their comfortable lives. If I manage to leave here, I'll never come back, even if I have the chance someday."

Hearing the pain and anger in her voice, Luke tried to comfort her. "One of the most painful things in life," he murmured, "is having your illusions taken away. Don't think it's only here that people take advantage of others. It happens everywhere. Even the most honorable men are capable of cruelty and betrayal. It's human nature ... there's dark and light in all of us."

"Thank God I have you," Tasia said wearily, resting her head on his chest. "You would never betray me."

"Never," he agreed, bringing a lock of her hair to his lips.

"You're the best man I've ever known."

"You haven't known that many," Luke said with a short laugh, embarrassed by her praise. He moved over her and cradled the side of her face in his hand. "But I love you more than my life. You can depend on that, Tasia ... always."

* * *

The following morning Nikolas unlocked the door to the suite and requested a minute alone with Tasia for a reason he would not explain. Luke refused immediately, claiming that anything Nikolas wished to say to his wife could be said in front of him. An argument brewed until Tasia interceded. She went to her husband and whispered in his ear, rising on her toes to reach him. "Please, Luke, just allow us a few moments."

Glaring at Nikolas, Luke left the suite with the greatest reluctance. Tasia smiled faintly at her husband's surly departure and turned to her cousin. "What is this about, Nikolas?"

He stood looking at her for a moment, his face like carved granite. The thought flashed through her mind, how coldly beautiful he was. Suddenly her breath stopped as he stepped forward and knelt before her in a lithe movement. His head lowered, and he lifted the hem of her gown to his lips in an ancient gesture of homage. He let go and stood up. "Forgive me," he said stiffly. "I did you the greatest of wrongs. My debt to you will live through my children's children."

Tasia made an effort to gather her scattered wits. She had never imagined Nikolas would apologize for his actions, much less in such a manner. "All I ask is that you protect my mother," she said. "I'm afraid she may be punished for helping me tonight."

"There will be no consequences for Marie. I have friends in the ministry of the interior, as well as the department of police. They'll be angry at your disappearance, of course, but all they can do is question Marie as a formality. I'll bribe a few high-ranking officials to ensure that she isn't confined or interrogated, and to say that she is a foolish woman who was duped by her clever daughter. I'll take care of everything. You can trust me on that."

"Yes, I do."

"Good." He turned to leave.

"Nikki," she said softly. He stopped and glanced at her with a rare expression of surprise. No one ever called him by the dimunitive form of his name. "You know sometimes I have ... feelings about things."

"Yes." Nikolas smiled slightly. "You and your infamous witch spells. If you've had a 'feeling' about me, I don't want to know about it."

"There is disaster ahead for you," Tasia persisted. "You must leave Russia. If not now, then very soon."

"I can take care of myself, cousin."

"Terrible things are going to happen if you don't make a new life for yourself somewhere else. Nikolas, you must believe me!"

"Everything I want, everything I know, is right here. For me there is no world outside Russia. I would rather die here tomorrow than spend a lifetime in any other place." A mocking smile touched his lips. "Go with your English husband, and bear him a dozen sons. Save your concern for those who need it. *Da sveedah'neeya*, cousin."

"Goodbye, Nikolas," she replied, her face drawn with anxious pity as she watched him leave.

Madam Marie Petrovna Kaptereva entered the Angelovsky Palace wearing a green satin hooded mantle that covered her from head to toe. The sentries stationed in the entrance hall stared at her with respectful interest.

Colonel Radkov, the officer in charge of the imperial security detail assigned to the palace, approached the woman. "The prisoner is not permitted to have visitors," he said in a forbidding manner.

Before Marie could reply, Nikolas Angelovsky stepped forward to intervene. "Madam Kaptereva is allowed to spend ten minutes with her condemned daughter, on my authority."

"It is against my orders to allow—"

"Of course, I'll understand if you decide to take your complaints to the minister of justice. I'm known as a very forgiving man." In spite of his words, Nikolas gave him a smile of such chilling menace that the officer turned pale and shook his head with an incomprehensible mutter. The Angelovsky reputation was well-known and, by all accounts, well-deserved. No sane man would voluntarily make an enemy of the prince.

Silently Marie placed her bejeweled white hand on Nikolas's proferred arm. They ascended the stairs together.

Luke was waiting in the antechamber of Tasia's suite as the door was unlocked and opened. He and Nikolas exchanged a subtle glance—so far all had gone well—and Nikolas left with a murmur of warning. "Ten minutes," he said, closing and relocking the door behind him.

Luke stared at the woman before him, noting the superficial likeness between his wife and her mother. They were both small and sable-haired, with the same porcelain skin. "Madam Kaptereva," he murmured, lifting her hand to his lips.

Marie Petrovna could pass for a woman of thirty rather than forty. She was a great beauty, with more classically perfect features than her daughter. Her eyes were round instead of cat-shaped, her brows as delicate as butterfly feelers instead of bold slashes. Her lips were drawn with a pouting perfection that was entirely different from the passionate ripeness of Tasia's. But there was a brittleness about Marie that would only grow as the years passed. Luke far preferred Tasia's radiant and unconventional beauty, which would never lose the power to fascinate him.

Marie swept him from head to toe with an expert glance, and gave him a flirtatious smile. "Lord Stokehurst," she said in French, "what a pleasant surprise. I expected a small, pale Englishman, and instead I find a big, dark, handsome one. I do *adore* tall men. They make one feel so safe and protected." Gracefully she unfastened her mantle and allowed him to take it. Her well-endowed figure was clad in a yellow gown. Jewels covered her waist, neck, arms, and ears.

"*Maman*," came Tasia's tremulous voice from nearby. Marie turned with a brilliant smile, holding out her arms as her daughter rushed forward. They embraced with a mixture of laughter and tearful exclamations.

"They wouldn't let me see you until now, Tasia."

"Yes, I know—"

"You look so beautiful!"

"And, you, as always, Maman."

Together they went to the adjoining room for privacy and sat on the bed with tightly linked hands.

"There is so much I want to tell you," Tasia said, her voice muffled as she leaned forward to hug her mother.

Uncomfortable with displays of emotion, Marie

patted Tasia's back with a light flutter of her hand. "How is it for you in England?" she asked in Russian.

Tasia smiled, her face suddenly glowing. "It's heaven," she said.

Marie glanced at the next room where Luke waited. "Is he a good husband?"

"Good, and generous, and kind. I love him very much."

"Does he have land and property?"

"He's very wealthy," Tasia assured her.

"How many servants does he have?"

"At least a hundred, perhaps a few more."

Marie frowned, for the number was modest by the standards of Russian nobility. At one time the Kapterevs had possessed almost five hundred retainers. Nikolas Angelovsky's servants numbered in the thousands, necessary to maintain his twenty-seven estates. "How many estates does this Stokehurst have?" she asked suspiciously.

"Three, Maman."

"Only three?" Marie's frown deepened, and she let out a disappointed sigh. "Ah, well ... as long as he is kind to you," she said, trying not to sound glum. "And he is handsome. That counts for something, I suppose."

Tasia smiled wryly. She took Marie's hand and squeezed it lovingly. "Maman, I'm expecting a child," she confided. "I'm almost certain of it."

"Truly?" There was a mixture of delight and dismay on Marie's face. "But Tasia ... I'm far too young to be a grandmother!"

Tasia laughed and listened attentively as Marie advised her what to eat and how to preserve her figure after the baby was born. Marie promised to send the white lace christening gown that had been used by four generations of Kapterevs. All too soon their ten minutes were over, and there came a knock on the door of the next room. Tasia started at the sound and looked at her husband with wide eyes as he approached.

"It's time," Luke said quietly.

Tasia turned back to her mother. "Maman, you haven't told me how Varka is."

"She is well. I wanted to bring her with me tonight, but Nikolas forbade it."

"Will you give her my love, and tell her I am happy?"

"Yes, of course." Busily Marie began to unclasp her necklace and bracelets. "Here, put these on. I want you to have them."

Tasia shook her head in amazement. "No, I know how you love your jewels—"

"Take them," Marie insisted. "I just wore the small ones tonight. Really, I'm tired of these baubles."

The baubles, as she called them, were a collection of priceless gems. There were twin ropes of pearls and diamonds, and a gold bracelet with huge cabochon sapphires. The stones were polished but unfaceted, like gleaming blue eggs strung together in a thick web of gold. Ignoring Tasia's protests, she clasped the bracelet around Tasia's wrist and slid heavy rings on her fingers. There was a cluster of blood-colored rubies— "Always wear rubies, they help to purify the blood"—a ten-carat yellow diamond, and a creation of emeralds, sapphires, and rubies shaped in the pattern of a firebird. "Your father gave this to me when you were born," Marie finished, pinning a bouquet of jeweled flowers to the bodice of her dress.

"Thank you, Maman." Tasia stood up and allowed Luke to drape the green mantle over her shoulders. When the hood was pulled over her head, the garment would cover her completely. She looked at Marie with a worried frown. "When they discover you waiting here instead of me—"

"I'll be perfectly all right," Marie assured her. "Nikolas has given his word."

Nikolas came into the bedroom, his mouth tight with impatience. "Enough of this female chatter. Come, Tasia."

Luke squeezed Tasia's shoulder and gently pushed her toward Angelovsky. "I'll join you later," he murmured.

"What?" Tasia spun around to face him. The blood drained from her cheeks. "You're coming with me, aren't you?"

Luke shook his head. "It would look suspicious if I left now. Better for Radkov and his officers to think I stayed up here to comfort you. They're watching all of us closely. I'll leave soon and meet you and Biddle at Vasilyevsky Island." Located on the east side of the city, the island possessed a sea port that opened into the Gulf of Finland.

Tasia was stricken with panic. She reached for her husband, clinging to his lean waist. "I won't go unless you're with me. I can't leave you now."

Luke smiled reassuringly. In full view of Marie and Nikolas, he pressed a kiss to her lips. "Everything's going to be all right," he murmured. "I'll follow you soon. Go, and please don't argue."

Nikolas interrupted, unable to help himself. " 'Please don't argue'?" he repeated acidly. "Now I believe what they say about Englishmen being ruled by their women. Pleading with her to obey your commands, when you should be disciplining her with a leather strap. The day any self-respecting Russian speaks to a disobedient wife that way—" He broke off and regarded the two of them with horrified disapproval.

Tasia scowled back at him. "Thank God I'm not married to a 'self-respecting Russian.' You don't want wives, you want slaves! Heaven help a woman here with any intelligence or spirit, or opinions of her own."

Nikolas looked over her head at Luke, his golden eyes suddenly glinting with amusement. "You've ruined her," he said. "She's better off in England."

Obeying her husband's nudge, Tasia let go of him and went toward Nikolas. She began to pull the hood of the mantle over her head. All at once she stopped as she saw a shadow in the sitting room and heard the sound of a carpet-muffled footstep.

The others heard at the same time. Luke was the first to react, moving into the sitting room with quick, noiseless strides. He grabbed the intruder, an eavesdropping sentry, and clapped his hand over the man's mouth. The sentry struggled so hard that they both slammed sideways into the wall. Gamely Luke held on, grunting with the effort of subduing the intruder. One shout would alarm the entire houseful of guards, and ruin all chances of getting Tasia out of Russia.

Luke was dimly aware of Nikolas's approach. There was a flash of steel, and a silent, startling explosion of violence, and then the man stopped struggling in his arms, beginning to sag heavily. Gasping for breath, Luke realized that Nikolas had stabbed the sentry and had shoved a wad of fabric—a towel, or perhaps a coat—over the fatal chest wound to staunch the flow of blood. The soldier gave one last death convulsion in Luke's arms.

"Don't let his blood splash on the carpet," Nikolas muttered, easing the limp body away from him.

Luke felt sick. He caught a glimpse of the women's faces: Marie's tense and pale, Tasia's blank. Resolutely he swallowed back the twinge of nausea and helped Nikolas carry the dead sentry out of the suite. Several doors along the hallway there was a room piled with rows of paintings and unused furniture. They worked quickly, depositing the body in the corner and concealing it with a desk and a stack of framed canvases.

"Another skeleton for the family closet," Nikolas said facetiously, taking a critical glance at their handiwork. His face was like granite, his yellow eyes eerily flat. Luke's first reaction was to despise Angelovsky for his callousness, but he noticed that Nikolas had clenched his fist so tightly that his knuckles formed white peaks amid the bloodstains on his skin. "You're a fool if you think the sight of death disturbs me," Nikolas murmured. "It used to, but now it's the absence of feeling that bothers me."

Luke eyed him skeptically. "Whatever you say."

"Let's go," Nikolas said. "All this scuffling, and moving furniture—soon they'll discover the soldier is missing and we'll have an entire regiment up here."

Tasia was very calm as she descended the stairs on Nikolas's arm. She kept her head bent, as a sorrowful mother might, letting the hood of the mantle drape over her face. The death of the soldier had shocked her into a state of absolute clarity. She took strength from Nikolas's cold determination. She was leaving the palace where Misha had died and her strange journey had begun, except now there was Luke, and a home to which she desperately wanted to return. Inside the cloak, she slid her free hand over her abdomen, where her unborn baby nestled. *God, just give me the chance to go back, let us all reach safety . . .* Her lips moved in a soundless prayer as she walked with Nikolas through the hall of soldiers and felt their gazes on her.

Someone stepped in front of them, forcing them to halt. Tasia curled her fingers into Nikolas's wrist. He didn't flinch from the bite of her nails. "Colonel Radkov?" Nikolas said coolly. "Is there something you want?"

"Yes, Your Highness. Madam Kaptereva is renowned as a woman of surpassing beauty. I would like to be honored with a brief glimpse of her."

Nikolas's reply dripped with contempt. "The kind of request a stupid peasant would make. Have you no respect for a mother's grief, that you would insult her in such a manner?"

There was a long, challenging silence. Nikolas's forearm was taut beneath Tasia's hand.

Finally Radkov backed down. "Forgive me, Madam Kaptereva," he murmured. "No insult intended."

Tasia nodded beneath the green mantle, continuing to walk with Nikolas as the officer stepped aside. Carefully she stepped over the threshold and through the outside vestibule. She felt the cool night air on her face. Her foot touched the pattern of colored bricks artfully embedded in the side of the street. They went to a waiting carriage, which was poised outside a circle of light from the streetlamp.

"Quickly," Nikolas said, pushing her up the tiny steps and into the carriage.

Tasia turned and grasped his hard wrists. Her eyes were luminescent as she stared at him from the shadow of the hooded mantle. Her sense of impending doom, not for herself but for him, was suddenly overwhelming. She had a flashing vision of him crying in agony, his face covered with blood. She trembled in distress. "Nikolas," she said urgently, "you must leave Russia very soon. You must consider joining us in England."

"Not if my life depended on it," he said with a short laugh.

"It does," she whispered intensely. "It *does*."

Nikolas stared at her, his smile fading. He leaned into the carriage as if to tell her something important, confidential. She stayed very still. "People like you and me always survive," he murmured. "We take our fates into our hands and mold them to our liking. How many women would have gone from that rotting prison cell to being the wife of an English aristocrat? You used your beauty, your wits, and everything else you have to get what you wanted. I'll do no less for myself. Don't worry on my account. I wish you happiness." She felt his cool, firm lips touch hers, and she shivered as if she had tasted death.

The carriage door closed, and Tasia settled back against the cushions as the driver snapped the horses into action. She gasped in surprise as she realized there was another presence in the vehicle. "Oh—"

"Lady Stokehurst," came Biddle's mild voice. "It is gratifying to find you in good health."

Tasia laughed breathlessly. "Mr. Biddle! Now I'm finally beginning to believe I'm going home."

"Yes, my lady. As soon as we collect Lord Stokehurst at the shipyards."

She sobered at once, her face tense with concern. "It won't be soon enough to suit me."

Marie joined Luke at the window to watch the departing carriage. She gave a relieved sigh. "Thank God she's safe." She turned to Luke and touched his arm. "Thank you for saving Anastasia. It is a comfort to me to know that she has a husband who is so loyal. I must admit, at first I was dismayed by your lack of wealth, but now I see there are more important things, such as trust and devotion."

Luke opened and closed his mouth several times. As the heir to a dukedom who had added an industrial fortune to his already considerable landed income, possessing estates and forests that covered territory in seven counties—not to mention the majority of shares in an expanding railroad company—he had never anticipated being confronted by a mother-in-law who had decided to overlook his "lack of wealth." "Thank you" was all he could manage to say.

Marie was suddenly misty-eyed. "You're a good man, I can see that. Kind and responsible. Tasia's father, Ivan, was like that. His daughter was his greatest happiness. 'My treasure, my firebird,' he always called her. His last words were about Tasia. He begged me to make certain she would marry a man who would take care of her." Marie began to sniffle. "I thought my daughter would be well off as the wife of an Angelovsky. She would never want for anything. I convinced myself it was for the best. I didn't listen when she begged me not to force her into marriage with Mikhail. To me she was just a child prattling about love and dreams ..." She bent her head and dabbed at her eyes with the handkerchief Luke gave her. "I'm responsible for what happened to Tasia."

"It does no good to assign blame," Luke murmured. "It's been difficult for everyone. Tasia is going to be fine now."

"Yes." Marie leaned up to kiss him on each cheek, in the European fashion. "You must go to her right away."

"My thoughts exactly," he said, patting her silk-covered back. "Don't worry about your daughter, Madam Kaptereva. I'll keep Tasia safe in England—not to mention happier than she ever dreamed."

Tasia and Biddle waited alone at the corner of a warehouse used for storing cargo. There were pockets of activity around them: sailors on leave from their ships, dock laborers, a few merchants squabbling over damaged cargo. Drawing into the shadows, Tasia watched anxiously for a sign of her husband.

Biddle sensed her growing worry. "It's too soon for him to have reached the island, Lady Stokehurst," he said quietly.

She took a deep breath and tried to calm herself. "What if they have discovered I'm gone? They could detain him for questioning by the state police—he could be accused of committing political crimes against the imperial government, and then—"

"He'll be here shortly," Biddle assured her, though a note of worry had entered his voice.

Tasia went rigid as she noticed a tall man approaching them, dressed in the black, red, and gold uniform of the corps of gendarmes, a special section of police serving under the jurisdiction of the Imperial Chancellery. As the gendarme came closer, the suspicion on his whiskered face was blatant. He would want to know who they were, and what they were doing there. "Oh, God," Tasia whispered, thrown into panic. Her thoughts moved at lightning speed. She turned and wrapped her arms around the surprised valet beside her. Ignoring his shocked sound, she pressed her lips to his. She continued the embrace until the gendarme reached them.

"What is this?" he demanded. "What's going on?"

Tasia sprang back from Biddle and gasped in feigned dismay. "Oh, sir," she said breathlessly, "I beg you, don't tell anyone of our presence here! I have come here to meet with my English beau ... My father doesn't approve of him ..."

The gendarme's suspicion turned to frowning censure. "No doubt your father would beat you with a birch rod if he knew what you were doing."

Tasia looked at him beseechingly, her eyes filling with convincing tears. "Sir, this is our last evening together ..." She drew closer to Biddle and clung to his arm.

The gendarme looked at Biddle's small, slight frame with skepticism, clearly wondering how he had been able to inspire such passion. A long, agonizing moment passed before he relented. "Say your goodbyes and tell him to go," he told Tasia gruffly. "And trust your father to know what is best for you. Obedient children are a joy to their parents. A pretty girl like you—why, they'll find a far better match for you than this scrawny little Englishman!"

Tasia nodded meekly. "Yes, sir."

"I'll pretend I haven't seen you, and continue my patrol around the shipyards." He shook his finger at her. "But you had better be gone by the time I return."

"Thank you," she said, plucking one of the jeweled rings from her fingers and handing it to him. The gift would ensure that his stroll would be a leisurely one, allowing them to stay several minutes more. The gendarme accepted the ring with a curt nod. Casting a dark look at Biddle, he continued on his way.

Tasia breathed a sigh of relief. She turned to Biddle with an apologetic smile. "I told him you were my lover. It was all I could think of."

Biddle stared at her dazedly, unable to say a word.

"Are you all right?" she asked, puzzled by his silence. "Oh, Mr. Biddle ... did I shock you terribly?"

He nodded, gulping and loosening the collar of his shirt. "I ... I don't know how I shall ever face His Lordship again."

"I'm sure he'll understand—" she began contritely, and gave a start as she noticed another man walking toward them.

Biddle froze, bracing for another possible assault, but instead Tasia flew to the stranger with a soft cry.

"Uncle Kirill!"

Kirill's bearded face split with a smile, and he engulfed Tasia in his brawny arms. "Little niece," he murmured, holding her tightly. "It is no good for me to sneak you away from Russia if you keep coming back. You must stay away for good this time, *dah?*"

Tasia smiled back at him. "Yes, uncle."

"Nikolas sent me a note to explain everything. He wrote that you had married in England." Kirill held her at arm's length to have a better look. "Blooming like a rose," he said approvingly, and looked over her head at Biddle. "He must be a good husband, this little Englishman."

"Oh, no," Tasia said hastily, "that is his valet, Uncle Kirill. My husband will join us soon . . . if all goes well." Her forehead furrowed miserably at the thought of Luke being in danger.

"Ah." Kirill nodded sympathetically. "I will go look for him. But first I will take you to the ship—"

"No, I won't go anywhere without him."

Kirill seemed inclined to argue, but then he nodded thoughtfully. "Is your husband a tall man?"

"Yes."

"Dark-haired?"

"Yes . . ."

"With a hook in place of one hand?"

Tasia stared at her uncle, stupefied. All at once she spun around and saw Luke coming to them. The sight of him filled her with overwhelming relief. She ran to him and flung her arms around his waist. "Luke," she whispered, closing her eyes in thankfulness. "Are you all right?"

Luke tilted her head back and kissed her lips. "No. I won't be all right until I take you away from here and see you safely back in England."

"I agree, my lord." Tasia slipped her hand into his. Drawing him forward, she introduced him to her uncle. Kirill said a few words in broken English, smiles were exchanged, and they agreed to board the waiting ship without delay.

Suddenly remembering his valet, Luke glanced at Biddle, who stood nearby wringing his hands. "Biddle, why is your face purple? You look as if you're on the verge of apoplexy." He watched with a frown as the valet muttered incoherently and rushed away toward the ship. "What's the matter with him?"

Tasia shrugged casually. "Perhaps the strain of the evening is catching up with him."

Luke stared at her carefully innocent face with frank skepticism. "Never mind. You can tell me later. For now, let's get the hell out of this place."

"Yes," she said with calm certainty. "Let's go home."

Twelve

🌿🌿

London, England

In the three months since their return to England, Tasia had blossomed with well-being. They continued to live in the London villa, to make it convenient for Luke to attend to his business interests. For the first time in her life Tasia was happy, not with the brief, brilliant flashes of emotion she had known before, but with something stronger and more enduring, a steady flame that warmed her from the inside out. It was a miracle to wake up beside Luke every morning and realize that he belonged to her. He was all things to her, sometimes fatherly, sometimes devilish, sometimes as tender as a boy with his first love. He teased and played and courted her with passionate enthusiasm. As Tasia's pregnancy advanced, Luke became fascinated with the changes in her body. Sometimes he would undress her in the middle of the day just to look at her, ignoring her laughter and half-annoyed protests. He would brush his hand over the naked curve of her stomach as if it were a magnificent work of art.

"I've never seen anything so beautiful," he had murmured one afternoon, admiring her rounding abdomen.

"It's going to be a boy," she said.

347

"It doesn't matter," Luke had replied, spreading kisses over the tender skin of her stomach. "Boy or girl . . . it's part of you."

"Of us," she said with a smile, idly playing with his black hair.

Since Tasia was able to conceal her condition with high-waisted gowns, she was able to attend parties, theater productions, and other social gatherings. Later, when her stomach became too large to hide with loose gowns and silk shawls, propriety would dictate that she confine herself at home. "As slight as you are, I don't believe you'll show until you're quite far along," Mrs. Knaggs predicted. Tasia hoped she was right. After a lifetime of shelter and confinement, she intended to enjoy her freedom.

In the meantime she was busy making friends with other young matrons, involving herself in various charity concerns, and fulfilling her responsibilities as Luke's wife. She was also making progress in her campaign to push Emma into friendships with girls her own age. Emma seemed to be growing out of her shyness, and she had actually begun to enjoy going to children's parties. When the dreaded day of her first monthly bleeding arrived, she told Tasia about it with a mixture of embarrassment and pride. "Does this mean I can't have doll parties anymore?" she asked, and was relieved by Tasia's emphatic assurance that she could.

As autumn swept over England, crisp and cool, abundant with color, a shipment of crates and trunks arrived from Russia. Alicia Ashbourne came to help unpack them. "More presents from Maman," Tasia read aloud. She was seated on the sofa, scanning the letter from her mother, while

Alicia and Emma lifted priceless ornaments from the well-stuffed crates. Tasia was glad to receive further news of her mother's wellbeing, and especially to read that there had been no repercussions for her. Nikolas's expert bribery had ensured that Marie had been questioned only briefly and then released by the authorities after Tasia's escape from the Kurkov Palace. Since then Marie had sent letters and a collection of family heirlooms to the London villa. So far they had unearthed treasures of porcelain and crystal, a stack of icons, a lace christening gown, and a case of silver tea-glass holders studded with precious stones.

A chorus of delight erupted as a huge silver samovar was unwrapped. "From Tula, I think," Alicia said as she inspected the elaborate engraving. "The best ones are always made in Tula."

"Now if only we could get the proper tea to brew in it," Tasia lamented.

Emma looked at her in surprise. "Isn't English tea the best, Belle-mère?"

"No, indeed. Russians brew the most precious Chinese caravan tea." Tasia sighed wistfully. "It's more fragrant and delicious than any other kind. Many people like to drink it through a lump of sugar held in their front teeth."

"How odd!" Emma exclaimed, examining the samovar with great interest.

Alicia pulled out a length of shimmering Russian golden lace and held it up to the light. "What else does Marie say in the letter, Tasia?"

Tasia turned a page and continued reading. "Oh," she said softly, her fingers trembling a little.

Alerted by the strange note in her voice, the women looked up at her. "What is it?" Alicia asked.

Tasia answered slowly, staring at the thin sheaf of letter paper in her hand. "Governor Shurikov-sky was recently found dead in his palace. 'He took poison,' Maman writes ... 'and it is commonly believed that he committed suicide.' " Her voice faded, and she exchanged a grim glance with Alicia. Regardless of appearances, there could be no doubt that Nikolas had finally taken his revenge. Tasia looked back at the letter. " 'The tsar is distraught,' " she continued, " 'and his health and state of mind have been severely affected by the loss of his favorite adviser. He has withdrawn to such a degree that all his ministers and high officials are squabbling for power.' "

"Does it say anything about Prince Angelov-sky?" Alicia prompted.

Tasia nodded, her forehead wrinkling. " 'Niko-las is suspected of treasonous activities,' " she read, " 'and he has been arrested and held for questioning for many weeks now. There is a rumor that he may be reprieved and exiled soon. If he's still alive.' "

A heavy silence fell over the room. "They've done far more than question him," Alicia said softly. "Poor Nikolas. I wouldn't wish such a fate on my worst enemy."

"Why? What have they done to him?" Emma asked curiously.

Tasia was quiet, thinking of the hideous tortures that were sometimes whispered about in St. Petersburg, used for punishment or as a way to ferret out enemies of the imperial government. The torturers most often used the knout, a whip that could lay open flesh to the bone, and they plied it in conjunction with hot pokers and other fiendish methods of applying pain that could separate a man from his sanity. She wondered what they had done to Nikolas, and how badly he was hurt.

Suddenly all the pleasure in the gifts from her mother was gone, and Tasia was flooded with pity. "I wonder if there's something that could be done for Nikolas."

"Why would you want to help him?" Emma asked. "He's a bad man. He deserves everything he gets."

" 'Condemn not, and ye shall not be condemned,' " Tasia quoted. " 'Forgive, and ye shall be forgiven.' "

Emma scowled and returned her attention to the box of treasures in front of her. "He's still a bad man," she muttered.

To Tasia's dismay, Luke's reaction concerning Nikolas's plight was similar to his daughter's. When she showed him the contents of Marie's letter that night, Luke was disappointingly unsympathetic. "Angelovsky knew the danger he was in," he said evenly. "He decided to kill Shurikovsky even if it meant sacrificing his own life. He had a taste for playing dangerous games, Tasia. If his political enemies have found a way to destroy him, it's not more than what he expected. Nikolas's eyes were wide open."

"I can't help feeling sorry for him," Tasia said. "I'm sure they've made him suffer terribly."

Luke shrugged. "There's nothing we can do about it."

"Couldn't you at least have someone make an unofficial inquiry? One of your acquaintances in the English foreign office?"

Luke's blue eyes were sharp as he looked at her. "Why do you care what happens to Nikolas

Angelovsky? God knows he's never given a damn about you or anyone else."

"Part of it is that he's a family member—"

"A distant one."

"—and part of it is that he's been victimized by the same corrupt government officials that I was."

"In his case there was good reason," Luke said sardonically. "Unless you believe Shurikovsky's death really was a suicide."

His condescending manner stung her. "If you've decided to appoint yourself judge and jury over Nikolas, then you're no better than the tsar and his rotten ministers!"

They glared at each other. A flush of fury began at Luke's shirt collar and swept upward. "So now you're defending him."

"I have a right. I know what it's like to have everyone against you, facing all the accusation and scorn, having nowhere to turn—"

"Next you'll be demanding that I take him under my roof."

"*Your* roof? I thought it was *our* roof! And no, I hadn't thought of such a thing—but would it be too much to ask for you to offer shelter to someone in my family?"

"Yes, if it's someone like Nikolas Angelovsky. Dammit, Tasia, you know as well as anyone what he's capable of. He's not worthy of this conversation. Not after what he did to us."

"I've forgiven him for that, and if you can't, at least you can try to understand—"

"I'll see him in hell before I forgive him for his interference in our lives—"

"Because he hurt your pride," Tasia shot back. "That's why you're so enraged by the mere mention of his name."

That was a direct hit. She saw it in the sudden lowering of his brows and the violent twitch of his jaw, saw that he was clenching his teeth to hold back a scornful remark. Somehow he controlled himself enough to speak, though his voice was distinctly unsteady. "You think I value my pride more than your safety?"

Tasia was resolutely silent, torn between anger and guilt.

"What are we arguing about?" Luke asked, his eyes as cold as ice. "What is it you want me to do?"

"All I'm asking is that you try to find out if Nikolas is dead or alive."

"And then what?"

"I . . ." Tasia looked away from him and shrugged evasively. "I don't know."

His lips curled in a sneer. "You're a poor liar, Tasia."

He left without agreeing to her request. Tasia knew that it would be foolhardy to raise the issue again. For the next few days they carried on as usual, but their conversations were strained and their silences were filled with unanswered questions. Tasia couldn't explain why the thought of Nikolas's plight bothered her so, but she was increasingly anxious to know what had happened to him.

One evening after supper, when Emma had gone up to her room, Luke drank a snifter of brandy and regarded Tasia with a speculative stare. She squirmed uncomfortably but held his gaze, sensing that he had something important to tell her.

"Prince Nikolas has been exiled from Russia,"

he said curtly. "I heard from the foreign minister that he's taken a house in London."

Tasia burst with excited questions. *"London?* He's here now? Why did he come to England? How is he? What about his condition—"

"That's all I know. And I forbid you to have anything to do with him."

"Forbid?"

Luke toyed with the brandy snifter, rolling it gently in his fingers. "There's nothing you can do for him. He has everything he needs. Apparently he was allowed to leave with a tenth of his fortune intact, which is more than enough to sustain him."

"I should think so," Tasia said, reflecting that a tenth of the Angelovsky fortune would amount to at least thirty million pounds. "But to lose his home, his heritage . . ."

"He'll do fine without them."

Tasia was stunned by his callousness. "Do you know what the government interrogators do to men suspected of treason? Their favorite technique is to flay a man's back until the bone appears, and then roast him over a fire like a pig on a spit! Whatever's been done to Nikolas, I'm sure no amount of money could compensate for it. He has no family in England except me and Cousin Alicia—"

"There's no way in hell Charles will let her visit Angelovsky."

"Ah. So both you and Charles are in complete control of your wives?" Tasia sprang from her chair, unable to sit and talk calmly any longer. Resentment boiled up inside her. "When I married you, I expected to have an English husband who would respect me, who would allow me to say what I think, and give me the freedom to make choices for myself. From what you've told me, that was no less than what you gave your first wife. You can't claim that I would be in any danger from Nikolas, nor would I do harm to anyone by seeing him! You can't forbid me something without offering any explanation why."

Luke's face darkened with rage. "In this you'll obey me," he said in a guttural tone, "and I'll be damned if I give you an explanation. In some matters my decision is final."

"Simply because you're my husband?"

"Yes. Mary abided by that, and so will you."

"I will not!" Tasia quivered like a tightly drawn bow. Her hands knotted into fists. "I'm not a child you can order about! I'm not a belonging, or an animal you can harness and lead wherever you wish, or a slave to do your bidding. My mind and body are my own—and until you reverse your decision about letting me see Nikolas, you are not to touch me!"

Luke moved so swiftly that she didn't have time to react. All at once she was caught up against him, his hand twisted in her hair, his crushing mouth fastened on hers. He kissed her hard, grinding her lips against her teeth until she tasted blood. She whimpered and pushed against him, gasping with fury when he released her. Slowly her trembling fingers moved up to her bruised lips.

"I'll touch you whenever and however I want," Luke said harshly. "Don't push me too far, Tasia . . . or you'll regret it."

Although Alicia had no desire to see Nikolas, she was curious about his situation. "They say it took twenty wagons to bring his valuables from the docks to the house he let," she told Tasia as the two of them talked over tea. "He's had all sorts of callers already, but he won't see anyone. It's all anyone is talking about—the mysterious exiled Prince Nikolas Angelovsky."

"Are you going to visit him?" Tasia asked quietly.

"My dear, I haven't seen Nikolas since I was a little girl, and I have no desire or obligation to see him now. Besides, Charles would explode if I set one foot on Nikolas's property."

"I can't imagine Charles in a temper," Tasia said. "He's the most mild-mannered person I've ever known."

"It does happen," Alicia assured her. "Once every two years or so. You wouldn't want to be in the vicinity when he blows."

Tasia smiled slightly, then gave a deep sigh. "Luke is angry with me," she confided. "*Very* angry. Perhaps he has every right to be. I can't explain why I must see Nikolas . . . All I know is that he's alone and suffering, and there must be some way I can help him."

"Why would you want to, when all Nikolas has ever done for you is cause trouble?"

"He also helped me to escape from Russia," Tasia pointed out. "Do you know where his house is? Tell me, Alicia."

"Surely you're not going to disobey your husband?"

Tasia's brows quirked with a frown. She had changed over the past months. Once there would have been no need to ask such a question. She had been raised to regard a husband's word as law, to accept his authority without question. She remembered the bitter irony of Karolina Pavlova, a Russian writer: "*Learn, as a wife, the suffering of a wife . . . she must not seek the path to her own dreams, her own desires . . . all her soul is in his power . . . even her thoughts are fettered.*"

But that was no longer her fate. She had come too far, had changed too much, to let someone else own her soul. It was important for her to prove that to herself as well as to Luke. She would act according to her own conscience, and love her husband as a partner rather than revere him as her master.

"Tell me where Nikolas lives," she said firmly.

"Forty-three Upper Brook Street," Alicia murmured, wincing. "The big white marble house. And don't let anyone know that I was the one who told you—I shall deny it to my last breath."

Tasia waited until the next afternoon, when Luke was gone and Emma was immersed in French philosophy. She ordered a carriage to be prepared and left on the pretext of paying a call on the Ashbournes. Upper Brook Street was only a short distance from the Stokehurst estate. Tasia wondered why Nikolas had taken a house there, and if anyone had accompanied him from Russia. Her feeling of urgency increased, not to mention her nervousness, as the carriage stopped in front of a huge marble mansion. A footman preceded her up the front steps to knock at the door. They were greeted by the housekeeper, an old Russian woman dressed in black, with a gray scarf tied over her hair. Evidently Nikolas had not seen fit to hire a butler. The housekeeper muttered a few words in broken English and gestured for Tasia to go away.

Tasia spoke briskly. "I am Lady Anastasia

Ivanovna Stokehurst. I have come to see my cousin."

The woman was surprised by her perfectly accented Russian. She answered in kind, seeming relieved to have a countrywoman to confide in. "The prince is very ill, madam."

"How ill?"

"He is dying, madam. Dying very slowly." The housekeeper crossed herself. "A curse must have been placed on the Angelovsky family. He has been this way ever since he was questioned by the special committee in St. Petersburg."

" 'Questioned by the special committee,' " Tasia repeated softly, knowing that was far too civilized a description for what had really gone on. "Does he have fever? Infection in his wounds?"

"Not any longer, madam. Most of the outside wounds have healed. His sickness is of the spirit. The prince is too weak to get out of bed. He has commanded that his room be kept in darkness. No food or drink will stay down, except a glass of vodka now and then. He will not allow himself to be moved or bathed. When anyone touches him, he trembles or cries out as if a hot coal has burned him."

Tasia listened to the short speech without expression, though her insides were wrenched with pity. "Is anyone with him?"

"He will not permit it, madam."

"Show me to his room."

As they went through the shadowy house, Tasia was amazed to see that the rooms had been filled with many of the priceless treasures from the Angelovsky Palace in St. Petersburg. Even a magnificent icon wall had been transported and reassembled in flawless detail. They neared Nikolas's bedchamber, and the smell of incense became very strong. The air was thick with an Oriental scent that was used to ease the passage of the dying. Tasia remembered that the same fragrance had clung to her father's deathbed. She entered the room and asked the housekeeper to leave them.

It was too dark to see anything. Tasia made her way to the heavy curtains and drew them back a few inches, shedding afternoon light into the dim room. She opened the windows. A crisp fall breeze began to whisk away the haze of incense smoke. Slowly she walked to the bed, where Nikolas Angelovsky lay sleeping.

Nikolas's appearance shocked her. He was covered up to his chest, but one long, thin arm was visible. The fingers twitched slightly as his mind wandered in and out of dreams. Freshly made scars twisted like serpents around his wrists and inner elbow. Tasia's stomach turned at the sight of them. She switched her gaze to his face, seeing with regret that Nikolas's once-splendid handsomeness was in ruins. There were deep hollows in his face and neck. The healthy bronze of his skin had faded into a grayish-yellow death mask. His bright golden-streaked hair was dull and matted.

There was a bowl of herbed soup, untouched and cooling, on the table by the bed. There were also carved animal figurines to ward off evil spirits, and a pot of burning incense. Tasia snuffed the little flame and covered the pot to eliminate the vertical stream of scented smoke. Her movements, and the fresh air, disturbed Nikolas. He awakened with a nervous start.

"Who is it?" he said groggily. "Close the windows. Too much air ... too much light ..."

"One would think you didn't want to get well," Tasia observed quietly, coming closer to his bed-side. Nikolas blinked and stared up at her with his odd wolf-eyes, which seemed even more sterile than she remembered, if that was possible. He re-minded her of a listless, suffering animal, uncaring if he lived or died.

"Anastasia," he whispered.

"Yes, Nikolas." Carefully she sat on the edge of the bed, looking down at him.

Though she made no move to touch him, Nikolas shrank away from her. "Leave me," he said hoarsely. "I can't stand the sight of you . . . or any other human being."

"Why did you come to London?" she asked gently. "You have family in many other places, France, Finland, even China . . . but you have no one here. No one except me. I think you wanted me to come to you, Nikolas."

"When I want you, I'll send an invitation. Now . . . go."

Tasia was about to reply when she sensed that someone was at the door. She glanced over her shoulder. To her horrified surprise, Emma was there. Her slender form was nearly lost in the shadows of the doorway, but her red hair glowed with burning cinnamon lights.

Tasia rushed over to her with an annoyed scowl. "Emma Stokehurst, what are you doing here?" she whispered sharply.

"I took one of the horses and followed you," Emma replied. "I heard you and Papa talking about Prince Nikolas Angelovsky, and I knew you were planning to go to him."

"This is a private matter, and you have no busi-ness interfering! You know how I feel about your eavesdropping, as well as your habit of prying into things that are not your concern."

Emma tried to look repentant. "I had to come alone to make certain he didn't hurt you again."

"A gentleman's sickroom is not a proper place for a young girl. I want you to leave at once, Emma. Have the carriage take you home, and send it back for me."

"No," came a low voice from the bed.

The two women turned to look at him. Emma's blue eyes rounded in curiosity. "Is that the man I saw before?" she asked under her breath. "He doesn't look the same at all."

"Come," Nikolas said imperiously, gesturing with a slender hand. The effort cost him, and his hand dropped back to the bed. His gaze fixed on Emma's freckle-spattered face, surrounded by brilliant curls. "We meet again," he said, watching her without blinking.

"It smells bad in here," Emma observed, folding her arms over her flat chest. Ignoring Tasia's protests, she went to the bedside and shook her head disdainfully. "Look at all these empty bottles. You must be completely plowed."

The ghost of a smile touched Nikolas's dry lips. "What does it mean, 'plowed'?"

"It means stinking drunk," Emma replied pertly.

In a swift move that surprised her, Nikolas reached out and caught a lock of her gleaming hair between his thin fingers. "There," he said softly. "I know a Russian folk tale about a girl who saves a dying prince . . . by bringing him a magic feather . . . from the tail of the firebird. The bird's feathers were a color between red and gold . . . like your hair. A bouquet of flames."

Emma jerked away from his weak grip and

scowled down at him in annoyance. "More like a bunch of carrots." She glanced at Tasia. "I'll go home, Belle-mère. I can see that you're in no danger from *him*." She invested the last word with infinite disdain, and left the room.

Nikolas struggled to turn his head on the pillow and watch her departure.

Tasia was amazed at the change that had come over him. The listlessness had gone from his eyes, and there was a touch of color in his face. "Devil child," he said. "What is her name?"

Tasia ignored the question, beginning to roll up her sleeves. "I'm going to have the servants heat up more soup," she said, "and you're going to eat it."

"And then you'll promise to go away?"

"Certainly not. I'm going to bathe you and put salve on your bedsores. I'm certain you have many."

"I'll have the servants throw you out."

"Wait until you're strong enough to throw me out yourself," Tasia suggested.

The bruised-looking lids half-closed. The conversation had wearied him. "I don't know if I'll get stronger. I haven't yet decided if I want to live."

"People like you and me always survive," she replied, repeating the words he had once said to her. "I'm afraid you don't have a choice, Nikki."

"You're here against your husband's wishes." It was a statement, not a question. "He would never agree to let you visit me."

"You know nothing about him," Tasia said calmly.

"He'll beat you," Nikolas continued in glum satisfaction. "Even an Englishman wouldn't stand for this."

"He won't beat me," Tasia said, though privately she had her doubts.

"Did you come here for my sake, or to defy him?"

Tasia was silent for a moment. "Both," she said finally. She wanted Luke's complete trust. She wanted the freedom to do as she thought best. In Russian society a noblewoman always expected to be ruled by her husband. Here she had the chance to be a partner rather than a slave, and she would make it clear to Luke which role she preferred ... no matter what the consequences.

It was late in the evening when she returned to the Stokehurst villa. Nikolas had been a difficult patient, to say the least. While Tasia and the housekeeper gave him a bedbath, Nikolas had alternated between vicious insults and quiet, wretched stillness, as if he were being tortured all over again. Feeding him was another ordeal, but they had managed to coax him into keeping down a few spoonfuls of soup, and a bite or two of bread. Tasia had finally left him in a far cleaner and more comfortable condition than when she had first arrived, although he was now furious at being deprived of his vodka.

Tasia planned to return the next day, and every day after, until her cousin's recovery was certain. She was tired and depressed at the sight of Nikolas's broken body, the heartbreaking evidence of the cruelty that human beings could inflict on each other. She longed to crawl into Luke's arms and be comforted. Instead she faced a battle. Luke knew what she had done, and why she had returned at such a late hour. He would see her action as a slight to his masculine authority. Perhaps he had already decided the punishment for her disobedience. Or worse, he might be coldly contemptuous, and ignore her.

The villas was left in near-darkness. It was the servants' night off, and the house seemed deserted. Wearily Tasia went upstairs to the suite she shared with Luke, and called his name. There was no answer. She lit a lamp in the bedroom and began the process of undressing. She stripped down to her shift and sat at her dressing table to brush out her long hair.

She heard someone enter the room, and her hand froze, gripping the brush tightly.

"My lord?" she said tentatively, looking up. Luke was there, dressed in a dark robe. His face was grim. The look in his eyes caused her to drop the brush and jump up from the dressing table. Her instincts warned her to run from him, but her feet were leaden. All she could do was totter backward a few steps.

He came to her, pushed her against the wall, and held her jaw in his hand. There was no sound except their breathing; his deep and heavy, hers far more rapid. Tasia was aware of his brutal power, knowing he could crush her bones like eggshells.

"Are you going to punish me?" she asked unsteadily.

He forced a knee between her thighs, pinning her between the wall and his aroused body. His gaze burned into hers. "Should I?"

Tasia quivered slightly. "I had to go," she whispered. "Luke ... I-I didn't want to disobey you. I'm sorry ..."

"You're not sorry. You shouldn't be."

She didn't know what to say. She had never seen him like this before. "Luke," she whispered, "Don't—"

He smothered her words with an aggressive kiss. His hand slid down her throat, found the fragile strap of her shift, and pulled roughly until it broke. His hot palm covered her breast, squeezing, circling until the peak sprang into a sensitive bud. At first Tasia was too unnerved to respond, but his mouth, his touch, his body compelled her, and suddenly she was flooded with excitement. The thunder of her pulse was loud in her ears, obliterating all other sound. Only dimly could she hear herself gasping a few words of surrender ... but he wasn't listening. He held her in arms that hurt, and bit and licked her throat. Tasia let her head fall back, offering more, abandoning herself to the savage storm of passion.

Yanking the hem of her shift to her waist, he reached between her thighs. He pressed the heel of his hand against the place she most wanted it, grinding gently until the delicate fluff of curls was flattened beneath his palm. His mouth covered hers again, his tongue thrusting toward the back of her throat. She pushed against his hand, while her face became damp with sweat and her breathing turned ragged. When she was too weak to stand, he pulled her to the bed and lowered her to the mattress.

She lay passively on her side, robbed of speech or thought, her eyes closed as she waited in trembling anticipation. The hard length of his body pressed against her, his chest at her back. He pushed her top leg up high, arranging her to his satisfaction, and he entered her warm body with a skillful stroke. His hand played lightly on the front of her torso, sliding over each ripe, tender curve. Tasia writhed against him, oblivious of everything except the sweet torment. "Please," she moaned.

"Not yet," he said against the nape of her neck, his teeth closing on the delicate softness.

Her body contracted around him in the first spasm of release. "Oh—"

"Wait," he whispered, slowing the rhythm, making her cry out in frustration. He kept her at the edge of the precipice for agonizing minutes, knowing her well, controlling the rising sensation until he owned her body and soul . . . and only then did he drive deeply into her center, making the feeling spill in a bountiful flood, sex and sensation and love blending into intoxicating pleasure.

Afterward she turned over to press against him, burying her hot face in his chest. She had never felt so close to him. For a few blinding moments they had found a place outside of time, a state of perfect understanding and bliss. A trace of it lingered even now, and she knew what Luke was going to say even before he spoke.

"You're a strong-willed woman, Tasia . . . and today I realized that I want no less than that. I'm glad you're not afraid of me. You're willing to stand your ground, and I don't want to change that. I had no reason to forbid you to visit Angelovsky. The truth is, I was jealous." Luke stroked her hair. "Sometimes I want to hide you away from the world and keep you all to myself. I want all your attention, your time, your love—"

"But you have all those things," she said softly. "Given willingly and without measure. Not because you own me, but because I choose to."

"I know." He sighed deeply. "I was unreasonable, and selfish, and I'm not proud of it—"

"But you'll try to do better," Tasia prompted.

"I'll try," he said wryly.

She laughed and slid her arms around his neck. "Our life together is never going to be smooth, is it?"

"Apparently not." He slid his palm over her round stomach. "But I'm enjoying every minute of it."

"So am I," she said. "I never dreamed I would be this happy."

"There's more to come," he whispered against her lips. "Just wait and see."

Epilogue

The bitter November wind chilled Luke to the bone as he rode the short distance between the railroad offices and his villa on the Thames. In hindsight, he should have taken a carriage, but the day had turned out much colder than expected. Dismounting from his horse, he gave the reins to a waiting footman and bounded up the front steps. The butler opened the door and took his coat and hat.

Luke shivered at the pleasant warmth of the house. "Do you know where Lady Stokehurst is?"

"Lady Stokehurst and Miss Emma are in the parlor with Prince Nikolas, sir."

Luke blinked in surprise. Nikolas had never come to visit before. It was one thing to tolerate Tasia's sickroom visits with her exiled cousin, but quite another to welcome him into their own house as a guest. Setting his jaw, Luke went to the parlor.

As he approached, the sound of his footsteps must have alerted Emma, who appeared in front of him with an air of explosive excitement. "Papa, the most *extraordinary* thing has happened! Nikolas came to visit, and he brought a gift for me!"

"What kind of gift?" Luke asked darkly, following her into the parlor.

"A sick kitten. His poor little paws are infected. The man who owned him had his claws pulled out, and now the kitten is so weak with fever that we're not certain he'll live. We've been trying to coax him to drink some milk. If he pulls through, Papa, may I keep him? Please?"

"I don't see why a kitten should be any trouble—" Luke stopped short as he took in the scene before him.

Tasia was crouched on the floor next to a striped bundle of orange, black, and white. It was about the size of a small dog. Underneath Luke's incredulous gaze, the "kitten" tottered on bandaged paws to a dish of milk and began to lap it tentatively. A pair of house maids were gathered at the other side of the room, viewing the animal with apprehension. "They eats people, don't they?" one of the maids asked in concern.

It was a tiger cub, Luke realized. Probably the Siberian variety that grew to the size of a horse. Blankly he looked from Emma's hopeful face to Tasia's apologetic one . . . and finally to Nikolas Angelovsky, who was seated on the settee.

It was the first time Luke had seen Nikolas since he had been in Russia. Angelovsky looked as before, except much thinner, the edges of his cheeks and nose as sharp as knifeblades. His golden skin had faded to an unhealthy pallor. His piercing yellow eyes were as startling as ever, and his smile held the same mocking curve. "Zdráhstvuyti," he said softly.

Luke couldn't keep a scowl of dislike from his face. "Angelovsky," he muttered. "I would appreciate it if you refrained from bestowing any further 'gifts' on my family. You've done quite enough for the Stokehursts."

Nikolas's smile didn't falter. "I had no choice but to bring the kitten to my cousin Emma, the patroness of injured animals."

Luke glanced at his daughter, who was crouched over the wobbly bundle of stripes like a worried mother. Angelovsky had chosen his gift well. No other gesture could have so effectively softened Emma's heart. "Look at him, Papa," Emma said, while the cub made contented gurgling and puffing noises in between slurps of milk. "He's very small . . . He won't take up much room at all!"

"He'll grow," Luke replied ominously. "Eventually to forty stone or more."

"Really?" Emma gave the cub a dubious glance. "That much?"

"There is no way in hell we're going to keep a tiger!" Luke divided his glare between Nikolas and his wife. "Someone had better think of a way to dispose of it, or I will."

Tasia interceded with gentle diplomacy, hurrying to him with a swish of silken skirts, laying a light hand on his arm. "Luke," she murmured, "I would have a word with you in private." Glancing at Nikolas, she added, "I'm certain you need more rest, Nikolas. You wouldn't want to ruin your recuperation by overtaxing yourself."

"Perhaps I should leave," Nikolas agreed, rising from the settee.

"I'll see you out," Emma said, draping the tiger cub over her shoulder, where he lay in limp contentment.

After the pair left the room, Tasia stood on her toes to whisper in Luke's ear. "Please . . . it would make her so happy to keep him."

"We're talking about a *tiger*, for God's sake."

Luke pulled his head back and frowned at her. "I don't like to come home in the afternoon and find the likes of Angelovsky sitting in my parlor."

"It was a complete surprise," Tasia said contritely. "I certainly couldn't turn Nikolas away at the doorstep."

"I won't allow him to worm his way into our lives."

"Of course not," Tasia said, walking with him into the hallway. "This visit was just Nikolas's way of making peace. I don't believe he means to harm any of us."

"I don't have your forgiving nature," Luke muttered. "As far as I'm concerned, he's not welcome here."

Tasia was about to argue when she happened to glance at the entrance hall. Emma was standing with Nikolas, looking up at him as she cuddled the tiger against her shoulder. Nikolas reached to stroke the cub's round head. As he did so, his fingers gently rubbed a lock of Emma's shining red hair. The gesture was brief, almost unnoticeable, but it sent a chill of warning down Tasia's spine. She had a sudden premonition of Nikolas with an older Emma ... staring at her with a seductive smile, leading her step by step into a fathomless shadow ... until they had both disappeared from the light.

Did it mean that Emma might someday be in danger from Nikolas? Tasia's brow wrinkled, and she wondered if she should tell Luke of her vision. No, she didn't want to worry him unnecessarily. Together they would take care of Emma and protect her. Nothing would threaten them now that they were a family.

"Perhaps you're right," she said to Luke,

squeezing his arm. "I'll find a way to make Nikolas understand that he mustn't visit often."

"Good," he said in satisfaction. "Now about that cub—"

"Come with me," she coaxed, urging him to the dimly lit space beneath the grand staircase. Together they drew into the private corner.

Luke began again. "About the tiger—"

"Come closer." She pulled his cool hand to the velvet-covered slope of her breast. Automatically his fingers slid over the plump mound, finding the downy warmth of her cleavage. Tasia sighed with pleasure. She pressed her body, lush with pregnancy, against the length of his. "You left before I woke this morning," she murmured. "I missed you."

"Tasia—"

She pulled his head down and nipped his neck with her teeth. Blindly Luke turned and found her mouth. The kiss deepened, and he felt the warmth of it spread through his body. As always, he was aroused by her nearness, his blood stirring rapidly at the feel and taste of her. Tasia's small hand covered his, and she pressed it inside her bodice, underneath the velvet, until his palm fitted over her peaked nipple. He kissed her once more, and Tasia responded with avid pleasure, molding herself against him. "You smell like winter," she whispered.

Luke shivered as he felt her lips brush against the side of his neck. "It's cold outside."

"Take me upstairs and I'll warm you."

"But about the tiger . . ."

"Later," she said, loosening the knot of his cravat. "For now, take me to bed."

Luke raised his head and gave her a sardonic glance. "I know when I'm being manipulated."

"You're not being manipulated," she assured him. She pulled his cravat free and dropped it to the floor. "You're being seduced. Stop trying to resist."

The prospect of being in bed with her, holding her body against his, was too much for Luke. As long as he lived, there would be no temptation, no pleasure, no passion more intense than what he felt with her. Carefully he lifted her in his arms. "Who's resisting?" he muttered, and carried her up to bed.

NEW YORK TIMES BESTSELLING AUTHOR
LISA KLEYPAS

Scandal in Spring
978-0-06-056253-3/$7.99 US/$10.99 Can
Daisy Bowman's father has told her she must find a husband, or she will have to marry the man he chooses.

Devil In Winter
978-0-06-056251-9/$7.99 US/$10.99 Can
Evangeline Jenner stands to become the wealthiest "Wallflower" once her inheritance comes due.

It Happened One Autumn
978-0-06-056249-6/$7.50 US/$9.99 Can
Lillian Bowman quickly learns that her independent American ways aren't "the thing."

Secrets of a Summer Night
978-0-06-009129-3/$7.99 US/$10.99 Can
Four young ladies enter London society with one goal: use their feminine wiles to find a husband.

Again the Magic
978-0-380-81108-3/$7.99 US/$10.99 Can
John McKenna's ruthless plan is to take revenge on the woman who shattered his dreams of love.

Worth Any Price
978-0-380-81107-6/$7.99 US/$10.99 Can
Charlotte defies convention by fleeing a marriage to a man who wants to control her.